REMEMBER THE PASSION

LYNN ELDRIDGE

WOLFPACK
PUBLISHING
— EST 2013 —

To My Family,
Remember to always love and laugh.

REMEMBER THE PASSION

"Love looks not with the eyes, but with the mind;
And therefore is winged Cupid painted blind."
William Shakespeare

CHAPTER 1

"She killed herself because of you, Blaze!"

"The hell she did, Shade!" Blaze Bowie shouted.

Shade's fist caught him on the corner of his mouth and Blaze hit his brother square in the eye. Shade yelled in primitive rage and grabbed Blaze's throat.

"Blaze! Shade!" the wizened preacher said. "Pull in your horns before you both wind up in the hoosegow."

Blaze ignored the warning of jail from the bespectacled man who'd just dropped the bad news in the foyer of the Bowies' two story, plantation home. Clamping his hands around Shade's wrists Blaze slammed him against the brick hearth in the parlor. Centered on the fireplace directly above their heads was the Bowie family coat of arms.

Blaze felt guilty for fighting with his little brother, but it was only the four years between them that labeled Shade as *little*. He was two hundred ten pounds of well matched fury, wounds and muscle. Shade's grip tightened like a hangman's noose and Blaze coughed. Desperate to breathe, Blaze jammed his forearms between Shade's, breaking the strangling hold. Blood dripped from the cut above Shade's eye as he shoved Blaze back a step. Blaze wiped blood off his mouth with the back of his hand and clenched his jaw.

"Only God knows why Lucy Ray took her own life," Parson Wilkie said from behind Blaze. "But I heard the poor girl swallowed enough laudanum to kill a horse."

"You should have married her, Blaze!" Shade jabbed a finger in Blaze's chest. "Instead you buried her."

"I'm sorry Lucy Ray is dead," Blaze said, backhanding Shade's forearm. "But I hardly knew her."

"Like hell!" Shade erupted with what was fueling his volcanic rage, "You took her to bed, Blaze!"

"Help us, Lord." Parson Wilkie gazed heavenward.

"I did not." Blaze held up both hands, palms out. "You're the only one of us who bedded her."

"Lucy said she slept with *me* only to make *you* jealous." Glowering at Blaze, Shade swiped blood away from his eye with his sleeve. "Dammit, Blaze. How do you think that makes me feel?"

"Like you have another reason to hate me."

Blaze had loved Shade from the day he was born. He had cheered when Shade took his first steps, built him a birdhouse for his sixth birthday and bailed him out of fights at school. Named Trailblazer by their beautiful half Natchez Indian mother, Dawn, and their handsome Scottish father, Tyler, for being the first born Shade reckoned their folks had appointed Blaze as the leader thus relegating Shade to second best. Their younger son, with his brown hair and their mother's coloring, was a little darker than Blaze who took after their blond father. And in the same way their mother was named for her birth at sunrise, his brother was named Shade Tree having been conceived underneath a large magnolia's flowering branches. Yet, Shade swore he lived in Blaze's shadow. Blaze didn't know what or who it would take to convince Shade otherwise.

"I don't hate you!" Shade planted his fists on his hips. "But every girl I've ever wanted threw herself at you. You bed 'em and then you tell 'em you aren't the marrying kind."

"No." Blaze shook his head and replied, "I tell 'em I'm not the marrying kind before I bed 'em. That's more than you do."

"Please." The parson looked from one brother to the other. "Let's shake and make up, boys."

"We aren't boys." Blaze glared at Shade. "We're grown men and it's time we started acting like it again."

"Yes," Parson Wilkie said, bobbing his head. "I'm here to tell you that your heathen behavior must stop." Pulling a handkerchief out of his breast pocket, he swiped at his forehead. He stuffed it back into his pocket and pushed his round glasses up his nose. Holding his Bible in one hand and tapping shaking fingers against the front of it with the other, his voice shook. "Your father didn't hold with gambling, dueling, tippling, or wenching. Yet, it's common knowledge since your folks died in the fire, you two have frequented Natchez-Under-the-Hill, knowing full well it's the most licentious port on the Mississippi River!"

"What the hell's licentious?" Shade asked dryly.

"Rowdy! Naughty! Immoral! Depraved! Sinful!" Parson Wilkie replied.

"And that's exactly why I like Natchez-Under-the-Hill." Shade rolled his eyes when Blaze glared at him.

"We've been in Natchez proper on top of the hill, too," Blaze said referring to the affluent part of town overlooking the decadent boat landing beneath the bluff.

"No doubt to gamble on the horses at that shameful racetrack! Even the genteel enjoy vice!" The preacher clutched the Bible to his chest like a shield. "I hear you two have done more betting, fighting, drinking, and... and... pleasuring the flesh than any hundred other men in Louisiana and Mississippi put together!"

"He drove me to whoring." Shade inclined his head in Blaze's direction. "After stealing all the decent girls around Vidalia."

"That's a lie."

After their parents died, Blaze had taken the ferry across

the river to Natchez, Mississippi. Unlike Shade, Blaze had also gone in an effort to negotiate with the bank to save their property.

"You won't spend time to court a girl, Shade. You'd rather just buy one."

"I courted Lucy and she didn't make me any happier than the whores. Explain that."

"You didn't court Lucy Ray, you took her to bed." Still squared off in front of the massive fireplace, as Shade hung his head, Blaze placed a hand on his shoulder. "Look Shade, maybe if she'd been the right girl for you, you'd have courted her. If she'd been the right girl for me, I would have courted her."

"Right or wrong, she's dead and we're back to you!" Shade knocked Blaze's hand off his shoulder. "Exactly what did you do with Lucy the night you let her into your room?"

"Talk." Blaze blew out a sigh. "Lucy told me she loved you. She twisted the truth about that night to make *you* jealous, Shade, not me. She said whenever she tried to get your attention you just tossed up her skirts."

"Little did she know you've tossed up more skirts than I ever have!"

"Have mercy on them, Lord!" the parson said. "Are there no chairs left in this house?"

"No!" Blaze and Shade both replied.

"I'd leave, but I'm afraid you'd kill each other." The parson tapped his fingers to his lips as if he wished he'd never shared the news about Lucy Ray. "How was I to know that telling you about a local girl's death would cause all this blame casting?"

"Do you think Lucy took the laudanum to get my attention?" Shade asked, his brows furrowing. "That would mean I'm to blame for her death."

"No," Blaze said. "All it means is that a nice, but troubled girl fell in love with you."

"Why didn't she tell me she loved me?"

"Are you sure she didn't?"

"I'm not sure of anything." Shade narrowed his eyes. "Including your part in this, Blaze."

All of a sudden the front door to the large house burst open. The doorknob banged into the wall where the antique, mirrored hall tree had stood before the bank started pressuring them.

"Who the—" Shade was cut off by the parson's scream.

In the middle of the black and white tiled foyer a tall man, clad in a ragged coat and worn breeches, brandished a deadly flintlock rifle.

"Mr. Ray," Blaze said recognizing the intruder as Lucy's father.

"Shut up, Shade... Blaze... whichever son of Satan said that!" Rufus Ray said, blurry-eyed from crying or drinking or both. "I'm here to revenge my Lucy. You land swindling, slave smuggling Bowies're gonna pay with yer worthless hides."

Shade lifted his upper lip in the arrogant snarl Blaze recognized as having escalated more than one fight over the years.

"We acquired all our land titles through fair speculation, Ray," Shade said.

"We never have been nor will we ever be slave smugglers." Blaze squared up at Shade's side, stopping Rufus Ray from advancing on them.

"How can you stand there in them fringed deerskins with Bowie knives swinging from yer sashes and swear such tripe?" Rufus Ray asked, using the barrel of the rifle to point at them. "You dress like Jim Bowie, ya got all kinds of land like him and in my book that means yer in cahoots with pirates fer slave smuggling like him."

"The Forks of the Road slave market in Natchez, where the Bowies have been of late, is one of the busiest and most profitable slave markets in all of Mississippi," Parson Wilkie said.

Blaze scowled at the preacher. "You've said enough."

"Afore I send yer sorry carcasses straight to hell," Rufus

bared his teeth, "you should know Lucy was three months gone with child when she swallered that laudanum."

Blaze stared at Shade. Never had he seen Shade take a step back when faced with a man holding a gun. Until now. Blaze figured Shade would have dropped into their father's favorite wing backed chair... that is if they still had the chair.

"Mr. Ray, we just heard about Lucy and we're very sorry," Blaze said.

"Yer sorry you ain't got no handy little innocent across the bayou to attack no more." Rufus Ray shook as his face contorted.

"Now listen here, Ray," Shade said. "Neither of us attacked Lucy. I haven't been with her for six months so I sure didn't get her with child."

"Shade." Blaze clamped a steadying hand on Shade's shoulder. "Mr. Ray, we considered Lucy to be our friend. Shade would have done right by her if he were the father."

"Wasn't Shade!" Rufus' contempt formed spittle on his lips. "It was you, Blaze Bowie, you stinking piece of swamp scum. Lucy told me on her deathbed you was the father of her unborn child."

"No, sir, it wasn't me."

Lucy Ray was more disturbed than Blaze had thought, but would Shade realize it?

"It was me Lucy was seeing." Shade never even glanced at Blaze. "But like I said I hadn't been with her—""Seeing as in raping," Rufus said. "And it sure 'nough was Blaze."

"Mr. Ray," Blaze began and was cut off by blood running thicker than water.

"It was not my brother!" Shade said as if he had never doubted Blaze. "I took Lucy to bed, but that's all I did. Blaming Blaze is her revenge against me. If you send anybody to hell today it'll be me."

For the first time in his life, Shade stepped in front of Blaze.

"Then get ready." Stalking from the foyer into the parlor,

Rufus Ray put his finger on the trigger of the rifle. "Yer 'bout to meet the grim reaper, Shade Bowie."

"Over my dead body, Ray." Blaze yanked Shade back beside him.

"Warn the devil, both Bowies are on their way, preacher!"

The preacher's abrupt shriek was shrill and jolting. Rufus Ray, looking like the grim reaper in the flesh, glowered at the minister. Parson Wilkie collapsed to his knees and covered his bowed head with his Bible.

As they had done in countless backwoods brawls in the bayou and in turbulent tangles in Natchez-Under-the-Hill, Blaze and Shade pushed apart. Blaze brandished his ten-inch blade knife and Shade did the same.

"Put the rifle down, Ray!" Blaze ordered.

With his targets divided and armed, Rufus Ray dragged his hand down his haggard face and flinched.

"What the hellfire's going on here?" asked a new voice from the front door.

CHAPTER 2

"WE'RE TRYING TO TALK SOME SENSE INTO RAY," BLAZE SAID as he glanced past Rufus Ray to where the town's burley sheriff filled the doorway of the house.

"Are you here to arrest Shade Bowie for murdering Lucy?" Rufus asked.

"Nobody murdered your daughter. Lucy took her own life," the sheriff said. "Now, put that dad-shamed rifle down, Rufus."

Instead, Rufus Ray aimed the rifle at Shade and put his finger on the trigger. Blaze snapped his wrist and his knife sailed through the air. Before Ray could pull the trigger, the razor sharp blade found its mark in the back of Ray's right hand. Rufus Ray hollered in pain as plaster rained down from the rifle ball burying itself in the ceiling.

Leaping forward, Shade tackled Rufus to the hardwood floor and pulled the knife out of his hand. Lightning quick he swiped the knife blade clean on the sleeve of Rufus' black coat and tossed the weapon back to Blaze. The sheriff grabbed Ray from behind and hauled him off the floor. Still gripping his own knife, Shade got to his feet and stood beside Blaze. Blaze picked up Ray's rifle.

"Come on, Rufus!" the husky sheriff said. "Your wife

thought you might be ruckus raisin' over here at the Bowie plantation and sent me to fetch you home."

"I'll be back to kill both of ya!" Rufus Ray said as the sheriff shuffled him to the front door.

"Shut your trap, Ray." The sheriff pushed him onto the porch and hollered at someone who was outside the house. "You can go on in now."

A trembling Parson Wilkie said, "The sooner you boys find the right young women, the better." On his way out he said, "But... but there are no ladies in my church able to handle heathens! So Godspeed and farewell."

"Guess the preacher's given up on us," Shade said.

"As long as we don't give up on each other, little brother." Blaze held out his hand to Shade and thought Shade was about to shake his hand when a third visitor entered the foyer.

"Well, well, come to squeeze blood out of turnips?" Shade folded his arms over his chest and tapped the blade of his knife to the buckskin covering the muscles in his upper arm. "I'm in a real sour mood, Spencer. So, I suggest you get out of here and head on back to the bank while I'm of a mind to let you leave in one piece."

"A sour mood is your usual mood, Shade," the diminutive, dapperly dressed bank manager said. "I'm here to..." He paused to look over his shoulder and called out of the door, "Sheriff? Sheriff!"

"The sheriff's taking Ray home," Blaze said.

"Sheriff, could you wait for me?" Spencer's short-lived bravado vanished as he peered out of the door. "The Bowies have their knives, a rifle and are splattered with blood!"

The sheriff shoved Rufus onto his horse and waved the banker off. Turning pale, Spencer backed up until the winding staircase in the foyer stopped him.

"What do you want this time, Spencer?" Blaze asked.

"I'm... um... here to... uh... foreclose," he said, his voice and the piece of paper in his hand both shaking.

Shade grabbed the paper, ripped it in half and flung it to

the floor. Blaze sheathed his knife in the scabbard tied to his buckskin pants and then resting the rifle on his right shoulder, folded his arms over his chest.

"It's been three months since the sawmill burned down with your folks in it. You've had time enough to repay the loan taken out on this house and land."

"How can we repay the loan when you won't lend us the money to rebuild our sawmill?" Blaze asked.

"You could farm." Spencer swallowed hard making the fancy silk ribbon tied around his neck bob up and down.

"Our crops burned!" Shade said. "How are we supposed to clear the fields and plant new crops when our barns and silos burned and all our plows and farming tools were destroyed?"

"All good points." The banker tittered nervously. "I guess farming isn't the answer."

"No, I guess farming isn't the answer," Shade said with a smirk.

"We're lucky it started to rain when it did or the fire would have burned our house to the ground," Blaze said. "After we buried our folks and made sure all of our workers had enough money to make it through this winter, we gave your bank what savings was left."

He'd had the majority of this conversation with the banker before, but tried once more to appeal to him. "Help us hire our workers back and we'll rebuild the sawmill. I want to relocate the mill closer to the recently purchased timberland anyway. The new mill will be bigger, I can make it even more efficient and we'll have no trouble paying what we owe. Charge us extra interest on the loan."

"It's not my fault Tyler Bowie refused to use slave labor and was mortgaged to the hilt when he died. I cannot lend you more money when you can't repay the debt you and your father incurred." Spencer pursed his lips. "Besides, I heard you fellas lost what savings you had not by paying your workers, but by gambling in Natchez-Under-the-Hill."

After taking care of their workers, Blaze and Shade had indeed gambled at the racetrack. They knew horses and almost always won, but the winnings just weren't enough to bring their bank loan current, much less rebuild. As for Natchez-Under-the-Hill, gambling there was small time with little reward.

"You heard wrong," Blaze said.

"Your strumpets and two-fisted tippling are the talk of the county," Spencer said. "You're being called," his mouth shriveled up like a prune, "rowdies!"

"Rowdies? You heard that *talk* from the preacher!" Shade hooted. "When a man suffers so much loss he needs some comfort, women and whiskey usually work. So if we're going to name-call then I have to say I know a certain henpecked," Shade poked his finger in the banker's scrawny chest punctuating his words, "teetotaling little prig who wouldn't know how to enjoy a woman's comfort if it straddled his shriveled lap."

"Well!" Spencer turned bright red and as Shade stood back, he fluttered his small hands over his chest. Without making eye contact he drew himself up to his full height, a foot shy of Shade's, and said, "You can sell this house to me personally instead of losing it to the bank."

"No!" Shade yelled. "You're being a horse's ass because this is the biggest plantation house on this side of the Mississippi!" He swung his arms wide. "And your pants-wearing shrew of a wife wants it."

"She does fancy the Greek Revival architecture," the banker said.

"I'll burn this place to the ground before I see *you* move into it." Clamping a hand on Spencer's shoulder, Shade slipped his knife under the silk ribbon at the banker's throat.

"Shade," Blaze said, as Shade sheared the ribbon in half.

"My wife purchased this tie." Keeping a wary eye on Shade, the banker fiddled with the dangling halves of the ribbon. "We can discuss the house again at a later date. I will proceed with foreclosing on the farmland first."

"You'll die trying," Shade said.

Blaze inwardly raged and gripped the rifle. The plantation was their birthright. A former Natchez Indian village, this land by the blood of his mother's people belonged to him and Shade. A century ago, after the French-Natchez conflict, the Natchez tribes had scattered. Eventually, survivors joined the Muscogee, Chickasaw or Cherokee tribes. Others sought refuge with English colonists. The son of a Natchez chief had stayed and married a beautiful settler who bore him a daughter. That daughter was Blaze and Shade's mother. It was she and their father who had inherited the rich soil of the flat, delta lowland, farmed it and turned it into a thriving plantation. As the brothers grew up they did their share of backbreaking farm work that packed their bodies with muscle.

"Well then, I'll foreclose on Blaze's timberland first."

"The hell you will, Spencer," Blaze growled.

Blaze's dream of owning and operating a sawmill began with a small operation using the trees cleared from the farmland. The Bowies were known as kind and generous employers and the business had flourished. From their lumber and profits from the sawmill, the Bowie family built their sprawling manor house. Recently, the family had agreed to mortgage property to purchase another fifty thousand acres of prime timberland. And Blaze vowed the house, the farmland and the timberland would remain Bowie property.

"You can move the graves," Spencer said.

Their parents were buried side-by-side, on their mother's beloved Indian village soil surrounded by the family's towering pine trees. Trying to reason with Spencer had been no use. There had to be another way and Blaze knew what it was.

"We can't sell the farmland because we need it to grow

the corn for bourbon and barley to make our scotch," Shade said, breaking into Blaze's thoughts.

The banker's eyes widened and he licked his thin lips. "Yoder's Whiskey'll run you out of business."

"No, because they don't make scotch," Shade replied.

"What's scotch?" Spencer asked.

"Whiskey without the 'e'. We have a one-of-a-kind family recipe for whisky straight from Scotland."

"Is that right, Blaze?" Spencer asked.

"Yes," Blaze said. "While Shade runs the distillery, I'll be operating my new sawmill."

Spencer rubbed his throat where Shade's knife had been and mumbled, "That's brave talk as you stand in an empty house about to be foreclosed on."

"We sold most of the furniture to make your loan payments," Shade said.

"Land rich, penny poor," the banker tsked as if rehearsed and raised his nose in the air.

"You give us six months to pay your bank loan off and we'll build you a house." Blaze had had enough of Spencer. Shade wrapped his arm around Blaze's shoulders and walked him into the parlor.

"How the hell are we going to pay him off, Blaze?"

"I'm going to meet up with Colonel Crockett," Blaze said quietly. Keeping an eye on Spencer, he set the butt of the rifle on the floor and leaned the barrel against the wall.

"Davy Crockett?" Shade's eyes widened. "How is going to Texas with Crockett and his Tennessee Mounted Volunteers going to get us any money?"

"I'll give you an additional three months, Blaze." Spencer hurried to the open door. "But I'll need free scotch and bourbon for life in addition to the new house, Shade."

"You're going to give us six months or I'll help Shade burn this house down." Stalking back into the foyer, Blaze fixed a stare on the crooked banker that had backed down many a ruffian. "Except we won't do it before you move in. We'll wait until after you're in it."

"Coming from Shade that would be a worrisome threat." The blood drained from Spencer's pinched face as he backpedaled out of the house. "Coming from you, Blaze, I consider that a solemn promise."

Blaze walked to the door and watched the chicken-hearted banker flap his way down the porch steps and along the wide, brick walkway leading to the hitching post.

My wife's birthday is May fifteenth," Spencer said from a safe distance as he untethered the horse hitched to his little yellow buggy. "I'll grant you a reprieve until then."

"That's just short of five months, so forget charging us the extra interest." Damn, Blaze thought, none of this seemed remotely legal.

Nodding, Spencer hopped into his buggy and snapped the reins to the horse's back. Shade slammed the front door shut and faced Blaze.

"You can meet up with Crockett, Blaze, but it's not to go fight for the independence of Texas, is it?"

"What do you think? Our backs are to the wall. I'm going to find Jim."

"How can you be sure he's still in Texas?"

"I'm not." Blaze recalled the day Jim had gifted them with the knives his older brother, Rezin, had made. Based on that conversation, Blaze said, "But Jim said if we ever needed him, he'd be in Texas."

"Let's say you find him, what makes you think Jim Bowie would give up his precious secret to you?"

"Pa always said all Bowies from Scotland are kin. Since our ancestors came from the same Scottish town where Jim's lived, maybe Jim will share the secret. We'll keep it among cousins."

"Distant cousins."

"It's not like I won't repay him, Shade."

"Fine. I'll go with you. But when Jim won't tell you anything, you have to go with me to Galveston Island on the Gulf of Mexico."

"What?" Blaze laughed. "Oh, I see. We're going to get the money we need by joining up with Jean Lafitte."

"Why the hell not?" Shade folded his arms over his chest and cocked his head to one side.

"Because the Pirate of the Gulf hasn't been seen for twelve years."

"We'll find him. In the meantime, I'm gonna ferry on over to naughty ol' Natchez."

With that, Shade yanked the door open. Rifle blasts filled the air and bullets whizzed between Blaze and his brother. Blaze jumped back at the same time Shade did and together they glanced outside.

"Looks like Rufus Ray and all nine of Lucy's older brothers are out there," Shade said, the gleam of adventure burning in his eyes.

"Hell's bells." Blaze kicked the door shut. He stuck out his right hand and Shade grabbed it. "No better time to meet up with Crockett than now!"

CHAPTER 3

ASIATIC CHOLERA WAS A MERCILESS KILLER.

Noelle Charbonnez knew she had reason to fear the worst. Standing in the tiny, curtained off area Noelle stared out the glassless window. Fifty yards away, near the San Antonio River, a copse of cottonwood trees swayed in the January breeze. A shiver ran up Noelle's spine and she wrapped the threadbare serape more tightly around her thin shift.

"I pray the rumor about Jim Bowie being in San Antonio is true," Mama whispered upon waking.

Noelle turned and taking only a couple of steps, sat on the edge of the cornhusk mattress. Her mother had fallen ill two days earlier and steadily worsened. Since Mama was married to a Catholic, the San Fernando Church had sent over a priest who took one look at her and performed the last rites.

"Please don't waste precious strength talking about him," Noelle said.

"Jim is an old and dear friend." Mama's voice was strained, her laughter forever lost. "If the rumor is true and he's at the Alamo, I want you to meet him."

"I don't wish to meet anybody named *Bowie*."

She offered her mother the treatment for cholera; water.

Like most cholera patients she'd only managed to sip a little. Mama shook her head and Noelle set the cup aside. Almost before Noelle's eyes, Trilby Charbonnez Herrera's skin had withered and turned ashen. Her aristocratic hands were icy, her lovely face drawn, her brown eyes sunken.

"Ma chère." Mama smiled softly, gazing up at Noelle. "Your hair reminds me of those dark copper irises that bloom every spring around the fountain in your grandmother's yard."

"Shh, please rest."

"I can't rest until you promise to go back home."

"I'll go home when you go. For now, I'm happy—"

"I won't be here tomorrow, Noelle." Mama grasped Noelle's hand.

"Don't say that." Noelle's throat ached with emotion and anticipated grief.

"Even though General Cos surrendered our beloved mission to us in December, I fear that battle was just a taste of what's to come before the Texas rebellion against Mexico is settled." Mama grimaced with pain. "Carlos and Felice will be safe because they're Mexican. But you are Anglo. The Mexican Congress has passed immigration laws that make it dangerous for you to be here."

"You're Anglo, but you stayed."

"Because this is my husband's home. Carlos wants Texas independence. As a Tejano, he supports the cause and will never leave. Since the fighting in December, I have been hoping to find someone passing through to take you back East."

"You want Jim Bowie to be the one to take me, don't you?" Noelle's stomach clenched when Mama nodded.

"Oui. Jim lived in Louisiana. He's the logical one to take you."

"I have no one in Natchez, Mississippi."

Mama gave her a look that clearly said *you know that's not true.*

"You have your grandmother, Noelle."

"Who despises us."

"She despises me for marrying Marcel. You, she will forgive. Oui?"

"Oui. Yes, but with one very strict condition."

"Not so strict when you consider the fortune your grandmother can lay at your feet. Go back to where—" Mama choked. Noelle offered the water, but again she refused. Picking up where she left off, her mother said, "Where we lived from the time you were two until you were seven. Remember those magnifique five years?"

Sudden muscular cramping drew Mama's body up in a tight ball. The dreadful scrounge had dehydrated her and during the last few hours had made her delirious several times. Helplessly, Noelle witnessed her mother's agony. Each time Mama's eyes closed Noelle expected her to fall comatose, a common step along the path to death for cholera victims. Finally, Mama's body relaxed but her eyes remained shut.

"Noelle," Mama whispered. "You were the best present your father ever gave me."

"About Papa..." Noelle knew this was her last chance to ask the question that had haunted her for years. Mentally she squared her shoulders and said, "I heard him say more than once that I was not his child. Was Marcel Charbonnez my real father?"

"Why didn't you ask me this before now?" Mama's eyes fluttered open.

"Because I feared the answer. But I want to know."

"Noelle, before you were born I loved two men. After I lost them both, you and I found Carlos and Felice. For years, Carlos has loved you like he was your real father."

"I love Carlos and Felice, too. But which one of those first two men was my real father?" Her mother didn't answer and Noelle was about to repeat her question when Mama shuddered violently.

"When Carlos and Felice get back from Gonzales tell

them how much I loved them, Noelle. Tell them, gracias for everything."

"They love you, too." Noelle felt tears burning in her eyes.

"It is my dying wish for you to return home and reestablish your relationship with your grandmother." Mama's eyes grew lucid. "But—" she broke off as if undecided about continuing.

"But what?"

"If you cannot happily comply with her condition, then don't. When you find—" Mama sighed, too tired to continue and closed her eyes again.

Using the corner of a blanket, Noelle swiped away the perspiration on her mother's forehead. Mama's eyes finally opened. Noelle smiled and listened to her raspy voice.

"Noelle, when you find a man who you can love as much as I've loved the three men in my life then never let him go for any amount of money. I didn't."

"How will I know I have found such a man?"

For the first time in forty-eight hours, a peaceful expression crossed Mama's face. Her mouth curved into a smile and Noelle suspected this was the last one she would ever see.

"You will know it's him the moment he takes you into his arms." Looking up at Noelle, there was a dreamy quality in Mama's eyes and smile. Then her tone grew urgent. "Promise me when you find that man you will never let him go and you will always—" Mama choked, but refused the water.

"Always love and laugh," Noelle said for her, having heard it so many times before.

"Oui, and promise me you will go back home."

"Oui, I promise." Noelle would have promised her the moon.

"Tell my mother I loved her to the very end. And remember I loved you most of all, Noelle."

"Je t'aime, Mama."

Then Mama's eyes closed forever.

Glad she hadn't promised not to cry, Noelle crumpled at her mother's bedside and wept. Exhausted, she hadn't realized she had fallen asleep until she heard Carlos' voice. Noelle struggled to her feet.

"Trilby?"

Shadows of dusk played across Carlos' face as he stood at the end of the bed. Noelle had covered her mother with the blanket. But the stench of cholera had surely hinted at the blow Noelle must deliver.

"Carlos, I had to close your cobbler's shop," Noelle said. He and Felice had traveled forty miles to a settlement where Texas Rangers were posted in hopes they could sell or repair boots and shoes. "While you and Felice were gone, Mama died of cholera."

Tears spilled from Carlos' dark eyes, streaked his brown cheeks and glistened on his thick, black mustache. Wrenching sobs rocked the frayed sombrero hanging down his back and fluttered his faded poncho. Noelle hurried around the end of the bed and gave him a hug.

"She said to tell you she loved you, Carlos." Noelle wondered if she would see the day when she repeated a similar sentiment to her grandmother. "Mama said gracias for everything."

"She was a great lady. More than I deserved."

"Where's Felice?" Noelle asked in regard to her stepsister.

"At the shop."

"Help me bring a coffin back here before Felice comes home."

Her mother's body was already swelling and soon the flesh would fall to pieces. Noelle led a bereft Carlos out of the house. Due to the outbreak of cholera, coffins were readily available and they quickly returned. But the one they obtained wouldn't fit through the narrow front door. Carlos carried Mama outside and placed her in the wooden box. Noelle covered her with the blanket.

"Is that Mama?" Felice called from a distance and started running. Mama always complimented pretty Felice on having the most beautiful, light yellowish brown skin tone she'd ever seen. *It's a unique and magnifique pale olive*, Mama would say and kiss Felice's cheek. Collapsing in the dust beside the coffin, Felice touched a trembling hand to the bloated chest. "I knew it!" Through her tears, she looked up at Noelle. "I had a nightmare Mama died while we were gone. When we got back, Papa made me stay at the shop and unload all the boots and shoes and hats we could not sell. Why did you not come and get me?"

"We hoped to spare you from seeing Mama like this." Noelle knelt and wrapped an arm around Felice's slim shoulders as Carlos wept. "Let's take Mama to the burial ground for cholera victims and say adios to her there."

Felice's mother had died in childbirth. She had longed for a mother and was thrilled when her father had married Noelle's mother. Felice had improved her English, right along with Carlos, as a way to show her love for Mama. Noelle felt her chin quiver and she clenched her jaw to stop it from showing. Felice suddenly grabbed handfuls of Noelle's serape.

"You will not leave us now that Mama's gone, will you, Noelle?"

"Mama said to tell you how much she loved you, Felice. She wants us to love and laugh." Noelle smiled as she smoothed a thick, straight lock of black hair out of Felice's large, almond shaped, brown eyes. "She wanted us to go on with our lives."

"But will you go on with yours here?"

"You know Trilby wanted Noelle to go back to her child-hood home, Felice."

"Si, Papa I know." Felice sniffled and nodded.

"If and when I find someone to take me home you and Carlos can come with me."

Such naked longing showed on Felice's lovely face that Noelle took hold of her sister's hands. For years she and

Felice had raptly listened to Trilby's tales of endless wealth from the gatehouse, up the circular drive to Cupid's fountain among flower gardens and manicured lawns, to winding staircases, twenty foot high ceilings, polished marble floors, carriages, horses, and boats. A large staff, with their own quarters, ran a magnificent three story castle-like mansion where high society gathered to dine scrumptiously and politic in a formal dining room, to flirt outrageously and dance in the glittering ballroom.

"If only we *could*, Noelle."

"IF WE DON'T GET to San Antonio soon, I'm turning back," Shade said. "I'm saddle-sore as all get-out."

"Hell, you've been singing that song ever since we crossed the Sabine River and headed to Nacogdoches, Shade," Blaze said, stretching as he rode alongside him. They were miles southwest of Nacogdoches now and Blaze was saddle-sore, too. "We're a little over halfway there."

"That means what... another two hundred and fifty miles to the Alamo?"

"Yeah."

The days were brilliant under the biggest sky Blaze had ever seen. At night they rode beneath a bright moon and shining stars. Leaving the near tropical weather and wet marshes back home, the journey through these drier grasslands seemed to be an endless trip across the Mexican province of Texas. At least, the abundance of wild turkeys, rabbits and prairie chickens kept stomachs full.

"What do you make of those two Tennessee Mounted Volunteers who claim to be from Galveston Island?" Shade asked.

"The pirate and the Indian?"

"Especially the pirate," Shade said under his breath, as they rode at the back of the group. "He swears he sailed with Lafitte."

Giving his name as Pirate, he had black hair and

whiskers. A deep scar etched his forehead and others marred the backs of his hands. The Indian with him, whose face resembled ancient leather, had spoken only once to warn them of a buffalo stampede.

"I think we'll never know if he sailed with Lafitte."

Blaze's saddle creaked as he glanced around at the dozen other men traveling with them on the El Camino Real Trail. Colonel David Crockett led the way. Clad in a coonskin cap and fringed leather, Crockett was a man to be reckoned with. He was also an excellent yarn spinner and liked to tell of his adventures with Old Betsy. A gift from the people of Tennessee, Old Betsy was Crockett's favorite rifle, named after his favorite sister. Blaze and Shade enjoyed his tall tales and fiddle playing around the evening campfires.

Pirate, in a seaman's jacket and work pants, and the buckskin-clad Indian were in stark contrast to another Volunteer sporting a frock coat and red breeches. This man prided himself on his singing which he managed to do even during the dust storms when everyone else pulled a neckerchief over their nose and mouth to breathe more easily.

"I wish we were done and heading back home," Shade said.

"Who's put you in a sour mood?"

"That cheroot-smoking dandy in the lace cuffs and top hat." Shade frowned. "He won another dollar off me this morning with his dad-blamed thimble trick."

"Don't bet against Thimblerig. Colonel Crockett doesn't hold with gambling," Blaze reminded Shade who agreed with a single nod.

"I'm tired of that other fool singing about his dalliances."

"Who me?"

Blaze raised his chin in greeting as Bee-Hunter guided his horse to trot closer to them. A man in his early twenties, he scouted out bee trees and sold the honey. Clad in deerskin pants and a jacket ornamented with Indian beads, he wore a white shirt with a black ribbon tied at his neck. He polished his boots daily and got on Shade's nerves hourly.

"I won't sing any more today if you tell me what you plan to do in the next town," Bee-Hunter said. "You two never tell me anything until I've missed the adventure."

With his usual amount of diplomacy, Shade said, "That's because you're so busy caterwauling about made up women you never get to the cantinas where real women are."

Jovially, Bee-Hunter replied, "You know I don't drink, Shade."

Thimblerig joined them and gave his opinion while bouncing a thimble in his hand. "I think Bee-Hunter spouts romance while the Bowie brothers do the dance."

They all laughed. Colonel Crockett turned around in his saddle, raised his right hand and signaled.

"Blaze!"

CHAPTER 4

"Yes, sir!" Blaze tipped the brim of his buckskin cowboy hat at his companions and rode to the front of the group. "Colonel Crockett?"

"I need to speak my mind before we get to San Antonio de Bexar, because once we arrive I may not get the chance," Crockett said with a cursory glance. He was always on the lookout for Indians and cougars. "You said when you met up with us that you and Shade were going to find Jim Bowie. I appreciate your honesty. It's been a pleasure to travel with you."

"Thank you, sir. It's been an honor," Blaze replied, wondering where this was headed.

"Jim Bowie's known all across the South as a superb knife fighter." Colonel Crockett motioned to the Bowie knife strapped to Blaze's leg.

"He taught us a thing or two. Probably felt it was his job, since he gave us the knives."

"Speaking of jobs, I understand Sam Houston sent Jim to San Antonio to carry out a specific task."

"I was glad to hear that back in Nacogdoches. It was my confirmation Jim may still be in Texas."

"Your timing is bad, Blaze."

"Yes, sir, but things were bad in Louisiana, too."

"General Antonio Lopez de Santa Anna will pay a visit to San Antonio soon because of Cos's surrender of the Alamo last month."

Blaze had heard Colonel Crockett say Santa Anna was embarrassed and angry over a December defeat suffered by a General Cos. As for Santa Anna, he called himself the president of Mexico, but by all accounts he was a sadistic, blood hungry dictator.

"I figure Cos would be dead by now if he weren't Santa Anna's brother-in-law." Crockett chuckled and then sobered. "As to brothers, that's where I want to speak my mind. I like Shade but he's a hotblood. If you two are still with my Tennessee Mounted Volunteers when Santa Anna rolls into town, keep Shade on a short leash. Otherwise you'll be hauling your brother back to Louisiana in a box."

"Shade and I have dealt with bloodthirsty men before," Blaze said, hoping to allay the colonel's fears. "Shade named his horse Buckshot because that bay's as good at dodging bullets as we are."

Crockett shook his head. "Nothing will compare to what you'll face if you're caught in the Texas fight for independence. I know from serving in the United States Congress, Texas has been claimed by many countries, one of which was Spain. When Mexico won their independence from Spain, they claimed Texas. Wanting Texas settled, Mexico initially encouraged immigration from the United States. But that's all changed."

Riding ever deeper into the land being dangerously disputed, Blaze listened to Crockett learning there were some thirty thousand Anglos in Texas now, compared to less than eight thousand Mexicans. The *change* had been outlawing immigration. General Santa Anna was infamous for his brutality in trying to control the Anglo colonists already living in Texas.

"If I understand the current situation correctly, Santa Anna is trying to force a centralist government with Texas under his dictatorship," Blaze said. "But the Anglo-Americans living here, who call themselves Texians, along with the Tejanos, who are Mexicans wanting independence from Mexico, favor a federalist government where they can be a fairly autonomous state. So, these two groups are rebelling against Santa Anna."

"You have the famed Bowie brains as well as their brawn, Blaze."

Blaze acknowledged the compliment with a self-conscious nod. Crockett went on to say how Santa Anna planned to consolidate his power over the Texians and Tejanos because he viewed Texas, as its own state, being just a step away from becoming part of the United States. The escalating conflict between the dictator and these Texas rebels was rapidly building toward a deadly revolution.

"I empathize with their passion in fighting for one's home. Shade and I are fighting for our independence and land, as well, Colonel Crockett."

"Do what you must, then get the hell out of Texas."

Continuing to lead the pack, they traveled in companionable silence. It was an hour later when Blaze saw a sign stating; *'Pedro Garcia keeps mustangs and people...1 1/4 leagues off right hand path 3 times'.* Having had a good year, farmers were glad to feed the men going to fight for Texas freedom. Pedro Garcia was one such farmer firmly refusing to be subordinate to a Mexican dictatorship. Thanks to him, Crockett's men sat around a campfire and ate venison, black-eyed peas and cornbread for supper. Blaze and Shade offered to pay, but Señor Garcia would not hear of it. His stomach full, Blaze yawned. The Bee-Hunter hummed.

"Let's get, before that fool starts singing." Shade groaned and stood.

Blaze agreed and got to his feet. Sure enough as they walked away from the campfire Blaze heard Bee-Hunter coaxing some of the other men into a rousing chorus.

> *Hurray for the Texas Volunteers!*
> *We are the boys so handy.*

We'll teach the Mexicans to fear-
Our Yankee Doodle Dandy!

Blaze hoped that would be the case as he settled down for the night on a pile of hay in Garcia's small barn. When he had closed his eyes, Shade was near him. But deep in the night he heard Shade's low chuckle a few yards away. A female giggle followed and Blaze knew his brother had sought out Garcia's daughter.

From Vidalia to Nacogdoches, Shade had brooded over Lucy Ray. But by the time they had crossed the Trinity River, Shade's thoughts started flowing in a new direction. He had an itch for a woman. Any woman.

Blaze rolled away to his side and fell asleep.

Between the Trinity and Brazos Rivers, the only women they encountered were those in cantinas. In a cantina in San Felipe de Austin, the owner's daughter flirted shamelessly with Blaze. After serving Blaze supper, she boldly offered herself to him as dessert. Shade grinned at him and followed one of the working girls upstairs.

Blaze smiled at the proprietor's daughter and politely declined. He paid her twice what he owed for supper and left the cantina. It wasn't long before Shade found him at the hitching post, untethering the reins to his horse, Blue. The reddish brown sorrel had a light colored mane and tail and allowed no one but Blaze to ride him.

"How do you feel after bedding your first woman in weeks?" Shade asked, before untethering his horse with the black mane and tail.

"I didn't," Blaze replied and swung himself into the saddle.

"What?" Shade's expression turned doubtful and he missed putting his foot in the stirrup. Blaze raised his brows and smothered a laugh. "Why not?"

"I feel too restless." Blaze held up his hand as Shade opened his mouth.

"It's being in these strange surroundings while worrying

about home that's making you restless." Shade managed to mount Buckshot on his second try. In the saddle he turned to Blaze. "Don't you think so?"

"Yeah, partly." Sitting in the yellow light of the cantina, Blaze was surprised by Shade's insight. "But a real home is more than just a house and land. A real home is the freedom to live your life the way you want it to be, with people you would die for. You have the independence to leave, but you would never want to." Blaze rotated his shoulders, trying to dislodge this new uneasiness... awareness... emptiness... whatever the hell it was. Confusion crossed Shade's face, but Blaze simply shrugged. "Come on. Let's catch up with Colonel Crockett."

They pushed south. Along a grassy trail, under a cloudy sky, Shade confided in Blaze.

"Garcia's daughter was kind of shy and I liked it."

"Shy and you liked it?" Blaze blinked and shook his head as if he hadn't heard right.

"Yeah." Shade sat taller in the saddle. "I'm not giving up wenchin', but I'm going to keep an eye out for a shy and innocent girl in Texas."

"An innocent girl will make you work for her favors, little brother."

"I'm turning over a new leaf."

"Good." Blaze wondered if the leaf turning had to do with a real home being more than just a house and land.

"I want to find a raven-haired beauty like Jim said his wife, Ursula, was." Shade gazed into the horizon. "My señorita will be exotic, but so innocent I'll have to teach her everything."

"Can you slow down enough to notice it's your raven-haired beauty's first time?"

"Yeah, I can." Shade seemed to decide that on the spot. "When I find this virgin, with her long black hair, you're keeping your hands off her."

"What?" Blaze started to protest, saying he had never

taken a girl from Shade. Instead, he encouraged his brother along this new path. "I promise I will."

"Maybe bedding a virgin would cure your restlessness." Shade titled his head and grinned.

"There'd have to be more to it than just that."

"It couldn't hurt. You've been in a sour mood."

Blaze threw his head back and laughed.

"JIM BOWIE ARRIVED WEEKS AGO," Felice said to Noelle in Carlos' cobbler shop.

"I know." Noelle moved away from a small, glassless window as the breeze blew in.

"It's February and you haven't gone to see him. Does that mean you're staying in Texas with Papa and me?"

"It means I don't care for Jim Bowie, his brother, Rezin, or anybody else named Bowie." Noelle softened her tone. "It means I'm torn between my love for you and keeping my promise to Mama."

Just then distant shouts floated their way from Main Plaza. Hurrying into the cobbler shop from Potrero Street, Carlos removed his sombrero and delivered big news.

"Muchachas, the reason on why Colonel Bowie came to Bexar is out!" He'd spoken of San Antonio de Bexar as it was referred to locally. His kind brown eyes were wide. "Have you heard?"

"No, Papa, why is he here?" Felice asked.

"Sam Houston sent Jim Bowie to blow up the Alamo." Carlos glanced at Felice and then at Noelle.

"What?" Jarred, Noelle stared at Carlos in disbelief. Mama had loved the old mission and lived to see it surrendered by General Cos. "Are you sure?"

"Si," Carlos replied. "If you're going to talk to Colonel Bowie, Noelle, do so fast. They say after he blows up the Alamo, he will leave."

"So be it." Noelle knew only a Bowie could be cold

hearted enough to destroy their beloved Alamo and ride out of town. Between clenched teeth, she said, "Let him leave."

"But Trilby..." Carlos stopped when Noelle frowned. He stood in the middle of the shop running the brim of his sombrero through his fingers. Shifting the subject, he said, "A Colonel William Barret Travis, all the way from Alabama, has arrived. Talk is Colonel Davy Crockett and his Tennessee Mounted Volunteers are not far behind."

"They're probably coming to help Jim Bowie blow up the Alamo," Noelle said.

An out of breath Señora Esparza stopped in the doorway, her skirt swirling dirt off the street and into the shop. Cleaning the leather shoes, boots, cowboy hats, and sombreros never ceased.

"Colonel Crockett just rode into town!" the señora said. "Hurry to Main Plaza!" Turning, her words came to them over her shoulder. "Jim Bowie's on his way here from the Alamo to welcome Crockett and the Volunteers!"

Carlos and Felice walked to the door as Noelle shrank back until she met with the cool adobe wall.

"Carlos, you and Felice go. I'll keep the shop open and dust."

DISMOUNTING BLUE in this dusty town called Bexar, Blaze squinted against the sunlight breaking through the clouds. Long auburn waves caught his eye in a sea of hundreds of black-haired people. The redhead must be an American immigrant, Blaze thought. If he were still atop Blue he'd have taken another look. But on the ground he lost sight of the fiery colored head.

"Look at all the raven-haired señoritas!" Shade elbowed him.

"Buenas tardes," said a woman pushing her way between Blaze and Shade.

Blaze swung his head left and a pie-faced señorita batted

her lashes at him. Blaze returned her greeting. Shade looked to his right and grinned at the woman.

"Bien venido... welcome," a second woman said on Blaze's other side.

As Shade talked to them, Blaze studied the shifting crowd. Vaguely he heard Shade agree to something called a fandango. Blaze glimpsed the copper curls again. Set in a flawlessly beautiful, ivory face were big, hazel eyes. Despite the excitement of the moment, calm intelligence shone in those eyes.

"I'm going to fix it so our pokers stay hot all night," Shade said, as he leaned close to Blaze.

Blaze frowned and shook his head. He looked to the spot where he had seen the young woman with dark red hair and greenish gold eyes. She was gone. Damn.

Undaunted, Shade said, "Blaze, this is Rosa and this is—"

"Maria." The second woman licked her lips.

"So, Maria, what's a fandango?" Blaze asked.

CHAPTER 5

"QUIET, YOU RING-TAILED HYENAS!"

The stranger shouting stood on top of a wooden box in the center of Main Plaza. Noelle listened as he explained that James Neill, the colonel in charge of the garrison at the Alamo, had to leave Bexar to care for his family who'd been stricken with illness. Neill had turned over his command of the regular army to Colonel William Barret Travis. When the crowd's enthusiastic approval of Colonel Travis died down, the speaker said he hoped everyone would now endorse his nomination of the man taking charge of all the volunteers at the Alamo.

"I would personally follow him to hell and back," the man atop the box said. "He's fought alligators with his bare hands and opposed men when he was armed with naught but a little knife no bigger'n my foot." The man held up his huge foot and the crowd roared. "I'd like to nominate Colonel Jim Bowie as leader of the volunteers and if I don't hear any other nominations I'll declare the nomination closed and Colonel Bowie elected."

Everyone cheered and clapped except for Noelle. She wished Carlos hadn't locked the shop and made her come with him and Felice. Noelle ducked her head as people threw their odd assortment of hats, caps and sombreros into the air to celebrate Colonel Bowie's win.

In the distance, to her left, a buckskin cowboy hat was seized and set on a dark blond head. Thick hair touched the collar at the back of his shirt and covered his ears with a sweep falling across his sun-bronzed forehead. His nose was straight and his chin had a stubborn tilt. Along his jaw lay a shadow of whiskers. The set of his chiseled profile projected confidence. She assumed he was one of Crockett's Tennessee Mounted Volunteers. He nodded to someone and Noelle recognized Maria, who was either batting her eyelashes at him or had a bug in her eye.

The blond man, as if feeling Noelle's stare, pulled his gaze up from the cantina woman's low cut blouse. He looked dead on at Noelle with eyes a color she'd never before seen. They were a smoky gray. Like burning ashes blown out of a raging fire, the heat of his bold gaze singed her. Noelle's face flushed. She turned away and placed the backs of her fingers to her cheek. Sure enough, her fingers were cold on the heated skin of her face.

The man was as handsome as the Anglos Mama had described to her from back home. Handsome? No, this man was gorgeous!

Noelle risked a second glance to confirm he was truly as attractive as her first impression. Yes, he was and he was still looking at her. His sensuous, full lips parted in a riveting smile. Spellbound, Noelle scrutinized him. He appeared savvy and tough, lean and sinewy. When he tilted his head at her, Noelle realized he knew she was staring at him and nervously averted her gaze.

"Three cheers for Colonel Bowie!" someone yelled to the crowd

"Hip, hip, hurrah! Hip, hip, hurrah! Hip, hip, hurrah!"

Without moving her head, Noelle strained her eyes to the left. The man with blond hair appeared to be listening to someone resembling him enough to be his brother. Brown hair curling over his collar, the second man wore a coonskin cap, just like Colonel Crockett's. Maybe they were related to Davy Crockett. Whatever the case, these two men were so striking Noelle figured they created a sensation among women wherever they went. The shifting crowd, or the cantina women working it, stole both men from Noelle's view.

"Look! There's Colonel Bowie!" Felice said.

A tall, broad shouldered man with deep-set eyes took his turn on the box.

"I am Jim Bowie and I thank you. No man can be honest and say that praise does not warm his heart. Also no man can be honest and fail to say the things that are true and right."

Noelle listened as this man, whom her mother had called friend, spoke of the Mexicans as his amigos. He pointed out that he had become a Mexican citizen and married a Mexican woman named Ursula. She had been with child when she died of cholera in 1833. He had loved Ursula very much and was deeply saddened by her death. Having lived and worked with the Mexicans, he knew there were many who felt as he did about the tyranny of the Mexican *president*, Santa Anna. Those Mexicans were fighting on the American side for the independence of Texas. Identifying with their cause, Bowie said he had not been able to remove the garrison's artillery, blow up the Alamo and walk away as Sam Houston had ordered.

"How about that, Noelle?" Carlos asked.

Noelle frowned, crossed her arms under her breasts and remained silent. But her heart ached with compassion for the expectant mother who had suffered the same horrible death as Mama.

"Since the Alamo's intact, Colonel Neill is within his rights to appoint Colonel Travis as leader. It's military procedure," Colonel Bowie said. "It's also customary in Texas for volunteers to select their leader in the fields. And that's what you've just done in nominating me. It creates confusion in this instance as to who's in command of the Alamo. But with all due respect, I intend to place myself at Colonel Travis' disposal. We'll see what arrangements can be made to keep everyone happy and intent on the only end we serve—God and Texas!"

The crowd erupted with wholehearted support. When the cheering died down, Davy Crockett and his group were welcomed. The colonel spoke of Texas as their common country and said he had brought his Volunteers to aid the Texas cause. Exhausted after their long trip, he would speak again at the fandango.

"I am going to introduce myself and shake hands with Colonel Bowie," Carlos said to Noelle and Felice.

"I wish you wouldn't, Carlos," Noelle said and placed her hand on his arm.

"I'll see my señoritas at home for supper." Carlos patted her hand, turned and waded through the crowd.

"Let's go home, Felice."

"Miss?" came a deep voice from behind Noelle.

Noelle twirled to face a man whose dark blond bangs swept across his right brow. Close up, his gray eyes captured and mesmerized her. Her heart pounded. He had to be around six foot three because he towered over her. Never had she confronted such a mass of muscle planted before her in the form of one magnificent male.

"Are you going to the fandango?"

"The dance isn't until the day after tomorrow," Noelle heard herself say as Felice clutched her hand.

The man grinned and Noelle widened her eyes as if that might help her take in all of her overwhelming reactions caused by this striking stranger.

"Will you be there?" he asked again.

Noelle shyly raised one shoulder and lowered her eyes from his. A fringed buckskin jacket stretched across wide shoulders. Knotted at the open throat of his blue shirt a yellow neckerchief lay against sun bronzed skin. A broad chest filled out a shirt tucked into snug buckskin breeches.

Around his trim waist he wore a blue sash. There, a knife handle protruded from a scabbard tied with the sash.

"Our fandangos are a happy time."

Felice's merry comment yanked Noelle's roving study back up the man's solid body.

"What's your name?" the blond asked Felice.

"Felice Herrera," she answered.

So he was interested in Felice. Noelle could neither deny nor explain the stab of disappointment she felt at that realization. She covered it up with a smile.

"Hey!" the man with brown hair called out across the throng of townsfolk. "Get back over here."

The blond presented them with his back and motioned for the other man to come over to him. Beneath the fringe of his jacket his buttocks was tightly rounded. Felice nudged her and Noelle quickly lifted her gaze. The other man had a slight scowl on his face as he worked his way through the crowd still roaming Main Plaza.

"Noelle," Felice said with an ear-to-ear grin, "Mama told us to love and laugh. There's one for each of us."

"Shh, you're loco." Noelle wasn't taken with the man with the darker hair. "We've never even seen them before."

"You're the one who's loco." Felice stood her ground, held fast to Noelle's hand and said, "Many girls my age are married with babies. We are *spinners!*"

"Spinsters." Noelle knew Felice often forgot her English when anxious. "And no, we are not spinsters."

"Rosa just caught the one who has brown hair." As Felice looked past the blond man whose back was still to them, her expression changed from excited to dejected. "Si, we will go home."

With a last glance at the back of the muscular, fairer haired rogue, Noelle turned and maneuvered a path through the crowd. They hadn't gone far when someone touched her elbow.

"Wait."

Pivoting, Noelle faced two men. Close up, the man with

brown hair had a reckless, devil-may-care gleam in eyes which were also gray. That glint was present in the eyes of the other man, but tempered. She wondered which one had touched her arm.

"My name is Shade," the darker haired man said, looking at Noelle and then at Felice. "My brother, Blaze, and I rode in with the Tennessee Mounted Volunteers and we're at your service. I stopped you so we could introduce ourselves."

"I'm Felice," she said grinning up at Shade. "Felice means happy in Spanish."

So they *are* brothers, Noelle thought. But it was Shade and not the blond who had stopped her. She felt another jab of disappointment. She glanced at the one called Blaze. His lips spread into a smile so exhilarating, it scorched her cheeks. How could she be so hot in February? Blaze's head tilted toward them in polite acknowledgment of Shade's introduction. Someone had taught them manners.

"It's nice to meet two of Colonel Crockett's men," Noelle said, remembering her own manners. "If you will be staying at the Alamo, I hope you're prepared for a battle in the near future."

"I think a fandango's in the near future," Shade said.

"Will *you* be there?" Blaze peered at Noelle. The tone in his deep voice said he wanted an answer this time.

"Si, she will be," Felice decided for Noelle with another big smile directed at Shade. Belatedly, Felice nervously said, "But we do not work at the cantina. We are not trumpets!"

Noelle tensed and for a moment she didn't know whether to laugh or cry. Maybe they hadn't noticed. No such luck. Blaze bowed his head and smothered a chuckle.

"You mean strumpets?" Shade asked and laughed.

"Si." Felice nodded at Shade with naked adoration on her face. "We are *nice* girls."

With Jim Bowie and Davy Crockett gone, the throng of people thinned revealing the lingering cantina women. Waving at the brothers nearly bounced Rosa and Maria's generous bosoms out of the tops of their blouses. Too bad the first man Noelle had ever felt drawn to was attracted to others. In turn, never had Noelle seen her step-sister entranced by any man. If Felice wanted to stay a *nice* girl she had better stop looking at Shade like that.

"We know you are nice girls and we mean no disrespect," Blaze replied.

Shade wrapped an arm around his brother and whispered something to him Noelle couldn't hear, other than the name Ursula. Too gracious to leave without saying goodbye, she did however squeeze Felice's hand in warning. Shade appeared to be in his mid-twenties. As for Blaze, the way Shade had come to him across Main Plaza said Blaze was the older brother. The leader. They were both old enough to have had years of experience with women. For women who had no experience, these rakehells would be an impossible challenge. What's more, their confident, cocky attitudes suggested they heard nothing but 'yeses' from women. When the brothers turned their attention back to her and Felice, Noelle's heart thumped so wildly, she thought she might faint. She was as afraid of the blond as she was attracted to him.

"We can't go to the fandango because we're in mourning," Noelle quickly said, trying to breathe evenly.

"Mourning?" Felice asked with a whine. "But Mama made us promise to—"

"Adios," Noelle said politely as she turned away, tugging Felice along behind her.

Splaying a hand over his heart, Blaze felt for Cupid's arrow. Surely he had been shot by the god of erotic love because desire had slammed into him the moment he saw that redhead. Blaze pictured lassoing the willowy young woman whose auburn curls would surely dance when she twirled in surprise. Her hazel eyes would no doubt snap with gold and green fire when he tugged her to him. How sweet would her full, pink lips taste should he kiss her right here in Main Plaza?

Blaze let go of the vision and enjoyed the view.

Long thick hair, crimson with the sunlight on it, bounced halfway down the back of her peasant style blouse. At her small waist, a tattered skirt gathered gently and fell over the curve of her slim hips. Slender ankles showed beneath the uneven hem of her skirt and dainty feet were encased in shoes surprisingly far nicer than the rest of her wardrobe.

"I didn't get the redhead's name," Blaze said.

"Me neither." Shade clapped Blaze on the back. "But they're nice girls and I want them."

"Them?" Blaze swung his head sideways and scowled at Shade. "You just told me Felice was the raven-haired beauty you'd hoped to find, like Ursula."

"Raven... red... who cares?" Shade grinned and splayed his hands. "They're both shy and beautiful."

"What about Rosa and Maria?"

"Now that I want an innocent, you're interested in whores?" Before Blaze could say no, Shade said, "We can bed the cantina wenches tonight and tomorrow night. The fandango isn't until the tenth."

"Yes, so the *redhead* told me when I was talking to her," Blaze said, his voice taking on emphasis, *"before* you came along."

"If she and Felice attend the fandango, remember you gave me your word." Shade pointed at him.

"No." Blaze shook his head and clarified, "I didn't promise a damn thing about a redhead. I only gave you my word in regard to an exotic señorita with long black hair. Felice fits the bill perfectly, Shade."

"Yeah, I like Felice. I'm gonna have 'em both."

"I *promise* you, you're not," Blaze said. "Hell, if you'd have been half as polite back home as you were today, nice girls would have thrown themselves at you."

"Maybe I'll impersonate you more often," Shade said with a grin.

"Shade Bowie!" Rosa motioned to him. "Come here and bring your brother for Maria."

"COME HERE, FELICE." Noelle rubbed beet juice between her thumb and finger. She grew beets fall, winter and spring to sell and eat. Mama had taught them an extra bonus about beets. "Let's pink your pretty cheeks."

Felice tilted up her chin and using the juice Noelle lightly rouged her soft cheeks to perfection. Since they had no mirror, Felice did the same for Noelle and they hugged in a dank corner of the tiny combination kitchen and bedroom where they ate and slept. From behind the curtained-off bedroom he had shared with Mama, Carlos appeared.

"What convinced you to attend the fandango, Noelle?" he asked.

"It's what Mama would have wanted."

"Si, and that is why I am also happy to attend as my daughters' chaperon."

"And I'm going," Noelle wagged her finger at him, "to make certain you don't meet Colonel Bowie tonight, since you weren't able to catch up with him the other day in Main Plaza."

"Your mother did not hold a grudge." Carlos gently patted Noelle's shoulder. "Trilby said what happened to Marcel was his own fault and not that of Jim or Rezin Bowie."

"I'm not convinced and besides there's more to it than that. I will never travel anywhere with a *Bowie*."

CHAPTER 6

THE NIGHT AIR WAS COOL AS BLAZE AND HIS BROTHER RODE their horses to the town hall where the fandango could be heard already in full swing. While passing flat roofed adobe casas where candlelight flickered inside small windows, Blaze wondered if any of them was the one the redhead called home.

During the sunny days, San Antonio de Bexar locals frequented Main Plaza and Military Plaza as well as the little shops and houses lining narrow streets. He had learned that naps, called siestas, happened every afternoon. But the nameless redhead who had captured his attention was not to be seen anywhere, awake or napping.

At night, in the garrison built around a nearly eighty year old chapel known as the Alamo, he and Shade bunked on cornhusk mattresses. Though his quarters were drab, Blaze's dreams were not. In them, Blaze danced with a girl painted by nature's palette. Crimson fire brushed long curls that bounced against ivory skin. Fringed by thick midnight lashes, big eyes blended emerald green with glistening gold. Like raindrops, a few pale freckles splashed a petite nose and the pink of sunrise colored full, kissable lips.

"Think they'll be at the fandango?" Shade asked.

"If they are, there'll be a hundred volunteers and soldiers who'll be in line ahead of you to dance with them."

Despite Shade's dismay on the day they'd arrived, Blaze had insisted on bidding the cantina women adios in Main Plaza and tracking down Jim. They had met up with him inside the Alamo, to the left of the garrison's main gate. Jim had whooped for joy, taken them under his wing and found them bunks at the opposite end of the low barracks near the fort's largest cannon. Blaze had hardly seen a busy Jim since so hadn't asked about the secret, yet.

Now, they dismounted their horses and entered the front door of the town hall. Obviously, the Bexar citizens enjoyed a fandango as much as they did their siestas as surely most of the town was here. The temperature inside was far warmer than outside due to the press of people enjoying their dancing with gusto. Blaze watched clumsy men from Tennessee, Virginia, Missouri, New York, and other states trying their best to keep in step with graceful señoritas. His shoulder grazing the wall to avoid colliding with the dancers, Blaze surveyed the crowd.

"I don't see those girls from Main Plaza anywhere," Shade said.

But Blaze did. About five foot five, a magnificent woman lit up the room as she entered the hall from a small, side door. Wearing a worn blue dress, which looked dated from what he knew of party frocks back home, the redhead was in the company of Felice and a Mexican fellow.

Blaze had no sooner wondered who the man was when Maria and Rosa descended like vultures. Blaze swore under his breath as Shade wrapped his arms around them. Shade had made good on his plan to bed them and had stumbled into the low barracks stinking of cheap perfume and whiskey. As Shade turned to leave with the women, Blaze caught his arm.

"If I get a chance to dance with the redhead while you're wenchin', I'm taking it."

"One dance," Shade said, distracted by the women and grinning at Rosa.

As Rosa tugged Shade toward the door, Maria's fingers brushed Blaze's crotch. "Come with us."

"Shade can handle both of you."

"Si, he says you can, too. *Dance* with me, Blaze."

"OH, NOELLE," Felice said. "Rosa will dance Shade out of here to the cantina. He will not be back and I had so hoped to dance with him. I am leaving."

Not convicting Shade as completely as Felice had, Noelle replied, "If he *does* come back, you won't get to dance with him if you're at home pouting."

Noelle had spotted the brothers the moment she entered the room. Both tall and so handsome, they were hard to miss. She wondered if Maria would dance Blaze out of the fandango. The evening was early and time would tell, but something told her the gorgeous blond in buckskin danced to his own tune. Besides, just because her skin heated and her heart pounded when he had spoken to her the other day didn't mean she gave a fig with whom he danced.

From the various men approaching Noelle and Felice, a young man wearing a deer-hide jacket decorated with Indian beads, a white shirt, deer-hide breeches, and polished boots was the first to reach Noelle. A second, dandified looking fellow with lace around his wrists, a top hat on his head and a cheroot between his teeth, arrived and asked Felice to dance. With an air of defiance, Felice accepted.

When the man clad in deer-hide asked Noelle to dance she ventured a sweeping glance in Blaze's general direction. Seeing him point Maria toward the door, Noelle accepted the man's invitation to dance. Noelle's feet moved to the music, but her head bowed and her shoulders sagged. She knew only too well that Maria could please Blaze much better than she.

Mercy! What did pleasing a man even mean? Her thoughts had inexplicably taken a dangerous new direction. No! Who was she trying to fool? The curious urge to explore uncharted territory had hit her precisely two days ago in Main Plaza.

"May I cut in?"

Noelle looked up and her shoulders squared as her partner halted their dance.

"I was trying to get some experience with a real woman so I could sing about her."

"Get it from some other woman, Bee-Hunter."

Bee-Hunter bowed out and Blaze took command. Noelle's heart waltzed into place as she was swept up in Blaze's embrace. Sinewy arms held her to a rock hard body. Resting her left hand on his broad shoulder, she felt muscles ripple under her palm. A large hand engulfed her right one while his other hand flattened to the small of her back. When he smiled down at her, Noelle waited for the wooden floor beneath her feet to burst into flame.

"What's your name?" Blaze asked.

She couldn't remember how to breathe. Clean shaven and hatless Blaze was wickedly dashing. With his sun-bronzed face, straight white teeth and full smiling lips so close, she couldn't recall how to swallow. When she didn't speak, slashing brows raised over smoldering gray eyes. This man was overwhelming at a distance. Here in his arms...

You will know it's him the moment he takes you into his arms.

"This is where you say your name," he said.

"Noelle," she replied softly as he smiled that riveting smile.

"If Felice means happy, what's the significance of Noelle?"

"I was born on Christmas day."

Noelle's heart thudded so hard she feared he could hear it. She tried to inch her body back from touching his, but her palms were clammy, her knees wobbled and she tromped both of his booted feet! He didn't point it out nor miss a step.

"How many Christmases ago were you born?"

"Twenty, but I certainly do not see how that is any of your business!"

"Good." He chuckled. "You're old enough."

"Old enough for what?" she asked, looking up at him.

"Me." There was strength behind that single word. More gently he told her, "My father was ten years older than my mother and they were closer'n a knife in a scabbard."

Although his voice had taken on a tender tone when he mentioned his parents, the word *me* resounded in Noelle's head. Then it dawned on her. He was flirting with her! Yes! Mama had said men and women often did that at the fancy balls back home. Well, she would not have Blaze think she was unsophisticated. She could learn to play this flirting game, too. A man approached to cut in, but a shake of Blaze's head stopped him.

"I want you, Noelle." Blaze frowned at another man who approached them and thus they were not interrupted. "But my brother wants you, too."

"Then we shan't tell him about us."

Noelle considered that quite the flirtatious reply. When Blaze cocked a brow as if he'd not expected such a witty and coquettish response, she wiggled her fingers at Carlos who nodded his approval of her dancing.

"Who's he?"

"Carlos," she replied mysteriously. Yes indeed! She was doing superbly given this was her first foray into flirting. She'd test a bit of aloofness now by pulling back, but with more finesse and less trampling of his feet. When she leaned back, Blaze's embrace tightened and he pulled her back to him. Sort of like being lassoed, it was the perfect reaction from Blaze. Pleased with herself, Noelle decided to further heighten the intrigue. "I love Carlos."

"He's not your husband, fiancé or boyfriend or he wouldn't be smiling at us. Is he your father?"

"Step-father," she said. Blaze was quite skilled at this game. When Blaze winked at her, Noelle's heart flip flopped and she blurted, "But I do love him and Felice!"

Blaze's gray eyes looked straight into hers. "I've never been in love and I never believed in love at first sight until I spoke to *you*."

"Well now, Blaze." He may have one-upped her about Carlos, but she would even the score. "I knew you were the right man for me the moment you took me into your arms."

Such an endearing grin quirked up one side of Blaze's sensual mouth, that it brought a smile to Noelle's face.

"Good. Because I'm going to marry you, Noelle."

The music stopped and Noelle trampled her own feet. Marry her? What? Don't be a nincompoop! He's just flirting! Blaze steadied her and desperately trying to recover, she held out a trembling hand to him and flirted back.

"I accept your proposal."

Blaze took her hand, but instead of shaking it he brought it to his lips and gallantly kissed it.

"Don't tell Shade or all hell will break loose."

"It will be our secret," she said and gave him an exaggerated, conspiratorial wink.

With a glance over his shoulder, Blaze lowered his head and planted his mouth on hers! His lips were warm and the sensation explosive. Noelle's arms dangled limply at her sides while his hands held her face. His palms were slightly rough and his fingers strong. He slid a hand to the back of her head and a muscular arm snaked around her waist. He molded her breasts to his broad chest and Noelle knew he couldn't help but feel her heart thumping madly against his fringed buckskin.

She could fall in love with a man who kissed like this. Her heart said she had fallen for this man in Main Plaza. Remembering how Mama had spoken of never letting go of the one she loved, Noelle brought her hands up between Blaze's arms and tangled her fingers in his thick hair. He groaned and lifted her against him. She wound her arms around his neck until only her tiptoes touched the floor between his boots.

"Noelle!" Felice giggled somewhere behind her. "What a romantic first kiss."

"Felice, hush!" After breaking off the kiss, Noelle took a step away from Blaze.

"Come back here." Blaze caught Noelle's arm and pulled her to him. He pressed his lips near her ear and asked, "If that was your first kiss, does that mean you're a virgin?"

"Yes," she replied without hesitation. "Not that it's any of your—"

Blaze straightened his stance and scowled down at her, stopping her sentence. This man was as intimidating as he was glorious. Superior masculine power emanated from him, heightening Noelle's sense of femininity."For God's sake, don't tell Shade that, either."

So serious and persuasive was he, Noelle nodded even though she wasn't sure what all he didn't want her to tell Shade. She glanced at Felice, but her step-sister was staring at the front door. Noelle looked back at Blaze and decided to get some answers from him as he had from her.

"I want to know your last name, where you're from and why you're flirting with me."

"I'm not flirting with you, darlin'."

Not flirting? Was he serious about marrying her? Tantalizing craving for and petrifying apprehension of marriage to this magnificent male tickled a new place in her lower body. What was that tickle? Moisture? Heat? Did she have a fever? She did feel clammy and lightheaded. Bewilderment mixed with a fearful sense of having taken on far more than she could handle with this stranger.

"I'm not flirting with you either, Blaze," Noelle mumbled, feeling confused.

"Only with me, Noelle."

Blaze seemingly sealed their *betrothal* with a small wink and by taking her hand. Raking his other hand through his hair, he glanced across the room. Heart hammering and legs shaking, Noelle looked at Felice who was watching Shade strut his way through the crowd.

Noelle tightened her hold on Blaze's hand. Just let Maria or Rosa try to pull this man outside. And do what with him? The terrifying point exactly! Just as quickly, Noelle loosened her grip.

"Here he comes," Blaze said and let go of her hand. "Let's hope he asks Felice to dance."

Not only frightened, never had Noelle been so flattered or so flummoxed in her life. What about that first kiss? Mercy! Her fevered body wanted more of Blaze.

"It's hotter'n here than a whorehouse on nickel night," Shade said, stopping alongside Blaze who grimaced at his choice of words. Shade shrugged and looked at Noelle. "May I have the next dance?"

"It's intermission and Colonel Crockett's going to speak," someone said from the front of the town hall.

Noelle's knees nearly buckled with relief. She prayed Felice thought Shade was asking her and not herself to dance. Noelle looked past Shade who had worn a coonskin cap the day they'd met, to the man wearing the coonskin cap on center stage. Was their last name Crockett? Though the rifle in his hand looked menacing, the colonel's smile was friendly. When the cheering subsided, Colonel Crockett spoke to the crowd.

"Before coming here I made a farewell speech to my constituents back in Tennessee who decided that they didn't want me to serve them in Congress any more. I stood up and in the most neighborly fashion I said; 'Since you have chosen a timber toe to succeed me, I have decided that I am going to Texas and fight for liberty and you, my friends, can go plumb to hell!'"

Whoops and hollers, laughter and clapping ensued. When it died down, Colonel Crockett told them how he and his Tennessee Mounted Volunteers had been caught in a buffalo stampede one day and surrounded by a hundred

Indians on another day. Not one of his brave men had panicked or turned back.

With Shade and Felice on her left, Noelle ventured a peek to her right at Blaze. She smiled up at his handsome profile. He turned his head and frowned slightly at her. Did that have to do with Blaze not wanting all hell to break loose? Perplexed, Noelle looked away. Blaze caught her hand between the folds of her dress and twined his fingers through hers. Her cheeks felt flushed and surely the floor was smoldering under her feet.

"How'd you recruit such fine volunteers?" somebody called out from the crowd.

"It wasn't easy," Crockett replied. "The ones here with me are half-horse and half-alligator meaning they have the nobility of the horse and the mean-cussedness of an aroused 'gator."

While Felice gazed longingly up at Shade, Noelle wondered if Felice suspected how scary it would be to handle an *aroused 'gator*. She tugged hard on Felice's skirt, but Felice ignored her. When Blaze squeezed Noelle's hand, she trembled. At least she fully realized she was not prepared to handle an aroused 'gator.

"When it comes to women," Colonel Crockett continued, "two of my men could grin until the bark curls off a gum log. But the night I saw them in a cantina in the middle of a knife fight, they looked mean enough to carve up Santa Anna and leave him for dead."

The crowd roared and demanded the names of these two fine men.

Colonel Crockett looked around the crowded town hall and then motioned to someone.

"Maybe you'd like to introduce them, Jim, since you've known them a lot longer than I have," Crockett said.

Colonel Bowie stepped up on the stage beside Davy Crockett and studied the throng of people. Wrapping his fingers around the handle of a large knife protruding from the sash around his waist, a knife that looked like the one at

Blaze's waist, with a big smile Colonel Bowie pointed toward Blaze and Shade!

"Please welcome my cousins, Blaze and Shade Bowie, from Vidalia, Louisiana!"

Thunderous applause filled the room. When Noelle pulled her hand out of Blaze's he thought it was so she, too, could clap. But she didn't clap. Peering down at her, he saw her auburn brows lift in question. Maybe with hurt? The surety of betrayal clearly misted her hazel eyes just before damning fury clenched her delicate jaw. The clapping ceased as the music and dancing began again. The beautiful redhead stood rigidly at his side.

"Bowie?" Noelle spat. The pretty pink lips which had tasted so sweet when pressed to his, quivered with emotion. "It all makes perfect sense now."

"What makes perfect sense?" Blaze asked.

"And to think I was wondering if you might be the man to take me home to my grandmother," Noelle hissed, through straight, white teeth.

"What the hell is she talking about, Blaze?" Shade asked, leaning around Felice.

"What am *I* talking about?" Noelle asked Shade and glared at Blaze. "Your brother could talk all three colors off a calico cat!"

"At least two." Shade glared at Blaze.

If Shade weren't here, Blaze would grab Noelle's hand, haul her outside and get to the bottom of this. She was slipping through his fingers and he was powerless to do anything to stop it because he did not want a scene in front of Noelle.

"What makes perfect sense?" Felice asked, looking from Shade to Noelle.

"They're *Bowies*, Felice," Noelle replied, visibly shaking as she turned to her step-sister. "That means they're *fortune* seekers."

"Oh, si," Felice said sadly.

Blaze felt the swish of Noelle's skirt against his leg as she twirled away from him and snatched Felice's hand. The young women worked their way past countless men asking them to dance and dashed out the small, side door as if fleeing for their very lives. Carlos followed them.

"Is she mad because we're Bowies?" Shade was obviously as surprised as Blaze. "Except for Rufus Ray, that's a first."

"And probably the last you'll see of Noelle Charbonnez," Jim Bowie said as he joined the brothers. "Her mother was an old friend." Jim nodded slowly as if remembering something from long ago.

"Who is Noelle?" Blaze asked.

"Some folks say Noelle is the illegitimate daughter of Jean Lafitte."

CHAPTER 7

Angels the men from the Alamo were not.

Tension knotted Blaze's gut as he stalked alone to the small, side door. He was relieved to see Noelle and Felice had not been captured by the men just outside the town hall. There, soldiers and other volunteers mingled with some of Colonel Crockett's new arrivals. They resembled sharks nibbling the neck of a señorita here, tasting the cleavage of a cantina wench there, gobbling up whatever a woman offered.

Stepping into the cool night air, Blaze walked around the building to the front where he'd left Blue. The sorrel whinnied and shook his mane upon seeing Blaze.

"Blue," he said and patted the horse's neck.

He could ride Blue back to the Alamo now, but he would just lie awake all night wondering about Noelle Charbonnez. Maybe he could get more information from Jim.

Making his way back into the town hall, Blaze looked for Shade who was nowhere in sight. Jim was in a far corner immersed in talking to Colonel Travis. Travis who Jim said was 'wet-behind-the-ears' had come for Jim right after his cousin had said Noelle could be the daughter of the Pirate of the Gulf.

Ignoring the dancing, Blaze skirted the crowd, stopped

next to Jim and listened to what he figured was history being made. Youth versus experience, Jim and Travis fiercely discussed who would ultimately be in authority at the Alamo. It was a foregone conclusion that Jim would retain control of all volunteers and Travis the troops at the garrison. What they could not agree on was who would make the important decisions. Colonel Crockett played his fiddle while a volunteer, named Johnny McGregor, blew his bagpipes. Around midnight Jim and Travis took a break.

"Come on, Blaze." Jim coughed, headed to the front door and waved Blaze to follow him. "I need some fresh air." He explained when they were outside. "I've been feelin' poorly lately."

"Why? What's wrong with you?" Blaze asked.

Shrugging off Blaze's question, Jim coughed again and wheezed. "You want to talk about Noelle?"

"Yes." Blaze squared his shoulders certain he could right any wrong Noelle associated with the Bowies. "What did you mean when you said that I'd probably seen the last of Noelle?"

Under a bright moon, Blaze's hopes dimmed as a tale of history, already carved in stone, assailed his ears. A tragic past which linked the Bowies to the Charbonnez family, squeezed Blaze's heart with what-might-have-been.

"Hey! There's half a dozen señoritas dying to dance with you, Blaze," Shade said, hanging out the front door.

"Then dig 'em a grave."

At Blaze's uncharacteristically cold remark, Shade swayed backward as surely as if Blaze had hit him. There was a flask in his hand. Hell, Shade was as drunk as he was shocked.

"Where'd you get that flask?" Blaze asked as Shade made his slightly staggering way to him.

"A gift from Buzzard." Shade lifted it into the air and motioned to the man coming up behind him.

"There are other fish in the sea," Jim said kindly and clapped Blaze on the back.

"The sea is my lady."

The man with Shade, who had spoken, claimed to be an acquaintance of Pirate's. Raoul Buzzard was medium height and stocky. He had a habit of licking his chops like a wolf salivating over his prey. Likening him to a polecat due to his stink, Blaze pegged this man to be as savage as a meat ax and had told Shade so. Stating the surname Buzzard was French, the man pronounced it with a long *u* and a soft *a*. Blaze pronounced it like he saw it, buzzard as in rapacious.

"This flask is pure silver, right Buzzard?" Shade asked, as he and Buzzard stood near Jim and Blaze.

"Pure silver!" Buzzard's oversized grin displayed a mouthful of rotting teeth surrounded by thin lips and a scraggly beard. Holding out his flask, Shade then did the same and Buzzard clinked his flask to Shade's.

"Colonel Bowie!" one of soldiers from the garrison called from the front doorway. "Colonel Crockett and Colonel Travis are looking for you, sir."

Jim grabbed the flask from Shade. "Tin!" he said, never breaking stride as he hurled the flask into the night.

Blaze watched Buzzard's fist clench as he glowered at Jim's back, but the man didn't dare utter a word. According to Jim, Buzzard was a newcomer from Nacogdoches. He lived in town as opposed to the Alamo, so he wasn't a volunteer. Knowing Nacogdoches was a convivial place for gamblers, smugglers, pirates, and other dubious sorts who liked operating near an international border, it was fairly obvious why Buzzard had been there.

"If the sea's your lady," Blaze swept one hand out, palm up, "why are you in the middle of mesquite prairie, Buzzard?"

"Like most women," Buzzard began, squinting as he leaned over and searched the ground for his flask, "the sea is fickle."

Buzzard wore a dirty scarf around his bald head. His eyes were small, close set and slightly crossed. The light from the fandango caught on a hoop in his left ear. The day

he and Shade had first bumped into Buzzard, he had tried
to buy them a drink at a local cantina. They had refused.
Now, the gift of the tin flask. He wanted something.

Buzzard found the flask, returned it to Shade and
draped his arm around his shoulders. Shade flung an arm
around Buzzard in return.

"Were you really Lafitte's first mate, Buzzard?" Shade
asked.

"Oui," Buzzard replied. "And his bon ami."

The man had no trace of a French accent and even
though he sprinkled French here and there, that wasn't
proof he'd ever sailed with the French pirate, Jean Lafitte as
his *good friend*. The name Lafitte made Blaze's stomach
churn.

"I'm leaving." Blaze headed toward Blue.

"Back to the Alamo?" Shade asked.

"No." Blaze reached the sorrel as Shade came up
beside him.

"Where are you going?"

"To a small adobe casa owned by the local cobbler." He
couldn't live with what-might-have-been without a fight.
"Inside will be a girl who hates all Bowies."

Blaze glanced at Buzzard who made a show of yawning
and stretching as if paying them no mind.

"I'm going with you." Shade frowned as best he could in
his intoxicated condition. He swayed and said, "Because
Noelle's mine."

"No, she's not. I made no damn promise about a girl
with long red curls. I want her, Shade."

"Hell's bells, Blaze!"

Just before all hell could break loose, from out of the
night running toward them and gasping for breath, a man
shoved past Buzzard. Waving a note in his hand, the fellow
craned his neck, scanning the crowd in front of the town hall.

"Where're Bowie and Travis?" the man asked.

"Follow me," Blaze replied.

Blaze led the courier and Shade into the town hall to the corner of the room where the men in charge of the Alamo huddled in disagreement.

"What do you reckon this is about?" Shade asked.

"Santa Anna," Blaze said.

Jim, Travis and Crockett discussed the message. Word of General Santa Anna marching north toward the Alamo sounded urgent to Blaze. However, those in charge weren't alarmed and the fandango rolled on. But it did so without Blaze or Shade.

UNDER THE LIGHT of the full moon, Blaze stared at a tiny, forlorn hut perched near a creek called the San Antonio River. Shade lowered the flask from his lips and squinted.

"I think that's her house," Blaze said at the edge of a copse of trees.

"House?" Shade asked. "That shack would fit in our foyer back home."

"One of the locals tonight told me that Carlos Herrera lives in a jacal, the Spanish word for a hut having a thatched roof and walls made of sticks covered with mud or clay. They said Herrera's jacal has a rawhide door. I think that's an animal skin flapping in the wind there."

"My God," Shade said as they sat on their horses. "Noelle and Felice live in poverty."

"Quiet," Blaze said as a breeze floated a sound his way. "Hear that? Someone's crying."

"Yeah." Shade drained the flask, pocketed it and tugged at the sash around his waist. "Mother Nature calls."

As Shade dismounted and turned away from the house, Blaze dismounted, tethered his horse to a tree and listened. Silence. Quietly treading within twenty feet of the adobe hut, he heard nothing. To the far left, Shade stood in the shadow of some tall trees relieving himself in the creek. Slowly scanning downstream to the right, a huddled form sat facing away from him near the edge of the creek. Blaze was drawn like a magnet.

Moonlight shimmered amongst riotous auburn waves. A cape of tumbling tresses surrounded the girl whose forehead rested on her knees as she wept. A million stars shone in the sky but to Blaze none twinkled like the one on the ground.

"Noelle?" he said and squatted near her.

Her head jerked up, she gasped and moved backward in the dirt. Bracing one knee on the ground, Blaze leaned forward and gently grasped her wrist. When she struggled he let go, holding his palms out in surrender.

"How did you find me?" she asked, using the hem of her skirt to swipe at her tears.

"I asked around. Did I make you cry?"

"Absolutely not!" She shook her head furiously. "Don't flatter yourself."

Blaze heard movement and glanced over his shoulder as Shade disappeared into the trees.

"What's wrong?" Blaze asked, turning back to Noelle.

"Felice became angry on the way home." Noelle sniffled. "She said if I planned to ask you to take me back to my grandmother, then I should just go ahead and leave tonight. So I guess I will."

"Noelle, I'll take you to your grandmother," Blaze heard himself say. What about their deadline at the bank? "Listen to me."

"I-will-not-listen!" Noelle said in staccato and flattened her hands to her ears. "Talking to you at the fandango cost me my home. I'm homeless again!"

"Again?" When she didn't answer, Blaze almost reached for her hands, but thought better of it. Leaning back on his haunches, he flattened his hands on his thighs. When Noelle placed her hands in her lap, Blaze said, "My brother's with me and he'll be here any minute, so I have to talk fast."

"I'm glad my cat isn't here!" Noelle glared at him. "Because Mistletoe's a calico."

Blaze grinned. This woman was not only beautiful, but funny. Through the glitter of tears, her big hazel eyes flashed emerald and gold sparks. He craved the feel of her full, quivering pink lips on his and could almost taste the saltiness he'd find there.

"Jim told me you're from Natchez, Mississippi. Is that where your grandmother lives?"

"Yes!" Swiping at her cheeks with the back of her hand, Noelle said, "Which is directly across the river from Vidalia, Louisiana where you're *coincidentally* from!"

"It is a coincidence, Noelle."

"What nerve! I've never seen anybody with more nerve than you and your brother. You didn't come to fight in the Texas rebellion, did you?"

"No."

"You came for me, didn't you?"

"No." Blaze shook his head, a little confused. "It's true I'm not here to fight, but what I came for wasn't you." Since she'd made the remark about fortune seekers, Blaze didn't elaborate on his reason for being in Texas. "I intend to get what I came for but now I want to take you with me when I leave."

"You'll never take me anywhere, Blaze *Bowie*."

She tried to stand, but Blaze tugged her back to the ground. Her eyes widened and her lips pursed. Damn! Did Noelle regard him as suspiciously as he viewed Buzzard? The wind rifled through Blaze's hair and he realized Noelle wore only a paper thin shift. A threadbare serape lay twisted at her waist and when he placed a hand to her bare feet, they were like ice. She slid her feet under her and he shifted the subject.

"Why doesn't your step-father make you some slippers?"

"I can make my own slippers! Felice and I work alongside Carlos every day. We use what precious little leather we have for *paying* customers." Noelle tilted her head as if he should know that. "People here are afraid, not only of losing their lives when Santa Anna comes but of losing their money. Families are burying what little savings they have in their backyards. The last thing on their minds is buying shoes. Carlos made an eighty mile trip recently and only sold two pairs of boots to the Texas Rangers. When he and Felice returned, my mother was—" Noelle's voice broke. She rested her forehead on her knees and said, "Dead from cholera."

CHAPTER 8

"Come here, Noelle."

Blaze didn't give a damn if Shade saw or not. He slipped his hands under Noelle's arms and pulled her to him. Folding her arms over her heart, she bowed her head and wept. How arrogant he'd been to think she had cried over him when she was grieving for her mother and fearing she had lost her home. Blaze wrapped her serape around her trembling shoulders, pressed her head to his shoulder and patted her back. In the circle of his arms she felt small and delicate. The powerful feelings he had for this woman were strangled by the fact Shade wanted her, too. Yes, he'd pointed out she had red, not raven, hair. No, Shade couldn't have both Noelle and Felice and Blaze had even admitted he wanted Noelle. But Shade wasn't accepting it and Blaze feared things would get worse between him and his brother in this time and place where they needed to stick together.

And why did Noelle have to hate him so much?

"I'm sorry about your mother, Noelle," Blaze said. "Did you hear Jim say that day in Main Plaza that his wife died of cholera?" Noelle nodded. "I can't change what happened to your mother, but I want to change your feelings about me. Jim asked Shade and me to stay close to the Alamo tomorrow because it'll be his first day in joint command with Travis. Will you meet me on the twelfth?"

"No, I certainly will not." Noelle shoved out of his arms and shook her head.

She looked up and it was all Blaze could do to keep from kissing those pink lips.

"Noelle, let's meet so we can reconcile the Bowies' connection to the Charbonnez family and so you'll allow me to take you to your grandmother."

"Get what you came to Texas for and don't worry about me." Noelle tilted her head with childlike innocence and trusting vulnerability etched her voice. "A man named Raoul Buzzard has already offered to take me."

"DON'T EVER SNEAK up on me again, Buzzard," Shade said in the copse of trees. He'd no sooner turned from the river when he bumped into the man. He'd shoved Buzzard into the thicket because Blaze didn't like him and Shade didn't need a lecture. "You'da scared the whiskey outa me, if I'd had any left."

"Same here, matey," Buzzard said. "It's been a pleasure talking to ya about Lafitte. But I bet you'd druther be talking to that purdy señorita coming toward us."

The exotic señorita with long black hair gliding his way didn't surprise Shade half as much as running into Buzzard. Why was the man here, anyway?

"Hey, Buzzard, why—"

"Say no more, matey. I'll leave you to yer lady," Buzzard said and vanished into the night.

"Hola," she said at the edge of the trees.

"Hola." Shade turned to face her, and still somewhat inebriated, nearly lost his balance.

"What are you doing?" Felice asked and smiled.

"I added to your creek." He walked out of the trees and into the open toward her.

"Oh, I thought maybe you had come to see me."

"How'd you know I was out here?"

"I didn't." Felice clasped her hands behind her back and made small, half-turns. "I was looking for Noelle." She nodded her head to the right. "She's with Blaze. I was about to go back inside when I heard your voice."

Shade frowned. In the distance, Blaze was kneeling beside Noelle. They sat too close to each other but at least Blaze wasn't touching the beautiful redhead. That battle could wait.

Felice was more than *purdy*, as Buzzard had said, and lively. She flipped a lock of raven hair over her shoulder and Shade's attention riveted on her thin gown. Its sleeves barely reached her elbows and the hem stopped just above her ankles. As she made her half twirls, the moonlight teased him with the dark tips of her breasts and the shadowy vee between her legs. Shade's body hardened in response. Odd. He had never been attracted to women with small breasts and slight curves. He preferred voluptuous, like Rosa or Maria. Maria had left the fandango in a huff after Blaze's rejection and Shade had been quick with Rosa. She hadn't satisfied him and here was Felice.

"Who were you talking to, Shade? The trees?"

"Yeah, my name is Shade Tree." He grinned down at Felice and improvised, "So I was telling the trees I came to see you."

"Really?" Felice's dark eyes twinkled up at him full of promise.

Her lips parted as if she wanted to be kissed. Shade planned to do more than that. He grinned and backed his way into the copse of trees. As he hoped, she came after him.

"So, uh, what kind of tree are these, Felice?"

"Cottonwood," she said stopping in front of him. "In Spanish, Alamo means cottonwood."

"Blaze and I own some trees back home, but none like

these cottonwoods." Glancing around and nodding, Shade casually said, "Let's sit down so I can study them for a while."

Yeah, tumbling Felice would appease his interest in her so the next time he saw her, she wouldn't have this surprisingly arousing effect on him. Shade sat, leaned against a tree and held out his hand to Felice. He tugged her onto his lap thinking she didn't weigh much over a hundred pounds. He wondered if she got enough to eat. He'd have to remember how small she was when he rolled on top of her.

"Shade, I've never sat on a man's—"

Shade cut her off with a kiss. Her lips were as warm as her reception. With only a moment's hesitation, Felice slid her arms around his neck. He placed a hand on her side and when he trailed his fingers higher she buried hers in his hair. This was going to be so damn easy, Shade thought as his palm met with her breast. Then she pulled away from him.

"Remember I'm not a strumpet, Shade."

"Uh-huh." Shade groaned, noting she didn't push his hand away from her breast. Kissing her again, he caressed her. Her breasts reminded him of rose buds that had yet to fully bloom. "How old are you?"

"Twenty," Felice said against his lips.

"Good." Figuring she'd done it all by now, Shade eased her off his lap to the ground and leaned over her. Stroking her cheek, he said, "Pull up your gown for me."

"I don't know if I should."

"If you won't, Rosa will." Shade cocked a brow.

"Si." Felice wiggled as she yanked up her shift, legs stiff and straight.

"Don't you know you're supposed to spread your legs now?" Shade raised the sash at his waist and undid the buttons on his pants. With his pants open he rolled on top of Felice. "Spread 'em." He felt her legs move apart.

"I will because... te amo, Shade."

"Huh?"

"That's Spanish for I lo—"

Tired of talking and ready to mate, Shade fastened his mouth over Felice's. He was about to ease himself out of his pants when he was hauled off Felice by strong hands. Instinctively, he clutched his pants shut and yanked his knife out of its scabbard. Felice shoved her gown back into place.

"Dammit, Shade!" Blaze said. "She's only seventeen!"

"No, she's not." Shade knew this looked bad in front of Noelle, but he could think of no explanation for his actions. Buttoning his pants and defending himself at least in part he said, "Felice is twenty."

"Felice will be eighteen on St. Valentine's Day and that was her first kiss," Noelle said to Shade as Felice scrambled to her feet. "And that was some first kiss, Felice Herrera."

"It wasn't my first kiss," Felice said. "Shade gave me several."

Shade squinted down at Felice. Hell, if she wasn't already appealing enough, the fact that she was probably a virgin made him itch to find out. But he couldn't let that show in front of Noelle.

"Felice, you lied to me."

"About my age, si, but I reminded you I wasn't a strumpet."

"Actions speak louder than words," Shade said

"I acted like a strumpet?" Felice asked.

"Hell, yes! You…" Shade tapped his finger to her chest, "yanked your gown up, not me."

With a gasp, Felice turned and ran toward the jacal with the animal skin flapping in the breeze.

"Felice!" Pausing in surprise only a moment, he stomped after her and called over his shoulder, "Blaze, keep your hands off Noelle and meet me up on the road."

Blaze gritted his teeth. Shade caught Felice. She threw a wild punch, but Shade captured her fist. The moment

Shade's mouth lowered to Felice's, Blaze looked down at Noelle.

"To hell with what Shade wants."

Gently, Blaze grasped Noelle's upper arms and pulled her to him. He lowered his head, but she turned away. Shoving out of his embrace, Noelle clutched the serape over her breasts.

"Goodbye, Blaze Bowie."

"You mean goodnight."

"I mean goodbye, forever."

"That's not acceptable. Let's talk on the twelfth. In the meantime, do *not* go anywhere with Buzzard."

"You can't tell me what to do! I'll go wherever I please with whomever I please."

"You agreed to marry me tonight and you aren't going anywhere with any man but me, Noelle."

"I thought you were just flirting with me."

"I told you I wasn't." Blaze felt his temper flaring.

"Well, I was only flirting." Noelle tried to wrench out of his grasp, but he held tight. "Buzzard is taking me home."

"It's more than five hundred miles from here to home." Blaze yanked her closer. "You go with Buzzard and if you're still alive by the time you get there, you'll wish you were dead."

"I—I don't know what you mean." She shivered and it wasn't from the night air.

"Then just take my word for it."

Ever so slightly, she nodded. Burying one hand in her luxurious auburn waves, he tilted her head back and splayed his other hand across her back. She wiggled against him and he savored the rub of her femininity against his body. Her breasts were the size of ripe peaches and he was sure they'd taste as sweet. He yearned to touch her, but after what just happened with Felice and Shade, Blaze held himself in check. Lowering his head and, holding hers in place, he pressed his lips to hers.

Noelle's serape dropped around their feet and her

fingers lightly lit at waist. He coaxed her mouth open and when her tongue met his, he groaned his approval. She leaned into him and her soft moan threatened to be his undoing. Blood pumped hot and hard into his loins. No. He had to back away for now. With iron control, Blaze released his grip on the naïve temptress.

Blaze detected an impish gleam in Noelle's hazel eyes just before she scooped her serape off the ground. Standing, her lips quivered but Blaze sensed it was with a grin and not tears. Protectiveness slammed into him.

"The next time you're half-naked don't stick your tongue into a man's mouth unless it's mine, darlin'."

"If I can show someone as big as you who's boss, I can show any man." Noelle arched a brow.

"Unless you want to be stripped of your virginity against your will, don't bet on it." He glimpsed fear in her eyes again before she lowered her gaze and hugged herself. A giggle pulled his head up. Shade was kissing Felice. Her arms slid around Shade's neck and at least one of his hands molded to her breast.

"Go ask Carlos if you still have a home, Noelle. If not, you're coming with me to the Alamo."

"Muchachas?"

"Carlos!" Noelle gasped and turned toward the little hut.

"Tell me where we can meet on the twelfth," Blaze said and at the risk of being shot by an angry father, he caught Noelle's arm. "Or I won't let you go."

"At the cobbler shop, during siesta."

Noelle yanked away from him. As he had at the fandango, Blaze stood his ground as the girls fled. Carlos herded them into the hut and Blaze walked to his horse. Shade met up with him and they headed toward the mission.

"Damn," Shade said. "That little raven-haired beauty set my poker on fire."

"It's time you started thinking with your brain and not

your poker. How could you try to steal a seventeen year old girl's virginity along a muddy riverbank?"

"Don't lecture me. I've never had a virgin and I want one. Do you think Noelle is an innocent?"

"Leave Noelle alone."

CHAPTER 9

"Carlos, you worked straight through siesta," Noelle said after another fretful glance out the window. "Why don't you go home and take a late nap? Soon. Before it gets any later."

"No." Carlos sighed behind his workbench. "Someone with pesos might walk through the door."

Or someone else. Noelle didn't want Carlos encouraging Blaze Bowie to take her home. Five hundred miles was a long way and he might talk her into being friends. She snapped her fingers.

"I have an idea! The Alamo has new arrivals. You should go and ask the soldiers and volunteers if they need shoes or boots." She swept her hand over the shelves of men, women and children's footwear.

"Si. Or maybe they need a cobbler." Carlos nodded as her idea took root. He got up from his workbench and grabbed a bag of tools. He quickly crossed the hard-packed dirt floor and gave Noelle a hug. "I will go pronto."

As Carlos trotted down the street, Noelle wrung her hands. Thank God, Blaze was late. She didn't know if she was happy he wasn't here or worried he might not show up. In either case, she was as nervous as she had ever been in her life. If and when he arrived, what would she say? She would demand to know what kind of Bowie he was; smuggler, fortune seeker or killer.

"As if he'd tell me the truth," Noelle mumbled, looking out the window again.

"Who are you talking to?"

"Felice!" Noelle twirled to her step-sister. Felice had apologized since telling her to leave. In fact, she had begged Noelle to stay in Bexar with her and Carlos forever. "I thought you were home taking your siesta."

"I could not sleep," she said, meeting up with Noelle in the center of the shop. "Where's Papa?"

"He went to the Alamo."

"Shade is there!" Felice squealed. "I am going, too."

"Wait!" Noelle said as Felice turned. "Be cautious around Shade or he'll teach you things you're not ready to learn."

"I want Shade to teach me."

"He's a Bowie, Felice."

"The way I felt when Shade was kissing me," Felice closed her eyes and touched her lips, "and holding me," she opened her eyes and continued, "I don't care if his name is Bowie. I can't wait for him to kiss me and hold me again." Sincerity filled her soft voice as she placed her hands over her heart. "I want to be loyal to you, Noelle, but I love Shade."

"Oh, for heaven's sake, Felice, you don't love him," Noelle said, as her own heart whispered that she had fallen in love with Blaze the day she'd met him in Main Plaza. "You don't really know Shade."

"Ahh, but I know Shade," Rosa said from behind Noelle.

Noelle pivoted to face the voluptuous prostitute. A gauzy, peasant style blouse was tied so loosely it displayed the woman's generous cleavage to the rim of her dark nipples.

Gauzy cloth? Noelle's mind whirled. Countless washboard scrubbings had rendered her nightgown as thin as gauze. How much had Blaze seen of her the other night? Then something occurred to her. Whatever he had seen... it hadn't appealed to him, because he had not been carried away with her as Shade was with Felice.

"And Maria knows Blaze," Rosa taunted Noelle as Maria swayed up to the doorway. "Si, Maria?"

"Si." Maria trailed long, painted fingernails across the tops of her large, brown breasts. "And he knows these. Pity you have so little, Noelle."

Staring at Noelle's bosom, Rosa snickered and nudged Maria. Shifting their gaze to Felice's chest, they burst out laughing. So Blaze liked large bosoms. Noelle had her explanation of why Blaze hadn't tried to do with her what Shade had with Felice.

"Maria, Rosa, why do you hate us so?" Noelle asked and placed her arm around Felice. "What is it that we have done to you?"

"You think you are so high and mighty." Maria stepped forward and put her hands on her wide hips. "Don't you?"

"High and mighty?" Noelle asked. She looked down her worn green dress and back up at Maria. "You and Rosa have rings on every finger. You wear fancy blouses and satin skirts trimmed with colorful ribbons and bows. How are Felice and I high and mighty, Maria?"

"You walk and talk like you are somebody," Maria hissed through her teeth.

"Noelle *is* somebody," Felice offered. "Her abuela is muy rich."

"Shut up!" Rosa shoved Felice's shoulder.

"Don't touch her!" Noelle said.

"Then make her leave Shade Bowie alone." Rosa narrowed her eyes at Felice. "Next time he falls into my bed, he'd better not be coming from your arms, Felice Herrera."

So, the Bowie brothers were to thank for this visit, Noelle thought and seethed.

"I will do all I can to make sure Shade Bowie never visits you again, Rosa," Felice said.

Rosa slapped Felice so hard Felice fell in a sideways heap onto the floor. Noelle flung herself at both cantina whores.

Maria dug her sharp claws into Noelle's arms and Rosa grabbed her hair. As Felice jumped up and screamed at them to stop, Rosa viciously kicked Felice, knocking her much smaller opponent down again.

"You stay away from Blaze Bowie, Noelle." Maria's grin oozed evil as she and Rosa held a struggling Noelle in place. "I'm keeping him for myself."

"I'll see Blaze Bowie whenever I want to!" Though leery of Raoul Buzzard since Blaze had warned her about what men were capable of, Noelle didn't fear these women.

"You will not!" Maria screeched, "Blaze is the best I've ever had in bed! You could not handle him!"

"Blaze can decide for himself!" Since Noelle was determined not to have anything to do with Blaze she was confused as to why it hurt to think he had bedded Maria. Frustrated with her jumbled feelings and concerned about Felice, Noelle tried to twist out of their painful grasp. "Let me go!"

Maria released Noelle's arms only to raise a hand, her fingers like talons. Rosa let go of her hair and turned toward Felice. Before Maria could strike her, Noelle was whisked out of her reach and her spine was riveted to a hard chest.

"How the hell would you know what I'm like in bed, Maria?" came Blaze's deep voice at Noelle's back.

Maria's face turned red and Rosa backed away from Felice. Maria jostled her breasts and opened her mouth to say something. Blaze held up his hand.

"Outside, *ladies*," Blaze ordered.

With her back to Blaze's chest, Noelle's heart pounded against his forearm. She hadn't seen Blaze's face yet, but his voice sounded lethal. Releasing her, he ushered the prostitutes to the street. Noelle helped Felice to the padded bench where Carlos often took his siesta. Not wanting Blaze to fight her battle, she rushed to Blaze standing with his back to her, blocking the door. Coming up on Blaze's right, he shoved her behind him. What was going on here? Was this partaker of trollops' favors trying to hide her while arranging his next bedding?

"I turned you both down the day we met and every time you've propositioned me since," Blaze said. "I wasn't looking to make you my enemies. But my eyes are always wide open and when I look at the two of you, I don't like what I see."

Noelle's jaw dropped and she peeked around Blaze's broad shoulder.

"Puta!" Along with whore, Maria spewed several Mexican curses, ending by damning Noelle to hell.

"Shut up, Maria," Blaze said.

He put his fists to his hips, keeping Noelle behind him. Noelle flattened her hands to Blaze's broad back. If he could back her up, she would do the same for him.

"As much as I wanted you, now I hate you, Blaze Bowie!" Maria said. "Noelle will live to regret this day."

"Touch Noelle again and I'll kill you."

Dear God, this Bowie *was* a killer! Noelle heard gasps from Maria and Rosa and then the swishing of their satin skirts. She stepped from behind the shield of muscular man and saw the women scurrying down the street. At the swinging doors of the cantina, they met up with Raoul Buzzard. Tossing their heads, they each took one of his arms and escorted him inside.

"There goes a helluva trio," Blaze said.

He turned, stepped inside the shop and Noelle noticed his right eye looked red and the skin bruised. Felice, marred by a handprint on her cheek and dirt on her clothes, announced she was going to the San Fernando Church to pray. When Felice was gone, Noelle spoke to the gorgeous man in buckskin.

"What happened to your eye, Blaze?"

"All hell finally broke loose when I told Shade I plan to marry you. That's why I'm late."

Noelle all but fell onto the small siesta bench. Blaze sat down beside her, stretching his long legs out.

"I can't believe you still think we're going to be married."

"I can't believe you got into a cat fight over me."

"Cat fight?" Noelle pursed her lips. "Rosa slapped Felice because of Shade. I was defending my sister."

"I heard you tell Maria you'd see me whenever you wanted to." Blaze tilted his head, crossed his arms over his chest and looked at her.

"But I'm not going to see you and you know why."

"That's what we're here to discuss today."

"Is Shade hurt, too?" she asked.

"His left eye looks like my right one." Blaze rubbed his forehead and sighed. "He says I broke my word which I've explained I didn't."

"What do you mean?" Noelle listened as he briefly told of a raven hair versus redhead contention with Shade. "I don't want to come between brothers."

"Too late." He frowned at the fingernail marks on her arms. "Noelle, I'm sorry they hurt you and Felice." He leaned closer and when he touched a tangle in her hair his muscular leg brushed her thigh.

"I'm fine." Noelle got up and smoothed her hair. "I'll see to your eye."

Lacing his fingers behind his neck, Blaze rested his head on the adobe wall of Carlos' shop and shut his eyes.

Blaze Bowie was all male. His hurt eye smacked of a wild streak. The breadth of his shoulders and size of his muscles lay claim to his strength. His aura of masculine virility burned Noelle like the heat of a thousand suns.

Noelle hurried to a bowl and pitcher on a table near the workbench. She wet a clean cloth and put it to her own cheek to cool the hot blush she felt crawling up her neck

"So I left Shade there drinking and arguing."

"What?" His comment came out of nowhere. She realized along with her eyes, her mind had wandered in regard to this man. Taking a deep breath, she walked to him and hoped she sounded like she'd heard every word. "Who's Shade arguing with besides you?"

"I just told you he was fighting alongside Jim against

Travis." Blaze opened his eyes and looked at her sideways. "Jim and Travis aren't sharing the authority well. Sam Houston likes Jim and is letting him run his own show. Travis is mad as a March hare about that and ordered an election hoping to win command of all the volunteers away from Jim."

"What happened?" Noelle was engrossed as she sat back down beside him. Before thinking herself out of it, she boldly swept a lock of blond bangs away from Blaze's hurt eye. "Who'd they vote for?"

"Hell, they like Jim and voted for him, of course."

"Close your eyes," she said and gently placed the cool cloth to his right eye.

Sunlight glinted off the knife in the scabbard tied by the sash around Blaze's waist. The danger of latent violence sliced shivers up her spine. Following the sash ends led her gaze between his legs where she saw a masculine bulge. The newly awakened mystery place deep inside Noelle tingled.

"But Jim's sick," Blaze said.

"I hope Colonel Bowie doesn't have Asiatic cholera." Noelle could almost hear her mother voicing concern for her longtime friend.

"It's not cholera. He's drinking a lot, too."

"Is Colonel Bowie drinking because he's sick?" Surprising herself, she patted his knee.

"He said he started drinking after his wife and children died of cholera." Blaze covered her hand with his. "I think he's drinking more now because he's upset over the way things are at the Alamo. Doc Pollard, the fort's hospital surgeon, said Jim has a peculiar disease of a peculiar nature. He's worried enough about Jim that he called in a Dr. Sutherland to see about him."

"What does Dr. Sutherland think is ailing him?" Noelle couldn't believe she was asking after Bowies. First Blaze, then Shade and now Jim and with her hands on Blaze's eye and knee no less. When she tried to tug her hand out from under his, he laced his fingers through hers!

"Maybe consumption." Blaze plowed his other hand through his thick hair and Noelle remembered how luxurious his hair had felt in her hands at the fandango. Rolling his shoulders he added, "It could be pneumonia or typhoid fever. Nobody knows."

"I'm so sorry to hear about Colonel Bowie and of your fight with Shade," Noelle said softly. "On the subject of fights, thank you for helping me get rid of Maria and Rosa."

"We have a fight of our own." Blaze moved her hand and cloth away and his steely gray eyes bored into her. "Because I want to marry you and you want rid of me. Don't you?"

"No." Had she said that out loud? She couldn't marry him, but she didn't want to be rid of Blaze. What? Yes, of course she... did not. Confused, she looked away, pulled her hand from his and twisted the damp cloth in her lap. "I admit I hold a grudge against Jim and Rezin Bowie for taking Marcel Charbonnez, my fath... umm... my mother's first husband on the expedition where he got killed. But a grudge doesn't mean I wish harm to befall any of you."

"Let's talk about Marcel Charbonnez."

"There's no use in talking."

"Hogwash. Today's my day for setting things straight with people. The night of the fandango, Jim told me all about Marcel Charbonnez."

"I already know this story." Noelle stood up.

"Sit." When Blaze cocked a brow, she sat. "Marcel's hero was Louis Juchereau de Saint-Denis from Beauport, Quebec. He was a French-Canadian explorer who was in Natchitoches, Louisiana almost a hundred years ago. From Natchitoches, St. Denis traveled to Texas and discovered what's since come to be known as the lost San Saba Mines."

"Treasure mines supposedly filled with gold and silver." Noelle stood again and tossed the cloth on the bench.

Blaze snared her hand. "I said sit." He tugged and she sat. "Marcel, who was also from Quebec, decided to follow in his hero's footsteps. Marcel retraced Saint-Denis' journey and met your mother when she was visiting friends in Natchitoches. Right?"

Noelle slid away from Blaze and yanked out of his grasp, crossing her arms under her breasts and hugging herself around the waist.

"Marcel met your *cousins*, Jim and Rezin Bowie, in Natchitoches, too!"

The feisty redhead was so beautiful Blaze smiled. As she'd listened to him, anger had heightened the pink in her cheeks and misted her hazel eyes. He wanted to trace his finger along the freckles on her nose and tilt up her trembling chin so he could plant his mouth on those pouting lips. Careful not to touch her breast, he grabbed a folded arm and tugged her closer. She shoved off his hand but didn't move away. As he pictured bedding the sexy spitfire, he smiled.

"Are you trying to grin the bump off a tree frog?" Noelle snapped at him.

"That's bark off a gum log." Blaze laughed. "But in your green dress, you sorta look like a little tree frog sitting on this wooden bench and all."

"Ooh!" Noelle balled up a fist and punched the knee she'd just patted!

"Try to be a good girl." Blaze caught her wrist. "And just talk to me."

CHAPTER 10

"I AM A GOOD GIRL!" NOELLE NARROWED HER EYES.

"I know." He let go and expected her to jump up and away from him.

"If Marcel hadn't met the Bowies in Natchez-Under-the-Hill, he and Mama wouldn't have met Jean Lafitte!" she said, staying at his side. Anger and desperation blended in her voice. "And I wouldn't doubt my parentage."

"From what Jim told me if your mother hadn't met Lafitte, you might not be here. Besides what's wrong with having Jean Lafitte for your father?"

"He's the Pirate of the Gulf!" Noelle cried and smacked his arm.

Blaze grabbed her hand. Hell, he'd have knocked any man on his butt for doing half as much as what he let this little girl get away with.

"Noelle, why don't you know which man is your father?" He loosened his grip on her hand and she pulled it free. "Tell me the parts of this story I don't know."

"Marcel and Mama eloped." She stared straight ahead and Blaze studied her profile made pretty with high cheekbones and dainty nose. "My grandparents didn't approve of a fortune seeker for a son-in-law and tried to force Mama to have the marriage annulled. She refused." Noelle swallowed a lump in her throat. "My grandparents disowned Mama. So, she and Marcel headed to Texas and the San Saba Mines." Blaze's gaze traveled to Noelle's breasts and his palms itched. "Their money ran out on Galveston Island. Then along came the Bowies, who introduced Mama and Marcel to Jean Lafitte!" She turned to him, eyes sparking. He could get lost in those eyes.

"And threw your mother into Lafitte's bed!"

"Well, no." Noelle winced. "But Marcel followed in Lafitte's footsteps and pirated American ships."

"Lafitte pirated mostly Spanish ships, darlin', because he hated them for raping his wife. Lafitte was loyal to the colonies and helped President Jackson defend New Orleans against the British during the War of Eighteen Twelve."

"Really?" Noelle asked in surprise.

"Yes, really."

"Perhaps I was wrong about that one thing."

Noelle crossed her arms under her breasts again and stared at the far wall. With her head turned, Blaze savored the sight of her ivory cleavage. The swell of her bosom filled the scooped neck of her green dress. He reached out wanting to touch her breast, but instead nudged her elbow.

"Go on with your story."

"Marcel was not loyal to the colonies and sailed with men who pirated American ships." Noelle clasped her hands in her lap and Blaze was drawn to the vee formed between her slender thighs. He knew the ecstasy he would find between her legs and almost groaned. "Marcel was thrown into prison and Mama... grew lonely."

"Ahh," Blaze breathed. "So maybe Lafitte returned from sea, comforted your mother and gave her a baby to love and keep her company?"

"Probably." Noelle's shoulders sagged. A tear ran down her cheek and Blaze gently swiped it away with the backs of his fingers. She flinched. "If Lafitte's still alive, only he could say now."

"What did your mother say?"

"She didn't while she was alive." Noelle bowed her head. "Carlos gave me Mama's diary after she died. Luckily, Carlos can't read because it was all about Lafitte. I can't believe she fell in love with a pirate." Without looking at him she asked, "Are you a pirate, Blaze?"

"No."

"Loneliness shouldn't have driven Mama into Lafitte's bed."

"Love and sex don't always go hand in hand."

Noelle slowly turned toward him. Her expression of naiveté heated Blaze's loins. He fought his lower body for control.

"I hope Jean Lafitte loved my mother as much as she loved him," Noelle said almost to herself as she looked at Blaze. "Have you bedded women you don't love?"

"I told you the night we met I'd never been in love."

"So you're an innocent, like me."

"Not for hell—" Blaze nearly choked. "Fifteen years."

"So you lost your innocence at fifteen?"

"Yeah." Blaze wanted off this subject. "Why're you in San Antonio instead of Galveston Island with Lafitte?"

Noelle studied the floor. Blaze noticed her small feet were bare as she made patterns in the dirt with her toes.

"After I was born, my grandparents forgave Mama. When Marcel got out of prison he was broke. So we moved home when I was two and lived with them until I was seven. After my grandfather died, Marcel told Grandmother finding buried treasure would be easier than living with her. She slapped some money in his hand and we left Natchez. Marcel had gone through Grandmother's money by the time we reached Bexar, so we were one of three hundred families to settle here."

Hearing the rising anxiety in her voice, Blaze thought to calm her by asking, "Where are your shoes?"

"When Jim and Rezin Bowie came through Bexar on their way to the San Saba Mines, Marcel was elated," Noelle said, ignoring his question. "Still fortune hunting, he followed them to the mines with a dozen other men."

"But Marcel didn't come back."

"The Comanche Indians killed him!"

"And you hold Jim and Rezin accountable." When Noelle nodded, a lock of hair fell across her cheek. Blaze gently tucked it behind her ear. "Maybe Charbonnez' greed and disloyalty got him killed?"

"You sound exactly like Mama and Carlos!" Noelle said and stiffened.

Just then an elderly lady entered the shop and Noelle eased off the bench. The woman's clothes were nearly rags, but she held out a purple ribbon to Noelle. When the woman indicated her shoes, Blaze recognized them as the pair Noelle had worn the day he met her in Main Plaza. Noelle put her arm around the tiny, stooped woman and tried to refuse the ribbon. When she insisted, Noelle told her it was her favorite color and graciously accepted it. The ancient woman's eyes teared. She nodded politely at Blaze and patted Noelle's cheek before leaving.

After Jim had told him about Charbonnez' link to the mines, Blaze had asked if he'd share his secret, their location. Jim said there was gold and silver aplenty and yes, it should be used to save Bowie land. He'd escort Blaze to the lost mines and no, he did not want to be reimbursed monetarily. But maybe Blaze could repay him by doing some things Jim's failing health was limiting him in doing regarding the Alamo. Absolutely, Blaze had vowed. But for now he had to get Noelle over her bitterness caused by those mines. Noelle pocketed the ribbon, and with the elderly woman gone, she whirled on him.

"Did Jim Bowie tell you Marcel sold everything in order to finance his search for those blasted mines? That after he died, Mama and I landed on the street until Carlos took us in!"

"No, I don't think Jim knows that. But he described Marcel as a follower, not a leader and that sounds like a fair

accounting from what you've told me. Anyway, I can understand why you'd have a fear of being homeless again," Blaze
said and stood. "What kept you here after your mother
died?"

"Well... umm..." She stared at the floor. "I can't face my
grandmother until I know who my father was."

"You're her blood relative, no matter who your father
was. I think you're still here in Texas because you're afraid
of her."

"I'm afraid of no one!" She drew back her fist and he
caught it.

"You've walloped me in the knee and in the arm. Smack
me a third time and I'll turn you over the knee you
punched."

Wanting to kiss her rather than fight, Blaze grasped her
shoulders. His hands slid down her back and molded her to
him. Her squirms ground against sensitive flesh. She was
oblivious to what she was doing to him and his body was on
the verge of a fine display. He lowered his head and she
turned her cheek.

"Noelle, you may as well know that Carlos showed up at
the garrison today and Jim put me in charge of taking you
home. When we get there we can get married."

Noelle went limp against him, but for not nearly long
enough. She quickly pushed out of his arms and stood back.

"I don't want a knife wielding *killer* and lifelong *fortune
seeker* for a husband any more than I want a pirate for a father!"

"I haven't killed anybody when I could avoid it."

"You've killed people?"

"Only in self-defense," he said. "But just because my last
name's Bowie doesn't mean I'm a *lifelong* fortune seeker."
What in God's name would Noelle say if she knew he was in
Texas in search of the same mines that cost Marcel his life?
"What would be so wrong with finding a fortune, Noelle?"

"Hunting for it breeds an unstable life!" Noelle put her
hands on her hips and knitted her arched brows. "I cannot

be married to a man who takes off for months, leaves his wife and children starving and who might never come home to me again."

"Children?" Blaze asked with a grin. "How many do you want?"

"Doesn't matter." Her voice grew crisp and matter-of-fact. "Because I can't marry a man who isn't attracted to me and now is a good time to point out that you aren't."

"What do you mean I'm not attracted to you?"

"You aren't attracted to—" Now that she had opened her big mouth, Noelle didn't quite know how to explain herself. "Maria said you like big," she moved her hands near and then away from her breasts, "ones."

"She doesn't know what the hell I like."

"Yes, but the other night after the fandango when you had the chance, you didn't..."

"Didn't what? Tell you that your breasts are the size of ripe peaches or that I bet they taste sweeter and feel a whole lot softer?"

"How dare you pretend an interest in me!" Noelle said. "Just because Colonel Bowie probably told you my grandmother is rich."

"Jim said only that she's a flush big bug in Natchez worth meeting."

"Grandmother has a strict condition which is she must approve of the man I marry or I inherit nothing." Noelle's eyes narrowed and she put a finger to Blaze's hard chest to punctuate her words. "And she would never approve of the likes of you."

"Is that right?"

"That's plenty right!"

"Fine. I want nothing from your grandmother, except you." He shoved her finger off him and touched his finger to her chest. "You agreed to marry me and you'll lie in the bed you made... with me."

"You're a pigheaded, one-track minded ruffian! I can't

think of names low enough for you!" She punctuated that with a punch in his gut.

"Dammit! Don't say I didn't warn you!" He grabbed her hand and yanked her to the bench. He laid her over his knee, braced his left arm on her back and flattened his right hand to her rounded fanny. "Men have tasted the blade of my knife for a helluva lot less than you've done to me today, little girl!"

"Your washboard belly hurt my hand!" She kicked her feet as she wiggled across his lap.

"Don't hit *me* when it's Lafitte and Charbonnez you're mad at. Leave the past and get on with the present with an eye toward the future. You believed me when I told you Lafitte defended New Orleans. So believe me when I tell you Jim and Rezin weren't responsible for Charbonnez' death."

"I don't have to believe you!"

The gorgeous man lightly smacked her fanny and looking at the shop in her upside down position, Noelle knew Blaze's truths were steadily righting her upside down world. The Bowies had been easy to blame for her poverty ridden lot in life until today. She had to admit Mama was a dreamer who had never worked a day in her life and Blaze was right; Marcel wasn't smart enough to be a leader. He'd followed Saint-Denis, then Lafitte and finally the Bowies. The handsome Bowie, whose hand lay where no other man's hand had ever been, gave her fanny a second playful swat.

"All right!" Noelle gasped. "I admit what happened with Mama, Marcel and Lafitte was their doing and not any fault of the Bowies. There! Are you satisfied?"

Blaze released his hold on her. She scrambled off his lap and stood. He stood as well and placed his strong hands to her cheeks. Noelle likened his eyes to gray fire and his nostrils flared like those of an angry bull. His kiss was as hard and furious as the man himself. The instant she whimpered, his iron grip loosened and his lips softened. Noelle pictured him stalking out of the shop to the cantina and vividly recalled her devastation when Maria claimed she had slept with Blaze. When he broke off their kiss, Noelle clutched his shirt.

"I don't trust you as far as I could throw you, Blaze Bowie, but I do want *you* and not Buzzard to take me to Grandmother. I promised Mama I'd go."

"I'll prove myself to you." His voice was husky. "Because when we get to Natchez, you're going to tell your grand-mother that you're spending the rest of your life with me."

"Well..." Noelle's heart said yes! Absolutely. Her mouth said, "Not unless you promise you'll never go fortune hunting like your relatives."

"I promise you'll never be homeless again."

Noelle decided that was promise enough for now. When Blaze slid his arms around her, Noelle slipped hers around his neck and closed her eyes. As his lips touched hers, she molded her breasts to his chest. He lifted her against him until her tiptoes left the dirt. Her nipples beaded and she knew he felt her response from the deep groan in his throat.

"I'm not made of steel. I'm flesh and blood," he whispered between kisses. "I don't know how long I can kiss you and keep my hands in safe places."

"Then don't," she said, as he put her feet on the ground.

Noelle heard Mama's voice resounding in her head, making her promise not to let go of the man she could love. She'd had no desire to ever fall in love until Blaze Bowie breezed into town. And in love with him, she was. She closed her eyes and when he kissed her again, she savored every single sensation. His hands trailed from her back to her ribs and moved higher. Taking the weight of her breasts in his hands, he gently kneaded her through the thin fabric of her dress. His thumbs brushed the sensitive tips and heat flooded that uncharted territory between her legs. Having a man touch her breasts was a first. She wondered if the dirt under her feet could catch fire.

What was he thinking?

"Too small?"

"They're a handful, Noelle, just like you and that's all a man needs. You fit my needs so perfectly I think you and your breasts were made just for me."

"Blaze, hush!" Noelle was both thrilled and shocked by his bold compliment. She admitted to herself it made no difference what this man's last name was as long as his first name was Blaze. Bravely letting his hands linger at her breasts, she asked, "When will we leave for Natchez?"

"When my business here is done."

"What is your business here?" She'd almost lost sight of her intention to ask her third question. She'd already covered fortune seeker and killer. "Smuggling?"

"It's a secret." Blaze's wink was a sexy one.

"I've told you my secrets today," she said and pushed his hands to her waist.

"Which allowed us to bury your Bowie grudge."

"Noelle!" Felice said, skidding to a halt in the doorway. "Blaze! Colonel Bowie's in town and full as a tick!"

"He's been on a bender." Blaze rubbed his forehead and looked out to the street.

"Is he all right?" Noelle knew they meant Jim was intoxicated and was glad Blaze had forewarned her.

"He just claimed command of the whole garrison," Felice said. "He is yelling at private citizens and ordering town officials to unlock the calabozo!"

"Dammit!" Blaze said, storming past the women and out of the shop.

Noelle followed and found utter chaos in Main Plaza. Alamo volunteers paraded back and forth, drunk, shouting, cheering for Jim and waving their rifles over their heads.

"Buzzard!" Blaze yelled to the pirate standing on a sideline of the melee. "Have you seen Shade?"

CHAPTER 11

"Matey, ain't ya heard he's the prisoner Colonel Bowie wants sprung from the calaboose?"

Blaze barreled into Main Plaza. The mass of marauding, drunken men didn't bother him. This bedlam was nothing compared to stampeding buffaloes or the intensity of a knife fight. He stopped abruptly and Noelle piled into the back of him, all copper curls, hazel eyes and green gingham.

"Go home! It's dangerous out here."

"It's my turn to help you."

"Did Señor Buzzard say Shade's in the calabozo?" Felice asked, darting toward them through the hollering, rebellious volunteers.

"If calabozo means calaboose, then Shade's in jail!" Blaze said, scanning the mob for Jim.

"We have to get Shade out of that dungeon!" Felice grabbed Blaze's arm.

"Shade can wait." Blaze pulled away from Felice. "I'm concerned about Jim because he's sick. Shade's landed in jail before. He sleeps it off and comes out with a clearer head."

"No, Blaze!" Felice began to cry.

"Jim!" Blaze shouted. "Go home, girls!" With that, he charged across the plaza and met up with Jim.

"Is that Noelle?" Jim asked, looking past Blaze.

"Yeah." Blaze said, glancing over his shoulder. Noelle stood where he'd left her comforting a weeping Felice. "I told them to go home."

"She's muy bonita, Blaze, truly beautiful," Jim said, weaving three sheets to the wind. "You're gonna take her back home with you, aren'tcha?"

"Yes. But for now let's get you back to the garrison."

"No." Jim shook his head stubbornly. "Not 'til Shade and some others who tore into town kickin' up a row are outa the calabozo."

No sooner had Jim spoken than the door of the jail swung open. Shade, along with a volunteer named Antonio Fuentes and several other men were freed. Jim and his band of volunteers cheered.

From a distance, Blaze made eye contact with Shade. As his little brother walked out of the shadows and into the light, Felice squealed Shade's name and he smiled at her. Before their fight, Shade had called Felice a raven-haired, exotic innocent and told Blaze he didn't think she got enough to eat. Blaze had not heard that tone of concern in Shade's voice for any woman, not even for Lucy Ray. And that's what had prompted Blaze to admit he planned to marry Noelle.

Rosa ran to Shade and kissed his cheek, but he nudged her aside. Good for you, Shade, Blaze thought. Shade walked over to Felice and Noelle. Felice smiled up at him and Shade winked at her but wrapped an arm around Noelle, kissing her full on the mouth.

"So, you have a battle of wills on your hands, just as Travis and I do," Jim said.

Never before had such blinding fury seized Blaze's heart and soul, clenching his jaw, stomach and fists. Never before had he experienced jealousy. But then never before had he witnessed another man kissing the woman he intended to make his wife. Noelle pushed away from Shade who glared a challenge at Blaze as Noelle turned to Felice. Felice backed away and ran. Maria joined Rosa, both laughing but keeping their distance from Noelle.

"Let's go, Jim." Blaze had seen enough.

"Aren't you gonna call Shade on this?"

"I'll concede this battle. Shade won't win the war."

"SHADE DOESN'T CARE a fig for me," Noelle said, still reassuring Felice two days after the fiasco in Main Plaza.

Noelle stepped out of the tin tub of warm water. Their bath tarp, as she and Felice called it, was flung over a rope that concealed them from the front half of the small shop and its one window. She and Felice bathed at the shop because it had a wooden door and not an animal flap at the entrance. Noelle dried off with a rough towel and donned her age-soft blue dress. She brushed her freshly washed hair as Felice crawled out of her tub and dried off. Though Carlos always waited out back after filling their tubs, Noelle kept her voice low. There was no reason to involve him in their dealings with the Bowie brothers.

"I think there's an ongoing rivalry between the brothers and that's why Shade kissed me instead of you."

"Si," Felice said. "I hope so, Noelle."

"Shade's interest will fade now that Blaze's has."

"Just because we have not seen Blaze for a couple of days does not mean he is no longer interested," Felice said as she dressed.

"He walked away the other day as though he didn't care." Noelle shrugged.

"It hurt seeing Shade kiss you, Noelle. That's why I ran away," Felice said, tying her new purple birthday ribbon in her hair. "How do you feel about Blaze since you no longer hold Jim and Rezin Bowie responsible for Marcel's death?"

"Muchachas!" Carlos called from out back. "Are you going to turn into prunes or take those boots we repaired and polished to the garrison?"

"We're going to the Alamo right now." Noelle pushed the tarp to one side and gathered up a pile of boots.

Felice scooped up the remaining ones and they hurried out the front door. As to Blaze, what could she say?

"Blaze is wild, romantic and hermoso?" Felice said, as they headed down Potrero Street.

"Yes, Blaze is wild, romantic and handsome," Noelle said, turning toward the old fort. "But that's what Mama said about Marcel and Lafitte and I can't end up like she did."

"Poor and living in a jacal?"

"I didn't mean it like that, Felice."

"I know." Felice smiled, but her shoulders sagged. Noelle longed for her sister to be happy like her name.

"Until I'm sure Blaze isn't a fortune seeker I'm determined not to feel very much for him." She could say that out loud, but inside she felt way too much for him. "I want a husband who will be home at night to tuck his children into bed."

"And then tuck you into his bed."

"Felice Herrera!" Noelle gasped in surprise.

"When Blaze kisses you does he make a broomstick in his pants?" Felice's big brown eyes sparkled.

"What?" Noelle stumbled and nearly dropped her boots.

"When Shade rolled on top of me by the river it felt like he had a big broomstick in the front of his breeches."

"No, I don't think Blaze has done that."

"Oh," Felice drew out the word ever so wisely. "Well, Shade said men cannot help it when they are with a woman they like. I'm sure that does not mean Blaze isn't attracted to you."

"Like Shade also said, actions speak louder than words."

Blaze had certainly walked away from her in Main Plaza without so much as a backward glance. No matter what Blaze said about wanting her, maybe all he really wanted was Grandmother's fortune. She stewed about the dashing man's true intentions all the way to the garrison's main gate.

Allowed in by two guards, Noelle knew she could run

into Blaze at any moment and her stomach flip-flopped. Just inside the gate, she stopped beside rough steps leading to the roof of the low barracks. Felice also stopped and they took in the activities of the Alamo.

It was a mild day and scores of people were hard at work in and around the three acre, open rectangle known as the plaza. Some men carried supplies to and fro while others kept watch at posts high atop crumbling walls. Several soldiers and volunteers were laboring over various forms of weaponry while another group of men fed horses and cows. Someone was cooking. The smell of beef, peppered beans and tortillas filled the air.

Noelle recalled what Carlos had said about the volunteers. They consisted of farmers, clerks, doctors, lawyers, blacksmiths, hatters, house painters, and a Baptist preacher. Only a few like the Bowies and Colonel Crockett were frontiersmen.

"Felice," Noelle began casually, "why don't you ask Shade what he does for work back in Louisiana?"

"Why don't you just ask Blaze?"

"Blaze won't even tell me why he's here, so I can't imagine he'll tell me what his business is back home."

"I *imagine* you could worm whatever information you want out of Blaze, if you ask him so very nicely."

Might be worth a try.

Carlos had explained the layout of the mission and Noelle easily matched his description to what she was seeing. Behind them on both sides of the main gate were the low barracks. She and Felice moved forward and straight ahead, they passed a cannon placed alongside a well. To their left was an artillery command post, the officers' headquarters and personal quarters. On the right was the chapel and although the roof had never been completed, a northeast corner supported a large cannon.

The chapel's courtyard appeared ready for a lively noon meal on one side and in stark contrast on other side, atop earthen breastworks, sat four cannons positioned to kill.

Beyond a gate in the courtyard were the horse corral and cattle pen. The hospital was the cornerstone of the artillerymen's quarters, next came the regular infantry barracks, known as the long barracks which led to the north wall, also fortified by breastworks and another cannon.

"Carlos said the quartermaster will be near the artillerymen's quarters," Noelle said to Felice.

Indeed, they found the busy quartermaster who was expecting them. Grateful for the resoled, patched up and polished-to-perfection footwear, he paid them what he could. Retracing their way back through the plaza, Noelle watched for Blaze, but he was nowhere to be seen. Felice stopped at the corner of the chapel courtyard where most of the men who'd been working here and there were now gathering for the noon meal.

"I... umm... I think I'll go to the chapel and pray."

"The chapel's in ruins," Noelle said.

"Uh-huh." Felice studied the crowd.

"See you at home after you've visited Shade," Noelle said.

"I'm sure he'll want to wish me feliz cumpleaños." Felice grinned and giggled.

Noelle and Carlos had wished her happy birthday when Noelle gave Felice the purple ribbon. Noelle couldn't help wondering what Shade might give her. But without lecturing Felice on her birthday, Noelle smiled and headed toward the main gate. Nearing the low barracks, she glanced down the left side where Carlos claimed Jim Bowie's room was. She saw no sign of Colonel Bowie... or Blaze.

Scanning the right side of low barracks, Noelle was startled to see Raoul Buzzard. At the far end of the low barracks, he lurked near the largest cannon of all. From the shadows, he motioned to her. This was as good a time as any to tell him that she didn't need him to take her back to Natchez. As soon as she reached the stocky man, Noelle was vividly reminded of how badly he stank and how downright unfortunate looking this unsavory man was. Due to the smell alone, she knew her grandmother would refer to him as a polecat.

"Hello, Mr. Buzzard." If Blaze only wanted her for Grandmother's money, did she still prefer him instead of Buzzard to take her home? "How are you?"

"Not good." Buzzard shook his large, square head. "Because Blaze Bowie relieved me of the pleasure of escorting you back to Mississippi. He claims he lives across the river in Louisiana."

"So he told me." Noelle nodded in relief. "Thank you anyway." With that, she turned to go.

"Mademoiselle, wait!"

When Buzzard stepped forward Noelle backed up to avoid the man and his smell, but in doing so found herself trapped against the wall of the low barracks.

"What do you want, Mr. Buzzard?" She grimaced as his foul breath and odor assailed her.

"Just to warn you of those two whores from the cantina. I think they aim to harm you."

"I'll watch out. Please let me by now."

"I have a suggestion." Instead of moving aside, Buzzard leaned in and further imprisoning her, flattened one grimy hand to the wall. "For safety's sake, let me travel with you and Bowie when you head outa town."

"You'll have to ask Blaze about that."

"No," came Blaze's resonating growl.

His sandy, collar length hair was tousled and his gray eyes hooded, as if he'd just rolled out of bed. Commanding her full attention was the fact he wore no shirt.

This frontiersman's sunbaked skin was a warm fox brown. His broad shoulders and massive chest rivaled solid granite. The flexing muscles in his sinewy arms bulged like mountains. Honey gold hair teased his bronze nipples. Like rapids in a river, muscles rippled down his washboard stomach. His missing sash let his buckskin pants breeze far below an indented navel swirled with darker gold, masculine hair. What was yet to be discovered in his deerskin breeches ended the limits of Noelle's knowledge.

"Come here, Noelle," Blaze said.

Buzzard lowered his arm and Noelle hurried to Blaze. Her cheeks burned after her bold perusal of him.

"I'm surprised you didn't turn your back on me like you did in Main Plaza and walk away," she said softly.

"Shh." Blaze draped his arm around her. "Why are you in the Alamo, Buzzard?"

"Lookin' for Shade."

"He's on watch and Colonel Crockett doesn't want him bothered."

"That's fine, matey," Buzzard replied.

"Don't bother Noelle again, Buzzard. If you have something to say to her, you say it to me. Understand?"

When Buzzard nodded, Blaze seized Noelle's hand and stalked off trailing her behind him. She took two steps to every one of his long strides and was led into a nearby room with two bunks.

"Is this your room?" Noelle gulped, eyes wide.

"And Shade's," Blaze said as he shut the door.

"Why aren't you two in the regular infantry barracks?"

"Because we aren't regular."

That's the God's truth, Noelle thought. Blaze plowed his hands through his hair and yawned. In doing so, his chest expanded and his stomach bowed inward. His breeches dipped dangerously low. Noelle yanked her eyes up.

"Did you just wake up?"

"Hell, I just went to bed. I was on watch all night at the cannon where I just found you."

"Watching for General Santa Anna and his troops?" Noelle asked.

"Yeah." Blaze rubbed his eyes. "I pulled Shade out of bed when I came in and sent him to take his watch at Crockett's post near the chapel."

"Are you two getting involved in this Texas rebellion?" It

was the first time the idea he might be had occurred to her. "Please don't get caught up in it, Blaze."

"Since you weren't *caught* by Shade that probably means he's asleep at his post."

"Felice will wake him soon enough," Noelle said. "I'm glad to see your eye didn't turn black. What about the places where I punched you?"

He spread his arms wide, showing his unmarred, upper body. She shivered from his scowl and cool attitude.

"Why didn't you punch Shade when he kissed you in Main Plaza, Noelle?"

CHAPTER 12

"BECAUSE THAT KISS WAS DIRECTED MORE AT YOU THAN ME," Noelle answered.

"Touché." Blaze nodded as though he knew that and his frown faded.

"How did you know I was here?"

"Buzzard's voice and stink woke me. I couldn't believe it when I saw you backed against that wall. What if *he'd* tried to kiss you, Noelle?"

"I'd have walloped him," Noelle said.

"You pack the wallop of a gnat."

"What would you have me do?"

"Ram your knee between his legs, dammit!"

Noelle digested that as best she could as a barefoot, half-naked Blaze swaggered to his bed.

"What are you doing here, Noelle?" he asked, sitting on his cot.

"Felice and I delivered some boots and shoes that Carlos repaired," she said. "Did Colonel Bowie and Colonel Travis make up?"

"Kinda. They've agreed to agree on the important decisions." Blaze yawned and then studied her. "Were you coming to my room to make up with me or were you on your way home without a word?"

"I was on my way," Noelle swung a hand behind her back, crossed her fingers and smiled sweetly, "to wish you a Happy Saint Valentine's Day."

"You little liar." Blaze leaned forward and grasped her wrist. He pulled her to sit next to him on his slept-in bed and her heart thudded. "You were on your way outa here."

"I'm mad at you for leaving me in Shade's clutches the other day after he got out of the calaboose!"

"Well, now." A slow, deliciously seductive grin formed on Blaze's lips. "I never thought about it from your perspective. I apologize." Lying down, he pulled her with him! Coming to rest on their sides, facing each other, she was tucked between a cool adobe wall and a warm muscular body. "Would you rather be in my clutches?"

"I'm too angry to answer."

"Let's make up by makin' love."

"No! Blaze!"

"I like the way you squeal my name. Let's make you moan it along with yes instead of no."

"I'm leaving."

"You're staying, darlin'." Blaze swung a muscular leg over hers and leaned over her. "Since it's Saint Valentine's Day, you can celebrate with me."

Lying in bed with him was thrilling and truth be known, there was no place else in the world she'd rather be. When he nibbled her earlobe, goosebumps sprinkled her skin. Raining kisses down her throat beaded her nipples against her bodice. His hand closed over her breast and all reasonable thought abandoned her. As he caressed her breast, he slid his knee between her legs. The excitement this man rained throughout her entire body made Noelle hope he'd do even more. Afraid that he would, she trembled and thought to distract him.

"Who took your virginity when you were fifteen?"

"Noelle." He drew out her name in a scolding grumble.

"Please tell me."

"Gentlemen don't tell." Blaze raised up, braced himself on an elbow and moved his hand to her ribs.

"You asked about me and I answered."

"Because you didn't have anything to tell." He grinned, seeming smugly happy about that.

"Who was she?" She tugged on a strand of his thick dark blond hair.

"A twenty-two year old woman who came to the house to tutor Shade. He was only eleven, had been sick and missed some school."

"So after she tutored Shade she tutored you." A knife of pain, like the one she'd felt when Maria claimed she'd slept with Blaze, viciously stabbed Noelle. "Where were your folks?"

"She invited me to her house."

"You lost your virginity in her bed?"

"I think of it as finding my manhood."

Noelle huffed in a jealous pout. Jealous? Yes, jealous. She pursed her lips when Blaze chuckled.

"When she made Shade a man a few years later, he told our folks that he'd traded in readin', writin', 'n 'rithmetic for pleasin', pettin', 'n pokin'." Blaze lay back down beside her and stared at the ceiling. "My mother fainted, pa belted him and Shade took off. When I found him in Natchez-Under-the Hill, he'd worn his poker raw."

"What does that mean?" She didn't wait for him to answer before firing off her next question. "Did you do the same, Blaze Bowie?"

"I didn't say that."

"But you have, haven't you?"

Blaze pulled her away from the wall and rolled on top of her. Draping his long muscular legs on the outsides of her thighs, he pressed his hips against hers.

"Your knife is gouging my stomach."

"My sash and knife are on the floor, darlin'." His smile was wicked.

"Oh!" He'd made the broomstick! Maybe Blaze was attracted to her!

When Blaze undid the top button on her bodice Noelle was torn between a raging desire to experience these intimacies and assuaging her rampant curiosity regarding Blaze's purpose in Texas. Lying here in his bed, she was being very nice to him after all... As his fingers brushed the underside of her naked breast she realized he'd unfastened her dress to the waist as her thoughts roamed.

"Blaze!" Noelle clasped her bodice shut.

"Let me *tutor* you, little girl."

He brushed her hands aside, bared her upper body and caressed a naked breast. His lips captured hers in a hungry kiss and his tongue coaxed hers into play. When he stroked her nipple with the pad of his thumb, red hot tingles erupted in Noelle's most private spot. He spread her legs using both knees and nestled his hips between her thighs. Noelle pushed at his chest and broke off the kiss.

"Blaze, I'm tired of trying to worm information out of you. Tell me what business you're in back home."

"Timber."

"What's your business here?"

"Right now, it's you."

She raised a brow and so did he. He lowered his mouth to hers and she sucked her lips between her teeth. In one fell swoop his lips fastened over the tip of her left breast! He flicked the beaded nipple with his tongue, widened his mouth and suckled her right breast. White hot lightning streaked across Noelle's breasts, burned zigzags to her fingers, roared hot and fast to her stomach, thundered between her legs and curled her toes. She moaned his name and arched her back wanting more. More? Yes. She tried to imagine what that might be.

"...and that's the reason I'm here, Noelle."

"I missed what you said!" Her eyes flew open.

"Ain't it a shame, darlin'?" He chuckled. "Your mind tends to wander."

"It never wandered until you came along!" Noelle yanked her bodice over her well-kissed breasts and fumed, "Tell me again or let me up."

"I was awake all night." Blaze placed more weight on her. "I'm going to sleep now."

"With me under you?"

When Blaze rolled off her, Noelle's first instinct was not to bail out of bed, but to stay. What spell had this man cast over her? Still, she moved back a bit, but he hooked his leg over hers.

"Siesta with me," he whispered.

"Felice and Carlos will wonder where I am."

"The hell they will. It's nap time around here. If you stay, I'll encourage the garrison to give Carlos more work."

"Thank you—wait! Why should I play fair when you don't, Blaze?"

"If I didn't play fair, I wouldn't have rolled off you."

As he adjusted a feather pillow under their heads, she glanced between their bodies. Outlined in the crotch of his snug, low riding buckskin pants was Blaze's irrefutable interest in her. Long and thick, Noelle wondered how something so huge could be squeezed into someone else's body... her body. She stared.

"You'll be a custom fit," he said huskily.

"What does that mean?" Snapping her head up, she saw his gray eyes close. She let him answer this time.

"It means I'll be your first and last."

"How many innocents have you deflowered?"

"You'll be my first."

"And your last?"

"Yes." Opening his eyes, he looked straight at her.

"Where does it go inside..." she paused and he waited, "...me?" He smiled. "How does it get so big? What does it look like? How's it going to fit? Will it hurt me?"

"You ask too many questions." Blaze clapped a hand over her mouth, but she nudged it away.

"Will it hurt?"

"I don't know."

Blaze put his fingers to her eyes and shut them. Reaching to the floor he brought a blanket over them. Lying in the comfortable crook of his arm, Noelle was mentally exhausted and fell asleep in spite of herself.

It seemed only minutes later when Noelle heard her name called. She opened her eyes to find it was near candle-lighting time. Leaning over her and Blaze, Felice appeared dumbfounded.

"I've looked for you everywhere, but here. Papa is frantic."

"How'd you find me?" Noelle asked, looking up at her.

"Señor Buzzard was coming out of the cantina when we closed the shop. He told me."

Noelle eased her legs from under Blaze's. But when she tried to sit up, the arm he had around her tightened. His grip was possessive and his voice sleepy as he whispered in her ear.

"Button your dress."

Noelle's heart pounded and she fastened her bodice. Blaze threw off the blanket, rolled out of bed and tugged her out after him. He shrugged into a white shirt, tied his knife around his waist and jammed a saber in his sash.

"Where'd you get that saber?"

"Jim gave Shade and me sabers in case Santa Anna shows up."

"I don't want Santa Anna to come here," Felice said with a whimper.

"Neither do I," Noelle agreed.

"Come on. I'll walk you girls home."

Though they assured Blaze that wasn't necessary, he escorted them out of his room and past the guards at the main gate. As they left the Alamo behind, Noelle silently berated herself for not listening when he'd told her why he was in Texas. Maybe, just maybe Felice had gotten the information from Shade.

"How was your visit with Shade, Felice?" Noelle asked as

the three of them neared a footbridge over the San Antonio River.

"How did you know I saw Shade?" Felice asked with a grin.

"Well, your birthday ribbon is missing."

"At least I didn't lose it in Shade's bed."

"I didn't lose anything in Blaze's bed!" Noelle replied as Blaze chuckled. "Be quiet, Blaze!"

"Happy birthday, Felice," Blaze said. "Did Shade wish you a happy birthday?"

"Si. He made me eat a big dinner at the Saint Valentine's Day feast near the chapel." Felice tilted her head as if she hadn't expected that. "Then he showed me his four-pounder."

Starting across the bridge, Noelle stumbled over her feet and would have fallen into the creek if Blaze hadn't caught her arm.

"Four pounds?" Noelle pulled her arm from Blaze as her eyes dipped to his crotch. "It weighs four pounds?"

"The balls do," Felice explained innocently, standing beside Noelle.

Sauntering over the bridge, and leaving them in his wake, Blaze threw back his head and howled with laughter. Felice shrugged in confusion at Noelle.

"Blaze!" Noelle shrieked and ran after him over the bridge. "Is this true?"

"Mine's an eighteen-pounder, darlin'."

"What?" Catching up with him, she grabbed his arm and hissed, "You *know* that will hurt!"

"Hurt? Hell, it kills." Blaze took her hand and gave it a playful shake. "An eighteen-pounder is a cannon named for the weight of the cannon balls it fires."

"Ooh!" she said and drawing back her other hand she made a fist.

CHAPTER 13

"Do it." Cocking a brow, Blaze yanked her closer. "And I'll spank you."

Noelle huffed, but found her long pent-up anger had become easier to control since Blaze had righted her wrong conclusions about Marcel and the Bowies. She lowered her hand, uncurled her fingers and they continued in peace. At Ambrosio Rodriguez' place, the house closest to the footbridge, a man reined in a lathered horse.

"I wonder why Rivas, Señora Rodriguez' cousin, is riding in at dusk," Noelle said, acutely aware of her hand in Blaze's. Funny how safe she felt with him.

"Noelle! Felice!" Rivas waved and shouted in their direction. "I have just arrived from Laredo to warn my cousins they must leave here at once."

"Why?" Blaze asked.

"Santa Anna is at the Rio Grande and coming straight for us, Señor," Rivas replied, walking toward them.

"Where is Laredo and how far is it from here?" Blaze asked.

"It's on the Rio Grande River which runs between Mexico and Texas," Rivas answered as they met up. "About a hundred fifty miles south."

Noelle pulled her hand from Blaze and hugged Felice

who looked close to tears. Blaze had never felt for any woman the emotions burning in him for Noelle. Damn, how he wished he could pack her and Shade up and go back home. No. Not home. Just back to debt and ruin, without the gold or silver.

"The enemy hasn't come this close to the Alamo since we sent General Cos and his dragoons running like jack rabbits in December," Rivas said with concern in his voice.

"Yes, I know about Cos." Blaze also knew dragoon was the term Jim and Travis used to refer to a heavily armed cavalryman of the Mexican army.

"But since that victory," Rivas continued. "I hear the troops at the Alamo haven't drilled. They do not come out for roll call. They eat, sleep, chase señoritas and sit in the cantinas."

"They receive no pay." Blaze leapt to their defense. "Men sell their rifles just for a drink of whiskey." The garrison kept watch but that was all. Blaze didn't know much about the army but said, "I agree they should drill."

"Word is they think General Santa Anna is another elegant dandy like General Cos." Rivas shrugged.

"I don't know who you're including in *they*." Blaze rubbed his forehead. "But maybe the men in charge at the Alamo haven't heard reports about Santa Anna from someone they trust."

"Si Señor, that's because it is the Mexicans who know Santa Anna. But Colonel Travis does not believe what we tell him," Rivas said earnestly. "Por favor, tell Colonel Bowie what I have told you. He is more likely to take Santa Anna seriously." With that, Rivas headed for the Rodriguez house and called over his shoulder, "Adios."

Blaze gazed across the mesquite covered prairie to the majestic mission. It was easy to fall prey to the magic of the Alamo. He understood why Jim couldn't blow it up. But he had to remember his own goal.

"I have to report this to Jim," Blaze said. "You girls go home." Felice nodded and walked a few steps away. "And for

God's sake, stay away from Buzzard and the cantina women." He smiled at Noelle and turned to go.

"Blaze." Noelle stayed him with a hand on his arm. "I want to take Felice and Carlos with us when we leave. And I want to go now."

Blaze looked into the greenish gold eyes and smoothed a lock of wild copper curls away from the beautiful face. Damn, he wished he had enough money to buy horses and supplies and send her on ahead. But even if he did, there was no one he'd trust to take her on such a long, perilous journey.

"We'll take Felice and Carlos with us. But I've got something to do before I can go."

"I'm afraid."

"I thought you weren't afraid of anybody."

"I'm afraid for you."

Her arrow hit Blaze's heart. "That's seems like a lot to admit, considering you don't trust me as far as you could throw me."

"I'm tired of just dreaming about peace and security." Her eyes glittered with unshed tears.

"I swear you'll have both. Just give me some time."

"We don't have time."

"Listen to me." Blaze sighed and placed his hands to her shoulders. "Shade and I own a lot of land back home and we've got plans for it. But to make a long story short, our folks died in a fire that took away our livelihood and left us in debt."

"Oh no, I'm so sorry about your parents." A tear escaped down her cheek. "Perhaps Grandmother can help."

"No!" Blaze released her and stepped back. "Hell, no! I'm not Charbonnez. Your grandmother's not slapping any money in my hand. I can't go back just yet and that's all there is to it."

"Why are you in Texas when your problems are in Louisiana? How can you follow through on your plans for your land by fighting in a rebellion five hundred miles away from home?"

"Dammit! You and your questions!"

"You have *all* the answers, Blaze!"

"Hell's bells!"

Noelle flinched, Felice shied further away and Blaze felt like a bully for scaring them. But considering Noelle's opinion about *fortune seekers* he couldn't admit he was here seeking a fortune to save his land. How quickly Noelle would damn him when she found out what he needed was hidden in Texas. If only she didn't associate the San Saba Mines with Charbonnez' death and an unstable life. But she did and they'd only recently come to an uneasy truce on the Bowies' responsibility in the matter. He couldn't risk losing the ground they had gained.

"Blaze," Noelle gulped. "What's the secret you're hiding?"

"I can't tell you any more right now." He reached for her, but she stepped out of his reach. He lowered his hand and rested it on the hilt of his saber. "Everything will be all right."

"Not if you get killed." Noelle stared at the sword and shook her head.

"I won't get killed."

"That's what Marcel told my mother before he left with Jim and Rezin for the lost San Saba Mines."

"I *promise* I won't get killed."

"You broke your promise to Shade."

"No, we talked about this, Noelle. I told Shade I'd keep my hands off any *raven-haired* señorita he wanted." With a glance at Felice, who was a few feet away and crying, he said, "Shade thinks he was second best in our parents' eyes. That's not true. But taking you from me would prove to Shade he doesn't live in my shadow."

"I see." Noelle was impressed with Blaze's explanation of Shade's insecurities and his reasoning for the rivalry she'd suspected was ongoing. "If you and Shade are fighting and..." she lowered her voice, but her own insecurities and fears were quickly building, "Shade doesn't care about Felice, it would make for an awkward trip back to Natchez. I'll find someone else to take us and you can stay here in Texas with your *precious* secret!"

"You're not afraid I'll die." Blaze's jaw clenched. "You're afraid you'll lose your ride home to your *precious* Grandmother."

"That's not true!"

"Then prove it." He softened his voice. "Just wait until I can take you, all right?" Noelle pursed her lips and glared at him. "I'll take that as a yes." Blaze glanced at the garrison again. "I need to find Jim."

"Fine! Go to the Alamo!" Noelle snapped, backing up. "But you don't belong there. The fight for Texas land is not your fight. You need to go home and follow through on the plans for *your* land!"

"I will!" Blaze didn't like her angry cold shoulder or her moving ever further away from him. He wanted her as warm and close as she'd been beside him in bed. He strode forward, pulled her to him and expected her to struggle. But her arms twined around his neck like ivy. "*We* will go home, Noelle."

"I don't know what secret you're hiding from me," Noelle whispered in his ear. "But believe me when I say I don't want you to live so that you can take me home. I want you to live so *you can* go back home."

"I will live to get all of us home." Blaze fully believed this woman who comforted others, giving them the shoes off her feet and no doubt her only ribbon, her favorite color at that. "I give you my word."

"Don't worry about me." She stood back and flattened her hands to his chest. "If Santa Anna comes to the Alamo, you and Shade ride out of Bexar and never look back."

"Noelle," Blaze said in surprise at her vehemence. "I'm not going to run out on you or on Jim." Blaze took her hands in his, kissed her soft lips and reluctantly let her go.

Before changing his mind about leaving her, he turned and sprinted for the Alamo.

"COUSIN HERRERA TOOK them both on a run to see Santa Anna."

Turning to Carlos, who had spoken, Noelle all but dropped their bowl of supper on the small sawbuck pine table. This news along with Blaze's words of not running out on her and *Jim*, echoing in her head, warned her Blaze was in fact wrapped up in the Texas rebellion.

"Oh, Papa, no," Felice whimpered, put her hands to her cheeks and looked at Noelle.

"Herrera took Blaze and Shade Bowie to spy on General Santa Anna?" Noelle asked incredulously.

"Si," Carlos said. "Spying is what Cousin Herrera does. When I delivered boots to the Alamo today, Colonel Bowie said Captain Seguin himself recruited our cousin."

Juan Seguin came from an influential family in San Antonio. Noelle was aware that he was an important addition to the American defense because he and his men knew this part of the country so well.

"Captain Seguin asked Herrera to locate the enemy and report back their location," Carlos said.

"Dear Lord." Noelle sat down next to Felice on the table's bench seat. "Whatever made Herrera take Blaze and Shade with him?"

"Colonel Bowie said Blaze volunteered and then so did Shade."

"Is Blaze loco, Noelle?" Felice asked.

"No, I think he wants to report back to Travis, since Travis doesn't trust the Mexicans," Noelle guessed, wringing her hands. "No offense, Carlos."

"Si, I have heard the same."

Felice turned from Noelle to Carlos and blurted out, "Papa, I love Shade Bowie. I do not want that terrible dictator Santa Anna to kill him."

"What does she mean she loves Shade Bowie?" From across the table, Carlos stared at Felice and then as if she couldn't possibly give him a reasonable explanation, looked at Noelle. "Can you explain?"

"She told me that, too." Noelle cringed over the dangers involved in spying on Santa Anna's army.

"We have not seen Shade or Blaze since my birthday and here it is the twentieth." Felice jumped up from the table. "They have probably been dead for days by now!" Felice flung herself on her bed, crying.

"Don't say that, Felice." But thinking the same thing, Noelle hugged herself.

"What has been going on between my muchachas and the Bowie brothers?" Carlos asked, pressing his fingers to his temples and gazing from Felice to Noelle.

"I'm going to the Alamo, Carlos," Noelle said, standing.

"And do what?"

"Talk to Colonel Bowie."

COLD RAIN HAD STARTED DRIZZLING on her way to the Alamo. Though nervous Noelle had found and talked to Jim Bowie. During the two days since their conversation the rain had steadily poured. Despite today's storm, Carlos had gone to the shop to work on shoes and boots for the garrison. Since Felice blamed Noelle for Blaze taking Shade spying, she'd accompanied her father. Noelle hadn't pointed out that Herrera was their cousin, not hers.

Now she took a break from dumping out bowls of water, from the leaking thatched roof, and sat on the end of her narrow bed. Mistletoe crawled onto her lap and she petted the cat praying Blaze had kept his promise not to be killed. She replayed her short visit with Colonel Bowie over in her mind. She regretted he was ill. She found herself liking and respecting Jim Bowie even though, actually maybe because, he said he couldn't confide in her as to why Blaze and Shade were in Texas.

However, without her asking he had sworn an oath not to let them die.

"Please keep them alive, Colonel Bowie," she said all alone and so afraid.

Noelle's head turned as horse hooves sounded. She eased Mistletoe off her lap and hurried to the door. She threw back the rawhide, flinched at the pelting downpour and ran into the rain. A rider jumped off his horse and in two long strides soaked buckskin wrapped around her. Rain-cold lips came down on hers and strong arms lifted her against a muscular body, pulling her bare feet out of the mud.

Noelle clung to this man she had feared dead and thanked God for his safe return. The moment he set her feet to the ground, she pulled him into the hut. There was a look in his gray eyes that told her he had seen much.

Blaze tossed his hat on the sawbuck table and devoured Noelle with starving eyes. Every mile he had ridden away from this beauty had twisted a knife in his heart. Crossing the prairie, he'd searched in vain for the green and gold colors in her eyes. The rainy mornings dawned dreary instead of the pink of her petal soft lips. The roaring campfires at night had paled compared to Noelle's crimson curls.

"Blaze, I was so worried." Noelle swiped her wet hair away from her ivory face and her soft voice sounded almost mystified. "But you kept your promise to come back,"

"Thanks to Blue."

"Who?"

"True Blue, my horse. He got me back to San Antonio ahead of everybody else."

"Is he true blue?" Noelle asked as if she might mean Blaze himself and not the sorrel outside.

"Yes, he is," Blaze answered meaningfully. When Noelle smiled his burdens seemed lighter. But the gravity of the situation quickly returned. "You've got to get out of Bexar. Today."

"Fine." Her smile faded and she nodded. "Let's go."

"I said you, not me."

Blood pounded in Blaze's ears. He didn't want to stand here and talk. He wanted to carry Noelle to that bed in the corner. A small calico cat lying there stretched contentedly and Blaze pictured Noelle doing the same after he had made love to her. She unleashed a possessiveness in him that made him want to keep her close. But fierce protectiveness raced to the forefront warning him to get her far away to safety.

"When we last parted, you said to wait for you and that's what I'm going to do."

"Things have changed."

"Why? What did you see?"

"Santa Anna and his dragoons are less than fifty miles from the Alamo."

"Surely more than fifty." She held her breath and shivered.

"Fifty, Noelle."

Noelle sank down onto the bench seat at the table. Blaze straddled the bench and turned her to face him. The little calico cat hopped onto the bench between them. Noelle petted her and the cat purred. It then turned in a circle and lay down between Blaze's spread legs.

"Mistletoe," Noelle said and smiled at Blaze. "She likes you."

"Does she?" Blaze asked, looking into Noelle's eyes.

"She does," Noelle answered shyly, blushed and lowered her eyes to her cat. She reached a hand to pet her but realizing her hand would be between Blaze's thighs, she folded her hands in her lap instead. "What will be done to stop Santa Anna?"

"Not a damn thing." Blaze ran a hand through his thick hair that darkened to light brown when wet. "Not with only a hundred and fifty six men at the garrison."

"You went spying with Herrera to convince Travis that Santa Anna is closing in, didn't you?"

Propping an elbow on the table, Blaze rested his head in his hand. He was wet, cold and bone-tired. Noelle got up and pulled a blanket off her bed. She wrapped it around his shoulders and sat back down on the bench. When the sexy innocent before him smiled, heat flared in his lower body warming him and giving him the needed strength to persevere.

"Yes, that's exactly why we went with Herrera. I just told Travis and Jim what we saw. Travis believes me, but he doesn't think anything will happen until spring."

CHAPTER 14

"How can Travis think Santa Anna will wait until spring when he's this dangerously close?" Noelle asked.

"Because Travis swears Santa Anna won't bring his horses and mules over the arid-like desert that lies between here and Hondo Creek before March fifteenth." Blaze rubbed his forehead and sighed. "Travis thinks Santa Anna's animals need the wet spring grass to graze on."

"What does Colonel Bowie think?"

"Jim told Travis that Santa Anna can feed his animals on the dry mesquite grass, that it's the best hay you could find. But the worst is not how soon Santa Anna gets here."

"What's the worst?" Noelle visibly tensed.

"The odds." Blaze hesitated in being specific but when she placed her hand on the arm he'd propped on the table he replied, "Santa Anna has at least fifteen hundred dragoons with him." He took her hand in his. "Odds are bad when the enemy has ten times the men we have at the Alamo. To make matters more desperate, we have limited supplies and munitions."

"*We?*" She squeezed his hand. "You mean they." When he didn't reply Noelle asked, "Can't someone come to the aid of the Alamo?"

"Travis has requested help from Governor Smith." Blaze stroked the back of her hand with his thumb.

"I haven't heard why but Governor Smith was recently impeached."

"There's a General Council here in Texas and most of its members belong to the Peace Party. Smith was a leader of the Independence Party. Smith doesn't believe in compromising with Santa Anna nor does he understand the language of diplomacy. When the governor tried to dissolve the council they retaliated by impeaching him. With Santa Anna marching right for us and official leadership so critically needed… there is none."

"Dear Lord." Noelle shook her head and her brow furrowed. "What about Sam Houston? You told me he liked Colonel Bowie. Why doesn't Houston come with troops and help?"

"Houston's been on a furlough for almost a month, making sure the Indians around here don't side with Santa Anna against us."

"Who else can help us?" Noelle pulled her hand from him and clasped her hands under her chin so tightly her knuckles turned white. "Surely there's someone."

"There's a Colonel Fannin in Goliad with the New Orleans Greys, Alabama Red Rovers, and some others but he's dragging his feet on getting them here. Travis is waiting for the colonies to send help, but Jim doesn't think help is coming now or ever."

Noelle stood and paced to the foot of one of the two narrow beds in a corner of the tiny, damp hut.

"If it's hopeless," turning to him, Noelle asked, "what is keeping the men at the Alamo?" She swung her arms wide, palms up. "Why stay without pay only to be slaughtered by a sadistic dictator?"

"Land. If by some miracle they aren't killed they'll be allowed twelve hundred and eighty acres of Texas land." Blaze could tell by the wonder and then the resignation on her face that this was news to her. "You haven't seen a recruiting poster for this war?"

"No. I assumed the troops were ordered to come here. Until this moment, it was a mystery to me as to why men would voluntarily risk their lives." Clenching her fists over her heart, she hissed, "Damn men and their passion to die for land and treasure!"

Blaze knew that was a jab at him and the other Bowies and he couldn't deal with it right now. He grabbed his hat and shot to his feet. Mistletoe leapt off the bench and scampered to Noelle as Blaze stalked to the door. He yanked aside the animal skin which did a poor job of keeping the rain out.

"Blaze, wait!" Noelle came up behind him, pressed her cheek to his back and wrapped her arms around his waist. "Don't go."

"I told Jim and Travis to blow up the Alamo, like Houston said, so Santa Anna can't have it." Through the downpour of rain, Blaze stared toward the garrison. "I said they should leave here and join forces with Fannin's detachment in Goliad."

"Yes! That's brilliant!" Noelle moved around him into the rain. The storm drenching her, she looked up at him. "Tell me they will do that."

"They won't." Blaze stepped back into the house, pulling her with him and dropping the animal skin into place over the doorway. "There will be no surrender. It's victory or death. When I left headquarters they were talking about attending a fandango tomorrow night at Domingo Bustillo's place on Soledad Street in honor of *El Señor Jorge Washington's* birthday."

"While they are celebrating, Santa Anna will be marching." Noelle shivered.

Blaze stroked the soft skin of her face as he looked into her eyes. He wondered if he would ever see the love he felt for her mirrored in those green pools flecked with gold. Lowering his head he kissed her tenderly wanting again to toss her onto the bed. But this wasn't the time or place so he pulled back.

"I've never known anyone like you, Noelle," Blaze whispered and admitted, "I missed you like hell the past few days."

"I've never known anyone like you either. Will I see you at the fandango?"

"No!" he barked. "You're in danger here. I want you to convince Carlos to take you to Goliad and wait for me there."

"No, it's you who's in danger. Santa Anna will kill the men, not the women and children. Why won't you be at the fandango?"

"I'll be on watch until late." He craved another kiss, but if he got it he might not leave. "I have to go. Jim's health is failing more each day."

"That's it!" Noelle snapped her fingers. "Talk Colonel Bowie into letting you take him home to a doctor."

"That's about as likely as Shade giving up on winning you."

"Would it make a difference if I tell Shade he has no chance with me?"

"I don't know because—" He glanced around the hut. "You need a looking glass in here, darlin'," he said and finished his thought, "because you are beautiful."

"Beautiful?" She blushed sunrise pink. "Thank you." When he smiled, she looked down at her feet and said softly, "Shade is only interested because you've said you are."

"Partly, maybe." Blaze leaned against the wall and spread his feet. "Shade liked the bayou girls who were my age instead of girls his own age. When the older girls didn't pay attention to him he took it as proof he was stuck in my shadow as second best. It's gone on as long as I can remember."

"Because he admires you so much and he wants to be just like you, Blaze."

"I don't know about that." He shrugged and sighed. "He

went from the tutor to Natchez-Under-the Hill girls. He's treated all women like whores ever since. Even so, one girl loved Shade despite the way he treated her."

"Make that two girls." Noelle held up two fingers. "Felice told Carlos and me she loves Shade." Blaze took hold of her hand and tugged her to stand between his legs. "What happened to the first girl?"

Thinking if Noelle knew about Lucy Ray, it might help her and Felice better understand Shade, Blaze delayed going to the Alamo long enough to tell her the gist of what had happened with Lucy.

"On top of feeling insecure, Shade's angry with himself now," Noelle said. "I understand holding in sadness until it becomes anger over a death that could have been prevented."

"Yeah." Blaze smiled, appreciating her honesty and insight. "Lucy doted on him so completely she had Shade half-convinced he was second to no one. But when he lost interest, she lied to him."

"The lie being that she slept with him only to make you jealous."

"And we were right back where we started." He bowed his head and sighed. "On the way to Texas, we talked about home and freedom. Shade said he was turning over a new leaf and I was happy to make him the promise I told you about."

At the exhaustion in Blaze's voice, Noelle wished she hadn't asked about Lucy. He was worried enough about Jim and the Alamo without worrying over Shade. What could she say to help?

"Shade is lucky to have a brother who loves him so much. He loves you, too, or he wouldn't have stepped

in front of you when Lucy Ray's father threatened to kill you." As Blaze's right shoulder lifted in a shrug, Noelle glimpsed the little boy inside the powerful man. How sensitive and caring he was when it came to Shade, Jim Bowie, the Alamo... and to her. Did she not owe him the same in return? "If Shade could open his eyes to how much a certain raven-haired beauty loves *him* and not his older brother," Noelle smiled, "it might cure his bruised pride once and for all."

"Maybe." Blaze sounded uncertain, but hopeful.

He wrapped his arms around her and flattening his hands to her back, he kissed her. Noelle's body heated in response, despite the chilly air in the dreary house. Blaze pulled back way too soon and said he had to go.

"I'll warn Felice that loving Shade doesn't mean letting him take her for granted," she said with conviction. "No matter how late you get off watch, you and Shade come meet us at the fandango. I have a plan."

Blaze eased her aside and stalked to the door. He yanked open the rawhide and fixed a scowl on her. Mercy, what had she done to make him so mad?

"Nobody around here listens to reason," Blaze said. "When Santa Anna rolls into town he'll take charge of Bexar because the volunteers and soldiers will be trapped inside the Alamo. Santa Anna could commandeer this very house. Time is almost up."

With that said Blaze was out the door, on his horse and galloping toward the Alamo in the pouring rain. Several minutes ticked by before Noelle could move.

THE FOLLOWING EVENING, Noelle twiddled her thumbs at Domingo Bustillo's place for an hour. Carlos was enjoying himself, so she and Felice decided to leave him there to look elsewhere for Blaze and Shade. She had suggested a plan to Felice, who now also had a better understanding of Shade. Later, she would explain to Blaze that Carlos had refused to leave town and Felice wouldn't go without her father. Noelle would admit she couldn't run out on the Herreras any more than Blaze would run out on Jim and the Alamo. That was the truth, but not the whole truth. Even if Felice and Carlos had agreed to go, she couldn't leave Blaze. But why couldn't she?

"Because he's the man I lo—" Noelle cut herself off. She would never marry any man but a stable one.

"What?" Felice asked as they neared Main Plaza.

"Just rehearsing our plan." Noelle crossed her fingers to excuse the fib.

In Main Plaza they found a second celebration. Near a table laden with tamales and mescal, an alcoholic beverage, she heard people say Jim Bowie had asked his Mexican friends to provide these refreshments. If Blaze got off his watch in time, surely this was where he would come with Shade.

Rip-roaring horse races were mildly distracting until they ended at candle-lighting time. Illuminated by torches and lanterns, fiddle contests and street dancing provided new entertainment. Though asked to dance by this volunteer and that soldier, Noelle declined. When food and drink were gone and contests won or lost, people began moseying out of Main Plaza leaving Noelle and Felice in the ever darkening shadows of the San Fernando Church.

"They aren't coming, Felice."

"Si, let's go find Papa."

Noelle turned and was immediately engulfed by buckskin and muscles. He'd been so frustrated with her the last time he saw her, this embrace seemed unlikely. And he wasn't holding her like he always did. Why was his head down with the brim of his buckskin hat covering his face? Why had he clamped her cheek against his shoulder?

"Blaze, I was afraid you couldn't get away from the Alamo because of more bad news about Santa Anna." Noelle's head was to his shoulder as she tried to see Felice in the moonlight. "Did Shade come with you?"

"We saw Santa Anna riding on velvet cushions inside a shining carriage, drawn by matched horses."

"Did you catch a cold when you and Shade went spying?" Felice asked him. "You sound raspy."

"At night Santa Anna sleeps in a tent on a silk-covered bed." His voice didn't sound right to Noelle, either. "On a table he keeps a snuff box with the initial 'N' circled by a wreath, a short sword with the same initial, some gilt buttons, and a Moroccan leather writing case. They're all mementos of Napoleon. In fact, Santa Anna calls himself," he chuckled hoarsely, "the Napoleon of the West."

Staring at his buckskin shoulder and held so tightly she could hardly breathe, Noelle asked, "You were inside Santa Anna's tent?"

"Yeah, Shade and I blackened our hair and beard stubble with boot polish. *His Excellency*, Santa Anna," he said with a sarcastic tone Noelle had never heard him use, "and his men thought we were as Mexican as Herrera."

"Your reaction to spying on Santa Anna seems completely different than it was the other day." And so was Noelle's. Her heart wasn't pounding, her stomach wasn't flip-flopping nor did she have noodle knees about to buckle. Sensing a ruse, she shoved out of his arms. "Shade!"

"Shade!" Felice echoed, as the clouds shifted, shedding more moonlight on the situation. "Where'd you get that hat like Blaze's?"

"Couldn't wear a coonskin cap when spying." Shade laughed. "Your cousin, Herrera, gave it to me."

"How could you trick us and stab your brother in the back like this?" Noelle demanded.

"'Cause he's stabbed me and he's tricking you."

"No, Blaze is honorable!" Felice taunted him right on cue, instead of fawning over him, as they stood in the middle of the plaza. "He knows how to treat a woman."

"Then I guess the honorable Blaze has told you the real reason he proposed?" Shade asked Noelle.

"If it has something to do with my grandmother's money he won't take any, so that's not it."

"But, he'll take it from the bank," Shade said. "Except they'll only give us the money if one of us gets married. We flipped a coin and Blaze lost. He has to find a wife and quick."

The bottom dropped out of Noelle's stomach.

"I don't believe that!" Felice said.

"Where do you think Blaze is tonight, Noelle?" Shade demanded and answered for her, "In bed with Maria. The bank won't know she's a cantina whore."

Noelle swayed and Felice put an arm around her. Would Blaze siesta with her on Saint Valentine's Day, then turn around and sleep with Maria? This evening wasn't going at all as she'd planned.

"No!" Felice snapped at Shade. "You would live with any *easy* woman, Shade. Blaze will wait for the *one* woman he cannot live without!"

"Really?" Shade frowned at Felice as though surprised that not only was she defending Blaze, but for the way she had so accurately sized them up. He dared them, "Let's go to the cantina and find out."

Noelle's mind conjured up such a torturous image of Blaze in bed with Maria that when Shade threw his arm around her *and* Felice, Noelle numbly let him steer her out of Main Plaza.

What a fool she'd been to believe Blaze's lies about love at first sight. How naive to think a virile man like Blaze wouldn't turn to another woman after she had refused to make love to him in his bunk. No wonder his kisses were so chaste the other day. Every time he'd talked about marriage and proving himself, she had given him refusals or ultimatums. So, he'd turned to Maria. He was probably proposing to her this very minute. As they neared the cantina, guitar music and revelry assailed Noelle like jabbing jeers. She felt ill and just wanted to go home. As if she couldn't possibly feel any worse, she saw Raoul Buzzard shove open the cantina's swinging doors.

"Buzzard!" Shade hailed him and said to Noelle and Felice, "I want to travel with him. He told me he knows his way around Galveston Island."

The pirate hurried their way and met them in the center of Potrero Street. Noelle strained her eyes toward the lights of the cantina, but could see little over the tops of the swinging doors. Shade let go of her and Felice to meet up with Buzzard.

"I'm going home, Felice."

CHAPTER 15

"Noelle," Felice whispered as Shade walked toward Buzzard. "Shade's lying about Blaze. You said we were not only going to keep Shade from taking me for granted, but heal his bruised pride by making him have to win me. Let's keep to our plan. Por favor. Si?"

"Si." Noelle nodded as Shade came back. She noted that he draped his arm around Felice before he did her. Buzzard brought his foul odor with him and it worsened when he opened his mouth.

"Mademoiselle Noelle." Buzzard's beefy face drooped and he shook his meaty head as if feeling sorry for her. "Them cantina whores're saying they're gonna row you up Salt River because of Blaze Bowie."

"Salt River?" Noelle asked. "Where's that?"

"It means they're gonna beat you into oblivion," Buzzard replied.

"They'll have to get through me."

Blaze! Noelle pivoted, ready to strangle him.

"I told you to talk to me and not Noelle, Buzzard," Blaze said from about ten feet away. He was suspicious of this pirate's interest in Noelle. Having found Carlos at Domingo Bustillo's place, he had him in tow. They were headed to the shop to check for the girls when Blaze spotted them outside the cantina.

"Aye, matey I forgot," Buzzard said respectfully.

In the dim light of the cantina it was hard to be sure but it appeared to him that Noelle was frowning. He was the one who had the right to scowl for finding her with Buzzard. And why was she letting Shade drape his arm around her shoulders?

"Hola, Blaze!" Maria burst out of the cantina and waved at him. "I've missed you, caro. Come over here and make up with me."

He waved Maria the hell off. She had hurt Noelle enough because of him. He reached Noelle and thought her withering glare had lessened slightly from his reaction to Maria. Shoving Shade's arm off Noelle's shoulders, Blaze stared him in the eye, silently daring him to do anything about it. Shade smirked but kept his arm around Felice.

"Papa," Felice smiled, "I see you've met Blaze Bowie."

"We met Carlos at the Alamo, Felice," Shade said, when she didn't introduce him.

Carlos seemed to be taking a fresh look at Shade. No mystery, Blaze thought. Carlos had asked Blaze about Shade's intentions toward Felice on their way here. Blaze said he wasn't sure. But he'd told Carlos he had asked Noelle to marry him.

"So, Buzzard," Shade raised his chin, "wanna go to Galveston Island with us?"

"I could be persuaded." Buzzard's sneering smile was victorious as he looked at Blaze to say, "If the idea floats with you now, matey."

"I never said I was going to Galveston Island," Blaze replied. But he'd reconsidered it since hearing Noelle's confusion regarding Jean Lafitte. Lafitte was legendary in Texas and among the rumors Blaze had heard was that Jim and Jean once shared a quadroon mistress named Catherine. Although, Blaze had no reason to ask Jim about his love life, he had inquired if Lafitte was a man of reason. Yes, in

Jim's high opinion his good friend, Jean, absolutely was. In fact, Jim had added, a face-to-face meeting just might squelch Noelle's dislike of the man. Jim didn't elaborate, but finished simply with, 'See to it, Blaze.'

"If you go, I can guide you around the island, matey," Buzzard said. "And introduce you to Lafitte."

"My last name will introduce me. I don't need a guide and I'm not your damn *matey*, Buzzard." Hell would freeze over before Blaze traveled a mile with this stinking, untrustworthy polecat. He was getting madder at Shade by the minute for cultivating the man's friendship. "Where were you taking Noelle and Felice, Shade?"

"To the cantina to look for you," Shade replied.

"But we knew you wouldn't be there," Felice said and pushed Shade's arm off her shoulders. "Right, Noelle? That's Shade's kind of place."

"Why do you say that?" Shade asked Felice.

"Para todo mal, mezcal, y para todo bien, también."

Blaze noticed Felice's cold shoulder had Shade's full attention and reckoned this was part of Noelle's *plan*. It also occurred to him that Noelle hadn't spoken a word since he had joined them.

"What does that mean, Felice?" Shade put his fists to his hips and glared at Felice.

"For every ill, mescal and for every good as well," Felice said and took Carlos' arm. "I'd rather have the good than the ill. Let's go home, Papa, Noelle."

"Matey, are you coming back to the cantina?"

"No." Shade stepped away from Buzzard and spoke to Felice. "I'll walk with you, *Happy*."

A nickname? Another first for Shade where Felice was concerned, Blaze thought.

"Noelle, did you forget I left shoes for you in the shop?" Carlos asked.

"Carlos, I don't need shoes." Noelle curled her bare toes.

"I'll take Noelle to get her shoes and see her home," Blaze said.

"Gracias, Blaze," Carlos replied.

Noelle thanked Carlos and twirled toward the shop. As a light rain began to fall, Blaze strode after her. Crimson curls bouncing, Noelle began running through the raindrops. Taking long strides to catch up, Blaze enjoyed the way her slender hips swayed and her rounded fanny swished the hem of her skirt around her small feet. Damn, she was sexy. Nearing Carlos' shop, Noelle headed straight for the door.

"Stop right there," Blaze said.

"Go!" Whirling in the doorway, Noelle slashed her index finger toward the Alamo.

"What the devil is wrong with you, Noelle?"

"I'm trying to control my temper instead of walloping you."

Stopping in front of her, he clamped his hands on the hilts of his knife and saber. The moonlight flickered across her face, allowing Blaze to see her chin quivering.

"Lose your temper over what?" Blaze frowned at the beautiful woman. "I'm the one who should be mad for finding you with Shade and Buzzard!"

"I know your secret!"

Hell's bells. The lost San Saba Mines.

"Darlin', I was going to tell you when the time was right."

"When would that be exactly?" Her entire body shook with fury. "At the altar, in front of the parson? Would you say, 'I do... because I need a bank loan.'?"

So, she still didn't know about the mines. But she had tried and convicted him of some misconception and her hazel eyes held no mercy. This would be her reaction if and when she did find out his secret. Standing with her back to the door of the shop, she tossed her long curls over her shoulders. Her breasts heaved against her bodice and resting one hand on her hip, she jabbed a finger in his chest.

"Not that I ever intended to marry you, but it would be for love and not for money!"

"I don't need a wife to get a bank loan." Blaze reached behind her and opened the door to the shop. "Get in out of the rain." Noelle did so and he followed her. "Did Shade say I needed a wife to get a loan?"

"Yes! The jig is up! Run along to the Alamo, Blaze."

Moonlight streaming in the doorway and window, Noelle pursed her pink lips looking like a thundercloud barely holding back a deluge. Blaze longed to rain his fists down on Shade for brewing up this storm with Noelle. Instead, he calmly opened a hand in supplication.

"Noelle, you found me guilty without even talking to me. And yet, you know as well as I do Shade's trying his damnedest to come between us. Believe me, he was lying to you."

"Felice said Shade was lying, too." For a moment she was silent. Then her brows knitted and there was vulnerability in her voice when she whispered, "I don't know what to believe."

"Believe this if nothing else." The fear in her eyes tore at his heart. "Santa Anna is closing in and fast."

"Carlos won't leave town, so Felice won't leave, which means neither will I."

"So Carlos told me." Blaze shook his head. "To the day I die I'll never understand how the people here in Bexar can fandango half the night away when Santa Anna's near enough to spit on us."

"Don't talk about dying." Noelle hugged herself.

"Let's talk about the dragoons. You'll suffer worse than death if they get a hold of you."

"No, I'll be fine." She shook her head. "What was it you were going to tell me *when the time was right?*"

"That you'll be fine," he improvised a little now, "because you're moving into the Alamo with me tonight."

"Felice asked me if you were loco." Noelle's hazel eyes snapped green and gold sparks. "I think you are!"

"Hell, I'd have to be for putting up with you."

"Carlos would never allow that." Noelle backed further into the shop.

"He's already agreed," Blaze said, hands going to his hips.

"He and Felice are moving in, too, and he'll continue working for us there."

"Well, I'm not going." She crossed her arms under her breasts.

"Oh yes, you are." Blaze clenched his jaw. "Find your shoes and let's go."

Noelle turned and with help from moonbeams filtering through the window, she found the shoes. Blaze took her elbow as she leaned over to put one on. She yanked her arm from him and swung a wild punch. She missed and fell flat. He chuckled as she sat on the ground to put on the other shoe.

"It's not funny!"

"Sure it is. You spanked your own bottom!" He held out his hand, but she ignored it. "Come on."

"I'm sleeping in the shop from now on."

"You're trying my patience, little girl." Blaze yanked her up and tossed her over his shoulder.

"I'm going to row you up Salt River, Blaze Bowie!"

"I doubt it."

Blaze ducked out the door and closed it behind them. Taking off toward Main Plaza, Noelle clung to his buckskin shirt as the others came into view in the distance. Shade was the first to notice.

"Noelle, if big, bad Blaze puts you down will you come with us?" Shade called out.

"No!"

"Si, you must, Noelle," Carlos said. "My muchachas will be safer there. Since I believe in the independence of Texas, I want to do what I can to help win it."

"Por favor," Felice pleaded. "Or Papa and I will not move into the Alamo."

"All right!" Noelle seethed upside down as the right side of the situation took hold. "Only to please you and Carlos. But I'll sleep where I choose."

That's what she thought Blaze mused silently and set her down. Shade smiled, then turned his attention to Felice and

Carlos. Noelle gave her riotous curls a toss into place and marched in stoic silence at Blaze's side. Glancing at her amidst the misting rain and flickering moonlight, Blaze's irritation dissipated.

Noelle Charbonnez was the most beautiful woman he had ever laid eyes on. She would have captivated his father and his mother would have adored her. Blaze couldn't explain why love bloomed, but anger usually took root in reasons. He thought he had extracted the thorn in her side about the Bowies but she was as prickly as a cactus again. Dammit, they didn't have time to fight.

At the Herrera house, Noelle, Carlos and Felice hastened inside to retrieve some personal items. As Shade leaned against the adobe wall of the pitiful hut, Blaze stood rigidly about three feet away.

"Where's Noelle gonna sleep, Blaze?"

"I'm warning you, Shade," Blaze said through clenched teeth, "if you don't stay out of my way with Noelle you'll regret it."

"Just what can you do to me, *big bad* brother?"

"A helluva lot." Blaze grabbed the front of Shade's shirt and yanked him nose to nose. "I'll get the gold and silver without you, pay off my timberland and let Spencer take the house and your friggin' farmland."

"And live across the Mississippi River in Natchez?" Shade flinched.

"I was planning to move anyway."

"Don't threaten me or I'll tell Noelle about your plan to find the mines that killed her papa."

Noelle emerged clasping a small, cloth bag to her heart. Blaze shoved Shade back and they glowered at each other.

"What's the matter now?" Noelle asked.

Neither answered.

The rain intensified as Felice and Carlos joined them. They left the leaking, muddy jacal behind and made their way to the footbridge. Trudging over it, they crossed the mesquite prairie and passed through the main gate of the

Alamo. Inside, Jim came toward them until a cough doubled him over. Blaze reached him first but Shade wasn't far behind. Blaze was sure Jim had consumption. These cool, rainy days and nights weren't helping matters.

"You shouldn't be out here, Jim," Blaze said, fitting himself under Jim's right arm as Shade wedged under his left one.

"Buenas noches, Carlos," Jim managed to say and smiled. "Welcome, ladies."

"Colonel Bowie," Carlos began, "I am very grateful to you for taking my muchachas and me into the Alamo. Muchas gracias."

"You're welcome," Jim replied. "I expect to do the same for my late wife's sisters, Juana and Gertrudis. But for now they're at their parents' house on Soledad Street."

Ursula's father, Juan Veramendi, had been Jim's business partner. Señor Veramendi and his wife had died in 1833, of cholera like Ursula and the children. Carlos had pointed out the Veramendi house to Blaze after leaving Domingo Bustillo's place. It was little wonder Jim, who cared so much for his in-laws, would care enough about his blood relatives to share with them *gold and silver aplenty*. But with Jim sick and Santa Anna so close there was no chance of leaving the Alamo to go get the treasure right now. Blaze's threat to Shade suddenly mocked him.

Get the gold and silver? Did that mean they'd have to mine it? Was there time? It was late February and they had to be back in Louisiana the middle of May.

"Carlos, I've arranged for you and your daughters to stay in the chapel," Jim said.

"Si, Señor," Carlos said. "I will be honored to earn our keep by not only repairing boots but by doing anything else I can to help."

"Gracias, Carlos."

Carlos nodded respectfully and turned to the girls. "Come along, muchachas. Let's go to the chapel."

The pouring rain didn't quite mask a look that seemed

to pass between Noelle and Jim. Blaze hoped trouble wouldn't erupt with Noelle and Jim being in such close quarters. He and Shade helped Jim into his room. When they were back outside, near the stairs to the rooftop of the low barracks, Blaze caught Shade's arm and hauled him up short. Rain pelted the brims of their hats and ran down Blaze's back in rivulets.

"I told Noelle I didn't need a wife to get a bank loan, but she's still on the warpath. What else did you lie to her about, Shade?"

"Is this the thanks I get for keeping her away from Maria and the cantina to cover your back?"

"You were taking her *to* the cantina." Blaze scowled. "Did you make Noelle think I was with Maria tonight?"

"Noelle thinks you're a knight in shining armor, Blaze." Shade smirked. "But then, don't they all?"

"Open your eyes and you'll see a raven-haired señorita who thinks the sun rises and sets in *you*."

"My eyes will be wide open when I take your redhead beauty to bed."

"At least you admit she's mine." Blaze released his grip on Shade who then stormed toward his post near the chapel. "Keep whorin', little brother," Blaze said. "Dammit to hell. Ruin your life. You won't ruin mine."

"Blaze?"

CHAPTER 16

"Noelle," a surprised Blaze said as she walked out of the darkness from under the stairs. Wondering how much she'd heard, Blaze said, "I thought you went to the chapel."

"I told Felice and Carlos to go on because I wanted to thank you for bringing them into the Alamo. I didn't intend to eavesdrop," she said, hugging her cloth bag to her breasts. She bowed her head under the rain and admitted, "But I overheard what you and Shade just said."

"Let's get inside and dry off." Not giving her a chance to turn down his offer, he gently placed his hand to the back of her neck and guided her a few steps further to his room. He shut the door, hung his hat on a nail on the door and turned to her. "So you were actually on your way to my room this time and not sneaking out of the Alamo?"

"Yes." Her lips took on a pout before she lifted her chin and said, "I'm sorry I misjudged your motive for proposing to me. I realize now you were with Carlos looking for Felice and me and not with Maria."

"Apology accepted." Blaze backed her against the nearest wall. "Let's make up." Lowering his head, he leaned against her and froze. He stepped away and put a hand to the cloth bag. It moved. "What's in the bag?"

"My umm…two dresses and well—" She stalled and chewed her lower lip. "Umm…"

"You brought your cat to the Alamo."

"Mistletoe?" Opening the bag, Noelle peeked inside it. "However did you get in there?"

"Noelle," Blaze drew out her name in exasperation, then pinned her to the wall, the bagged cat between them. Mistletoe moved and Blaze chuckled. "I guess this is how it'll feel when my baby's inside you, kicking his father for trying to kiss his mother."

Noelle's mouth opened but nothing came out. She swallowed and tried to speak again with no success. Her hazel eyes widened and Blaze cocked a brow. The cat meowed and poked her head out of the bag.

"I think I'd better go to the chapel now."

Mistletoe, confined long enough, jumped out of the bag and vanished under Blaze's bunk. Noelle dropped to all fours and tried to sweep Mistletoe out from under it as Blaze untied his sash. She caught her cat and stood up only to have it bail out of her arms and land in the middle of his bunk.

"Off!" Blaze barked, sending the cat into hiding under his bed again.

"Blaze, what were you thinking scaring Mistletoe like that? I'll never get her now."

"Ain't it a shame, darlin'?"

Noelle's luxurious locks were in sexy disarray from digging for Mistletoe and the pink in her cheeks had heightened. Her rain-damp bodice lay molded to her breasts, her nipples beaded against the thin fabric. Blaze's blood heated. The last time she'd been in his room, he had discovered her breasts were as silky smooth as a ripe peach. The nipples he'd kissed were the same burgundy color and size of the seed inside a peach.

Damn. He wanted to feel his own seed spilling deep inside this woman. His veins pumped fevered blood hot and hard into his loins. If her hazel eyes lowered, she'd know *exactly* what he was thinking.

"Guess you'll have to spend the night with me, since your cat wants to stay." Blaze lowered his sash and weapons to the floor.

"You can't be serious. Everyone would know."

"Shade's on post and Felice won't mind. Carlos had plenty to drink at Bustillo's, so he's probably asleep." Blaze peeled off his wet buckskin shirt and hung it on a nail beside his hat. "My next watch isn't until morning. We have all night to make up."

Noelle's body heated from head to toe. What would this rugged male do to her in *making up*? She sensed a masculine urgency in him tonight. What lay behind the smoldering in those hot-as-ash gray eyes and in the spine tingling huskiness of his low voice? What did he know that she didn't? Absolutely everything when it came to making love.

"You keep Mistletoe," Noelle said, feeling nervous and bashful in the presence of this half-naked rogue. "I'll run along to the chapel and come back for her in the morning after you're on watch."

Blaze gave her a gentle shove and she fell back on his bed.

"No. Shade drinks on post. He'll roll in here half-drunk in the morning and I don't want him to find your pretty little bottom wiggling in the air as you dig for your cat under my bed."

Noelle gazed up at the gorgeous man. She understood why Maria wanted him so badly. Irrational jealousy swept over her as she thought of the countless women who had known Blaze Bowie before her. She burned to press herself to his muscular chest and be wrapped in his sinewy arms. What was hidden below his sexy, indented navel in those snug buckskin breeches? What would it be like for this powerful, experienced man to make love to her?

"Take off your clothes, Noelle."

Blaze grabbed a dry, white shirt off a nail on the wall and tossed it to her. Sitting on Shade's bed, he pulled on the heel of his left boot. Nearly reaching his knees, the leather boots were molded to his muscular calves. Dropping his boots onto the floor he folded back the flap over the buttons on his pants.

"Blaze." Noelle trembled. "Don't."

"These are the only pants I've got." With that warning, he stood and undid the top button. "They have to dry overnight."

Noelle covered her eyes and bowed her head. Peeking through her fingers, she saw his feet as he stepped out of his breeches. He picked up the pants and padded away. He had to be naked! She saw his bare feet as he sat beside her on his bunk again. A blanket flashed before her eyes and covered his feet.

"Are you naked, Blaze Bowie?"

"Find out."

"Are you!"

"Underneath this blanket I am."

Noelle squinted between her fingers. The blanket lay low across his lap. Inches of skin showed below his navel! She quickly stood up and looked anywhere but his lap.

"Santa Anna's breathin' down our necks," he said in reminder. "Let's work out what's wrong between us while we can."

"You thrive on risk and danger while I crave peace and security. I want my life to get back to normal."

"That won't happen here in Bexar. Besides, was normal so great? I've seen where you live."

Noelle hung her head. Back to normal was exactly what she did not want. But it hurt to imagine a wonderful life with Blaze, because he was a combination of Marcel and Lafitte; *wild, romantic and handsome*. But in Blaze's case he was so wild he was bigger than life and too romantic for a novice like herself to please. As for handsome, he was more attractive than any man had a right to be. She sighed in defeat.

"Noelle," Blaze whispered. "I'll put a roof over your head that doesn't leak and buy you a new dress and matching shoes for every day of the month. But for now, this may be the last peaceful night will have for...a while."

"What makes you say that?"

"Santa Anna reached the Medina yesterday."

"No, not the Medina." Noelle prayed he was mistaken. "The Medina is a little green river just twenty-five miles south of here."

"It's not so little right now. The rains have prevented Santa Anna from fording it."

In shock, Noelle put her hands to her cheeks. Jim Bowie had been right about Santa Anna bringing his horses and mules over the desert. Was he correct in saying he could keep Blaze and Shade from dying at the Alamo? He'd not said how he would do it, but could he still manage it at this late date? He was so sick. Did he even intend to try?

"Tell me there's hope we'll win, Blaze."

"Tell me you'll marry me if we get out of here."

"I believe that because times are troubled you think you love me." When Blaze clenched his jaw, Noelle said, "You won't want to marry me if...when this is over."

Blaze bowed his head, clasped his hands between his knees and stared at the floor. Troubled times or not, Noelle knew exactly how she felt about this man. Today and forever. The sudden urge to drop to her knees at his feet and wrap him in her arms as she admitted her love for him rooted Noelle to the spot.

"When we get out of this mess, I'll take you home and I hope you'll come to love me, Noelle. If you can't, I'll cut you loose." Blaze raised his head and his expression was almost fierce. "But if the day ever comes when you say you love me there will be no turning back. Understand?"

"Do you have more secrets?"

"Stay in the chapel under the part with a roof." Blaze

dragged a hand down his face. "The limestone walls are three to four feet thick. The doors are heavy oak and the windows are high enough above ground to provide some protection. Go."

Noelle crossed the room and opened the door. A soldier was herding townsfolk toward the chapel. Among them was Maria. Noelle closed the door.

"More people are moving in. The chapel will be full. Besides, I'd better not leave Mistletoe."

"Don't be afraid of me," Blaze said huskily. "C'mere and just *sleep* with me, darlin'."

Keeping the blanket in place, Blaze stretched out in his bunk. Noelle retraced her steps. He grasped her hand and when he tugged, she sat down beside him. Blaze let go of her hand and rested his forearm over his eyes. Crossing his ankles formed a mysterious, masculine bulge at the vee of his thighs. Placing one hand on his flat washboard stomach, Blaze groaned.

"It's said Santa Anna likes to torture the minds of his enemies. If he had you he'd drive men crazy by perching you on the side of their beds and telling them they couldn't make love to you."

"I don't know if that's a complaint or compliment, but I want—" Noelle cut herself off from blurting out that she wanted him to make love to her. Despite what he said about not being afraid, the physical aspect did frighten her. But it was the emotions he'd ignited in her that were truly terrifying. To lose Blaze Bowie was unthinkable.

"You want what?" he asked and moved his arm under his head.

"To tell you Shade is torturing us." Noelle decided that was both a fib and the truth. "He not only lied to me about Maria, he impersonated you in Main Plaza after the fandango."

"What did he do?"

"What he didn't do was kiss me this time."

"You probably still don't trust me as far as you could

throw me." Blaze smiled that smile of his. "But I trust you to the ends of the earth and back, Noelle."

"I wouldn't be here if I didn't trust you."

"Then strip, darlin'. Put on my shirt before you catch your death. And choose a bunk."

With that Blaze rolled to his side and faced the wall. His shoulders were broad and as he pulled the blanket higher around his tapered waist, muscles rippled in his back. Noelle was mesmerized and gave herself a shake. She changed out of her damp blouse and skirt into his shirt. She looked at Shade's empty bunk. That seemed like asking for trouble. Besides she wanted to sleep with Blaze like they had during siesta. She crawled between the cold, dank wall and the warm, muscular man.

"Good girl."

Blaze turned her to face the wall and molded her body to the hard length of his. The broom handle pressed against the place on her fanny he had spanked. He pulled the blanket over her and tugged the shirt up her belly. Only her thin underpants separated her skin from his! He slid his hand up to her naked breasts.

"Blaze," she whimpered nervously.

"Shh." He surely felt her heart hammering because he whispered hoarsely in her ear, "Just sleep."

THE MOMENT BLAZE WOKE, he knew he'd overslept.

Noelle was gone, her skirt was gone and his shirt was gone. Her blouse hung on the nail beside his pants and her calico cat lay in the crook behind his knees. Muttering an oath, Blaze rolled out of bed. He pulled on his buckskins, yanked open his door and found Jim about to knock.

"Jim, have you seen Noelle?"

"I was coming to tell you she left with Shade and the Herreras. And you're late for watch."

"I can't go on watch," Blaze said, plowing his hands

through his hair. "I have to find Noelle before Santa Anna gets here."

"Better hurry," Jim said and coughed. "Santa Anna was at Leon Creek last night."

"How close is Leon Creek?"

"Eight miles."

CHAPTER 17

"Eight miles?" Blaze repeated, feeling like Noelle must have when he'd told her Santa Anna was less than fifty miles away.

"Yeah." Jim signaled a passing volunteer. "Take Blaze's watch." The volunteer nodded. Pale and gaunt, Jim coughed. "I was about to go get Juana, her baby and Gertrudis. Come with me and you can look for Noelle."

Blaze grabbed his weapons. A few minutes later, crossing the footbridge, Jim pointed to the Rodriguez family piling into a two-wheeled oxcart.

"Looks like they're taking little Jose and their cousin Pablo and getting out of town," Jim said and wheezed.

Recognizing Rivas, the man who'd warned him Santa Anna was at the Rio Grande, Blaze called out to him.

"Hola!" Rivas replied and walked toward them. "Colonel Bowie, I think you should know Santa Anna rode into Bexar ahead of his troops. He played a trick on us by attending the fandango in disguise."

"Why didn't you tell us so we could capture him, Rivas?" Jim asked.

"I told those who would believe me, sir, and we're leaving now." They spoke for a moment before Rivas bid them, "Adios, vaya con Dios." Rivas joined his cousins and they set out for open country.

"There's nothing we can do about Santa Anna right now, Jim," Blaze said, seeing that Jim was red with anger. "He's already back with his dragoons."

"As loyal as the Rodriguez family was to the Texas cause, their departure will shake Travis." Continuing toward town, Jim coughed and said, "The fainthearted have been fleeing for weeks, but nothing like the runaway we'll see in Bexar today I wager."

As they approached the Herreras' hut, people from nearby homes scurried about or huddled in anxious conversation. Pulling back the rawhide door, Blaze found no sign of Noelle. Heading toward town, people darted in and out of houses and shops carrying clothing, bedding, pots, pans, and furniture. There were shouts of agitation and noises from townsfolk moving property onto wagons. Creaking of carts and braying of donkeys filled the air. Those who had no cart or animal were leaving on foot. The roads were jammed.

"Bexar will be deserted by the time *His Excellency*," Jim spat the Mexicans' name for Santa Anna, "returns. I think you ought to get Noelle and the Herreras out of town."

"Carlos won't go, so neither will the girls," Blaze replied. "They're as bullheaded as you and Travis."

"That could be said." Jim chuckled. "At twenty-six, Travis is not prepared to battle Santa Anna. Our rations are low, our cows have been slaughtered, and I don't know how long we can hold out."

"It's a shame all that food in the empty houses and the cows left in backyards will fall into Santa Anna's hands," Blaze said, on the watch for Noelle. "I expect Robin Hood and his band of Merry Men would steal that out from under the Sheriff of Nottingham."

"I expect so," Jim said. "Speaking of Travis, he got a room in town to be close to the San Fernando Church where we've posted a sentry in the bell tower. The sentry will ring the bell when he spots that damn devil, Santa Anna."

"I hope I don't hear that bell until I've found Noelle," Blaze said as they turned onto Soledad Street.

"I'm sorry I didn't ask where they were going before they left the Alamo. But since I saw her come out of your room," Jim said with a grin, "I figured you knew. Try Carlos' shop."

"I'm heading there now."

"If they aren't there, find Travis." Jim coughed. "If he doesn't know where Shade is, Dr. Sutherland might," he said as they stopped in front of the Veramendi house. "Sutherland's helping Nat Lewis count inventory at his dry goods store in Main Plaza. You can check the church for Travis."

The San Fernando Church was a squat pile of stone with a bell tower and was located between Main and Military Plazas. It was just a few minutes' walk from the Alamo.

"I'll find them. See you back at the garrison, Jim."

"Blaze," Jim said, "if you cross Santa Anna without reinforcements, don't give him a good look at you. If he suspects you were anywhere near his tent, you're a dead man."

Blaze thanked Jim for the advice and paused to make sure he made it to the door of the Veramendi house. Blaze wished he'd ridden Blue into town. Damn! A thought sliced him like a knife in his gut. If Noelle had decided she couldn't come to love him, Shade might have talked her into leaving with him. Why the hell had he said he'd cut her loose? He didn't know whether to go back and get Blue or forge ahead to Carlos' shop. On the other hand, hadn't he told Noelle just last night he trusted her? He'd go to the shop.

Suddenly a clanging racket split the air.

"Hell's bells," Blaze breathed. "The devil is here."

Blaze turned and ran toward the San Fernando Church. When he got to Main Plaza, the crowd was a bumping, crying, shouting mass of confusion.

"The enemy is in view!" the sentry shouted from the bell tower to the petrified people on the ground.

"Christ Almighty," Blaze said, glancing left and right. "Where are you, Noelle?"

"Bowie!" Dr. Sutherland yelled from the doorway of Nat Lewis' shop. "Is Santa Anna here?"

"That's what the bell ringing means, sir!" Blaze scanned the mob for Noelle. Surely he could spot crimson curls among all these dark heads. He'd done it once before. Yes, from atop Blue. Dammit! After dismounting his horse he'd lost sight of her that day. "I'm going up in the tower to have a look!" Blaze shouted to Sutherland.

"Yeah, me, too!"

Blaze was well in the lead. Running into the church, he took the steps two at a time. Reaching the bell tower he found not only the sentry, but Colonel Travis and John Smith.

"Travis, have you seen Shade?"

"No," Travis said and shook his head, looking underwhelmed over the sighting,

"Sorry, Blaze, I haven't seen Shade either," said John Smith, one of the men who had routed General Cos back in December.

"Where's Santa Anna?" Blaze asked feeling frustrated and worried about Noelle.

The sentry pointed southwest. Bare plains were dotted with mesquite thickets. The white glare of the landscape in the noonday sun made Blaze wish he wasn't in Texas. He longed for the green forests, rolling hills and babbling creeks of Louisiana.

And that's why he was here, to save his land.

"I swear I don't see any Mexican dragoons, Buck," John Smith said, addressing Travis by his nickname.

Cries of false alarm filled the streets. That was followed by a deluge of scorn hurled up at the sentry in the tower. The sentry stood his ground and cursed the townsfolk.

"I seen 'em! They're hid behind the brushwood!" the sentry hollered.

"I'll ride out a ways and have a look," Dr. Sutherland said, reaching the top of the tower. "If someone will come with me."

"Take Bowie and Smith," Travis said.

Mining for cooper in a mountain of coal, Blaze clenched his jaw. If only he knew where Noelle was, he'd be happy to go. But he didn't see her anywhere amidst the bewildered frenzy in the streets and besides he took his orders from Jim, not Travis. Without a word, Blaze preceded Sutherland and Smith down the tower stairs. Outside the church he turned to the other two men and made his own decision.

"I'll meet you back at the Alamo," Blaze said.

Smith and Sutherland nodded and raced toward the mission. Blaze ran, too, passing the deserted cantina and heading up Potrero Street to the cobbler shop. Blaze figured the only reason Carlos and the girls didn't live in the shop was that it was even smaller than their hut. He yanked the door open.

"Blaze!"

"Noelle!" Not knowing whether to kiss her or spank her, Blaze hugged her to him. "Why did you leave me this morning?"

"There was no reason to wake you," she explained as she embraced him. "Why aren't you on watch?"

"Because you're not safe outside the Alamo." He stood her back and asked, "What are you doing here?"

"Helping Carlos gather up his tools to take back to the Alamo." She plucked at her sleeve. "I borrowed your extra shirt to wear with my skirt because it's so chilly today."

"It'll let people know there's a man in your life to protect you. Keep it," he said and winked. He liked the way she'd tied the shirttails at her waist and rolled the sleeves tight around her wrists. But how unfair this beauty had only two worn dresses, a summer blouse and an old skirt to her name. "Where were you headed just now?"

"To find out why the church bell was ringing," she said, taking in the confusion out on the street.

"Si, Blaze, how close is Santa Anna?" Carlos asked from the back of the shop.

"The bell ringing means Santa Anna may be on the horizon. I've decided to ride out and see for myself."

"No, Blaze!" Noelle slipped her hand into his and held on tight.

"I'll be back. Jim said you and Felice left with Shade. Do you know where he is?"

"He insisted on walking us to the shop. A while ago, he told Felice he was sleepy after being on watch all night. She took him to the house to rest."

"I was just at your house. No one's there." Blaze could almost see the wheels spinning in Noelle's head.

"Shade's got her in Carlos and Mama's curtained-off bedroom," Noelle whispered with a glance at Carlos. "We have to stop him. He'll hurt her."

"No, he wouldn't hurt a woman," Blaze said.

"I mean he'll break her heart. Felice strongly believes in flechazo, just like you do."

"Flechazo? What's that?"

"An arrow shot...love at first sight."

Yeah, he remembered literally feeling for cupid's arrow after he'd spoken to Noelle.

"Chances are he's had her by now and gone back to the Alamo to his own bed."

"Maybe not. Remember, I told Felice not to let him take her for granted. Not to be easy."

"Ready to go fetch Felice?" Carlos asked, pushing a small wheelbarrow containing all his supplies.

"No!" Noelle said emphatically.

"Carlos, you go on to the Alamo," Blaze said calmly. "They probably need you. We'll go to the house." Indecision was on Carlos' face. "Please tell Dr. Sutherland and John Smith I'm on my way."

"Si, Blaze. I am happy to do that for you."

. . .

"SHADE?" Felice twined her arms around his neck and pressed him to her pounding heart. Never had she felt such a combination of excitement and anxiety. "Is it me or Noelle you prefer?"

"Who am I in bed with?" he asked.

"Papa says a man should not take a woman to bed unless he intends to wed her. Do you plan to marry me, Shade Bowie?"

"I'm not the marrying kind."

"There is a first time for everything."

"Yeah, and today was yours."

"Si," she said and blushed. Shade grinned so charmingly Felice would have done anything he wanted to please him. Except let him leave her. "What if I conceived your child?"

"Dammit, Felice." Shade pulled away, rolled out of bed and tugged on his pants. "You sure know how to kill a man's appetite for seconds."

Felice sniffled knowing she had given herself too easily. Would he take her for granted now? As he tugged on his boots, she crawled naked onto his lap. She wrapped her arms around him, loving him so much and never wanting to let him go.

"Have you had many women, Shade?"

"Hell, yes, I have!" he barked and nudged her off his lap.

"I want you to give up all other women for me." Tears welled in her eyes as Shade's gray eyes narrowed.

"That'll be the day, Felice."

CHAPTER 18

As he had one day not so long ago Blaze heard crying near the Herrera hut when he and Noelle approached.

"Felice?" Noelle called at the doorway.

Blaze pulled back the rawhide door and wasn't surprised when it was Shade who answered.

"I'll be right out."

As Shade came into view, Blaze jerked his thumb and waited outside. Shade joined him and stretched. Noelle ignored him and went into the home.

"What the hell were you doing in there, Shade?"

"Trimmin' Felice's wick." Holding up one finger at a time, Shade ticked off, "You were born four years ahead of me, you had your first knife fight four years ahead of me and you found your manhood four years ahead of me." He lowered his hand and bragged, "But I just bedded the first virgin, *Trailblazer*."

"Were you careful?"

"I'll ask you that after you've had your first tight little innocent," Shade said with a grumble. More quietly he confided, "Damn, Blaze, she was tiny. No swamp girl and especially no whore ever squeezed my poker like Felice. I couldn'ta pulled out even if I'd wanted to."

Blaze wanted to reprimand him. But isn't what Shade

did with Felice exactly what he longed to do with Noelle? Could he pull out when the time came?

"What if you got her pregnant?"

"Then she'll have to find somebody to marry her."

"Damn your cavalier attitude." Blaze clenched his fists. "Felice loves you."

"She hasn't said so."

"Are you sure?"

"I don't know." He flinched. "She says things in Spanish."

"Well, she shouldn't have to say she loves you for you to do what's fair by her. You knew exactly what you were doing, not Felice. Knowing how to be careful is why you haven't gotten anybody else pregnant. How could you forget that?"

"Because she's my shy, raven-haired beauty instead of a cantina whore, that's why." Shade clenched his fists, too, and smacked them on his hips. "Even though I've had her I still want her. Dammit, that's a first!"

Blaze fought a grin by scowling. Noelle's plan of Felice giving Shade a cold shoulder, along with Shade's past of *loose* women, was threatening to make *tiny* Felice his brother's undoing.

"Do you still want her enough to marry her if necessary?" Blaze asked.

"No." Shade frowned.

"Then pull out or stay out."

"Hell's bells." Shade kicked a pebble. "I hate it when you're right." Then he grinned. "Maybe I'll use the same trick on Felice and Carlos that we heard Santa Anna played on some girl and her father."

"What trick would that be?" Noelle asked, coming out of the house.

"Where's Felice?" Blaze asked.

"Getting dressed," Noelle answered and looked at Shade. "She seems...fine...actually."

"They always do." Shade grinned smugly.

"What was Santa Anna's trick?" Noelle asked again.

"He likes to pluck uh...fresh fruit," Shade replied.

"If by fresh fruit you mean innocents, he's married," Noelle said. "How could he do that?"

"With enough pinches of opium Santa Anna probably thinks he can do anything," Blaze said.

"Yeah," Shade chuckled. "You see there was this girl who *His Excellency* wanted. But her father said Santa Anna had to marry her first. So the sly dog disguised one of his men as a priest and staged a phony marriage. Santa Anna bedded the girl and right after he was done, sent her packing with two thousand pesos."

When Shade hooted, Noelle stepped between the brothers and punched Shade in the gut. Blaze laughed as Shade leaned forward, coughed and swore. From behind, Blaze wrapped an arm around Noelle's waist and pressed her back to his chest.

"Is that what you plan to do to Felice, Shade, if she has conceived your child?" Noelle asked.

"No, she'll have the Bowie name," Blaze said, glaring at Shade over Noelle's head.

"Noelle?" Felice called from inside.

Noelle went into the house.

"When Felice tells her how great I was, Noelle will be panting after me, too," said a red-faced Shade.

"You're the only one panting for a breath, Shade. Noelle belongs to me."

"She'll belong to the man who trims her wick."

"So far you haven't been man enough to light Noelle's candle."

"Shut up, Blaze," Shade said.

"I apologize for hitting you, Shade," Noelle said as she came back out. "There'll soon be enough fighting without all of us fighting among ourselves."

"She's right." Blaze smiled at her and plowed a hand through his dark blond hair. "I've got to get Blue and ride out with Sutherland and Smith."

"Why?" Shade asked.

"Didn't you hear the bell ringing?" Noelle asked.

"I thought Felice and I were making bells ring."

Blaze cocked a brow before telling Shade about Santa Anna's close proximity. As he finished, Felice joined them, a still-damp tear on her cheek. Shade nonchalantly thumbed the tear off her face.

"I'm going with you, Blaze," Shade said.

"All right. Let's go."

Blaze grabbed Noelle's hand and Shade walked beside Felice. They had made it over the footbridge when Dr. Sutherland and John Smith rode up leading a sorrel and a bay. They said Carlos had given them Blaze's message and they figured Shade would be with him. The brothers swung themselves into their saddles.

"You're riding straight into the enemy in broad daylight." Noelle cringed, shaded her eyes with her hand and looked up at Blaze.

"Go to the Alamo and *stay there*," Blaze said.

Noelle watched her gorgeous blond ride into the horizon until a teenage girl, an ancient crone, shopkeeper Nat Lewis, and Antonio Fuentes hurried over the footbridge seeking the Alamo's shelter. Antonio and Shade had been in the calaboose together. That seemed a lifetime ago, but it was a mere ten days.

The guard at the gate asked Noelle and Felice to show the women to the chapel. Women and children swarmed in and out of it like bees to a hive. Frantically, people were staking claims to cots or fashioning sleeping spaces on the floor. They left the new arrivals to settle in there. A few minutes later, Noelle found Susanna Dickinson, whose husband was a lieutenant under Colonel Travis.

"Mrs. Dickinson, did Colonel Bowie make it back safely with his late wife's sisters?" Noelle asked.

Mrs. Dickinson holding her baby, Angelina, said yes. He'd come back and was gone again. Noelle and Felice left Mrs. Dickinson and returned to the large plaza of the garrison. The air echoed with mournful moos as some thirty head of cattle were herded by volunteers into the cattle pen.

"Colonel Bowie and a squad of men are ransacking nearby jacals," Carlos said coming toward Noelle and Felice. "Already, bags of grain are filling up the long barracks. Men who sold or lost their equipment were sent to gather what was left behind." Carlos paused to watch returning volunteers, loaded down with hardware. He crossed himself. "It is a miracle."

"This was Shade's idea," Felice decided proudly.

"I have to set up my workshop now." Carlos made no other comment.

"Let Felice and me help you," Noelle said.

She hoped to keep her mind off Blaze by keeping busy. But work didn't help, the sun lowered and time dragged. Making their way to the chapel, after helping Carlos, Felice put voice to Noelle's worst fear.

"I think Santa Anna captured Shade and Blaze."

"No," Noelle replied with conviction she didn't feel. "They outsmarted Santa Anna and his men once before. They'll do it again."

In the chapel women and children huddled in bunches. There was fear on their faces and many were sobbing. The cots which Felice and Carlos had slept on the previous night had been taken. Using blankets for seats, Noelle and Felice sat down on the floor. Near a chapel door, Nat Lewis said he was happy to have donated dry goods to the Alamo from his store but he planned to leave for Gonzales. Noelle was edgy and wanted to leave, too. But Blaze had told her to stay. Well, she couldn't just sit here. When Mr. Lewis opened the door, she noticed Jim Bowie talking to two women near the eight-pounder cannon in the garrison plaza.

"They must be his late wife's sisters," Noelle said to Felice before following Nat Lewis out of the chapel. Having watched Blaze ride in Santa Anna's direction earlier had stretched her nerves to the limit. She had to remind their cousin about keeping Blaze and Shade alive. Finding Felice behind her, she said, "I'm going to speak with Colonel Bowie."

Suddenly the bell in the San Fernando Church clanged wildly. Frantic screams erupted as everyone knew that the ringing of the bell meant the sentry had spotted Santa Anna's army. Noelle hurried across the courtyard intending to ask the guards at the main gate if there was any news about Blaze. With Felice on her heels, they reached the edge of the crowded plaza just as Blaze, Shade, John Smith, and Dr. Sutherland rode in through the gate.

Noelle picked up the front of her skirt and raced toward Blaze as he and Shade reined in their horses in front of the officers' quarters. Dr. Sutherland dismounted and fell but Colonel Crockett was nearby and helped him limp toward Colonel Travis' room. Still mounted, Blaze scanned the plaza. Noelle called out to him and he dismounted.

"Shade Bowie!" Rosa squealed and waved from the long barracks on the opposite side of the plaza.

No wonder they'd not seen Rosa in the chapel, Noelle thought. And where was Maria?

Reaching Blaze, Noelle threw herself into his embrace and muscular arms closed around her. He lifted her up and his warm lips melted across hers. She twined her arms around his neck, wrapping her legs around his waist! She was now certain she had completely lost her mind over this man. When his mouth opened, her tongue met his. Her heart told her it, too, was lost to Blaze Bowie and never wanted to be found.

Blaze gave Noelle's fanny a familiar pat and she placed her toes between his booted feet. His strong hands framed her face as he grinned at her and chuckled.

"Glad to see me?" His gray eyes smoldered when she nodded. "I'm glad to see you, too, darlin'."

Glaring at Felice, Rosa stalked toward them and called out to Shade again. Hair in disarray, Maria stood outside the long barracks, which had once been the Alamo convent.

With her arms crossed under her generous bosom, the rage on Maria's expression said it all. Shade smiled at the cantina women.

"A woman for every ill or a woman for every good," Felice said, standing beside Shade.

Noelle held her breath as Shade scooped Felice into his arms and kissed her. Rosa stopped halfway across the plaza and stared open-mouthed, hands on her hips.

"Thank God, you're alive." Peering back up at Blaze, Noelle smoothed a lock of hair away from his furrowed brow, noting the sweat beaded at his temple as he glared at Maria.

"Are you all right, Noelle?" Blaze asked.

"Yes, are you?"

"Yeah." He looked down at her. "The only injury was to Sutherland. His horse stepped on something and fell with him."

"Did you see Santa Anna?"

"Oh yeah." Blaze raised his hand in a wave at Colonel Bowie who was headed their way. "We saw *His Excellency*, his army, his marching band and his female camp followers."

"We've got food, supplies and cattle, thanks to you, Blaze," Jim said, striding up to them.

Noelle wasn't surprised to hear that.

"Robin Hood and his Merry Men?" Blaze asked.

"Yes." Jim nodded and asked, "How close is the Sheriff of Nottingham?"

CHAPTER 19

"About a mile and a half," Blaze replied in a calm deep voice.

Jim frowned at the news.

"Has he added to his ranks since the last time you spied on him?"

"I'd say he'll hit us with at least eighteen hundred dragoons outfitted in white uniforms and polished armor. Sutherland and Smith are going to Gonzales to recruit reinforcements."

"Take Shade and go with them, Blaze," Colonel Bowie said. "You can help us most by staying out of the Alamo and recruiting volunteers." He pivoted and made his way toward the officers' headquarters.

"Yes, sir," Blaze replied and turned to Noelle. "Come with me."

"No."

"Why not?"

"I'm afraid you'd leave me in Gonzales, come back here and—" her soft voice broke and her hazel eyes glittered, "...be killed."

"Noelle, I promised you I won't get killed."

"What did Jim say?" Shade asked, walking up to them with Felice at his side.

"Jim wants us to go to Gonzales with Smith and Sutherland to round up volunteer reinforcements."

"Why?" Shade shrugged. "Travis is expecting James Bonham back from Goliad with Colonel Fannin and his four hundred troops."

"I guess Jim doesn't think Fannin and the troops are coming back with Bonham," Blaze said. "And Noelle, you're going with me."

"No, I'm not."

"I'll stay with the girls." Shade draped his arms around Noelle and Felice. "You go."

"Blaze!" Travis shouted from headquarters, standing beside a coughing Jim. "Smith is closing his house in town. He'll meet up with you. Sutherland's ready to ride. Jim says for you and Shade to get going."

"Five minutes," Blaze said to Jim who nodded. Looking back at Shade, Blaze frowned. "Let's go, Shade."

"No." Shade shook his head. "I didn't sign on for this Texas fight and neither did you."

"Blaze!" Maria called from across the plaza.

When Blaze ignored her, she cupped her hands to her mouth and screamed his name again. He wanted to vent his frustration with a yell but instead took a deep breath, turned his back on Maria and tugged Noelle from Shade.

"Please come with me," Blaze whispered.

"I'll wait for you here," Noelle replied calmly.

"All right." Blaze sighed. "The sooner I go, the sooner I'll be back." He grabbed Shade and walked him a few steps away. "Take care of the girls, but keep your hands off Noelle."

Shade rolled his eyes, but agreed as Maria called out again. A flash of his white shirt and a worn skirt caught the corner of Blaze's eye as Noelle twirled in Maria's direction.

"He's busy!" Noelle shouted to Maria then turned and winked at Blaze.

Blaze crooked his finger at Noelle and she hurried to him taking his hand. He trailed her behind him the few paces to Blue. Seeing the worry on her face he ran his other hand under her auburn curls.

"I'll miss you, Blaze Bowie." She swallowed hard as he caressed her neck.

"Darlin', except for meeting you, nothing has gone right since I got here. I'll miss you, too."

"With so many dragoons bearing down on us what good will a few more men do?" Noelle asked.

"I don't know. But Jim and Travis are determined to hold the Alamo. They say it's the key to Texas."

"What about your land?"

"The key to saving my land is here in Texas."

"Well, I'll be sure your body is sent home," she said, pulling her hand from his, "to your precious land."

"My land will be gone if I don't get the key."

"Then get the key. Today!"

"Noelle," he drew out her name in a sigh. "I can't."

"Why not?" Suddenly her eyes narrowed knowingly. "Does the key represent twelve hundred and eighty acres of Texas land?" He didn't respond and she asked, "Is the key a deed to your Louisiana land? Does Colonel Bowie hold the deed?" Her brow creased with worry when he didn't answer. "If money is the key, I told you Grandmother can help. What is the key, Blaze?"

Blaze wished he could say that the key was a fortune of gold and silver hidden in the San Saba Mines. But their situation was growing increasingly dangerous and he wasn't going to risk making it worse by telling her that.

"Look," Blaze began, "Jim wants these volunteers and if—"

"You've done enough for Texas," Noelle said, grasping his shirt front. "You've spied on Santa Anna twice, taken a post at the eighteen-pounder and helped the Alamo obtain supplies and food."

"Jim holds the key and I hate debt," Blaze said carefully and wrapped his hands around her wrists. "In exchange for the key, Jim asked for my help and I agreed. I don't want to owe him when I leave Texas. If I can bring back the volunteers Jim wants, I will feel I've paid for the key."

Still clutching his shirt, she said, "I don't understand any of this, but promise me you'll get that key."

"I'm gonna try. Now you promise me you'll watch out for Maria and the others."

"I'm not afraid of Maria. As for the men, you taught me that knee trick. Will Santa Anna attack us before you return?"

"No. What we saw today was just his advance cavalry. He'll want his entire army here before he storms the Alamo. He won't risk being routed like Cos was in December."

"How do you know so much about the military?"

"Brains and brawn," Colonel Crockett said, never breaking stride as he passed them on his way to his post at the rammed earth breastworks near the four-pounder.

"Blaze, promise me, too, that we'll leave the Alamo before Santa Anna tries to take it."

God Almighty! Noelle's request slammed into him with the force of a tidal wave. To a frightened, young woman that might seem like the only reasonable solution. But to Blaze it meant nothing short of abandoning Jim, Davy Crockett, and the fight for Texas independence.

Spying on Santa Anna had shown Blaze that the situation at the garrison was bleak. But until this instant he realized he had been halfway expecting a miracle, a truce, moving the troops to Goliad, intervention by the colonies, help from the impeached governor, something! Anything!

Every man at the Alamo was risking his life. If Blaze left to hunt for gold and silver he would never be able to live with himself. Noelle was right, he had become so caught up in the Texas rebellion that he, too, believed it was a matter of victory or death.

"The bleakness in your eyes is scaring me, Blaze." Noelle placed her hands on the sash around his waist. "What are you thinking?"

"I can't leave the Alamo ahead of anyone else." He'd been

staring blindly into the plaza and focused on her now. "Santa Anna is trying to steal this land. If I wasn't willing to let someone rob me of my land back home, I can't stand by while it happens to the people here. Santa Anna must be stopped."

"I'll get the key while you're gone." Noelle's voice shook and her hazel eyes glittered. "I can meet you on the road to Gonzales."

"You're not listening. You can't get the key and I can't leave."

Noelle put her hands in the air, palms toward him. Backing away she said, "Don't speak to me again unless it's to tell me you're ready to ride out of the Alamo for the last time."

Surely she didn't mean that. She turned and raced barefoot toward the chapel. Blaze wondered who'd needed her shoes this time. Felice followed. Damn, he'd not even kissed Noelle goodbye. Blaze started to call her name but Maria seized his arm. He shook her off as Rosa clutched Shade's hand.

"Shade, if you're mad at," Rosa jiggled her large bosom, "Felice, the tortilla chest, I will cheer you up."

"Shut up, strumpet," Shade growled and yanked his hand from her. "Felice is a nice girl."

Blaze was in no mood for this and Maria sensed it because she didn't utter a word. The cantina women glowered, cursed and shuffled away toward the infantrymen's barracks.

"Blaze!" Travis yelled from headquarters with Jim at his side. "Get going!"

"Blaze, I decided I'm coming with you," Shade said.

"No, I don't trust Maria and Rosa. Tell Jim I asked you to stay," Blaze said and mounted Blue. "And Shade," he paused, loving and worrying about his brother, "stick close to Crockett. He needs you. He says the other volunteers at the post don't have your fighting instincts."

"Be careful, big, bad brother," Shade said quietly.

With a glance across the courtyard, Blaze nudged Blue and rode out of the main gate. Avoiding Mexican scouts, Blaze, Sutherland and Smith took the old and mostly unused Goliad Road where they crossed the prairie to Salado Creek. On a rise, they reined in at the small ford and glanced back at Bexar. What met Blaze's eyes nearly knocked him out of the saddle. Brazenly pouring into Military Plaza were the advance units of Santa Anna's cavalry.

"God, help us," Blaze prayed under his breath.

From seeing them at close range, Blaze knew the dragoons were dressed in white. The officers wore short red coats, vivid blue trousers and black helmets decorated with horsehair or bearskin. As their breastplates reflected in the afternoon sun Blaze thought how easily a woman's tender skin could be punctured by the lances, sabers or pistols these men carried. As he'd warned Noelle, men could make a woman suffer a fate worse than death.

Sure, some of the men had brought along a camp follower; a wife or girlfriend who trudged behind the troops to cook, wash and care for them. When those women became exhausted or ill, they were left where they fell. What would such men, who abandoned women to die in the dirt, do to a gorgeous innocent with greenish gold eyes and long auburn waves?

Love, honor and anguish constricted Blaze's tormented heart. Staring back at Bexar, a blood red flag was hoisted into view in the tower of the San Fernando Church. As the crow flew, the church was only eight hundred yards from and very visible to the Alamo. So the flag had to be a message to Jim, Travis, and Crockett. But what message?

"Mi Dios!" cried a Mexican man stumbling over the rise and splashing across Salado creek. "I escaped Bexar just in time!"

"What's the red flag mean?" Blaze asked him.

"Santa Anna is telling us there will be no quarter." Running for his life, the terrified man shouted over his shoulder, "No surrender! No mercy!"

The Alamo answered the raising of Santa Anna's blood red flag by firing the eighteen-pounder. Its thundering roar echoed through heart and hills.

LYING on the ground near the chapel, Noelle uncovered her head. Men were shouting, women were screaming and somewhere a baby cried. Noelle struggled to her feet and frantically scanned the frenzied mob in the courtyard for Felice. Just minutes ago she had left her talking to Shade near the low barracks and had gone to find Carlos who was busy chopping up nails to use as shot. Now, Shade raced toward the south wall where he was posted alongside Davy Crockett. Having veered away from Shade it was only a matter of seconds before a panic-stricken Felice flung herself into Noelle's arms.

"Riders coming!" a guard yelled. "Open the gate!"

Taking Felice's hand, Noelle ran into the plaza. Jim's order for Blaze to leave the Alamo had not been lost on Noelle. But she realized too late it had backfired when Shade didn't go with him. Since Blaze was determined to return and fight, Noelle prayed the fighting would be over before he got back.

"Please let these riders be James Butler Bonham and Colonel Fannin's troops," Noelle said softly.

"Scouts and sentries!" a guard at the main gate shouted.

Noelle came to a stop inside the plaza as the main gate slammed shut. No Bonham. No troops. Blaze was right. Colonel Fannin was dragging his feet on coming to the aid of the Alamo. On wobbly legs, Noelle led a terrified Felice back to the chapel where Blaze had told her to stay.

Confirming with the scouts the presence of the Mexican army, Travis ordered a withdrawal into the Alamo as it was now too dangerous for people to be outside. Blaze had already told her that before Travis had decided it was so. But now Blaze was *outside*.

As Noelle and Felice huddled on a blanket in the chapel,

waiting for war, word spread that Jim Bowie wondered about the wisdom of defiance if there was chance of negotiation with Santa Anna. To that end, Colonel Bowie had dashed off a note to the Mexicans, explaining the garrison had fired the cannon before hearing whether or not the Mexicans wanted a truce.

"If Colonel Bowie can negotiate a truce, Blaze and Shade and all the men would be safe," Noelle said to a whimpering Felice.

Felice nodded and crossed herself. "Si, let's pray for a truce, Noelle."

Carlos burst into the chapel and barreled toward them. "Colonel Travis is furious with Colonel Bowie!"

"Why?" Noelle asked, jumping to her feet.

"For sending that message to Santa Anna. *El Presidente* has sent back word that he will not deal with bandits." Carlos tapped his chest and said incredulously, "*We* are the bandits! Travis says Jim Bowie made us look...uh...craven."

CHAPTER 20

"WHAT'S CRAVEN?" FELICE ASKED AS CARLOS LOOKED ON.

"Cowardly," Noelle answered. "I don't blame Colonel Bowie. He has a lot of lives to consider and if we're as outnumbered as Blaze says we are, then it was wise to seek a truce."

Gunshots blasted the air and a stone wall splintered. Screams exploded amidst more gunfire. Silent minutes ticked by and finally shadows fell. Eventually, smoke from fires inside the Alamo sent the smell of broiling meat into every part of the mission. Did Blaze have anything to eat, Noelle wondered. Had he been caught by dragoons or escaped Bexar? The timing of the cavalry's arrival had been perilously close to Blaze's departure. Was it too close?

Day one of the Mexican siege drew February twenty-third to a tense, edgy close. Noelle tossed and turned the night away on the hard packed ground in the Alamo's chapel.

ON WEDNESDAY, day two of the siege, Colonel Travis penned a declaration of defiance To the People of Texas and All Americans in the World. Rumor had it that the envelope was labeled VICTORY or DEATH. Travis had entrusted the letter to courier Albert Martin who was on his way to Gonzales with it.

Noelle hurried toward the low barracks to see if Colonel Bowie had any word about Blaze. Two volunteers were all but carrying the colonel into his room.

"Sister," Jim Bowie said to Juana Alsbury who was standing at his door. "Do not be afraid." He coughed and managed to say, "I leave you with Colonel Travis, Colonel Crockett, and other friends. They are gentleman and will treat you kindly."

The door slammed and Noelle was shut out.

Juana sniffled and walked away. Minutes later, when the volunteers came out of Jim Bowie's room their shoulders sagged. Noelle learned Colonel Bowie had turned over his authority to Colonel Travis. Doc Pollard took the volunteers' place and a stunned Noelle wrung her hands until he emerged from Jim's room.

"Doc Pollard, may I see Colonel Bowie?" she asked.

The doctor shook his head saying the strain of the last few days had been too much for him. He didn't want anyone adding to the colonel's discomfort. Jim Bowie had collapsed and the doctor doubted he would ever get up from his bunk again.

"The struggle for authority ends as the battle for life begins," Noelle said.

"God grant that we may create an independent government," Doc Pollard replied and walked away.

"Damn this Texas fever," Noelle said softly. It had infected all walks of men from the prairie to the ocean, from the Great Lakes to the Gulf of Mexico. Blaze had caught the fever and it could be the death of him if he returned in time to face Santa Anna.

The rest of the day, Mexican shells pelted the Alamo. Sometimes the garrison answered, but mostly saved its firepower. Shade, Colonel Crockett, and some other volunteers manned the four-pounders on the rammed earth palisade.

Noelle knew by Shade's frown he was as worried about his brother as she was.

"La Villita is burning," Noelle said on day three of the siege.

She and Felice were working alongside Carlos in his makeshift shop. They watched the smoke spiraling skyward. La Villita, not a part of San Antonio de Bexar proper, was made up of huts where soldiers often lived with their common law wives.

"Who set the jacales on fire? Us or them?" Noelle asked a passerby who said he didn't know.

In the next moment, Shade and a handful of men waving torches ran through the main gate. Davy Crockett clapped Shade on the back and took his torch. Shade sprinted toward them.

"We just took the Mexicans' most valuable cover and gained a new field of fire," Shade said proudly.

"Bueno, Shade!" Felice said with a smile.

"Any word on Blaze?" Noelle asked.

"No." Shade's grin quickly faded and he rubbed his forehead.

The burning of La Villita stopped the Mexicans' advance. But Santa Anna wouldn't leave them alone. He indeed enjoyed torturing the minds of his enemies. He kept the garrison from sleeping by having his marching band blare their horns, trumpets and tubas. Occasionally, he lobbed a grenade to punctuate the music.

Day four of the siege was bleak and near freezing. It became obvious the Alamo's well could not supply the one hundred and fifty plus people inside the fort with water. They'd have to venture outside the walls to get water from the acequia. A small channel of water fed by the San Antonio River, the acequia had been strategically dug to surround the garrison before flowing back into the river. Felice told Noelle that Shade planned to go for water. They found him and pointed out that he'd already risked his life by burning La Villita. But Shade was set on going until Davy Crockett called to him from the palisade.

The cold wind blew the fur on the coonskin caps of Colonel Crockett and Shade as they manned their palisade post. How badly Noelle wanted to run her fingers through Blaze's hair. Where was he? Was he alive? How could she have said for him not to speak to her until he was ready to leave? Of course she wanted to talk to him. She couldn't eat or sleep for want of hearing his deep, male voice and sexy, low chuckle. She missed the touch of his hands on her skin, the suppleness of his lips pressed to hers and her heated excitement within his strong embrace.

By Saturday, February twenty-seventh, day five of the siege, Noelle felt it had been a lifetime since she had seen Blaze. On this frigid day, the Mexicans decided to cut off the eastern acequia to stop the desperately needed water of the San Antonio River from reaching the Alamo. The defenders maintained constant fire on the enemy work party, but the Mexicans succeeded in eliminating the garrison's main source of water. Noelle wondered if Blaze and the others were under fire. Had they been cut down on their way to or from Gonzales?

On day six of the siege, word was that reinforcements were en route from Goliad. Morale in the garrison was high. Davy Crockett played his fiddle and challenged Johnny McGregor, who played his bagpipes, to a contest. Noelle listened from the chapel, which offered little shelter, but it was more than Blaze had in open country.

. . .

MONDAY, day seven, the Mexicans proposed a three day armistice. The ceasefire was a welcome relief but without word on Blaze, Noelle felt she would go insane. A westerly breeze chilled her to the bone and she hugged herself, wishing she could hug Blaze. The day dragged into evening. Leaning against the archway to the chapel that night, Noelle prayed Blaze wasn't lying hurt somewhere, needing medical attention. Looking east toward Gonzales, she covered her face and let pent-up tears flow.

"Blaze," Noelle sobbed softly. "I loved you on first sight, too."

"Half-horse, half-alligator."

Turning and swiping away her tears, Noelle took in a blur of coonskin cap, fringed deerskin and rifle.

"Colonel Crockett, have you heard anything on Blaze's whereabouts?"

"No. But he'll return at all costs." He smiled and stopped.

"That's what I'm afraid of."

"Blaze Bowie's as loyal to his friends and cause as he can be mean-cussed to his enemies and injustice," Davy Crockett replied and nodded.

"Yes, I'm learning that about him."

"It took a generous woman not to stop him from going to Gonzales. Come on, you shouldn't be in the open like this." Colonel Crockett took her arm and gently guided her to the chapel. "I wouldn't want to face Blaze if something happened to you."

Noelle thanked him and inside found her blanket next to Felice. Sitting in the darkness on her blanket, she suddenly bolted to her feet. Blaze had decided not to come back! Assuming the women and children would survive, he had left the duty of getting Shade out of the Alamo to her. And so far, all she had done was mope and cry. He would never forgive her if Shade died.

Leaving a sleeping Felice and Carlos in her wake, Noelle crept out of the chapel. In the moonlight, she glanced at the palisade. Neither Shade nor Colonel Crockett was there.

Having been on post most of the day, they were probably in their barracks. Noelle hurried to the room Shade shared with Blaze near the eighteen-pounder.

"It's Noelle," she said as she knocked. The door opened just a crack. Noelle frowned at the slice of Shade's face she could see. "I've come to say that you should go look for Blaze. He could be in trouble."

"Your cat's the one in trouble," Shade said. "She's under Blaze's bunk as usual and somebody in here hates the hell outa cats."

"Rosa hates cats?" Noelle asked, with a sinking feeling.

"Want me to set sail, matey?"

"Yeah, it looks like my night just improved." Shade swung open the door, revealing Raoul Buzzard.

"How'd you get past the Mexicans?" Noelle asked.

"Slit a couple o' throats," Buzzard replied.

"We were laying some plans for when we get outa here," Shade said with a nod for the pirate to leave. "But we're done for tonight, Buzzard."

Backing against the door to give the reeking pirate a wide berth, Noelle was caught off guard when Shade grabbed her arm. He dragged her inside and slammed the door shut. When Noelle brought her knee up, Shade blocked her at the last moment.

"What the hell! Did Blaze teach you that trick?"

"Yes, he did!" She yanked her arm from him. "My sister's in love with you and could be carrying your child at this moment. The brother who loves you could be bleeding in a ditch while you would force yourself on the woman he intends to marry. You're an ornery, selfish donkey and your lack of loyalty is despicable. For Blaze's sake, I'll try not to hold a grudge. For Felice's sake, I hope she is not pregnant. For my sake, I want you to give up trying to steal me away from the most noble and brave man on the face of the earth!"

"I was just trying to get you out of Buzzard's way so you could fetch your cat."

"I hope that's true. If so, perhaps we finally understand each other." She grabbed the blanket off Blaze's bed, shoved past Shade and yanked the door open. She'd enlist Felice's help in getting Shade to go after Blaze. "Come on, Mistletoe." When the cat scampered alongside her, Noelle scooped her up. Leaving Shade and hurrying across the plaza she said, "We all need Blaze, Mistletoe."

Wide awake with worry, Noelle slipped into the hospital. Soft snores told her that the few ill or injured were asleep. Putting Mistletoe down, she picked up a lantern and tiptoed to a tiny empty room. Before the water shortage, she'd filled a round tub from the well near the hospital and washed Blaze's shirt and her skirt. She'd been waiting for a quiet night to bathe and this armistice might prove her only chance to do so. For added privacy, she draped Blaze's blanket over the string she'd used to hang the clothes on to dry. She then slid into the tub and lathered her hair and body with soap. Though the water was cold, the bath was luxurious. Feeling closer to Blaze as she put his shirt back on, she prayed it would not be the only tangible memory she had of him. She pulled on her skirt and when her hair was fairly dry she left the hospital with Mistletoe. Not wanting to disturb people in the chapel, Noelle sat with her back to an outside wall of the hospital and wrapped Blaze's blanket around her and Mistletoe.

A SHARP CRACK of a rifle jolted Noelle awake and she realized she'd fallen asleep. Excited voices scraped her raw nerves. Noelle nudged Mistletoe off her lap and shooed her toward the chapel. Clutching the blanket and padding into the plaza Noelle heard a volunteer say it was three in the morning.

That made it Tuesday, March first, day eight of Santa Anna's horrible siege of the beloved mission. At the well, two soldiers hurried past her and she caught what one said to the other.

"The men who rode to Gonzales are going to try to sneak through enemy lines and make it into the Alamo!"

Stopping in her tracks directly across from the main gate, Noelle stood unmoving next to the eight-pounder cannons. The gate opened. Seconds ticked. Tension starched her spine. Minutes crawled. Nothing happened. Then all at once men and horses swarmed into the Alamo. Someone yelled that thirty-two reinforcements had been added to the ranks from Gonzales!

Noelle only cared about one man and there he was. She breathed his name like a prayer.

"Blaze."

CHAPTER 21

In a blaze of glory.

To Noelle, that's how Blaze Bowie returned to the Alamo. Tall in the saddle on Blue, and surrounded by cheering volunteers and soldiers, moonlight shimmered against Blaze's buckskin hat and sandy hair. The glow from torches and lanterns silhouetted his buckskin clad, muscular body against the night sky.

Noelle began maneuvering her way through lathered horses and exuberant men. Never taking her eyes off her frontiersman, she called out his name.

Blaze's gaze collided with hers.

He nudged Blue and cut a path through the crowd, coming to a stop near the well. Noelle smiled up at the horse's gorgeous master for only a second before Blaze plucked her off the ground and settled her across his lap. Strong arms embraced her and she twined her arms around his neck. His eyes closed as his mouth covered hers. Yes! One of Blaze's red hot kisses. His lips parted and her tongue met his. She melted against his hard chest and poured her all consuming love for him into the kiss.

Sheer heaven during a reign of hell.

"I love you, Noelle." His voice and his words were a healing salve to her very soul. "I missed you."

Since the day he had said she couldn't get that mysterious key for him, she had searched for a carrot to dangle that would lead Blaze out of the Alamo. Now in a blinding flash, she wondered if the promise of her love could be that carrot. She crossed her fingers behind his neck to excuse a truth so diluted it was nearly a lie.

"I care for you, too, Blaze," she said softly, while looking into the gray eyes she feared had never to see again. She, who had once vowed to hate all Bowies, was so hopelessly in love with this Bowie it had become her life's *mission* to save him. "My heart nearly stopped beating from missing you."

"My heart's a target your arrows never miss," Blaze said hoarsely.

Noelle's eyes stung and tears spilled down her cheeks from wanting to tell Blaze how much she loved him.

"Don't ever cut me loose, Blaze." She prayed he was hearing everything she wasn't saying.

"And here I thought you weren't going to speak to me until I told you I was ready to leave the Alamo."

Noelle kissed him knowing their future together depended on getting him out of the Alamo. Then with a smile, Blaze leaned back and wiped a tear off her cheek.

Noelle smiled and said, "As Mama used to say you're a sight for sore eyes."

"Got new buckskins and a bath in Gonzales." His grin was riveting.

"Hola, Blaze," Carlos said, coming toward them as the returning heroes and new volunteers dispersed here and there within the garrison. "Let me take Blue to the corral for you."

"Gracias, Carlos," Blaze said and eased Noelle to the ground before dismounting.

As Blaze took his bedroll and saddlebags off Blue, Noelle smiled at Felice who was standing in the chapel yard. Felice's hands were clasped under her chin in happiness. She waved and headed toward the low barracks.

"Welcome back!" Shade shouted from the doorway of the room he and Blaze shared.

From the direction of the north wall, Rosa was headed straight for Shade. If ever there was a love triangle of sorts this was the picture of it. When Rosa squealed Shade's name, Felice stopped and spoke to a new arrival.

"Did he give you any trouble?" Blaze raised his hand in Shade's direction and turned to Noelle.

"Not really but we had it out anyway. I'll tell you later."

A lantern cast its light across the scowl on Shade's face as Felice giggled at something the stranger said.

"Happy!" Shade gave a shrill whistle and motioned for Felice to come to him.

Felice bid the newcomer farewell, raised her chin and gestured to Rosa as if to say she could have the stranger. Rosa glared at her and then at Shade, but smiled at the new recruit. Felice reached Shade who swept her into his room and with a cocky salute at Blaze and Noelle, he shut the door.

"Felice flirts with other men so Shade won't take her for granted. Then she sleeps with Shade, and only Shade of course, every chance she gets," Noelle said.

"Felice has Shade's full attention. That's a fact and something no other woman as ever managed to accomplish. She could be the best thing that's ever happened to him."

Blaze was the best thing ever to happen to Noelle. She wanted better days with him. More days with him. All of her days with him. She couldn't get enough of his handsome face, his smoldering gray eyes, his muscular body, or his spellbinding touch.

"Come on." She took his hand and tugged him toward the chapel yard. "I smell food."

"I haven't had an appetite since Santa Anna raised that red flag in the church," Blaze said and squeezed her hand.

"Neither have I."

"I wanted to come back hours ago, but even with the armistice the Mexican army wasn't going to just let us ride into the Alamo. We had to wait until most of the dragoons were asleep. My God, the enemy is on all four sides of the garrison."

"Yes." Noelle heard the fatigue and concern in his voice as they walked hand-in-hand. She listened with love and compassion to the man who was putting Texas land before his own.

"The dragoons have dug earthworks for their guns." Blaze pointed toward the walls around the fort. "There are hundreds of men settled around countless campfires. We had to dodge between the mesquite thickets to get in here without being shot." He rubbed his forehead. "Are Jim and Travis aware of this?"

"Colonel Travis knows."

"Blaze," Travis called out, beside a four-pounder cannon at Crockett's post. "Good work. Thank you."

"You're welcome, Buck," Blaze replied with respect, but no enthusiasm.

In the chapel yard, Mrs. Dickinson was in charge of serving steaming tortillas filled with shredded beef to the hungry arrivals from Gonzales. Taking a seat at a sawbuck table with Blaze, Noelle delighted in watching him wolf his food as she nibbled a burrito. He washed his burrito down with mescal brought by a grateful soldier. More than one soldier or volunteer stopped to thank him or clap him on the back. One volunteer delivered a second tankard of mescal and his thanks for the new recruits. Blaze offered the second tankard to Noelle. She sipped and coughed.

"Have you ever had mescal before?" Blaze asked and chuckled. She shook her head and managed another swallow. "What did you mean when you said, 'Travis knows'? What about Jim?"

"Colonel Bowie gave over command of the volunteers to Colonel Travis almost a week ago."

"Why?" Blaze asked, looking in the direction of Jim's room in the low barracks. "How bad is Jim?"

Having anticipated this Noelle said evenly, "You know

how much everyone likes Colonel Bowie and we're all praying for him. But… it's bad." She paused and Blaze waited for her to continue. "He collapsed the second day of the siege and hasn't been off his cot since."

"Damn." Blaze bowed his head, then slowly raised his eyes to Noelle's. "Is he lucid?"

"They say he was at times, a day or two ago."

Two soldiers, carrying a third, neared the hospital. One of the soldiers said the man being carried had collapsed from exhaustion at the eighteen-pounder.

"Who's manning that post?" Blaze asked.

"Nobody now," the other soldier answered. "The cannon's ready to fire if the dragoons get riled up, but with the armistice maybe we'll be all right."

"That's my post. I'll take over."

"Blaze, no," Noelle said. "You need to rest."

"With Shade and Felice in the low barracks and the new recruits bedding down here and there, I was wondering where we could go talk. Now I know."

His grin suggested that he wasn't going to talk much. He stood, jammed his bedroll under his arm and slung his saddlebags over his shoulder. Her hand in the crook of his arm, they paused at the edge of the courtyard where Colonel Crockett stopped Blaze to thank him. Crockett patted Noelle's shoulder and headed toward Travis.

"After seeing the garrison surrounded tonight, I've realized if the men we recruited don't make it out of here their blood will be on my hands," Blaze said, as he and Noelle continued across the plaza.

"That's not true!" she replied. "No one twisted their arms to come fight for twelve hundred and eighty acres of free land. Colonel Travis is right. You did good work. To everyone here, you're a hero."

Blaze said nothing, but stopped when they reached the wooden ramp leading up to the eighteen-pounder. The cannon rested atop rammed earth and wood which was positioned near the top of the garrison wall to allow shots to go straighter and farther.

"I only want to be your hero, Noelle," he said, his voice husky. "I need you."

"I'm right here."

"I haven't been with a woman for months. If I can't have you...you should keep out of my reach tonight."

His arrows hit her heart one after the other. Boldly hinting that she had no intention of staying out of his reach she said softly, "I had a bath, too."

Blaze's gray-eyed stare was dark and intense. He gave her a nudge and followed her up the ramp. She stopped beside the eighteen-pounder. Dropping his saddlebags, he untied the sash holding the knife and saber at his waist. Goosebumps sprinkled Noelle's skin as he lowered his weapons to the ground. With a flip of his wrists, Blaze laid out his bedroll.

"Our bed, Maid Marian."

"What will you take from me, Robin Hood?"

CHAPTER 22

BLAZE'S SMILE WAS COCKY AND SEXY.

The threat of death from Santa Anna's dragoons, faded from Noelle's mind. Taking an eager step, she sat down on the bedroll and looked up at Blaze. Standing with his hands on his hips, Blaze loomed over her and then straddled her thighs. Dear Lord, he was big and the view between his legs made her wonder if she could handle this adventurous frontiersman.

"I may not know exactly what we'll be doing, but I've cried every day for fear I might never have the chance to give myself to the only man I have ever wanted."

"I wonder if being surrounded by an enemy could make someone take her first lover when otherwise she might hold out until marriage."

"No truer words have ever been spoken." Noelle gazed into his eyes, craving him madly. "I realize the dragoons could attack at any moment. But until something happens to stop us, live up to your name, Trailblazer."

"You heard Shade call me that at your house?"

She nodded and he pulled the buckskin shirt over his head. The moonlight revealed the muscles rippling in his upper body and arms. Lying back, she shivered with nerves.

He stretched out beside her and increasing the intimacy pulled the blanket she'd taken from his bunk over them. Bracing himself on an elbow, Blaze leaned over and lowered his head until his lips grazed hers. Noelle wound her arms around his neck and grasped his dark blond hair. His mouth sought hers and his lips parted. She opened her mouth to his ravishing kiss and Blaze groaned.

"I want your skin against mine," he whispered, unbuttoning her shirt.

Somewhere beyond the Alamo's walls, noises from the Mexican army drifted to Noelle's ears. Knowing it could mean trouble was brewing, Noelle yanked at the knot on the waist of her old skirt. A rip sounded as she tore the worn material in her desperate haste. She didn't care. She wanted her skin against Blaze's, too. His gentle hand brushed hers aside and a moment later she felt the cold blade of his knife as it sliced through the knot of her skirt.

The moon and stars illuminated their bodies just enough so they could see one another. Blaze folded back the shirt, baring her breasts. Noelle's heart pounded as he lowered his mouth to hers again. Then his fiery kiss scorched her neck and she gulped when his hand cupped her breast. She drew a sharp breath when his warm, wet lips closed over the beaded nipple. His tongue played with the pebbled tip and she moaned. A tingling warmth spread through Noelle's arms to her fingers while heat radiated down her legs to her toes. Flickering hottest of all was her most secret place.

"Mmm, Blaze."

He trailed kisses to the swell of her other breast and took the nipple into his warm mouth. Shameless with desire, Noelle arched her back to his mouth.

"Your drawers and skirt gotta go," he whispered.

Noelle raised her hips and Blaze pulled her clothes down her body. Her bare skin met his buckskin pants and she pushed her clothing aside. Blaze shifted himself on top of her and resting his upper body on his forearms, nestled himself between her thighs. The hard length of his arousal pressed against her through the buckskin.

"Unbutton my pants," he said. When she hesitated he said, "It's up to you to get what you want."

He leaned to one side and she slid her hands between their bodies. Finding a button, she unfastened it. Working up her courage she undid the second button. Trembling, she undid the third button and holding her breath, she unfastened the last button.

"Good girl." He shoved his pants down his tapered hips.

The warm flesh of his swollen desire singed her naked skin. Noelle wrapped her arms tightly around him, molding her naked breasts to his muscular chest. She snapped her knees firmly against his hips, but Blaze raised up and reached between her legs. When his fingers touched the secret juncture of her thighs for the first time, the new sensation shocked Noelle. She sensed a slick dampness. What was happening to her? Holding her breath she tensed from head to toe as her body allowed Blaze's finger to slide inside her.

"Breathe. Relax, darlin'."

Noelle took a breath, but instead of relaxing she clamped her legs against him again.

"Are you gonna let me?" he whispered.

"Yes," she said quietly.

His finger was exhilarating and she realized she was as moist inside as outside.

"You're ready for me." Blaze gently pulled his hand from between her legs. "Feel me."

"What do you mean?"

"Wrap your hand around me, Noelle. I want you prepared for what you'll be getting."

"You mean how much."

"I don't want you to be afraid. Do it."

"I'll try." Her fingertips brushed torrid skin and she pulled back.

"C'mon," Blaze said. "This is a first for me, too. Take your turn."

Noelle smiled, appreciating the time and patience he was showering on her. She moved her hand until her fingers touched rock solid, velvety smooth flesh. Slowly curling her hand around him, she burned with desire to have him deep inside her.

"You're hard as a broomstick and twice as thick."

"Mmm," Blaze groaned with a low chuckle. "Put me where I need to go."

"I don't know where that is. It's up to you to get what you want."

"Touché."

He spread the folds of her womanhood opening her to his penetration.

"Is it going to hurt?"

"Calm down."

When he pushed against her with his hips, his tongue slid inside her mouth. Then the most hidden place in her body began accommodating his discovering, male flesh. She spread her legs wider and arched against him, but he went only so far.

"Wrap your legs around my waist like you did that day in the plaza."

"Because it's going to hurt now?"

"Maybe. I felt a barrier inside you that I'm going to break and because you're really tight."

Guiding her with a tender touch, he lifted her right leg and she wrapped it around him. He raised her left leg and she rested her heels at the small of his back. She was giving herself to this man as fully as she could. Then wondering about the pain again, she froze. But melting her with each thrust, he ventured a little further. Still afraid, yet trusting him she felt only pleasure. Gently, he rocked his hips and slowly her fears completely thawed. Blissful excitement built inside her and she moaned until... Fire struck!

"Blaze! Ouch! Is that you or your knife?"

"Me. Relax and ride through the pain."

"I'm done with this ride," she said, wrapped around him inside and out. "You're an eighteen-pounder like your cannon." She pushed against shoulders. "I'll bet most men are four-pounders!"

"Yeah, well." Blaze chuckled and masculine pride rang in his voice. "Shade and I got lucky."

"Lucky?" she gasped. "This hurts."

"If we do it all the way this time, I promise it won't hurt next time."

Noelle held her breath and hugged him again. He pushed and she clung to him. When another stab assailed her, she gasped and tears rolled down her cheeks.

"I've broken through, but I'll stop if it still hurts."

"No. Tell me what to do."

"When I push, you push against me."

With his first slow thrust a paradise, she had never known existed, beckoned. His mouth captured hers as he retreated. He pushed again and this time she pushed back feeling inch by white-hot, sizzling hard inch fill her. As more of his fevered flesh pressed into her, she trembled.

"I can't handle all of you."

"Mmm, there. I'm in to the hilt. Are you all right?"

"Yes." She could handle him with pleasure.

"We're gonna ride like the wind now." Blaze undulated his hips. "But I'll be out before the storm."

"No!" Noelle wasn't sure exactly what he meant, but didn't want his body unjoining with hers.

"Yes."

Then she understood. At his expense, he was trying to protect her from conceiving. She loved him so much. He slid almost out of her and then plunged all the way in. His movements grew in urgency and pushing against him, she arched her hips to meet his thrusts.

"Blaze, surely..." she began breathlessly, "...I won't conceive... oh, yes, keep doing that," she whispered, loving his hard, fast plunges. "Conceive our first time."

"When was your last monthly?"

Everything slid to a halt. His eyes were duel flames of gray fire.

"I want you to stay inside me."

"Shade and I were taught the Natchez Indians' theory about conception. I'm pulling out unless you answer me, Noelle."

"I had it while you were gone. It left yesterday."

With a sexy low groan, Blaze lowered his mouth to hers. His tongue probed and his kiss was ravenous as he filled her womanhood. Writhing with sweltering pleasure, she rode straight toward the storm with him. Faster and deeper they pounded flesh against flesh, fanning his fire within her flames.

"Blaazze, yeeesss," she moaned, on the edge of something taking her body ransom with its rapture.

"There's the moan I've wanted to hear."

And with that, Blaze rode all of his inches into her. The moon overhead couldn't hold a candle to the shooting stars between Noelle's legs. Wave after wave of glorious splendor burst within her. She locked her limbs tighter, loving the oneness with the man delivering such ecstasy. Squeezing Blaze with internal muscles she didn't know she had, his deep, masculine groan brushed her ear as his hard throbs pulsed inside her.

"Mmm, Noelle."

Noelle whispered, "What was that?"

"The seed that can make our baby if the timing is right."

For Noelle time stood still. He was talking about new life and new beginnings! Never had anyone said something so intimate to her. And never could she have imagined hearing it while he was doing it to her. She would get this hero out of the Alamo if it was the last thing she ever did because she planned to love and laugh with Blaze Bowie. Always.

Slowly, heartbeats slowed and breathing returned to normal.

"You are a blaze of glory," Noelle whispered. "I'm surprised we didn't set your bedroll on fire."

"And you're my redheaded fireworks." Still inside her, Blaze smiled down at her.

"I'd like to have three children."

"Tell me that after you have twins."

"Do twins run in the Bowie family?"

"My father was a twin. They run in Jim's branch of the family, too."

"Conceiving twins with you will be my pleasure."

Out of the blue, a cow bell jangled. Blaze quickly rolled over and Noelle clutched the blanket to her breasts. At the bottom of the ramp, laughter rang out.

"Shade," Blaze growled in the darkness. "Get lost!"

"Hey," Shade flung his arms wide, "you cut my first time with Felice short and told me the bell ringing wasn't my doing. I'm just paying you back. I rang the bell tonight, not you."

"That's what you think."

His joke played, Shade left them alone. All was quiet as Blaze eased back down beside Noelle.

The night was still inky around twinkling stars as Noelle and Blaze, in the hushed tones of lovers, discussed her visit to Shade. The night air cooled their fevered bodies and then one of Blaze's promises came true.

The second time didn't hurt.

BAGPIPES WOKE BLAZE AT DAYBREAK. Sleeping spoon fashion with Noelle he felt her stir and hugged her slender back to his heart. A fiddle joined the bagpipes and Noelle's bare bottom wiggled against his buckskin pants. With Santa Anna's dragoons just yards away, and manning the cannon, Blaze had never taken off his breeches or boots.

"Noelle," he said and yawned. "I'll hold the blanket over you so you can slip into your purple dress." Hazel eyes closed, she rolled over and as she was about to question him, he said, "Yes, you have one now."

Out in the plaza, Davy Crockett's yell proclaimed the arrival of the Gonzales recruits to be the greatest coup since the siege began.

CHAPTER 23

"DID MARCH COME IN LIKE A LION WHEN HE BEDDED THE little lamb?" a smirking Shade asked moments later at the bottom of the ramp.

"What do you want now, Shade?" Blaze asked, standing behind Noelle and fastening the buttons up her back.

"To give you a message from Maria."

"No thanks," Blaze replied.

"Last night I ran into Rosa and Maria when they were sneaking out of the Alamo. They think they can make more money with the dragoons. Anyhow before she left, Maria said she'll be at the cantina when you need her."

Hearing Noelle hiss, Blaze smothered a laugh as he fastened the last button. "Better watch out or she'll try to knee you again."

Ignoring Shade, Noelle turned to Blaze. "I've never had a new dress and it's my favorite color."

"I remembered you telling the elderly woman who gave you the ribbon that purple was your favorite color." Blaze smiled. She looked so beautiful clad in the long sleeved, warm purple frock.

"I love it." Noelle wrapped her arms around his neck, stood on tiptoes and whispered, "Thank you."

Davy Crockett's fiddle playing and Johnny McGregor's

bagpipes had helped the rising sun wake the mission. Blaze brushed a wild copper curl away from Noelle's cheek and then glanced over her shoulder.

"Go, Shade!" Blaze said to his brother who frowned and crossed his arms over his chest.

"I have to go, too, before people find out I spent the night with you," Noelle said.

"Everyone will figure you just got here to welcome me back from Gonzales."

"Doesn't Blaze think of everything?" Shade smacked his forehead.

"Shade, stop acting like you're sixteen instead of twenty-six," Blaze said. "If you want to devil people, go join up with Santa Anna."

"Nah." Shade turned down the corners of his mouth and shook his head. "I don't like their white fatigues."

"If you're not a turncoat, then go man your post," Blaze said to his all too often immature brother.

"Since the soldier who mans the eighteen-pounder keeled over last night, Travis sent me here to give you relief."

"We take our orders from Jim."

"Not since Jim collapsed," Shade reminded him, strutting up the ramp.

"Noelle, I have to talk to Jim, but first I bought you something else." Blaze ignored Shade and removed a package from his saddlebag. He handed the gift to Noelle and watched her eyes widen in shocked surprise. "Open it." He grinned as she tore into the present.

"Moccasins with purple and red beads," Noelle said, turning them this way and that. "Knee-length, buckskin ones with leather soles on the bottom!"

"Promise me you won't give them away, darlin'."

"I promise I won't. I've never had moccasins. This is too much, Blaze."

"I hope it's just the beginning."

Holding her moccasins under one arm, she wrapped her

other arm around Blaze in a hug. She felt as soft and warm as the dress and moccasins. As she thanked him again and kissed his cheek, Shade clenched his jaw and studied the sky.

"I hope Carlos won't be insulted," Blaze said, holding her close. "I didn't buy shoes or boots for that reason. I thought moccasins wouldn't hurt his pride. Try 'em on for size."

"So, how was trying Noelle on for size, Blaze?"

"Dammit to hell!" Untangling himself from Noelle, Blaze faced Shade, itching to strike him for his crudeness. "Shut up!"

Shade snickered. "Now that you trimmed her wick, I guess anybody can light her candle."

"The hell they can," Blaze snarled.

"She looks well tumbled, Blaze," Shade said. "Of course you've had lotsa practice piercing maidens."

At that lie, Blaze charged forward and slammed his fist into Shade's face. Shade rolled head over heels down the ramp with Blaze stomping down the ramp after him. Shade jumped up and threw a punch. Blaze dodged it and hurled a jab which Shade took on the chin. Shade jerked back his fist just as Davy Crockett grabbed him.

"In five hundred miles, you boys never once fought with each other," Crockett said. "What the hell's gotten into you?"

"It's who Blaze got into," Shade said as Crockett released his hold on him.

"Shade Bowie, stop being a damn-fool hotblood! You couldn't have a better brother and friend than Blaze," Crockett said sternly. "Noelle was crying over Blaze when I found her sitting in the chapel yard in the middle of the night, not you! Now, shoulder it like the half-horse, half 'gator I said you are and take your watch beside me." With that, Crockett gave Shade a shove toward the palisade. When Shade stalked off toward the south wall, Crockett turned to Blaze. "Go see Jim. He's been worried about you and asking for you."

"Yes, sir." Blaze nodded. Davy Crockett picked up his fiddle and sauntered away. Blaze smiled at Noelle.

"You lied to me, Blaze." Her chin quivered.

"You know I didn't because you overheard Shade say he'd had the first virgin just before he called me Trailblazer. You were my first and last virgin."

"That bad?"

"That good." Blaze chuckled.

"Promise?"

"Promise. Why don't you put your moccasins on and rustle us up some breakfast? I'll meet you in the chapel yard after I've talked to Jim."

On tiptoes, she kissed him. He tasted a tear on her lip and thought it might just be her first happy one.

At Jim's door, Gertrudis and Juana told him that Jim was too ill to talk. The sisters promised to summon Blaze as soon as Jim's fever let up. Blaze stood outside of Jim's room analyzing the current situation. Even if Jim told him where the San Saba Mine was and he felt free to leave the Alamo today, he'd decided they didn't have time to mine the gold and silver. Not to mention hauling it back to Louisiana by mid-May.

Tick. Tick. Tick.

Blaze could almost hear each precious second slipping away from him. Even with the recruits from Gonzales, the Alamo had less than two hundred men. Santa Anna's main army was marching toward them and when they joined the advance cavalry already surrounding the fort... *God help us.* Looking around the garrison Blaze felt discouraged. Tortured. Trapped.

How could he make promises to Noelle he might not be alive to keep? Leaving the low barracks he wondered if James Bonham was having any luck persuading Colonel Fannin to bring his troops to the Alamo.

In the chapel yard, Blaze caught up with Noelle. She did a twirl for him in her purple dress and then served him breakfast. As he ate at the sawbuck table where they'd been just hours ago, she asked about his old buckskins.

"They've seen better days," Blaze said.

"But it's nice to have a change of clothes. I want the old buckskins and sash to see good days again."

Blaze wondered if he and Noelle would see better days. What would become of her if she was here when Santa Anna won? And win, he would. Blaze had warned her about being caught by dragoons. True she was safer at this point inside the Alamo than in Bexar, but he wanted her out of the area altogether.

"The buckskins will probably shrink if you wash them," Blaze said as he tugged her down beside him at the table. "You can have them."

Noelle blushed as if his suggestion was intimate. Maybe it was. Smiling at her bashfulness, Blaze watched her wring her hands. Those dainty hands had gently commanded spiraling ecstasy throughout his body. Within this sexy siren's sensual embrace, lovemaking simmered past familiar waters to uncharted seas. Love and lust had steamed in a boiling cauldron of pounding, fevered plunges. Lost in her velvety walls, pleasure had crashed over him in blistering waves and exploded in red-hot volcanic pulses. Never had he soared to such heights of passion and only with Noelle would he reach them again. He put his hand over hers and she twined her fingers with his.

"Noelle, you were everything I knew you would be last night and more." Her sweet smile swept away the torment of the Alamo.

"I would love to have another night like last night with you," she said, eyes lowered.

"Me, too."

"While you were at the low barracks, I showed Carlos and Felice my dress and moccasins. Carlos said he's never made moccasins, but he's going to try to make Felice a pair out of the cowhide we have from the rounded up cattle." Noelle stood. "I have to help the ladies serve breakfast now."

"Let me know if you hear anything about Jim." He left her then, glad the purple dress was keeping her body warm and the sturdy moccasins protecting her feet.

That afternoon, Travis, in high spirits over the addition of the thirty-two men, fired a double blast from the twelve-pounder. It was a direct hit on Main Plaza where they knew Santa Anna had set up headquarters in the Yturri house. With little reply from the Mexicans, rumors circulated within the Alamo that they had killed *His Excellency* Santa Anna.

At the eighteen-pounder, Blaze stared across the glaring prairie of mesquite thickets. He longed more than ever to go home and see the lush green of forests and hear the flow of babbling creeks. The San Antonio River could hardly compare to the mighty Mississippi.

Maybe he could leave the Alamo if they had killed Santa Anna.

"Our spies tell us *His Excellency* is alive," Shade said, trudging up the ramp to the cannon. "Blaze," he sighed, plopping down and leaning against the eighteen-pounder, "we're on a landlocked battleship. I don't want to go down with it, do you?"

Coming to talk was Shade's way of apologizing. Blaze sensed the scared, little boy inside the often angry, insecure man.

"Shade, why don't you take the girls by force if need be and sneak them out of here tonight?"

"Only if you'll come with us." Shade picked up some pebbles, tossed them one at a time and said, "I'm not going home without you."

Blaze refused to walk away though Shade cited reasons why he should. It was wishful thinking for him to picture a future with Noelle. Felice came for a subdued Shade and they went to the low barracks. Would he and Noelle ever make love again?

.   .   .

"SUPPER," Noelle called later from the bottom of the ramp, holding a tin of corn and salt pork.

For her sake, Blaze forced a smile he didn't feel. He crooked his finger and she swayed up the ramp. Damn, how he wanted to see this beautiful lady glide toward him and a preacher.

CHAPTER 24

ON MARCH SECOND, DAY NINE OF SANTA ANNA'S SIEGE, Travis received news of corn at the Seguin Ranch. He sent a detachment headed by a Lieutenant Menchaca to retrieve it.

JAMES BUTLER BONHAM arrived on March third, day ten. Alone. Colonel Fannin and his troops remained in Goliad. Blaze cursed under his breath and went to Travis' headquarters to hear what Bonham had to say first hand. As Bonham delivered his report, Blaze's feelings were mirrored on the faces of Bonham and Travis.

Bonham then handed a letter to Travis from Robert Williamson, a delegate pursuing independence for Texas. News of the letter's contents didn't take long to spread from William Ward at the main gate to Micajah Autry at the stockade, to Eliel Melton slaughtering beef in the corral, to Shade at the four-pounder; sixty men from Gonzales were marching to the Alamo's rescue and another six hundred would soon be en route. The Texians fired several shots into Bexar to celebrate.

Blaze would believe hundreds of reinforcements were coming when they rode through the main gate of the garrison. On his way back to the eighteen-pounder, Noelle motioned to him from the low barracks. He hurried across the plaza to Jim's room.

"I just took Colonel Bowie a plate of food and he's asking for you," Noelle said.

"Thanks for letting me know." Blaze stepped toward Jim's room and Noelle offered to go with him. "No. Whatever he wants to see me about, he might not say in front of you." Blaze had decided to ask Jim for a map to the mines. He'd give it to Shade and figure out some way to make his brother leave him behind and take the girls to safety. Shade could find the gold and silver they needed to save their land.

Juana came out of Jim's room and confirmed that Jim wanted to see him. He entered his cousin's room and closed the door. Blaze pulled a chair away from a desk and sat beside the cot. Pale and thin, Jim Bowie was a shadow of his former rugged self.

"How are you, Jim?" Blaze asked.

"Weaker'n a spring colt."

"I'm sorry to bother you," Blaze told him. "But Crockett and Noelle both said you wanted to see me."

"Yes. I'm worried, Blaze," Jim said. "Nobody's as trustworthy and fearless as James Butler Bonham 'cept you, me and Crockett. If Bonham couldn't get Fannin here, nobody can."

"Do you want me to try to get Fannin here?"

"It'd be a waste of precious time." Jim's strangled sigh rattled in his chest. "But we need help. You know Santa Anna outnumbers us at least ten to one."

Blaze nodded. Without Colonel Fannin's troops or other reinforcements they didn't have a prayer.

"I apologize for asking one last favor." Regret deepened the hollows of Jim's cheeks and sounded in his voice as he said, "I want you to travel west into the Texas Hill Country to get help, Blaze."

Such vulnerability and pain shone in Jim's gray eyes Blaze felt tears sting the backs of his own eyes.

"Not that I don't want to go, Jim, but who's left for me to get?"

"Sam Houston," Jim rasped. "He's still on furlough making sure the Indians don't align with Santa Anna. But Sam and his men would be here if he knew we were surrounded by the enemy."

"I can't leave Noelle." Blaze felt the walls closing in. More to himself than to Jim, he said, "I worried about her the whole time I was gone on the Gonzales trip."

"Take her." Jim coughed and spit blood into a rag. "Disguise her as a boy." Wheezing racked his wasted body. "Santa Anna not only thinks he's Napoleon and can get away with anything, he's sadistic. If he catches you and finds out Noelle is a woman, he *will* rape her."

Blaze's mind worked fast. This was the solution he needed to make Noelle, Shade and Felice leave. He'd go with them and together they'd find Sam Houston. Blaze would leave them in a safe location and accompany Houston back to the Alamo.

"Blaze, will you do this for me?"

"Yes, sir. What about Shade?"

"You tell Shade I *ordered* him to go with you."

"Thank you. I will. Where's Sam Houston?"

"Crockett's heard he's just two days' ride away, maybe three. But he's talking to the Indians up in the hills and not hurrying."

"I'll try to find him in two days."

"All you can do is try, son," Jim whispered. "But do not come back without Sam. It wouldn't do any good. Understand?"

"I understand," Blaze said, knowing he'd be back no matter what.

"Juana wrote down my directions to Houston's last known whereabouts," Jim said as his eyelids drooped. "She also penned a letter from me to Noelle. They're on my desk. Get 'em, Blaze." He did so. "Please don't give my letter to Noelle 'til you get where you're going."

"Yes, sir," Blaze said. "Speaking of Noelle, could you tell by looks who her father was?"

"Marcel and Jean both had black hair. After Noelle was born, Charbonnez claimed she got her red hair from his father." Jim paused to catch his breath. "But Lafitte told me *before* Noelle was born he'd named his place on Galveston Island Maison Rouge, which means red house, in honor of his mother's red hair."

"So, if you had to guess?"

"Lafitte. If you find him, he'll have hazel eyes just like Noelle's." Jim wheezed and Blaze helped him sip water. "Jean has a gold tooth and on the subject of gold, I'm sorry I wasn't able to take you to the mines."

"That's all right. It wasn't meant to be." Blaze couldn't bring himself to ask this sick man to draw a damn treasure map. Besides, if Shade sold Blaze's timberland, he would be able to keep the new manor house and plantation. "The San Saba Mines will stay lost. I'll leave today, but I'm not bringing Shade back."

"My older brother, Rezin, watched out for me, too." Jim's expression said he empathized fully. "Be on the lookout for Apaches and Comanches. Obviously, Houston's location is full of both." He smiled before continuing. "Blaze, you've made me proud to be a Bowie. You were worried about being in my debt, but I'll die in yours." From under his pillow he pulled out his sheathed knife and handed it to Blaze. "Rezin made this knife and it saved me more than once. It's yours now, as my thanks for risking your life at the Alamo."

"Don't you die on me, Jim! You'll see me when I get back here with Houston. We'll beat Santa Anna and I'll take you home."

"Come back with Houston and you got yourself a deal. Wait 'til dark and then ride like hell."

As Jim closed his eyes, Blaze bowed his head. With a last look, he left his cousin resting on his cot.

Blaze found Shade with Davy Crockett near their four-pounder post. Blaze told them of Jim's order to find Houston, the orders included Shade and he planned to take Noelle. Shade said he'd take Felice as well. Blaze didn't admit to Shade he was going to write his own letter telling him to sell the timberland.

"Disguise Felice as a boy, Shade." Sweeping his coonskin cap off his head, Davy handed it to Shade. Blaze suspected Jim and Crockett had already discussed this plan to find Houston. He would not let them down. "Thanks and Godspeed, boys." Packing Old Betsy, Crockett moseyed away to the palisade.

"Will the girls go without Carlos?" Shade asked.

Blaze had not seen the gleam of adventure in Shade's eyes since that day so long ago when they'd decided to join up with Crockett and find Jim. Now as they prepared to leave them, Blaze saw it again.

"I'm going to talk to Carlos now, but I doubt he'll leave," Blaze said, "If he disagrees with us taking Noelle and Felice, we'll have to kidnap the girls."

"Damn right!"

"SI, POR FAVOR TAKE MY CHICAS," Carlos said from behind his workbench. "Once you get them out of the Alamo, keep them away. If Noelle makes peace with her abuela, maybe the woman will be kind to Felice. Trilby's mama can give my muchachas a much better life than I ever could."

"Come with us, Carlos," Blaze said. "You can be a cobbler there as well as here."

"Gracias." Carlos shook his head and his sombrero bounced against his back. "But Bexar is my home."

Blaze understood all too well the love of home. Carlos Herrera was a quietly brave soul who was as passionate in his loyalty to Texas and in his resolve to defend the Alamo as any man at the fort.

"Blaze, tell each of the girls; *te quiero mucho,* which means I love you so much." His voice strained with emotion.

"Remind them Trilby said to always love and laugh." Carlos held out his hand to Blaze. "I would have been proud to have you as my son-in-law."

His throat tight, Blaze could only nod as he shook Carlos' hand. Damn the Alamo.

NOELLE FOUND Blaze leaning against the wheel of the eighteen-pounder cannon. The grim set of his chiseled profile as he glared toward Bexar said he hated being here.

"Blaze?" She walked up the ramp and he swung his head around. "Have you heard the rumor that Colonel Fannin told James Bonham stories of Mexican butchery and tried to talk Bonham into staying in Goliad instead of riding to the Alamo?"

"It's not a rumor. I heard Bonham when he said it," Blaze replied. "But the Mexicans won't butcher the women and children."

At the word butcher, the sun glinted off the handle of an unmistakable weapon tied at Blaze's waist.

"Why do you have Colonel Bowie's knife?"

"He's not getting any better and wants it kept in the family."

Noelle nodded, so wanting to have a family with Blaze. She'd made love with this gorgeous, brave man most of the night. Three times she had thought she would lose her mind from the pleasure. As their bodies cooled, she'd blinked back hot tears of despair for fear they might never make love again. At the top of the ramp Blaze reached out a hand and pulled her between his muscular thighs.

"When I bought your purple dress, I pictured how beautiful you'd look in it. And you do."

"Thank you." Noelle felt a hot blush crawl up her neck to her cheeks.

"But I want you to put on my old buckskins."

"You want me to look like a boy in case Santa Anna attacks."

"Not in case, Noelle, when." He took his bandana from around his neck and handed it to her. "Tie your hair up. Carlos has a hat for you. Shade's giving Felice his coonskin cap and Carlos is finding pants for her."

"You're scaring me."

"I'm *preparing* you." He gave her a sexy wink. He then turned her toward the ramp and gave her fanny a pat. "Get your wiggle on and turn yourself into a boy, little girl."

Noelle left Blaze then as she'd found him, grim and glaring in the direction of Bexar.

At Carlos' work area Noelle found him with Felice. He was handing her a pair of moccasins. They weren't knee high or beaded, but sturdy.

"Gracias, Papa!" Felice said.

Noelle had washed Blaze's old buckskins hours earlier and dried them above a campfire near Carlos' workbench. They *had* shrunk. That was a good thing now. Carlos handed her a dark brown hat.

"Muchas gracias, Carlos," she said. Hugging him, Noelle could have sworn he'd mumbled under his breath something about being able to die happy.

Serving up corn and beef for the noon meal in the courtyard alongside Felice, the haggard faces and sagging shoulders of the soldiers and volunteers pained Noelle. In the courtyard mothers were glum, their children fussy.

Henry Warnell came by, but didn't talk quite so animatedly about the horses he cared for. Davy Crockett and Shade sat down at the table with him and were served. Davy, always the yarn spinner, got a laugh out of Henry. Shade made Felice blush just by winking at her.

Out in the plaza, Green Jameson and others piled dirt up against the walls to fortify them against the enemy who lay in wait on all four sides of the crumbling Alamo.

Blaze strode into the courtyard and wrapped an arm around Noelle. A moment later, Carlos rounded the corner. Smiling broadly, Carlos presented Blaze with a dark brown hat larger, but similar to Noelle's.

"Brown will make your heads less of a target."

"Gracias, Carlos," Blaze said. "Noelle, why aren't you wearing the buckskins?"

Before she could answer it was because she so loved her purple dress, fierce yelling floated over the walls.

"Colonel Fannin?" Noelle asked, hope in her heart.

Blaze sprinted across the chapel courtyard. With Shade on his heels, he ran up a ramp to the top of the chapel and stopped on a small section of roof supporting a twelve-pounder cannon.

"Blaze, who is it?" Noelle called out from the ground.

"It's a column of arriving soldiers!" he yelled.

"Ours or Santa Anna's?"

CHAPTER 25

"Santa Anna's!" Blaze shouted.

The brothers raced back down to the courtyard and split up with Shade beelining to the palisade as Blaze tore across the plaza to the eighteen-pounder.

Word was Mexican General Gaona's Brigade had just arrived. Dear Lord, how badly did the Mexicans have to outnumber them before they finally attacked? The garrison braced itself but experienced only the usual intermittent shelling from the enemy.

It was only one in the afternoon, on this endless tenth day of the ever oppressing siege, when Noelle caught Blaze as he came out of the officers' headquarters. She fell into step with him as they walked toward his post. With his saber lashed to one side of his waist, he left Jim's knife tied on his sash, but handed Noelle his own knife.

"I told you to put your buckskins on."

"But I love my dress," she said, clutching the sheathed knife. "What's going on?"

"I had to tell Travis a couple of things from my discussion with Jim."

"I saw James Bonham and John Smith go into the officers' quarters a few minutes ago, too. Did Bonham have anything else to say about Colonel Fannin?"

"When Fannin told Bonham he was unable to offer assistance to the Alamo, Bonham spit on the ground and galloped west. Evidently Fannin's own men don't like him for not coming here. But Fannin thinks Jim and Travis should have blown up the Alamo when they had the chance."

As they reached the ramp to the eighteen-pounder, Noelle thought by this time even Mama would have wished they'd blown up the Alamo.

"Was Fannin our last hope?"

Blaze glanced away. Was he hiding something from her? How much worse could things possibly be?

"Travis wrote an official appeal for help to the Texian Independence Convention at Washington-on-the-Brazos," Blaze finally said.

"Washington-on-the-Brazos is the capital of Texas."

"Right. Which is where forty-one delegates have assembled to thrash out and vote for the independence of Texas. If they formally proclaim independence they'll raise an army fit to take the field against the Mexicans."

"With dragoons camped on our doorstep there's not enough time to save the Alamo, is there?"

Blaze shrugged. "Travis hopes if the Alamo falls the Mexican victory will eventually cost Santa Anna as much or more than if he had been defeated here."

"What makes Colonel Travis think that will happen?"

"He assumes someone who's not in the Alamo when it falls will make it happen by avenging the men who died for Texas."

"Men who died for Texas...like you," Noelle whispered, wanting to scream.

Blaze didn't reply. Noelle moved closer to Blaze, wrapping her arms around him. She craved his embrace and desperately longed to change his resolve to stay here. Blaze returned her hug and she clung tightly to him.

"Blaze!" Shade suddenly called, coming toward them. "I just ran into John Smith. Smith says Travis disagrees with

Jim on where Sam Houston is. Travis is sending Smith to Washington-on-the-Brazos."

"Yeah, I know," Blaze replied, keeping an arm around Noelle. "Another disagreement between Jim and Travis should come as no surprise."

Noelle thought she detected an unspoken message pass between the brothers. Had Blaze just given Shade a silent warning? Shade's brows knitted with what? Confusion? Comprehension? Was she reading signals where there were none?

"Who's going with Mr. Smith?" Noelle asked and Blaze shrugged. "Why don't you and Shade go with him?" When Blaze didn't respond, she persisted, "You went with John Smith to Gonzales."

Blaze and Shade just looked at each other as a solider assigned by Travis to take Blaze's watch arrived.

"Time for siesta." Blaze held out a hand to Noelle.

She took his hand and the three of them walked toward the low barracks. How unfair for these two men who shouldn't even be in the Alamo, to die here. Glancing at headquarters Noelle decided to try her luck in getting Colonel Travis to send them to Washington-on-the-Brazos. As Felice caught up with them, Noelle said she'd meet them in the low barracks. She pretended to head toward Carlos and the workbench where she'd left her buckskins, but as soon as Blaze, Shade and Felice disappeared into the brothers' room, Noelle dashed to the officers' quarters. If Blaze could talk to Colonel Travis whenever he wanted to, so would she! Noelle knocked on the door and was told that Travis was far too busy to see her. The door shut.

With a heavy heart, Noelle slowly walked to the low barracks. Glancing left, Juana came out of Jim's room and shook her head. Noelle pulled open the door of Blaze's room and saw Felice lying next to Shade. Quietly closing the door, Noelle padded to Blaze's bunk. Blaze lay sprawled on his back with Mistletoe curled at his feet.

Noelle crawled between the wall and the man. Eyes

closed, Blaze hugged her to his muscular body. Laying her head on his broad shoulder, she didn't know why he'd picked today to siesta but she was so mentally and physically exhausted by the siege she closed her eyes and fell asleep in his arms.

NOELLE WAS DREAMING OF BLAZE, gorgeous and commanding, seated at the head of her grandparents' long dining room table when someone pounded on the door. Blaze rolled out of the bunk, ran a hand through his hair and opened the door. No one was there.

"What now?" Shade asked groggily.

"Who the hell knows," Blaze replied. "Let's find out."

Noelle and Felice followed the brothers. From all over the mission, men were gathering in parade formation to hear what Colonel Travis was about to say. Blaze, Shade, Crockett and Carlos carried Jim out of his barracks on his cot. Only then did Travis speak. Whatever bitterness he may have felt toward Fannin, Travis did not relate it to the soldiers and volunteers.

"I can rely on nothing now but spirit and bravery," Colonel Travis said. "Fate is near and surrender impossible." Using his sword Travis drew a line in the sand of the plaza. "I cannot impose a death penalty on any man caring to escape from the Alamo before the inevitable end."

Noelle glanced at Blaze. Standing tall, his head high and shoulders squared, she wished he wasn't so honorable. But that was one of the very traits she loved most about her hero. Yes, one of so many.

"Escape will be difficult, but not impossible," Travis said. "Those who wish to stay cross this line. Those wishing to escape should not cross it."

Noelle held her breath. Ordering his cot carried over the line, Jim Bowie was the first to cross. Blaze, Shade, Crockett and Carlos had carried him and remained on that side of the line.

Everyone crossed the line but a man named Moses Rose. Travis and the entire garrison stared at him.

"I'm simply not ready to die," Moses Rose said.

He scurried away as Blaze and the others carried Jim back to his room.

"Felice, let's try to convince Blaze and Shade to go with John Smith to Washington-on-the-Brazos," Noelle said.

"I don't want Shade to leave me."

"You'd rather he stay here to the *inevitable end?*"

"No." Felice's shoulders slumped and she shook her head.

When the men came out of Jim's room, Blaze motioned to Noelle. Carlos passed her and Felice as he headed back to his workshop. Colonel Crockett and Shade walked toward the palisade. Felice caught up with them and grabbed Shade's hand. From where she joined Blaze near Jim's room, Noelle could tell that Felice was trying to reason with Shade.

"Blaze, please go with John Smith to find Sam Houston."

"Dammit, you heard Shade say Jim and Travis disagree on where Houston is," Blaze replied as they stood outside the low barracks.

"But you want to help, don't you?"

"I will help." He took a deep breath. "Jim gave me directions to where he and Crockett think Houston is in the Texas Hill Country. That's in the opposite direction from where Smith will be heading."

"That's wonderful, Blaze! When do we leave? Can we take Felice, Carlos and Mistletoe?"

"Carlos refuses to go."

"Then Felice won't go." Noelle paused and sighed. "I can't abandon them. But I want you to go."

"And leave you here to be raped by dragoons?"

Blaze frowned and Noelle wrapped her arms around him.

"Short of a miracle, you are breaking your promise to take me to Grandmother."

"I've realized I had no right to make any promises to you, Noelle."

"Don't say that! I've begun to dream of raising my family in Grandmother's house, because I was so happy there as a child. But if you're not there, it would be nothing but a pitiful prison instead of a happy home. Without you I'll have no husband, no children, no happiness. Ever."

"I love you so much, Noelle."

"Blaze, I—te quiero mucho!" Noelle had almost blurted out the carrot she was dangling and switched to Spanish at the last second. "Te quiero muy mucho!"

"You're young and beautiful and you'll be rich. Men will flock to your grandmother's house to court you. You'll love one of them on first sight and have everything you're dreaming of."

"No! I want *everything* with you and *only you!*"

CHAPTER 26

"I'm sending Shade out around midnight to go look for Houston," Blaze said calmly and hugged Noelle. "I'm sure Felice will want to tell him goodbye. Meet us at the archway between the courtyard and corral. I've got things to do now. I'll see you later." He kissed her forehead and let go of her. "If you don't have on the buckskins by then, I'll turn you over my knee and give you a spanking you won't forget."

"*Promise?*" Her whisper was ragged with tears.

"I do promise that, darlin'," he said over his shoulder as he headed toward the corral.

Noelle's eyes stung and her throat ached. She stood unmoving, her world titling out of control. She willed her heart to stop beating and release her from this unbearable pain.

No! She would not give up as long as there was breath in her body. Breathing in deeply, she squared her shoulders. Clearly and purposefully picturing Blaze at the head of the long table in Grandmother's fabulous formal dining room, she was determined to see that dream come true.

With a last look at Blaze, she stalked to the palisade. There she found Felice in tears.

"Shade, order Blaze to leave with you at midnight!" Noelle said.

"I can *order* Blaze 'til the cows came home." Shade shrugged. "But you ought to know by now Blaze makes his own decisions."

Deciding her next target was Carlos, Noelle turned away and her attention was drawn to Moses Rose. Packing a small bundle, he scaled a wall and dropped out of sight.

"Moses fell into a pool of Mexican blood!" someone posted near that wall shouted.

There had been numerous Mexicans who'd come too close to the Alamo walls and been shot. They were left where they fell as attempting to retrieve a body meant sure death. The garrison always paid for shooting a dragoon by suffering a bombardment of enemy shells. So far, no one inside had been hurt.

Noelle found Carlos in his workshop making leather straps. She pleaded with him to leave the Alamo. She explained they would all go, if he would go. Declining to leave the Alamo, he smiled and slowly shook his head. She'd not seen him so sad since her mother died. Perhaps, Noelle realized, Carlos no longer cared to live.

In a daze of desperation, Noelle left. Out in the plaza she heard no sympathy for Moses Rose from those in the garrison and no gunfire from the Mexicans. Halfway through the chapel courtyard she heard someone shout that Rose had made it past the enemy. That same enemy would kill Blaze as soon as Santa Anna gave the order.

Night fell and eventually it was time to say goodbye to Shade. Noelle and Felice hadn't seen Blaze or Shade for hours and Felice was beside herself with grief. Exiting the chapel, they saw Carlos just entering the opposite side of the courtyard. She and Felice walked to meet him. He said Santa Anna could attack at any moment and was glad to see his muchachas had changed into their boy clothes. From the direction of the four-pounder, Davy Crockett fell in beside them.

"Almost didn't recognize you girls," Colonel Crockett said.

Noelle wore Blaze's old buckskins over his white shirt along with her new moccasins. Her hair was tied up in Blaze's bandana under the brown hat. Felice wore her hair tucked under Shade's coonskin cap, along with a jacket, shirt, pants, and moccasins from Carlos.

"We are going to tell Shade adios," Felice said, tears streaming down her cheeks. "I know I will never see him again."

Noelle figured that was probably true, as they crossed the courtyard to the cattle pen and corral.

"Where are you going, Colonel Crockett?" Noelle asked.

"To say goodbye," he replied solemnly.

Nearing the area where the horses and cattle were kept, the Bowie brothers were nowhere to be seen.

"They're probably in the long barracks jawin' with Henry," Colonel Crockett suggested and opened the courtyard gate. "I'll round 'em up and send 'em back this way. Wait here."

Packing Old Betsy, Crockett left them with Carlos on the other side of the gate from the animals. Pungent smells of dirt, horses and cattle assailed Noelle. Cows mooed and horses whinnied. Amazingly, at midnight, there were several men on horseback. They must be riding out with John Smith. Just as Noelle was about to say she didn't see Blaze or Shade, Crockett called Shade's name. Shade rode away from the group of riders, and meeting up with Crockett, listened to him as they made their way back toward the gate.

"Where's Blaze?" Noelle asked as they neared. "I thought he'd be here."

"He's on his way," Shade said and motioned to Felice. "Come kiss me goodbye, Happy."

Colonel Crockett opened the gate and Felice dashed into the corral. Bracing a hand on Shade's knee, Felice raised on tiptoes and tilted up her chin. Shade caught Noelle's eye as

his hand went to the back of Felice's head. When Shade
leaned down to kiss her, Noelle saw Felice's purple birthday
ribbon slip through his fingers. Perhaps he hoped to keep it
as a memento and hadn't meant to drop it or maybe he
planned to return it before leaving. Either way, Noelle knew
Felice wouldn't want it trampled by hooves.

Noelle hurried into the corral and retrieved the ribbon.
She smiled as Carlos came up beside her. Then without
warning Carlos lifted Felice off the ground. Shade's arm
snaked around Felice's waist and she was plopped behind
him on the horse! With Shade's help, Carlos lashed Felice to
him with a *leather strap*.

"Papa!" Felice shouted, staying in the saddle only because
of the strap tied around her waist.

"Hold onto me, Felice!" Shade said.

"Carlos, what's happening?" Noelle asked.

Hands gripped Noelle's waist as Blaze galloped out of
the darkness. Gray eyes bored into her as he leaned down
and lassoed her with one arm. Blaze hoisted her into the air,
hands pushed the backs of her thighs and she found herself
sitting behind him on Blue. She realized Davy Crockett was
the man who'd helped put her onto the horse and in the
next heartbeat Carlos used a leather strap to tether Noelle
to Blaze.

"Goodbye," Colonel Crockett said with a smile, backing
up and raising a hand in farewell.

From Blaze's sash swung his saber and the knife from
Jim. A rifle and a hatchet were secured to the right side of
his saddle. Saddlebags bulged and he had two canteens. He
was going after Houston! *They* were going after Houston!
Noelle didn't question how or why, she just gave silent
thanks.

Henry Warnell ran forward leading two horses by their
reins. He put the reins to one horse in Blaze's hand and
handed the other horse's reins to Shade. Davy picked Old
Betsy off the ground and hoisted his rifle in the air while
Carlos waved his sombrero.

"Noelle!" Blaze yelled as Blue pranced with excitement. "Hold on!"

She wrapped her arms around Blaze's muscular body as Shade and Felice came to a stop beside them. On the opposite side of the corral was a wall with a wide, picket fence gate. Beyond that northern wall, open mesquite prairie lay dotted with Mexican dragoons.

"I didn't think you were coming with me," John Smith said, riding up on the other side of them.

"We're riding out with you, but heading in a different direction," Blaze replied.

Everything was happening so fast! Who cared where they looked for Houston as long as they were escaping the Alamo? There was elation in Felice's brown eyes at being with Shade and tears on her pretty cheeks over leaving Carlos. Noelle called to Carlos asking him to take care of himself and Mistletoe. He nodded he would.

"What're we waiting for?" Shade demanded.

"Me!" Travis sprinted into the corral and handed Smith a packet. "This is the list of supplies we need."

"God and Texas!" Smith shouted.

"Victory or death!" Colonel Travis replied crisply and saluted.

"Vaya con Dios!" came Carlos' prayer.

Cattle were shooed out of the way as Smith and his group on horseback suddenly crowded the northern postern. In the dim moonlight, the picket fence gate swung open wide. Shouting and firing at random to provide cover, Smith and his men charged outside. Carlos slapped Buckshot's rump and Shade tore out of the gate behind Smith. Bringing up the rear Blaze kicked Blue into a full-out gallop across the corral, but the erupting Mexican gunfire was so fierce soldiers began shutting the gate.

"No!" Noelle screamed in terror of Blaze being trapped.

"It's now or never!" Blaze yelled.

CHAPTER 27

"Now!" Noelle shouted, the sharp pickets looming dead ahead.

Under the midnight moon, she clung to Blaze, the soldiers scattered out of their way and Blue soared over the gate. The horse behind them jumped and suddenly open mesquite prairie surrounded them.

Mexican gunfire increased as dragoons rushed out of the darkness. It was a scene from a nightmare. Smith and his party continued to provide cover as they galloped north toward the sugar mill.

Terrified, Noelle expected to take a Brown Bess musket ball in the back. Blaze had told her the British had sold that musket along with Baker rifle bayonets to the Mexicans back in the 1820s. He'd said the .69 caliber balls spun out of the weapons with deadly accuracy up to one hundred yards and on impact made a devastating wound.

Noelle protectively molded her body to Blaze's broad back.

Finally, the enemy gunfire faded. They caught up with Shade and Felice who galloped along on their left side as Smith's party closed in on their right. Noelle peered over her shoulder.

The Alamo had vanished into the night.

They journeyed north with Smith for another hour. The men discussed Santa Anna, the Alamo and Sam Houston. Smith said he and his party had a one hundred and seventy mile trip northeast to Washington-on-the-Brazos. She listened as Blaze said Jim had given him orders to look for Houston on a two or three day ride northwest into the Texas Hill Country.

Noelle vividly remembered her mission had been to get Blaze out of the Alamo. Alive. By shouting her agreement to jump the gate, she'd done that. Whatever he did now was up to him… as long as he didn't go back.

"I love you, Blaze," she whispered too quietly to be heard.

"I think we're safe now." Blaze reined in Blue and patted Noelle's thigh. "Slide off."

Felice did the same. Blaze and Shade then dismounted and quickly helped her and Felice onto the saddles of the horses provided for them. Smith and his men waited until Blaze spoke.

"Good luck," Blaze said to John Smith.

"Godspeed," John Smith replied and veered east toward the Brazos River.

IT WAS the early morning of Friday, March fourth as Blaze led the way west. Darkness eventually turned into dawn. Around noon, Blaze reined in Blue near a creek to water the horses and check Jim's directions against nearby landmarks.

Yawning, Shade dismounted and stretched.

Blaze dismounted and went to Noelle who slid out of the saddle on her gentle mare and into his arms. His spirits lifted as he kissed her. Shoving her cowboy hat off her head, she let it dangle by a cord down her back, then hugged him tightly. With a kiss to the top of her head, he stood her back and handed her a canteen. As the horses drank from a rushing stream, Blaze matched the increasingly hilly countryside before them to Jim's description on paper.

"Where are we?" Noelle asked.

"Right where we should be," Blaze answered.

Mountains loomed days away. Towering peaks resembled great columns reminding Blaze of the four columns at the front of the Alamo chapel. Limestone buttresses made Blaze think of the rammed earth breastworks piled against the garrison's walls to support them from enemy attack.

"I'd like to stretch and splash water in my face," Noelle said, pulling off her bandana. She gave her copper curls a shake and tied the bandana around her neck.

They all took care of needs as the horses rested and grazed.

"Let's get going," Blaze said after a few minutes.

"I'm hungry," Felice said.

"Me too," Shade said. "Let's stay here and eat."

"No." Blaze filled his and Noelle's canteens from the stream. "We have to find Houston and we can't waste daylight." Capping the canteens, he gave Noelle hers and helped her mount her horse. "We'll eat tortillas as we ride. Mrs. Dickenson made them. They're in your saddlebags."

Canteens full and riders on horseback, with food in their hands, Blaze led the way northwest.

Hours and miles later, rolling his shoulders, Blaze noted a few yards to their right was a sheer drop-off of maybe fifteen hundred feet. Keeping Noelle on his left, Blaze veered away from the cliff.

"Felice, I just remembered I picked up your birthday ribbon in the corral," Noelle said, pulling it out of a pocket of the buckskin pants.

"The corral?" Felice asked as she reached out to Noelle who placed it in her hand. Happiness showed in her voice and on her face. "I thought I lost my ribbon at your post, Shade."

"A woman's ribbon is good luck during battle," Shade said and shrugged.

"I think the ribbon was dropped to lure me into the corral," Noelle said.

Blaze's nod confirmed that as Shade held out his hand to Felice who gave her ribbon back to him.

All day they traveled as fast as Blaze felt they could push their horses. That night, Noelle and Felice almost fell out of the saddles in exhaustion. Blaze and Shade made camp in a clearing of spiraling evergreen trees as the girls unpacked supper. After they ate, Blaze said he'd take the first watch. Noelle rolled out her bedroll next to Blaze's. She curled up at his side and closed her eyes while he sat staring into the campfire. The scent of pine needles reminded him of his timberland. How he longed to gaze out across his land with Noelle at his side.

Blaze's shoulders sagged as he thought about never marrying Noelle or seeing home again. Maybe Sam Houston would have so many troops that they would route Santa Anna the hell out of Texas.

And maybe not.

Shade was stretched out beside Felice as they slept. Remembering how good it felt to hold Noelle while they slept, Blaze wanted to lie down with her. But he couldn't or he'd fall asleep, too. As though she had read his thoughts, Noelle moved closer and put her head on his thigh. He'd never spent the whole night with any woman until this one entered his life. How he wished they could have a lifetime of nights together.

AT DAWN on March fifth they rode further into the Texas Hill Country. With a word from Noelle around midday, Blaze reined Blue to a stop. Noelle slid off her mare and scampered into the trees. Felice followed. Blaze and Shade were faster and met up again near the horses.

"I wonder what's going on at the Alamo," Blaze said to his brother.

"Me, too. When Jim gave you the knife, did you talk about the mines?"

"He said he was sorry he wasn't able to take us to them,"

Blaze said. "After we find Houston, you need to take the girls home."

"You mean we." Shade tilted his head.

No need to respond. He'd write Shade the letter.

"C'mere, Noelle," Blaze said as the fiery redhead in buckskins emerged like a wood nymph from the forest.

She twined her arms around his neck and stood on tiptoes to kiss him. He groaned, hugged her to him and lifted her off the ground. She wrapped her legs around his waist.

"Ready to ride?" Shade teased.

Blaze ignored him and with Noelle's arms and legs twined around him, he walked away from Blue. Putting his hands to her waist, he lifted the love of his life onto her horse.

"Let's ride," he said.

For two days now, Blaze had watched for the Comanche and Apache Indians Jim had warned him about. Per Carlos, they should also look out for the Lipan Indians and cougars. He'd seen none even though they were deep in their territory.

"I'm beginning to wonder if Sam Houston is really holed up in these hills," Shade said as they trotted over a rock strewn knoll. "Are you sure you're reading the directions right?"

"Yes. The columns in the distance, the sheer drop-off, the creek, it's all there in Jim's directions."

"I'm sure we are exactly where Colonel Bowie meant for us to be," Noelle said supportively.

Blaze ached for Noelle. Hell, he'd fantasized putting her in front of him on Blue, opening his pants, slicing a hole in hers and making love to her right here in the saddle.

"We should be close to Houston's camp," Blaze said to sidetrack himself as he guided the sorrel through the tall pine, leafy maple and reddish brown walnut trees.

"Blaze, look!" Noelle said. "A log cabin up ahead."

Weathered wood, a sagging roof and boarded windows

indicated desertion. Trees surrounded the old place on both sides and in the back. Out front was a small clearing and a gatepost.

"Does Jim mention this cabin?" Shade asked.

"No, but there's an X right about here on the directions that says *resting spot*. Come on," Blaze said and tugged Blue's reins toward the cabin. "It looks like rain and it's time to make camp. This cabin came in handy."

"Well, speaking of directions," Shade said, riding up beside them, "when you were in Gonzales, Jim told me the directions to the lost San Saba Mines were among a slew of maps that came into his possession around the time he met Ursula. I've been thinking maybe we should try to find those maps."

"Let it go, Shade," Blaze said.

"Without those directions," Shade went on, "Jim said he would never have located the mines that French Canadian explorer got rich off of. What was his name?"

"St. Denis," Noelle provided the information.

"Yeah, St. Denis," Shade said, ignoring Blaze's glare. "Jim thinks it's possible his directions were not just a copy of, but the original map belonging to St. Denis." Adventure gleamed in Shade's eyes. "You know Jim and Rezin and St. Denis are the only men who made the mines pay off. If anybody else ever found them, they didn't make it past the Indians to tell about it."

"Drop it!" Blaze barked.

"But Jim said there was gold and silver aplenty."

"Dammit, Shade! Shut up!"

"Hell's bells!" Shade said, "You don't hafta get as pinched as an old church woman thrown into a house fulla naked whores."

Blaze clenched his jaw and didn't reply. As Blue trotted past the gatepost, he noticed carvings. His heart raced. If he had just read what he thought he had, this journey had taken an abrupt new direction. He dismounted and inspected the post.

"Good God Almighty," Blaze said under his breath.

"What is it?" Shade asked, getting off his horse.

Blaze nodded at the names carved into the gatepost; Jim Bowie, 1828, 1832. Rezin Bowie, 1828, 1832.

"Marcel Charbonnez, eighteen twenty-eight," Noelle said.

Blaze swung his head right and barely managed to catch her as she poured like molasses into his arms.

"She has the vipers!" Felice gasped.

CHAPTER 28

"Vapors," Shade said. "She has the vapors."

Blaze held Noelle against his heart. Her head rested on his shoulder and he savored the feel of her curls brushing his cheek. Bailing off her horse, Felice ran toward them.

"In eighteen twenty-eight, Marcel went with Jim and Rezin Bowie and never came back," Felice said, her eyes wide with fear as she glanced left and right. "If this is the cabin where he died, we have traded Santa Anna and dragoons for Indians and cougars. We are in mucho, mucho danger!"

"Felice!" Shade said sharply. "Settle down!"

"We are all going to die!" Felice wailed, crossing herself.

Growling an oath, Shade snatched her off the ground and shook her.

"Shade!" Blaze barked. "She's afraid. Be nice, dammit!"

"I'm sorry," Shade said, gently putting her down with a hug.

Blaze whistled and Blue followed as he carried Noelle to the cabin. On a small porch, to the right of the front door, was a large, flat rock. Blaze read what was carved in stone.

"St. Denis, seventeen fourteen. Noelle will never believe I didn't plan this."

"I don't understand." Shade stared at him.

"Neither do I," Blaze said.

"Hell," Shade said in a grumble. "I told you Jim wouldn't share his secret with us. But why'd he have to hornswoggle us like this?"

The answer hit Blaze like a physical blow.

"To save our lives, Shade."

NOELLE SLOWLY OPENED HER EYES. She was lying on her side on a bedroll spread out on the wooden floor. The room was small and dark except for the fire in the hearth. Shadows flickered on the walls like Indians stalking them. Hissings through cracks between logs of the cabin could be cougars instead of wind. Noelle trembled.

"Blaze?" she asked, as rain pelted the roof and thunder clapped. "Blaze!"

"Yeah," he replied, rolling over and molding her to his chest.

He pulled a blanket over her shoulder and slid his arm around her waist. He kissed the back of her head and slipped his hand under her shirt flattening it to her tummy. She put her hand over his and pulled it to her heart. Then she remembered seeing Marcel's name carved into the gatepost.

"Is this the St. Denis place?" she asked.

"Afraid so, darlin'," Blaze said sleepily. "We're in what was probably the bedroom. Shade and Felice are on the other side of the door in the front room."

"You're too noble a man and too loyal to Jim and everyone at the Alamo to have planned this."

"I fully believed Sam Houston was here in the Texas Hill Country negotiating with the Apaches and Comanches."

"So did I." Turning over, Noelle smiled into Blaze's gray eyes. He held her close and despite the raging storm, cougars, and Indians, Noelle felt safe and secure. "What are we going to do?"

"You're waking me up and there's only one thing I'll wanna do," he whispered.

His animal magnetism sprinkled goosebumps over her skin in anticipation of his wild kisses and caresses.

"Blaze..." her nipples beaded as his hand slid to her breast, "...if you didn't plan on..." he leaned over her and she rolled to her back... "us coming to this cabin..." his lips heated her flesh... "then who did?"

"I could ask you the same," Blaze whispered between kisses.

"Uh...well...I *truly* believed you were going after Sam Houston."

"Now I believe Houston is in Washington-on-the Brazos." Blaze brushed his lips along her neck. "And I think Jim knew it all along."

"Jim Bowie is a wonderful man." Noelle's throat ached with emotion. "I will always be grateful to him."

Blaze rolled on top of her. Though he braced himself on his elbows, the weight of his lower body was exhilarating and that weight included a long thick broomstick pressing against her.

"It's your fault we're in this cabin, Noelle."

"Why?"

"Not that Jim didn't want us to leave, but you put the burr under his saddle to get me outa the Alamo, didn't you?"

"Which backfired the first time because Shade didn't go with you to Gonzales." She realized too late, she'd tipped her hand.

"I thought so."

"You once said you weren't made of steel. Flesh and blood can be killed!"

"How about I warm some of my flesh and blood inside you?"

"No, Blaze." But craving exactly that, flames erupted between her legs and her feminine desires screamed for his male invasion. "I'm not going to get any more involved than

I already am with a man who is probably going to fortune hunt now that we're in San Saba Mine territory."

"How involved are you?" His lusty grin was smug.

Noelle started to purse her lips, but when he pressed his lower body against her hips, her lips parted in a sigh.

"I'm not going to look for the mines, Noelle."

Noelle twined her arms around his neck and pulling him to her for another kiss she slid her tongue along his lips. He rolled off her and butterflies fluttered in her stomach as he unbuttoned her pants. He was going to take her home! He would make love to her tonight and every night along the way.

"You've made me so happy, Blaze."

Tossing the blanket aside, he tugged her pants down and tossed them as well. Recklessness glinted in his eyes and exigency radiated in his body. Though he wasn't saying much urgency sounded in his voice.

"Same here."

"Umm…why aren't you going to look for the mines, seeing as how we're so close and all?"

"No map and not enough time."

Boldly, he stood and shrugged out of his clothing. Naked, in all his male glory he added logs to the fire. Bathed in the fire's red glow was that which he'd often buried so deeply and deliciously inside her.

It…he…all of him was magnificent. He came to her, straddled her thighs and sat her up. She had never before seen his twice-as-thick-as-a-broomstick from this angle. After tugging off her shirt he lowered to his haunches. Molding his hands under her breasts, he stroked her nipples with the pads of his thumbs.

Noelle craved this man's every ravishing kiss and each exploring caress. Her heart pounded as he eased her back on the bedroll and shifted his nakedness on top of her. Nestling his hips between her thighs, his velvety, hard erection brushed her slippery womanhood.

"Promise me we can head to Mississippi tomorrow," Noelle said, spreading her legs wider for him.

"Shh." He parted her slick folds with gentle fingers. "Wrap your pretty legs around me."

"Promise me," she whispered and wrapped her legs around him.

"Mmm," Blaze groaned, sliding all the way into her.

Noelle's body was open to pleasure as her mind closed in fear. She wanted Blaze on her safe terms; no fortune hunting *and* no Alamo. When he didn't promise, she uncurled her legs and squirmed, losing him out of her.

"No!" she said firmly.

Rolling to his back, Blaze flung his arm over his eyes and muttered a curse. Without another word, he tugged on his pants, yanked the blanket over his hips and turned away from her.

"Blaze." Noelle stared at his broad back. "You said you're not fortune hunting, now tell me you're not going back to the Alamo."

"I'm going to sleep." His voice was gruff but after a moment he said quietly, "I love you, Noelle."

Noelle opened her mouth and closed it just as fast. Her admission of love was the only weapon she had against the Mexicans' heavy artillery. Hoping to tell him when it would do the most good, she held on to the carrot.

"Je t'aime." She had just said 'I love you' in French. She sighed and closed her eyes. "Goodnight."

"Bonne nuit, darlin'."

Noelle eyes flew open. Blaze had just said 'goodnight' in French! Did they speak French in Louisiana? Yes, no doubt they did! She suddenly remembered President Jefferson's famous 1803 Louisiana Purchase, of more than eight hundred thousand square miles of land for fifteen million dollars from Napoleonic France.

When she'd said she loved Blaze very much, with 'te quiero muy mucho' back at the Alamo, he hadn't known what she had said then, too. Had he? She rolled to her side and placed her arm around his waist. He took her hand and flattened her palm to his heart. She kissed his shoulder loving this man; body, heart and soul.

"BLAZE!" Noelle whispered near dawn. "Wake up!"

Blaze opened his eyes on March sixth and groaned. He guessed it to be about five or six in the morning. Flames crackled in the hearth, warming the small room. Noelle must have stoked the fire. She was sure stoking his as she sat beside him, wearing only the buckskin shirt.

"Guess what?" she asked excitedly and straddled his hips.

"I *know* what." He bunched the blanket around her hips and covered her bare legs. "You're asking for big trouble, little girl."

"Blaze, we're right on top of it!"

"You're right on top of it and you're gonna get it."

A knock sounded and Shade said through the closed door, "Felice had a nightmare and needs Noelle."

"It's time to get up anyway," Blaze grumbled and lifted Noelle off him. When they were both dressed, he opened the door and they joined Felice and Shade in the front room. "So what did you find, Noelle?"

"The *key*."

CHAPTER 29

"WHAT KEY?" SHADE ASKED.

"To saving your land." Noelle sat on the floor beside Felice and asked, "Are you all right?"

"Si, but I had a bad dream that something happened to Papa."

Noelle patted Felice's hand and felt all eyes on her. But hers followed Blaze as he walked to the cabin's front door, opened it and filled it with muscles. Combing his thick, dark blond hair away from his face with his right hand, he hooked the thumb of his left hand in the waist of his buckskin pants. Blaze Bowie was majestic as any mountain and her love for him just as towering.

"Where do you think the key is?" Blaze asked.

"I don't *think*, I *know*." Noelle smiled at Blaze. "When I added a log to the fire this morning I found a letter to me from Colonel Bowie."

"It must have fallen out of my pocket. Jim said to give you the letter when we got where we were going. I didn't realize he meant here until after you fainted. What did he say?"

"Colonel Bowie said it was Marcel who pushed to go to the mines in eighteen twenty-eight." Noelle showed them the letter and paraphrased, "Colonel Bowie deeply regretted not finding any gold or silver until after Marcel was dead. Though he couldn't change that, Colonel Bowie said he could grant my request to prevent the Mexicans from taking you and Shade from Felice and me."

"Jim *and* Noelle hornswoggled us," Shade said, standing near Blaze.

"Colonel Bowie says in the letter that he wants you to have the treasure to save Bowie land and to go home."

"I didn't know you cared so much about us, Noelle," Shade said with a chuckle.

"Oh, but I do," Noelle said, eyes on Blaze.

Blaze smiled. Noelle's throat ached to say outright that she loved him, wanted to marry him, have his babies, live in Grandmother's mansion, and see Blaze at the head of the dining room table. Determination gritted Noelle's teeth and clenched her fists. She was fighting the Alamo for Blaze and by God, she would win.

"So where are the San Saba Mines?" Shade asked impatiently.

"Colonel Bowie gave me the location of the gold he extracted in eighteen thirty-two from the mines. He said he was saving it for a rainy day."

"Hell yeah!" Shade whooped. "It rained all night. Close enough to a rainy day. Let's go to the mines."

"She said the location of the gold, not the mines," Blaze said.

"Colonel Bowie's letter said the best place to hide something is out in the open." Noelle gave Felice a hug and got up. "Mama used to say a secret well-kept is one kept close," she went to the hearth and ran her hand over the dusty mantle, "to *hearth* and home."

"Felice, come look at the carvings and tell me what you see."

"I see a slab of dirty wood," Shade growled as Felice got up and walked to Noelle.

"I see," Felice blew at the dust on top of the mantel, "carvings of Mexico; men in sombreros, adobe homes, women, children, donkeys, a cactus, and the Mexican flag of eighteen twenty-four!"

"Yes." Noelle nodded. "There used to be a second mantel above this one. It had carvings of ships at sea. The name on the biggest ship was The Pride and that mantel was sold to Jean Lafitte."

Blaze knew where she was headed and went into their room.

"There are two mantels above the hearth in here," he said. "The top one shows a big house, a man, a woman, and three children."

"Are the mantels maps?" Shade asked, moving to the first mantel as Blaze returned.

"No," Blaze answered. "I think Jim added four mantels to the two fireplaces in this cabin. Right, Noelle?"

"Right. Colonel Bowie said in his letter that you'd never find the mines without him. He realized by this late date you wouldn't have time to mine them anyway before the bank forecloses on your land."

"Get back to the location," Shade said.

"This Mexican mantel goes to you, Shade," Noelle said, coming to stand at one end of the hearth, while Shade stood at the other end, with Felice between them. "You told your cousin you came to Texas hoping to find," she looked from Shade to Felice and back to Shade, "a raven-haired beauty like Ursula."

"What the hell?" Shade folded his arms over his chest. "I'm not dragging that hunk of wood all the way back to Louisiana."

"The top mantle you described in our room, Blaze, goes to me because Jim said he thinks you and I should..." Feeling too shy to go on, Noelle hesitated.

"Get married and have a family?"

"Yes."

"What about the third mantel?"

"The mantel underneath mine goes to you, Blaze, because although its carvings are of Texas land... the hills and pine trees reminded Colonel Bowie of Louisiana and Mississippi."

Without another word Blaze returned to the bedroom.

"What are you doing, Blaze?" Shade asked.

"I want to see what's underneath the dust, which I suspect is mud," Blaze said. "Come here, Noelle." She joined him and using his knife he flicked off some of the mud along one corner, revealing an unmistakable color. "Gold." Blaze smiled at Noelle. "Still don't want to drag your mantel home, Shade?"

"Is mine gold, too?" Shade asked and flicked off a layer of mud from his mantel. "Well, I'll be damned." His expression was one of stunned disbelief as the gold glittered in the fire-light. "Why go to so much trouble to make carved mantels and then camouflage them with mud? Why not just bury them?"

"Because in the last line of Colonel Bowie's letter he said to never bury your dreams," Noelle said. A lifetime of love and laughter with Blaze was her dream and she refused to bury that dream at the Alamo.

"These must weigh a ton. Wonder how much they're worth," Shade asked, putting a hand on his mantel.

"They're invaluable, Shade," Noelle replied.

"Yeah, yeah," Shade said. "Sentiment aside, how much do you figure they're worth, Blaze?"

Noelle shook her head and handed Blaze the letter.

"Jim says each mantel's worth at least a hundred thousand."

"One hundred thousand dollars?" Shade repeated incredulously. "Each?" When Blaze nodded, Shade hurried over and hugged his brother. "Our debt is dead with gold leftover!"

"Jim is trying to make things right by you, Noelle," Blaze said. "Where Charbonnez was concerned."

"Jim Bowie owes me nothing," Noelle said. "I'll give you my mantel in exchange for you taking me back to Mississippi."

"I plan to take you home from—"

"Then do it." Noelle cut him off and wrapped her hand around his wrist. "You came to Texas seeking a fortune to save your land. You got what you came for. Colonel Bowie doesn't expect us back. Carlos doesn't expect us back. Let's leave for Natchez."

Blaze closed his eyes, lowered his head and a muscle flexed in his jaw. Shade glanced at Noelle and shrugged as Felice crossed herself. Noelle held her breath.

"We'll leave from the Alamo," Blaze said, looking directly at Noelle.

Shade grabbed up his bedroll.

"Like Noelle said, we got what we came for. I'm going to Galveston Island. If I can find the Pirate of the Gulf, maybe he'll buy my mantel, too. I'd be rid of the damn thing, my pockets would be full and I'd be almost halfway home. The girls can come with me."

"You know pirates still inhabit that island," Blaze said, squaring off with him. "A man alone with two women and a fortune in gold is asking for a saber in his gut."

"Dammit!" Scowling, Shade threw down his bedroll and kicked it. He paced across the room to the door, turned and said, "The night Buzzard visited me in the Alamo, he swore he could get us past the pirates and lead us straight to Lafitte's door. Let's go get him."

"Shade!" Noelle said. "If Blaze goes back to Bexar, it will be to the Alamo, not to get Buzzard."

"When we get there," Shade stalked to Blaze, clamped a hand on his shoulder, "you're not stepping foot inside the Alamo."

"The hell I'm not." Blaze knocked his hand off. "But you're damn sure not looking up Buzzard."

Shade's lip lifted and he snarled, "The hell I'm not."

CHAPTER 30

"LET'S VOTE," NOELLE SAID, STEPPING BETWEEN THE brothers. "I say Natchez by way of," she'd gamble to entice Shade into voting with her, "Galveston Island." She nodded with a smile at Shade.

"Women can't vote," Shade replied. "I'm going to Bexar to get Buzzard and then to the island."

"I vote for Bexar," Felice said.

"Bexar. It's settled," Blaze said.

"Compromise with me." Outvoted, Noelle was at her wit's end. "I have one more idea."

"What now?" Shade rolled his eyes.

"Actually this is your idea, Blaze." Noelle took his right hand in both of hers. "Remember the morning we woke up at the eighteen-pounder and I was concerned about people knowing I'd...umm—"

"Spent the night with me. What about it?"

"You said people would figure I was just then coming to welcome you home from Gonzales."

"So?" Shade muttered. "What's that got to do—"

"Yeah," Blaze said interrupting him. "We'll let the Mexicans think we're just coming home after being gone for a few weeks."

"Most of the soldiers and volunteers rode in from the east, like you and Colonel Crockett."

"But we'll be riding in from the northwest." Blaze rubbed his forehead.

"Yes," Noelle said, hope stirring. "We'll act surprised that Santa Anna took over the town while we were gone. We can find out what's going on at the garrison. You won't have to go inside, Blaze."

"We'll head back to Bexar today."

"What about the mantels?" Shade asked.

"We've got hatchets and knives with us," Blaze said. "We'll make three travois and drag the mantels out of here. In Bexar, we'll hide them at the Herrera house so the Mexicans don't steal them."

"It isn't agreed we're starting back today until we vote on it," Noelle said, since Blaze had let Felice's vote stand. "I vote we build the three travois, rest, eat, sleep, and go tomorrow."

"Buzzard's not going anywhere," Shade said, not complaining about who could vote this time. "I vote we go tomorrow, too."

"I vote we go today as soon as the travois are done." Blaze frowned.

"I am worried about Papa," Felice said and looked at Noelle. "But I will vote with Noelle and Shade."

Glaring at them, Blaze grumbled, "All right. Tomorrow."

"Work slowly," Noelle said, an hour later, picking up a sapling a few yards away from the front porch. She didn't want to take any chance of the work being completed too soon, lest Blaze would want to leave early. Every day that she kept Blaze out of the Alamo was a day he wouldn't be killed. "They can't lash the logs together without the strips we'll make from these saplings."

Suddenly she heard a noise. Looking around, she saw nothing but trees, brush, boulders, and grass.

"What's wrong?" Felice asked.

"Did you hear something?"

"Probably just Shade or Blaze bringing another tree around front," Felice answered.

Blaze and Shade had waded into the forest behind the cabin where sturdier trees grew. They had dragged several around front and wondered at how little Noelle and Felice had accomplished. Noelle had grinned sheepishly. Blaze and Shade had smothered chuckles and left again.

"I wish Shade paid notice to me the way Blaze does to you," Felice said, peeling a sapling.

"At least Shade doesn't plan on going back in the Alamo," Noelle said, determined Blaze would never again step inside of the garrison.

"I will say no to Shade like I heard you say to Blaze last night. That will make him want me more."

"To be fair, my *no* to Blaze wasn't no in the way you think."

Then she heard the noise again and froze. Their horses whinnied this time.

"Noelle!" Felice gasped, having heard it, too.

"Someone's in those rocks," Noelle said and used the sapling in her hand to point.

The noise had come from the mass of boulders at the base of a steep, rocky hill. Noelle recognized the sound and cautiously made her way toward them.

"Come back. Por favor, Noelle!"

Rounding the boulders, Noelle spied wisps of black hair and someone backing further into a crevice. Noelle stepped between the rocks and a tear stained face tilted up at her.

"Don't be afraid," Noelle said softly.

"An Indian!" Felice gasped behind her.

"She's only three or four years old," Noelle said, kneeling down. "You must be lost."

Clad in a deerskin dress, leggings and moccasins, the little girl stared at the Bowie knife in Noelle's hand. Noelle quickly hid it behind her back as Felice stayed in the clearing about a dozen feet away.

"Noelle, her people must be close by."

A piercing squall split the air as a tawny brown blur leapt from an overhang. It glided in an arc above Noelle and landed in the middle of the clearing just feet from Felice.

A full grown, growling cougar.

Noelle willed Felice not to move, but she stumbled backward inciting the mighty cat's predatory instincts. It charged, lashed out and clawed Felice's right thigh. Felice screamed and turned to run as claws caught the back of her other leg.

To Noelle's horror, Felice fell directly in front of the cougar. Noelle instantly hurled Blaze's knife in hopes of drawing the animal's attention away from Felice. The knife gouged the animal's left flank before slicing into the ground. The huge cougar swung its head, cold eyes burrowing into Noelle.

Noelle slowly backed the small girl further into the crevice and stood in front of her. Realizing she was still clutching the sapling, Noelle slapped at the air as the cougar growled.

"Run!" Noelle called out to Felice.

Felice got up and limped toward the cabin. The cougar's head lowered, eyes focused, ears laid back, it slowly moved toward Noelle, its dagger-like teeth bared, as it drew itself into a pouncing position.

"Blaze!" Noelle would die with his name on her lips.

But a rifle blast ripped the air and a musket ball slammed into the cougar's head. The shot lifted the cougar into the air and dropped it dead against a boulder. Rifle in hand, Blaze raced forward. Shade, with his knife and hatchet, was at his side. Noelle stared at the fallen animal as the Indian girl grabbed her free hand. She dropped the sapling and scooped up the trembling child.

"Good shot, Blaze," Shade said.

"Where did the girl come from, Noelle?" Blaze asked.

"I found her hiding between the boulders." Noelle smiled at the child in her arms. "Somehow she's gotten lost from her folks."

Felice's eyes suddenly rolled up in her head and she collapsed. Noelle stood the Indian girl to the ground and hurried to Felice's side.

"What happened?" Shade asked. "Did Felice go and get the *vipers* on us?"

"I'd faint, too, if a cougar clawed me," Noelle said, as blood began soaking through Felice's britches.

"Shade, pull up Felice's pant legs," Blaze said.

Shade did so and Noelle sucked in her breath, gently turning Felice's legs to get a better look. Four very deep and wide claw marks nearly circled Felice's right and left thighs.

"Damn, that looks bad," Shade said.

Noelle quickly removed Blaze's bandana from around her neck and tried to staunch the blood flow.

"Shade, use your bandana for a tourniquet on her left leg," Blaze said.

"Yeah. Do the same to her right leg, Noelle, or she'll bleed to death," Shade said.

Noelle did so and turned to check on the Indian child. She was hurrying toward them with Blaze's knife. Proudly, she handed it to Noelle.

"Thank you," Noelle said as the girl sat down beside Felice. Noelle slipped the knife into the scabbard Blaze had given her. Then she pulled the child onto her lap and rocked her until her eyes closed. "We'll find your people."

"Don't panic," Blaze said.

"Hell's bells," Shade breathed and shot to his feet.

Two Indian men astride Mustangs decorated with war paint loomed just yards away. Dressed in fringed buckskin shirts, leggings and breechcloths, the men wore their hair in long braids. Their hands held hatchets, bows and arrows were slung to their sides. The scowls on their faces were aimed at Noelle and the child in her lap. "Is this your child?" Noelle asked.

"They fit the description Jim gave me of the Comanches," Blaze said. "According to Jim they're an offshoot of the Wyoming Shoshoni Indians. They speak the Shoshoni language, not English."

"I don't care what they speak," Shade said. "All I care about is that there are about ten thousand of 'em and the two before us look madder than a couple o'peeled rattlers."

Noelle had heard that Comanches were so ruthless they had driven the fierce Apaches off the plains. Could the two Comanches before her have killed Marcel? Would they kill today?

"Don't make any sudden moves," Blaze said firmly.

"To hell with that." Shade gripped his Bowie knife tightly. "Let's kill the bastards before they lift our hair."

CHAPTER 31

"No," Blaze said. "Do nothing unless you want to wear a hatchet hat to your funeral, Shade." He glanced at Noelle and an image of her cradling a blond or auburn-haired baby to her heart flashed in his mind's eye.

With the child in her arms, Noelle stood up, smiled and took a step toward the Indians. They fingered their hatchets as they spoke to each other.

"I guess she got lost," Noelle said to them.

A teary-eyed Indian clad in a knee length buckskin dress and leggings dashed from behind a boulder. Blaze walked Noelle forward. Fear and mistrust creased the Indian woman's brow, while gratitude and relief shone in her dark eyes. The woman took the little girl from Noelle and the child hugged her mother. The woman slowly rejoined the men still on horseback as one grabbed his bow and arrow and waved them in a threatening manner.

"Get ready for war," Shade said, squaring up alongside Blaze.

Blaze knew that was good advice. A wise man never predetermined the outcome of a confrontation. He shoved Noelle behind him.

Blaze said, "The Indian with the two feathers in his hair has a Bowie knife tied at his waist."

The knife was almost identical to the one Jim had given Blaze. When he'd said Bowie it had set off a furious discussion between the Indian men.

"Bowie?" the man with two feathers asked, pointing at the knife at Blaze's waist.

"Bowie." Blaze laid his left hand to his chest.

"Jim Bowie." Brandishing his own Bowie knife, the Indian with two feathers said, "El Endiablado."

The Indian slashed the knife through the air in exactly the same way Blaze remembered Jim doing when he had given Blaze and Shade the knives Rezin had made.

"El Endiablado sounds Spanish," Blaze realized. "Do you know what it means, Noelle?"

Noelle said, "It means devilish, wild, furious. Along with the knife-slashing, he must be saying that Colonel Bowie was a wild and furious fighting devil."

"Ask 'em how they got a Bowie knife," Shade said with a growl. "They probably killed Charbonnez for it."

Blaze clenched his jaw.

"Marcel's greed and lust for treasure seeking is what killed him, Shade," Noelle said.

"Noelle, ask them if they speak Spanish," Blaze said.

"Habla usted español?" she asked and placed a hand to her chest. "Me llamo Noelle."

The Indians stared as if deciding whether to let them live or not. The shorter of the two began to rant. The one with two feathers didn't speak. The first one waved his weapons and hollered until his companion held up his hand.

"The short one's got more wind than a bull eatin' green corn," Shade said.

"Yeah, Crockett would say he's a hotblood." Blaze cocked a brow at Shade who snorted.

Having been awakened by the Comanche's yelling, the child stirred in her mother's arms. She wiggled out of her mother's embrace and ran to the crevice where she'd hidden from the cougar. Pointing to Noelle, then Felice, the little girl growled and clawed the air. The Indians' frowns softened as the child chattered while indicating cat ears and a long tail. Gesturing to Blaze and then the cougar, she made a rifle noise. Then she pointed to Noelle, hugged herself and smiled.

The Indian with two feathers dismounted and stared at them as if an unspoken truce had taken place.

"Gato?" the Indian asked and pointed at Felice.

"Gato...cat. Yes, the cougar clawed her," Noelle said. "We have no medicine. No medicina."

He untied one of several pouches at his waist, stepped forward and handed it to Noelle.

"I guess you know you're holding a buffalo's balls," Shade said with a snicker.

"I guess you know yours are still intact, thanks to Noelle saving this child's life," Blaze said.

"Medicina," the Indian with two feathers said.

"Muchas gracias," Blaze replied.

Kneeling beside Felice, Noelle opened the pouch. Stirring now, Felice was pale from pain and fright. Noelle dipped her fingers into the pouch and sprinkled some of its contents over Felice's wounds.

Noelle then offered the return of the pouch but the Indian shook his head. Noelle could keep the medicine. Looking at Blaze, he motioned to the cougar.

"Si." Blaze swung his hand toward the prize.

"They didn't even thank us for saving their kid's life," Shade said.

"This medicine is their thanks," Noelle replied.

"Not to mention you faced two Comanche warriors and lived to talk about it," Blaze said. "Just think of the 'hair-lifting' story you'll have to tell your grandchildren someday." Glancing at Felice, he asked, "How are you?"

"I'm feeling poorly," Felice said. "Could you carry me back to the cabin, Blaze?"

Blaze cocked a brow at Shade and picked Felice up. Shooing Noelle ahead of him, Blaze carted Felice into the cabin. After Noelle smoothed out Felice's bedroll, Blaze placed her on the blanket and pried her clinging arms from around his neck. Noelle found a clean cloth and soaked it with water from a canteen. Felice winced as Noelle gently swiped away the blood on her legs, carefully leaving the medicine in place.

"It's painful, Blaze," Felice whimpered.

"I'm going to work on the travois," Shade said, stomping out of the cabin.

Blaze followed him outside.

As Shade began lashing logs together, the Indians tethered three Mustangs to saplings. Pointing to the travois Shade was working on, one Indian picked up some of the felled trees and with gestures and motions, began showing Shade how to make the travois stronger and sturdier. The parents of the girl picked up several other branches and showed Blaze the same techniques. When the Indians continued working on the second travois, Blaze started building the third one. The child gathered stripped saplings and branches coming forward time and again, as Blaze's helper, placing the materials at his feet.

They all worked tirelessly and only when all three travois were completed, did the Indian with two feathers lead one of the Mustangs toward the cougar. Blaze called to Shade and together they hoisted the heavy cougar onto the Indian's horse.

"Muchas gracias," Blaze said, indicating the three travois.

The Indian with two feathers gestured to the child and said, "Muchas gracias."

Placing his hand on his Bowie knife, the Indian with two feathers looked at Blaze and paused. Blaze then placed his hand on his knife. The Indian nodded once, they mounted their horses and quietly vanished.

"Aren't you worried about Felice?" Blaze asked Shade after a moment. "I think she might be taking a fever."

"Yeah, to you," Shade replied.

"I don't know what's wrong between the two of you, but I'm not going to be part of it."

"Well, thanks for nothing, big brother."

"This is the same thing that happened with Lucy Ray. She loved you and when you took her for granted she tried to make you jealous by coming to me. If you care about Felice, and I think you do, don't let history repeat itself or you'll lose her, Shade."

"What am I supposed to do?" he asked, fear in his eyes.

"Prove to her that she can count on you. Not me," Blaze said. Hardly believing Shade's concern, he smiled. "For now, let's rest tonight and then get Felice back to Bexar. The Indians' medicine will help, but she'll need a poultice if her wounds fester up."

Giving away no more of his emotions, Shade agreed. Blaze clapped him on the shoulder and they pulled the travois to the side of the cabin. Dusting dirt and twigs off his clothing, Blaze headed back inside. Shade followed and squatted beside Felice and Noelle.

"Felice didn't want me to leave her, but I watched the Indians helping you build the travois," Noelle said. "I saw the one with two feathers touch his Bowie knife. What do you think all of this was about, Blaze?"

"Jim said he and Rezin and some men held out for two weeks against the Comanches in this very cabin when Charbonnez was killed. Because of that, I think the Comanches grudgingly respect El Endiablado." Blaze shrugged. "We can ask Jim when we get back. They treated us fairly today and it didn't hurt that our name is Bowie."

"We could have bested 'em, Blaze."

"Yeah. But I wouldn't want the other ten thousand swooping down on us tonight, would you?"

"No." Shade frowned. "That would be worse than the ten to one odds we left back at the Alamo."

"Let's gather some firewood," Blaze said, not wanting to discuss the Alamo in front of Noelle.

CHAPTER 32

"Speaking of the Alamo, how was Noelle that first time at the eighteen-pounder?" Shade asked once they were outside.

"Beyond words."

It took a moment for that answer to soak in.

"Which means you aren't going to tell me a damn thing."

Blaze chuckled. He needed Noelle and badly. He craved the kiss of her supple lips on his and his palms itched to touch her soft breasts. A constant ache burned in his loins at the yearning to make his body one with hers.

At least one more time.

"Come on, let's get the firewood, eat and rest," Blaze said.

"Wait." Shade put a hand on his shoulder. "I'm taking Felice to a doctor when we get to Bexar. When you get Noelle there, will you give her the heel of your boot on your way into the Alamo? What happens to her if you get killed?"

"It's different with Noelle and me."

"Different how?" Shade's eyes narrowed as his hands went to his hips. "I know you love her."

"I do love Noelle," Blaze said to his brother for the first time. "And you love Felice but it's scaring you."

"It'll be a cold day in hell before I'm afraid of a woman," Shade replied.

"You're scared because love can lead to marriage." Blaze stabbed a finger in Shade's chest. "If you throw Felice away, don't complain to me when the next cantina whore doesn't squeeze your heart and poker the way your *exotic beauty with long raven hair* does."

"You won't be there to complain to, if you're dead, Blaze." Shade shot him a sharp glare and with brotherly insight said, "I told you once Noelle would belong to the man who trimmed her wick. Don't you know she gave to you what she could only give to one man because she loves you, too? Hell, if I can see it you should be able to."

"Stop." Blaze held up his hand and Shade shrugged. If Noelle loved him, why hadn't she said so? In English. Maybe because she didn't and that hurt worse than he wanted to admit. "I told you it's different with us."

ON THE MORNING of March seventh, Noelle mounted her horse and, pulling her mantel secured to the travois, followed Blaze. Leaving the past in the past, she didn't look back. Squaring her shoulders she focused on the present, with an eye toward spending her future with the love of her life.

Though she had feared having to put distance between herself and Blaze if he planned to treasure seek, that hadn't been necessary. In truth, she suspected she could not have done it anyway. Now, for reasons she couldn't fathom Blaze seemed to have erected a wall of some sort between them.

Noelle's mind wandered to the previous night. Blaze slept with her before a crackling fire, but he'd not made love to her. After he had stretched out on his bedroll, she'd straddled his lap and felt his long hard arousal, but he'd kept his pants buttoned. He told her no jiggling, no wiggling, just sleep. Lifting her off him and rolling to his side, she figured he was just exhausted and she finally fell asleep.

Noelle understood Blaze's determination to return to Jim and the garrison. Yet, empathizing with him and allowing him to go back into the Alamo to die were two different issues. Blaze hadn't let the cougar or the Comanches kill her and she did not intend to let Santa Anna kill him.

When Blaze had helped her into the saddle at dawn, she'd wished she were riding behind him as she had when they'd left the Alamo. She craved having him between her legs. She was so in love with him, she ached. She didn't like this gulf between them and wondered again why he hadn't made love to her. Had his feelings toward her changed now that he'd had her? Maybe so. Her shoulders drooped.

Around noon, when they stopped to water the horses at a stream, Blaze helped her dismount and she hoped he'd kiss her. But instead, he turned and led their horses to a creek. His brief touch had shot heat throughout her body, kindling the smoldering fire between her legs. She imagined his naked chest molded to bare breasts and his hard, velvety manhood pressed between her moist folds. Sparkling ecstasy would follow. She hoped they would make camp early because she needed this gorgeous man badly.

Felice called out to her.

Noelle pulled the Comanches' medicine out of her saddlebag and hurried to where Shade was helping Felice sit down under a pine tree. Felice didn't look well. Noelle dipped her fingers into the bag and sprinkled medicine on her festering wounds. On or off the horse, Felice had trouble finding a comfortable sitting position. Blaze and Shade talked about making a fourth travois for Felice. But Felice didn't want that so after a short rest and something to eat, they traveled again until dusk.

"There's a good place to make camp," Blaze said.

He reined in Blue beside a copse of cypress trees and helped Shade ease an ever worsening Felice down from her horse. Noelle hurried to roll out a blanket on a soft patch of spring grass.

"We'll make a campfire and this will be a cozy bed," Noelle said to Felice.

"Come on, Noelle," Blaze said after unsaddling Blue and Noelle's horse. "Shade can stay with Felice while we gather the firewood."

The twilight sky silhouetted Blaze's dark blond head and the green forest framed his buckskin-clad body. When he extended his hand, Noelle grasped it. She didn't want to see a day where Blaze wouldn't be there to hold out his hand to her. Being with him, she felt safe and happy. Then she trembled, terrified that it was only temporary. Everything had to be all right. She would make it be all right. But how?

Blaze led the way through the woods, trailing her behind him until he suddenly gave her a tug and pressed her against a cypress tree.

"Who do you belong to, Noelle?"

"You, Blaze. Why?"

Blaze's lips lowered to hers and opened in a wild kiss. She twined her arms around his neck and hugged him tightly. Sliding his hands under her buckskin shirt, his palms cushioned her breasts. She arched against him and moaned. His tongue played with hers and she buried her fingers in his thick hair.

"Wanna learn to make love bayou-style?"

"I don't care if we make love in your saddle. I need you."

"Don't think I haven't pictured putting you in front of me on Blue and making love to you in the saddle," Blaze said with a low, masculine chuckle. "But there're 'gators in the bayou, so this is the opposite of sitting."

"Teach me bayou-style."

He stepped closer and his lower body undulated against hers, his front as hard as the wood at her back. She wanted his rigid flesh warming her, rocking her against the tree and pulsing deep within her. Seeming to read her thoughts, Blaze leaned back giving her room. Sliding her fingers to the buttons on his buckskin pants, Noelle undid them. His gray eyes smoldered with approval and his cocky grin made her yearn to be one with him.

"Drop your drawers, darlin'."

Noelle fumbled with the sash Blaze had given her to hold up her buckskin pants. As the knot tightened, he pulled the sash up letting her britches and drawers drop. She tugged her feet out of the clothing and stood half-naked before the magnificent and experienced man. He slid his hands under her arms and lifted her off the ground.

"Big, bad Blaze...what now?"

"Well, little girl," he grinned and her heart raced, "wrap your legs around my waist like you always do."

Noelle locked her toes at the small of his back and wound her arms around his neck. His large hands flattened to her naked buttocks and he opened his mouth over hers. She realized a spring of desire had dampened her when his strong fingers opened the folds of her womanhood. He knew she was ready for him, too, and touched the hardened tip of his arousal to her warmth. Spreading his booted feet, he gently leaned her back against the tree. As he slowly slid into her bayou-style Noelle squeezed the sensual frontiersman with internal muscles.

"Blaze, let's make a baby," she whispered.

"Noelle," Blaze said and paused. "I think," he half groaned and half chuckled, "I think that's the first time a woman's ever shocked me."

Noelle had shocked herself. She was fighting the Alamo with all the ammunition she had within her feminine power. She tightened her arms and legs and pushed down on his masculinity, wanting all of him inside her. Gripping her buttocks, his blond head lowered and his breath caressed her neck. When he pulled almost out she arched away from him. Yes, this is what she wanted forever and ever with Blaze. He rocked her and she met his every thrust. Tingles built, teasing her, beckoning her, making her crave another and yet another deep plunge.

"Blaze, I love... I love bayou-style."

"Are you mine, Noelle?"

"All yours." Noelle tightened her arms and legs, pushing against him and arching away to push again. Sweet ecstasy

244 | LYNN ELDRIDGE

exploded between her legs, making her moan and shiver with pleasure.

"Noelle, I love you."

Blaze's body left hers a split second before his deep groan of satisfaction sounded against her ear.

After a moment, she asked quietly, "Then why did you pull out?"

"Because I don't want you to have to explain an illegitimate baby to your grandmother," he said. "Or raise my child without me."

"The baby doesn't have to be illegitimate," she said. "Nor do I intend to raise your child without you."

"We can't take any more chances." With that Blaze unlocked her legs and stood her to the ground.

All we've done since we met is take chances." Noelle put her hands to his handsome face. "Why stop now?"

"Because I'm just too damn noble," he said and buttoned his pants.

He winked and grinned, the tension snapped and Noelle laughed and hugged the incredible man.

"If I'd had you in the saddle, you couldn't have thrown me so easily."

"This cold sweat should tell you it wasn't easy," Blaze said and swiped his brow.

"I want the noble horse to look the other way while the aroused 'gator makes a baby with me."

"Behave or else."

"You can spank me, but I'm not going to behave."

Blaze cocked a brow and pointed at her discarded buckskin britches. He snapped his fingers and walked away. Noelle snatched up her clothes as Blaze gathered firewood. They headed back to camp arms full.

"It's about time," Shade said and sitting next to Felice, he lifted a large rabbit by its ears. "Supper."

Blaze built a fire as Shade skinned their meal. The roasted meat was delicious. When night descended, Blaze took the first watch. Noelle sat up with him and mingled questions about plans for his land with the fact he had the key to make it happen. He had little to say. With a sigh, Noelle pulled her legs to her chest, rested her cheek on her knees and closed her eyes for a moment.

"RISE 'N SHINE," Shade said around a yawn on March eighth.

Noelle awoke to a pink dawn lying in Blaze's arms. Standing at the end of his bedroll, Shade stretched and tapped Blaze's foot with the toe of his boot. Blaze's embrace around Noelle briefly tightened and then he rolled away from her. Noelle rose and checked on Felice while Blaze and Shade saddled the horses.

Back on the trail, Noelle rode beside Felice encouraging her and distracting her as best she could. All the while, Noelle kept thinking if she could just get Blaze home she was sure Grandmother would give them her blessing. She would reestablish her relationship with her grandmother and fulfill her promise to Mama. Happiness was literally within her grasp *if she could just get Blaze home. Alive.*

"Are you and Felice holding up all right?" Blaze asked, coming alongside Noelle.

"I am, but I'm worried."

"What's worrying you most? Felice, Carlos, or Mistletoe?"

"You."

Blaze said nothing. Each mile brought them closer to the Alamo. With every breath, Noelle lost confidence that she was going to win her battle for Blaze.

"I'm burning up," Felice suddenly whimpered, her head hanging and her limbs dangling.

"I've got an oven on my hands," Shade said. "It's been a long day of riding. Let's camp here for tonight."

"Shade, on the night we rode out, I remember cresting a hill that overlooked Bexar. I want to reach that hill in daylight, so we can take a look from a safe distance," Blaze said. "With luck, we can get Felice and the mantels to the Herrera house tonight."

Felice said in a raspy whisper, "Home. I want to see Papa."

So they rode without stopping. As planned, they entered dangerous enemy territory from the northwest. Nearing the hill Blaze had mentioned Noelle bowed her head and squeezed back tears. She had used every weapon she had against the Alamo, except the three little words she prayed would pack the wallop of the eighteen-pounder.

"Blaze, I lo—"

"What the hell?" Shade said, interrupting her.

Noelle opened her eyes. The mesquite covered prairie which surrounded the mission was splattered red with blood. There were no soldiers. No volunteers. The garrison was empty, the posts unmanned. Near the mission was a huge, charred area of ground. Above that still smoking, blackened prairie, an eerie sky was dark with hundreds of circling, swooping vultures.

"The Alamo has fallen," Blaze said.

CHAPTER 33

"I GOT THIRTY-TWO BRAVE VOLUNTEERS KILLED," BLAZE SAID, staring in stunned disbelief at the Alamo.

"No, you tried to save the hundred and fifty-six other men," Shade said. "Smith and Sutherland would have brought those volunteers back with or without you."

"I left Jim, Crockett, Travis, and everybody to die."

"Maybe they aren't dead."

"Colonel Fannin may have arrived and saved the Alamo," Noelle said.

"If that was so, the garrison would be celebrating the victory with hundreds of volunteers and troops." Blaze shook his head. "I failed them."

"You didn't fail them any more than Felice and I failed Carlos," Noelle said. "We all believed we were going after Sam Houston."

"What does that smoke mean?" Shade muttered.

"The way the vultures are circling," Blaze flinched and continued, "I'd say it's a funeral pyre."

"Yeah, well, I don't want any part of this," Shade said. "Dragoons could swarm over us any second. Let's get the hell outa San Antonio while the gettin's good."

"I'm not leaving until I find out what happened," Blaze replied.

"I think we should leave now," Noelle said.

"If Jim is dead," Blaze said looking at Noelle, "I'm going to make sure he didn't die in vain."

"What do you mean you're going to make sure he didn't die in vain?" Shade asked.

"I don't know, yet," Blaze said in a ragged voice he hardly recognized as his own. Satisfied that Noelle and Felice looked as much like boys as they were going to, he said, "Felice needs medical help as soon as possible and we need to get it for her."

"Right," Shade replied. "Let's get her to the Herrera house and find a doctor."

Heading south, they could see the burned remains of La Villita on the horizon. They kept their distance and watered the horses in the San Antonio River. The precarious masquerade was upon them as they headed straight toward San Antonio de Bexar.

"If we meet up with anybody, you girls keep quiet," Blaze said.

"Blaze, did you come face-to-face with Santa Anna or his officers when you and Shade spied on them with Cousin Herrera?" Noelle asked.

"Don't worry about it."

"You did." Noelle reached out and touched his arm.

"Dammit, Noelle, act like a boy!" Blaze yanked his hand away. "Ride like a young man. Put that hand on your thigh and sit tall in the saddle."

"Blaze, she's afraid," Shade said. "Be nice, dammit."

"I'm sorry, Noelle."

Blaze gritted his teeth to keep from pulling her onto the saddle with him. Spotting some huts in the distance took Blaze's mind off Noelle. Another quarter mile and he was able to make out the Herrera jacal.

"Everything looks peaceful," Shade said.

"So does a 'gator, 'til you wake him up," Blaze replied.

Another hundred feet and Blaze exchanged glances with Shade as a musket-toting dragoon emerged from the

Herrera place. Clad in dirty, blood stained fatigues the soldier yelled for a second armed man who came out of the house and glared at them.

"Let's turn back," Shade said.

"Hell no, let's find out why they're here."

Before anyone could stop her a glassy-eyed Felice pulled her coonskin cap off. Her long black hair tumbled down her back.

"Parada!" The first dragoon took a stance and aimed his musket.

"Parade?" Shade asked. "What's that mean?"

"Stop," Felice said.

These Mexican dragoons would rape one of their own women as easily they would an Anglo woman.

"Howdy. We've been gone up north a spell," Blaze said in a happy-go-lucky manner. "What's going on around here?"

The first dragoon waved a third, unarmed man out of the house and they talked in Spanish. Noelle quietly whispered that the first man said the idiot Americans had arrived from the northwest. The second soldier wondered what to do with them and the third man asked what was wrong with the girl. Blaze knew what to say.

"We need medicina."

"I am medico...doctor," the third man said in stilted English and came forward. "Muchacha is Mexican?"

"Si," Shade said.

"She is wife to you?" the doctor asked Shade.

"Wife? No, she's only twelve years old. She's our half-sister," he replied.

"You are Texians?"

"Si," Blaze said, as an Anglo living in Texas would.

The doctor nodded. "You are loyal to Mexico or Texas?"

"Mexico," Blaze and Shade lied together.

"We were chopping wood when she tangled with a cougar." Blaze jerked his thumb toward the travois where chopped wood hid mud covered gold.

"Is this house some kind of hospital?" Shade asked.

"Hospital," the doctor repeated with a nod. "Si."

One of the dragoons approached Noelle's travois and studied the camouflaging firewood.

"Do you have medicina?" Blaze asked.

The doctor pulled up Felice's right pant leg and untied the yellow bandana. He gently patted her knee and handed the bandana to Noelle. Noelle took it and quickly folded her arms over her breasts.

"Si," the doctor said. "Tengo la medicina."

The doctor turned to the two dragoons, spoke and they dragged Felice off her horse. Shade cast a helpless look at Blaze and he gave Shade an almost imperceptible shake of his head. One dragoon pulled back the animal skin over the door and the other dragoon carried Felice inside. As she vanished a tick caught the corner of Shade's eye and a muscle worked in his jaw. Noelle bit the insides of her cheeks.

"One week," the doctor announced.

"I thought we'd wait for her," Shade said.

"El President comes for medicina." The doctor shrugged. "Gato shot because he say it American rebel. Comprendes?"

Noelle remained stoic as the doctor went inside, leaving them alone.

"The doctor just warned us if Santa Anna comes for his opium he will likely take exception to us being Anglos," Blaze said.

"Mama said it was dangerous to be an Anglo here," Noelle said softly.

"Yeah," Blaze said. "If we don't leave now, the dragoons will say we're American rebels, too."

"What will happen to Felice?" Shade asked.

"Nothing if the doctor has his way," Blaze said, looking toward town. "Let's ride to Carlos' shop. Maybe we can settle in there and make some plans."

Noelle didn't like leaving Felice, but they had no choice. She wanted to be on Blue with Blaze so she could comfort herself by hugging his muscular body. Meandering Mexican dragoons made that impossible. Blaze tipped his hat to them as Shade cursed them under his breath.

Carlos' shop was empty. Darkness had fallen as Blaze and Shade unsaddled the horses and left them to graze on wild grasses. They unhitched the travois and dragged them inside where the brothers dropped their saddles, bedrolls and canteens. The little shop was a welcome and familiar haven amidst the stench of defeat and death.

"Let's go to the cantina, Blaze," Shade said.

"Yeah." Blaze nodded. "Maybe Herrera or Captain Sequin will be there."

"No! The cantina may be full of dragoons," Noelle said.

"I have to find out about the Alamo," Blaze replied. "We can see the shop from the cantina. Stay inside with the door locked until we get back."

Seeing the pain in his gray eyes and hearing the strain in his deep voice, Noelle nodded. Blaze turned on his heel and left with Shade. Noelle slumped onto the siesta bench and heard a movement on the floor. She got on her knees and coaxed her cat out from under the workbench. She scooped up the fluffy calico and nuzzled her.

"Mistletoe, I thought it was you they shot." She fingered a thin strip of leather tied in a bow around the cat's neck. It was surely a message from Carlos. "How can I tie Blaze to me?"

UPON ENTERING THE CANTINA, full of dragoons, Blaze and Shade were waved to a table by the Herreras' cousin. Smiling and nodding their way past the enemy they sat down with Herrera. He then introduced Mayor Francisco Ruiz.

Suddenly, Maria spotted Blaze and grinned. He gave her a warning look. Hell, he had forgotten she might be here and squeal out the name Bowie. As she served him Mexican beer, he suffered her kiss to his cheek. Rosa hurried to the table with a beer for Shade and kissed him full on the mouth. These women could turn on them in a heartbeat, but for the moment Raoul Buzzard waved the cantina whores to his table.

God, how Blaze wanted out of this town as he looked through the window at the little cobbler shop. He listened as Mayor Ruiz told of being put on house arrest by Santa Anna during the thirteen day siege at the Alamo.

"How did the Alamo fall?" Blaze quietly asked, keeping a bland expression.

Mayor Ruiz leaned in and said, "Screaming 'Viva la Republica and Viva Santa Anna', the Mexican army stormed the Alamo about five thirty in the morning on the sixth of March."

Blaze glanced at Shade. That had been the same morning and around the same time Felice had awakened from her nightmare about Carlos. Speaking softly and careful to smile now and then, Ruiz described the scene.

"Two hundred yards from the Alamo, General Cos jumped out of the grass and yelled, 'Arriba!'. Close to two thousand dragoons surged forward, some with ladders, and scaled the walls of the garrison."

Shade and Herrera clinked their cerveza tankards as if celebrating the Mexican victory.

"Then what?" Blaze felt eyes on him and it took an iron will to smile and raise his tankard.

"Travis was ready with a double-barreled shotgun." Herrera a spy, accustomed to maintaining his composure under pressure, said casually, "From the top of the north wall battery, Travis yelled he was going to give the Mexicans hell. He discharged both barrels of his shotgun into the Mexican troops. He turned to reload and took a single lead ball in his forehead. He rolled down the ramp and died in a sitting position."

"Travis was the same age as I am," Shade said.

"Colonel Crockett was the last man standing," Herrera said.

"Did he survive?" Blaze asked.

"No. " Ruiz sighed and frowned. "After the battle was over Colonel Crockett was taken before Santa Anna who had him tortured. Crockett remained courageous and then he was executed."

"Damn that bloodthirsty bastard straight to friggin' hell," Shade said under his breath.

Blaze raised his tankard of cerveza to a trio of frowning dragoons who glanced their way.

"What about Jim?" Blaze asked. Neither Herrera nor Ruiz could meet his gaze. "Herrera?"

"Before manning his post at the four-pounder, Colonel Crockett stacked five loaded muskets beside Colonel Bowie's cot in the low barracks. When the battle was over —" Herrera paused before continuing in a hoarse voice, "Colonel Bowie's brains were splattered on a wall in his room full of empty muskets and Mexican bodies. I am so sorry mi amigos."

CHAPTER 34

FOR A MOMENT, BLAZE DIDN'T BLINK. HE DIDN'T MOVE A muscle or take a breath. He just stared at Shade, whose jaw was clenched with rage.

"Santa Anna will be stopped," Blaze said.

"What about *your* cousin, Herrera?" Shade asked.

"Cousin Carlos was the kindest man I ever knew," Herrera said sadly, shaking his head. "He was shot in the back as he shooed a cat into a room not far from Colonel Bowie's room."

"Dammit," Shade growled. "I liked Carlos."

"So did I," Blaze said. "What about James Bonham who went to Goliad to ask Fannin for help?"

"Bonham died beside the cannon at the rear of the church," Herrera replied.

"What about the Bee-Hunter, Thimblerig, Pirate, and the Indian?" Shade asked.

"All of the Tennessee Mounted Volunteers fought with fury before dying," Herrera said.

"*His Excellency*," Mayor Ruiz sneered the title, "gave no mercy to, nor did he accept surrender from, any of our brave rebels inside the Alamo."

"Which was the warning of the blood red flag in the San

Fernando Church," Blaze said, remembering the day Santa Anna had raised that flag.

"Si," Ruiz said. "When all one hundred and eighty-eight men in the Alamo were dead, as mayor, I was made to identify Colonels Bowie, Crockett and Travis to Santa Anna. His dragoons started throwing our rebels into the river. But *His Excellency* decided they would foul the water and they were fished out." The mayor grimaced and rubbed his temples. "About twelve hours after the Mexicans stormed the Alamo, they burned the bodies on the prairie."

"'The tree of liberty must be refreshed from time to time with the blood of patriots and tyrants'. Thomas Jefferson," Blaze quoted what the former president had written in a letter to a friend in 1787, after the American Revolution.

"We've got our sabers and knives," Shade said through his teeth. "Let's spill as much tyrant blood as we can and run for it."

"No," Blaze replied quietly. "You know Travis wanted Santa Anna's eventual losses to cost him more than an Alamo victory was worth. Now is the not the time or place."

"When will it be, Blaze?" Shade asked.

"When Sam Houston finds out what happened," Blaze said and nodded politely at some dragoons at the bar. "Let's round up some supplies tonight. I want to ride out of here as soon as Felice can travel."

"Drunk dragoons sleep like logs." Herrera smiled. "Night is the best time to collect your provisions."

"Santa Anna supplied the women in the Alamo with a blanket and two pesos before throwing them and their children out to...nowhere," Ruiz said quietly. "Mrs. Dickinson, her baby, Angelina, and a cook named Ben headed to Gonzales. Juana Alsbury and Gertrudis Navarro were taken to their father's home."

Blaze was glad the women who had taken care of Jim were safe. Thinking of the woman he loved being given a blanket, two pesos and sent into oblivion, Blaze glanced at the shop and saw Noelle heading toward the cantina.

Though her brown hat hid her hair and the buckskins made her look like a boy, her walk was all woman. These filthy dragoons would be all over her.

"Noelle's coming. So as Crockett said on the way to Texas, 'having liquored, let's journey.'" Blaze drained his tankard and in a jovial manner bid his friends, "Adios, amigos."

Blaze scraped back his chair and purposely staggered across the cantina as Shade did the same. Let the dragoons think they were full as ticks and harmless. He pushed past the swinging doors and there was Noelle surrounded by a dozen Mexican officers.

Front and center was the Napoleon of the West.

Blaze, if you cross Santa Anna without reinforcements, don't give him a good look at you. If he suspects you were anywhere near his tent, you're a dead man."

"Buenas noches." Blaze pulled the brim of his hat down in front as if in greeting and nudged Shade.

"Buenas noches." Shade tugged down his hat as well.

Meticulously dressed in a blue jacket, a white silk shirt buttoned with diamond studs, white linen breeches and red worsted slippers was General Antonio Lopez de Santa Anna, the President of Mexico and Commander-in-Chief of the Mexican army.

"Buenas noches," he said.

His black hair was fashioned with one lock curled over the thick brow above his right eye. His face was narrow and he had a long, bulbous nose, turned-down, thin lips, and pointed chin.

Santa Anna and his troops had come around the corner so fast Noelle had gotten locked between two officers. In the dim light of the cantina, Blaze caught Noelle's eye and glanced at her neckerchief.

As covertly as possible, Noelle pulled the neckerchief over her nose and mouth while Santa Anna took a snuff box from his jacket. Herrera claimed that opium mellowed those caught up in its fetters and shackles. Please let that be so for Noelle's sake, Blaze thought.

"'Scuse me," Blaze slurred, hoping to slide himself, Shade, and Noelle past Santa Anna and his officers.

All eyes suddenly bore down on Noelle as a meow was clearly heard.

"Nicky," Blaze said with a scolding tone. Looking at Noelle and Mistletoe, St. Nicholas was the first male name that had come to him. "We told you to take your cat and go to bed, little *brother.*" He stumbled through the officers and clumsily draped an arm around Noelle. "C'mon, let's go home."

"Por que?" Santa Anna asked and motioned to the blood stained neckerchief masking Noelle's face.

"Oh." Blaze nodded. "He's sickly. Yeah...uh...Sick Nick, that's what we call him."

"Sick-Nick?" Santa Anna took Noelle's arm and turned her to face him.

A bearded officer spoke to Santa Anna, translating what Blaze had said. Gripping Noelle's shoulder, Blaze took a step, but the officer blocked his way.

"Your name?" the bearded officer demanded, studying Blaze's light hair.

"Rufus Ray," Blaze said.

Still holding onto Noelle's arm Santa Anna appeared euphoric, but his officer glowered at Shade.

"Who are you?" the officer asked.

"His brother," Shade replied.

The officer asked, "Why is muchacho sick?"

"Cholera." Blaze dropped the deadly news like an eighteen pound cannon ball.

Noelle, clutching her cat, began coughing.

"Largo de aqui!" Santa Anna knew the word cholera and quickly released his hold on Noelle, backed up and waved them away. "Rapido!"

"Adios," Blaze said with a grin.

With his hand on the nape of her neck, Blaze guided

Noelle down Potrero Street. Shade flanked her and they skirted the front of the shop. Around back, Herrera was waiting for them. Blaze had not seen him leave the cantina.

"That was too damn close," Shade said.

"Lucky for you, Santa Anna thought you were a sick boy, Noelle!" Blaze said.

"I—I can't believe we just came face-to-face with Santa Anna," Noelle said, shaking.

"Not the first time we have seen him," Herrera said to Noelle, then turned to Blaze and Shade. "I told Mayor Ruiz I want to help you and Shade with whatever supplies you need. It is the least I can do after you helped us spy on Napoleon."

"Gracias, Herrera," Blaze said and turned to Noelle. "What were you thinking coming to the cantina?"

"I came to show you that I found Mistletoe and to tell you I have a surprise for you."

"Wait here." Blaze walked Shade and Herrera a few steps away. "Shade, go with Herrera for the supplies."

"Let's check on Felice, too. They're using her house as a hospital," Shade told Herrera and looked back at Blaze. "Don't go after Santa Anna without me."

"Don't tell me you're taking on a cause, little brother."

"Maybe so," Shade replied.

Maybe so, Blaze thought. Shade and Herrera then vanished into the night and Blaze returned to Noelle.

"My surprise is inside," Noelle said, standing at the door to the shop. "I'd like to hear about the Alamo out here and then leave it out here." She put Mistletoe down and the cat scampered into the shop.

As Blaze told her of Jim, Carlos, Crockett, Travis, and the others, her greenish gold eyes filled with tears. He explained the charred prairie as Noelle wrapped her arms around him sobbing. In her embrace Blaze felt a cold fury thawing around his eyes. He bowed his head, molded Noelle to his heart and dropped a single tear on her floppy, brown hat.

"Shade and I would be dead, too, if not for you and Jim," Blaze said. "Thank you, Noelle."

He knew it was an immense understatement. Noelle stood back as the realization hit her as well. He watched horror blend with sadness which gradually turned into profound relief. Slowly, she took his hands in hers and gently squeezed.

"What were Santa Anna's casualties, Blaze?"

"He's claiming he only has seventy dead." Blaze shook his head and scowled. "But Herrera says he lost two hundred. Santa Anna swears only a few dozen were wounded, while in reality four hundred lie in makeshift hospitals all over town."

"Where are Colonel Fannin and his men?"

"Still sitting in Goliad."

"What happened to Mrs. Dickinson, her baby, Juana, and Gertrudis?"

Blaze told her. Noelle's heart bled at the sorrow in Blaze's eyes, the same deep gray as those of his brave and caring cousin. She'd been petrified Santa Anna would remember the brothers and their unique gray eyes.

"If I could cast a magic spell I would set everything right."

"I know you would," Blaze replied.

"Is there any confirmation on Houston's whereabouts?" When Blaze shook his head, she pulled him close and said, "I want to show you my surprise now. Come into the shop with me."

She'd strung the bath tarp across the middle of the room, cutting off the back half of the shop. Taking his hand she led him through the dark. Behind the tarp, candles burned bright from the workbench, the shoe shelves, a table, and a wooden stool. Countless dancing flames flickered over bumpy, adobe walls.

Noelle held her breath.

A crackling fire made the room cozy. In front of the tiny hearth their bedrolls were spread, sides touching. On the foot of Blaze's blanket Mistletoe was curled in a ball. In the corner was the round, tin tub Noelle used for bathing. She had heated Carlos' last batch of fresh water.

Taking it all in, Blaze asked, "Who says you can't cast magic spells?"

Noelle flung her hat to the ground, shook her hair and stripped off her buckskins. His smoldering gaze touched her breasts and her nipples beaded.

"Should I come back when you're done with your bath?"

"Except for the smudges I purposely left on my face, I'm done. This bath is for you." Noelle took his hand and squeezed. "A bath will soothe your worry and pain."

"I don't deserve my worry and pain to be soothed."

Removing his sash, she laid his weapons aside. "With death all around us, let's make sure we're alive."

"I don't have the right to burn with you when bodies are smoldering in a funeral pyre."

Noelle gripped his upper arms. "Jim Bowie and Davy Crockett would call you a fool if you pass up the night I'm offering."

"Yes, they would." He bowed his head. "I haven't made love to you in a real bed. You can do better than dirt, trees and cornhusk mattresses, Noelle."

"I'd rather lie with you on a cushion of pine needles in a forest," Noelle placed her fingers to his chin and raised his head, "than without you on a bed of roses in a castle."

"You deserve a hero. I'm not one."

"You risked your life time and again for your country-men. The legendary Davy Crockett spoke of you as loyal to friends and cause. Because of your courage and generosity of spirit the famous Jim Bowie handed you a fortune in gold. If honor, loyalty and bravery do not a hero make, then pray tell me what a hero is."

"I don't know." His voice was a hoarse whisper.

"My hero is the man who refused to forsake his family and friends at the Alamo, the man who saved Felice, a child, and me from a cougar. I fought the Alamo for you and I won. Did my victory cost me your love?"

"I don't hold being alive against you, Noelle," Blaze said.

"Then don't hold being alive against yourself. Please love me, Blaze."

"I do." Blaze yanked his shirt over his head and flung it over his shoulder. "And I'll live to hear you say you love me, too."

"Yes, you will," she said. Noelle unbuttoned his pants. "Mmm...the stallion rides out of his corral and looks ready to mount."

"You're gonna be sore when I'm done with you, darlin'," he said stepping out of the buckskin britches.

CHAPTER 35

As he sat in the tin tub, Blaze grinned up at the breathtaking naked beauty. When she handed him a soft cloth, he tugged her to him and wiped away the remaining smudges on her cheeks and freckled nose. She returned the favor by washing him from head to toe.

Noelle then swayed to the corner, spread her feet slightly, bent over at the waist, and reached for his saddle. Blaze put a hand over his heart and thought maybe he'd died and gone to heaven.

"My God, you give a whole new meaning to fireworks."

Noelle laughed and struggled with the saddle until she had it in the center of their bedrolls.

"Out of that tub and into the saddle, Blaze of glory."

To hell with Santa Anna down the street. Who cared if the cantina whores were serving *His Excellency* cerveza or if Buzzard was trying to buy Santa Anna's friendship with the next drink? Noelle had restored his will to live. Blaze stood and the water ran off him in torrents. Blood roared through his veins making his loins ever hotter.

Together, they would make a future.

Noelle soaked up the moisture on the ends of his damp hair with a towel and tenderly dried his chest. Patting the towel to his shoulder blades, she dried a fiery path down his spine. Her every touch added to the flames burning inside him. In toweling his buttocks she massaged his skin and then stood before him. Lowering her eyes, she dried his hard male flesh inch by inch.

"I am ready to tell a man something important, if he has no more dangerous missions to pursue." She closed her hands around his arousal. Looking up at him, she said, "Tell me you have none, Blaze."

"I can't say I have none, ma'am," Blaze said, smiling. "Can you?"

"That's not what I meant. Tell me you're ready to take me home."

How could he admit he had to find Sam Houston first?

"Blaze, don't you want to hear what I have to say?"

"Yes. But depending on what it is, we might have to go find a minister right now," he told her. "Because I've decided if you ever say you love me, we'll be married within the hour."

"Oh, Blaze, you can't be serious."

"Oh, but I am, Noelle."

"What are you hiding from me, Blaze?" She gently squeezed his swollen desire.

"Seein' as how I'm naked, not a helluva lot."

"Tell me what you and Shade were whispering about before Herrera took Shade to get supplies!"

"Tell me the important thing you have to say to me, Noelle." Blaze placed his hands to her breasts and brushed the burgundy tips with his thumbs.

"I want Felice and Shade with us when we get married." Using his manhood, she tugged herself closer. "And I need Grandmother's approval."

"I don't think she'd approve of where our hands are right now." He caressed her breasts. "Let's call a truce for tonight and make love."

Holding him, Noelle nodded and backed across the bedrolls. When Blaze swung his leg over the saddle, Noelle's gaze dipped to his spread legs. With a grin she released him and he sat down.

Candlelight flickered, casting a shimmering halo around her rioting red hair. The fire crackled, silhouetting her curvy body and illuminating copper curls at the vee between her thighs.

"Noelle, you're the most beautiful woman in the world."

"I've got the most magnificent stallion on earth saddled," she said, straddling his lap. "And he can't throw me, like he did when we were bayou-style against the cypress tree."

"He could," Blaze said and cocked a brow. "But he damn sure won't. Let's ride."

He lifted her to her knees and posed her in position, thinking about his baby growing inside her. He slid the tip of his erection against her slippery velvet. Softer than a flower her petals opened, welcoming his rigid flesh.

"Mmm, Blaze," Noelle moaned.

He grinned as she impaled herself in slow stages. She leaned back, her long hair brushing his legs and Blaze groaned with pleasure when her buttocks met his thighs. Bringing her forward, he kissed her as she rose to her knees.

"Make me disappear, darlin'."

Blaze slid his hands to her back, down her spine and pressed her to him as her beaded nipples molded to his bare chest. Their mouths met and tongues danced, as Noelle's body wrapped and rocked his.

"Mmm, little girl," Blaze groaned, kneading her bottom, "you don't know what you're doing to me."

Noelle's smile squeezed Blaze's heart and he vowed to cherish and protect this woman for the rest of his life. Locking her arms around his neck, Noelle hugged him tightly. With the backs of her thighs flat against his, he was trapped inside her and he hoped he never escaped. She buried her hands in his hair and whispered against his lips.

"Teach me what to do next, Blaze."

"Ride up and down as fast as you can. I'll help you."

Blaze closed his eyes and soared. When her rhythm quickened, so did his pulse. He clamped his hands on her bottom to lift and lower her. Harder he plunged and faster he thrust until Noelle gasped his name and quivered from head to toe. Deep inside of her, Blaze's passion burst out of him and sizzled into her in hard throbs. His heart pounded as he pulsed deep inside her again and again. Her breath caressed his neck and she instinctively undulated her hips. Noelle moaned and with a sigh melted like wax against his red-hot skin.

"I'M SADDLE SORE," Noelle said the next morning as she straddled the handsome man on his bedroll.

"You're sitting on me." Blaze's deep chuckle was cocky as he stacked his hands behind his head. "You can't be too sore."

"Well, I'm sure I can't walk," she said, teasing him.

"I don't know what you're complaining about," Blaze said. "You wore my skin raw by the third go 'round."

Noelle laughed, enjoying the feel of the powerful body between her legs which had ravished her during the night.

"How can you be so big and strong?" Brushing a lock of Blaze's dark blond hair away from his smoldering gray eyes, Noelle asked, "And yet handle me so gently?"

"How can you be so small and delicate and yet save me from myself?" He ran a finger down the freckles on her nose. "I'm glad to be alive."

Noelle's eyes gathered moisture as she stretched out on top of him and lay her head next to his.

"You're going to stay alive." It was time to think beyond today. "Whether you like it or not you owe me."

"What do I owe you?"

"A lifetime of love and laughter."

Blaze rolled her off of him to her back and leaned above her with a pained expression.

"A lifetime?"

"Yes!" Her eyes widened and she laughed. "We could live in Grandmother's house."

"I don't want to live in her house," Blaze said. He got to his feet and pulled on his buckskin breeches, then picked up his sash, saber and knife. "I want to live in a new house I'll build."

"Is it because Grandmother's house is on a hill in Natchez and you want to live near the bayou in Vidalia?"

"No. I've been considering Mississippi."

Noelle sat up and clasped her hands under her chin. "In that case, you wouldn't have to build. You'd already have a house." She stood up. "It has dual winding staircases from the foyer to the second floor. I used to love sliding down the banisters."

"No wonder you're so good at sliding up and down."

With a laugh she replied, "When you're on the second story balcony you can see all of Natchez to the Mississippi River and beyond!" She swung her arms wide.

Blaze yanked on his knee-high boots. "You told me your grandmother wouldn't approve of me."

"That's when I thought you were a fortune hunter. You've said Grandmother will accept me and I know she'll approve of you."

"Doesn't matter. I'm not living with your grandmother."

"You're the most stubborn man I ever met!"

"You're the sassiest woman I ever met!" He tossed the buckskin pants to her and cocked his brow. "You get dressed. I'm going to find Shade." He walked across the shop and, blocking the doorway with muscles, waited until she was fully clothed. "I don't want Buzzard getting his hooks into him. Stay here."

Noelle watched him disappear, then sat on the wooden stool and sighed. Blaze Bowie was afraid of nothing and no one. If he was this confident and cocky under such horrendous conditions in Texas, he would be a force to be reckoned with back home.

She could hardly wait.

. . .

BLAZE AND SHADE packed sacks of coffee, tortillas, salt pork, beans, cheese, and eggs onto one of the travois. Another travois was loaded with a frying pan, coffee pot, tins, forks, and cups. Oats for the horses were loaded onto the third. After having collected those supplies with Herrera, Shade and Herrera had gone to Domingo Bustillo's place. Shade didn't look like he'd slept as he sat on the siesta bench beside Blaze, drinking coffee.

"Shade checked on Felice last night and we made a run past your house just now," Blaze said as Noelle handed him a cup of coffee. "Santa Anna was nowhere to be seen, so the doctor let us visit Felice for a few minutes."

"How was she?" Noelle asked and sat down on the stool.

"Delirious and had a fever," Shade replied. "The doctor said without the Comanches' medicine, she'd probably be dead by now."

"I have to go to her."

"No," Blaze growled. "You've passed for a boy so far, but we're not pushing our luck."

"Yeah, word is a woman about your age was already—"

"Shade," Blaze cut him off.

"Had by a dragoon?" Noelle asked.

"Or several," Shade said. "Felice will be next if anything happens to that doctor."

The day suddenly felt dangerous.

SEVERAL MORE TENSION filled days of dragoon dodging dragged by as they waited for Felice to get better.Noelle and the brothers stayed to themselves other than Shade's cautious, hit and miss visits to Felice. Blaze refused to let Noelle go. More than once, the mayor had dropped in to talk with Blaze. Herrera stopped by a time or two, usually after dark. Noelle feared Maria and Rosa would give them away to the Mexican officers or dragoons patronizing the cantina. But rumor had it that the two women had disappeared.

If any of the few remaining locals had recognized Noelle, Blaze, or Shade they evidently saw no reason to alert Santa Anna. Blaze kept an eye on *His Excellency* who remained entrenched in the Yturri house on Main Plaza.

Shade was unusually quiet and Noelle figured he must be hiding something. When Blaze asked him if he'd told Buzzard about the gold, Shade had said to mind his own business. They'd nearly come to blows over that. The brothers had initially drawn closer after the fall of the Alamo, but that was unraveling.

Nearly a week after being back in Bexar, Blaze packed more supplies onto the travois. Shade bought whiskey. From leftover material in Carlos' shop, Noelle finished a traveling pouch for Mistletoe.

Even with the tarp dividing the room, having Shade in the shop at night meant Noelle had to be content just lying next to Blaze and not making love. Just when she thought she couldn't take another pressure-filled day of worry and fear, the Mexican troops started leaving town.

"Santa Anna is on the march for more blood-bath victories like the one at the Alamo," Blaze said looking out the window while Noelle cooked huevos revueltos over the hearth.

"Forget Santa Anna," Shade said sitting on the bench. "Let's take our gold and go to Galveston Island."

CHAPTER 36

"WITH ALL THAT'S HAPPENED, LET'S FOREGO GALVESTON Island and go straight home," Noelle said, handing each of them a tin of breakfast.

"We're going to take our gold and ride to where the Texas Rangers are headquartered." Blaze took a bite and swallowed. "We'll hire a Ranger because," focusing on Shade, he pointed his fork at Noelle, "I want her protected. The two of you and Felice can head down to Galveston Island. Have a gold or silversmith sheer off the bottom half of our mantels, Shade, but leave Noelle's intact. Pay the Texas Ranger from the proceeds and we'll take the carved tops home. Like Noelle said, the mantels are invaluable."

"Just when did you decide all of this?" Noelle asked, staring at him.

"Yeah and where will you be while we're heading to Galveston Island, Blaze?" Shade asked.

"Washington-on-the-Brazos," Blaze said casually.

"You confirmed that's where Sam Houston is, didn't you?" Noelle asked.

"Yes." Blaze's eyes met hers. "I'm going to make sure Houston knows exactly what happened at the Alamo."

"Santa Anna is Houston's problem," Noelle said. "I want to get Felice and go straight home."

"I'll drag the gold to Galveston Island, but not all the way home," Shade said. "There's gotta be people on Galveston Island who'll pay more for it than those misers back in Vidalia or Natchez."

"You're right about that, Shade," Blaze said.

"Damn right!" Shade said.

"We'll sell half the gold on the island. But we *are* taking the top halves of our mantles home, Shade."

"I know it's not Felice's fault, but she's cost us days," Shade said. "If we run into bad weather dragging those mantels, we won't make it home before that banker forecloses."

"Why wasn't I included in any of this decision making?" Noelle asked, bristling.

"You were," Shade said. "We're taking you to Louisiana with us."

She slashed a finger at Shade. "You go to Galveston Island, Shade." She frowned and pointed at Blaze. "You go to Washington-on-the-Brazos, Blaze." She stomped toward the front door. "I'm getting Felice and we're going to Natchez!"

Blaze grabbed Noelle's arm. "All right. We'll all go to Galveston Island," he said firmly and rubbed his forehead. "Shade, go ask the doctor if we can take Felice. The sooner we leave the better."

THAT AFTERNOON, Blaze couldn't wait to tell Noelle what he'd heard. At the shop he found her pacing. Even dressed as a boy, she was so beautiful he wondered how they'd fooled the Mexican soldiers.

She hurried to embrace him. "You were gone too long. I was so worried."

"Houston rode out of the Washington-on-the-Brazos convention several days ago after signing a declaration of Texas' independence."

"Independence," Noelle said and smiled. "That would

have pleased Colonel Bowie, Colonel Crockett, Carlos, and the others. Is Houston headed east or west?"

"West, toward the Colorado River," Blaze said. Did Noelle suspect that he was going to do more than just tell Houston about the Alamo? That he planned to be with Houston when the inevitable confrontation took place? "We have to pull out of here today."

Mistletoe hissed and Blaze pivoted to face the door. Shade and then the foul presence of Raoul Buzzard entered the shop.

"I ran into Buzzard after I left the Herrera house and he came with me to tell you something," Shade said.

"We're all going to Lafitte's big yellow house on Galveston Island," Buzzard said.

Knowing Buzzard wouldn't dare touch Noelle, Blaze shoved Shade past the tarp and into the back of the shop.

"You told Buzzard about the gold, didn't you?" Blaze asked, itching to slam his fist in Shade's face, but it would solve nothing. "Dammit, Shade, can't you see he's more dangerous than any pirate on that island?"

"How will we find Lafitte's place without him?"

"I didn't tell you that Jim gave me the name of his house and its location because I didn't want you telling Buzzard. What I can tell you is Lafitte's house isn't yellow."

"Hell's damn bells," Shade said.

"We know Jim gives precise directions. We'll have no trouble finding Lafitte. Get rid of Buzzard and hope he doesn't follow us. Because if he shows up and Lafitte isn't on the island, I won't feel safe leaving Noelle so I can meet up with Houston."

Dawning narrowed Shade's eyes. "You're still determined to stop Santa Anna."

"Let's get the girls to Galveston Island. According to Jim, Lafitte will welcome us."

"The pirate no one's heard from in thirteen years now?" Shade asked. "On a pirate-infested island?"

"Damn, I hate it when you're right." Blaze flinched.

"We'll go to the island together, stop Santa Anna together and take the girls home together," Shade said.

"Agreed." Blaze hid a smile of victory. He shoved the tarp back and glowered over at Buzzard. "As I told you before, we're going it alone."

"HOW IS FELICE, SHADE?" Noelle asked, when Shade came back from checking on her.

"The stitches are out, but she seemed drugged."

"What?" Noelle asked.

Shade's face was lined with concern. "There were two dragoons guarding the door and one spoke English. After I bribed him with a bottle of whiskey, he told me that someone important saw Felice when he came for his *medicina* and said he planned to take her with him when he leaves Bexar. The doctor said she was too ill and was shot by the bearded officer."

"You left her there?" Noelle asked, terror filling her heart.

"They gave me no choice," Shade said, rubbing his forehead. "Whoever wants her is busy today but he's coming back for her in the morning. Since I'm her *brother*, the dragoon was authorized to pay me five hundred pesos for her. Then he told me to vamoose."

"Blaze, we have to get Felice now!" Noelle said, turning to him.

"Tonight," Blaze replied. "The dragoons'll be drunk and asleep."

"When *somebody* finds her gone in the morning, it'll take more than a pinch of opium to mellow him," Shade said darkly.

"Heads will roll," Blaze said darkly.

HIDING in the shadows of the Alamo chapel near Colonel Crockett's post, Noelle watched Blaze and Shade ride out toward the Herrera jacal. The night and distance quickly captured them from her view.

"I think I will name you Betsy," Noelle said to her mare, trying to distract herself. "Old Betsy is the name Colonel Crockett gave his rifles. He's the one who put me on Blaze's horse, Blue. Remember how we jumped the picket fence gate that night and barely escaped the Alamo, Betsy?"

Betsy seemed to nod. Noelle leaned down and hugged the horse's neck. Then she petted Mistletoe, tucked in her pouch hooked onto the saddle bag.

The garrison which had once teemed with such passionate activity was silent, deserted and eerie. Blaze had told her to keep Betsy and Felice's horse facing east, the direction they would be heading. Over her shoulder, Noelle looked toward the southwest corner where she and Blaze had first made love beside the eighteen-pounder.

The Alamo would forever hold a special place in her heart.

Noelle swiped a tear and waited.

Minutes ticked.

The moon moved in the sky as if blown by the midnight wind.

Time crawled.

Finally...faint...galloping...coming...her...way!

Noelle's heart thudded. She strained her eyes in the dark. And yes, in a few more seconds Blaze and Shade came into view.

"Ride!" Blaze shouted, thundering toward her.

Noelle kicked Betsy's flanks and both mares broke into a run. Blaze caught up with her and grabbed the reins to Felice's horse. Shade rode past her and with relief she spotted Felice behind him.

They galloped across the mesquite covered prairie. No shots rang out and there were no sounds of pursuit. Noelle didn't look back, but she whispered goodbye to the ghosts of the Alamo.

Nearing Powder House Hill where they'd hidden the travois, Blaze slowed the horses.

"Felice?" Noelle called. "Are you all right?" Felice turned her head away. "What's wrong with her, Blaze?"

"I don't know. We found her asleep on a cot," Blaze said in hushed tones. "When Shade woke Felice up, she fought him like it was life or death. Then the bearded officer stumbled out of the curtain-off bedroom and grabbed his musket."

"What happened?" Noelle's heart pounded.

"It was kill or be killed, Noelle."

Noelle felt numb. She hadn't worked with Colonel Bowie to save Blaze and Shade from the Alamo, to send them into danger in what had once been her home.

"You said they'd be drunk and asleep."

"We hadn't counted on the bearded officer and some of his men being camped out there. It was five against two."

Since that long ago evening at the fandango and during her stay in the Alamo, Noelle had heard wild tales about the Bowie knife wielding Bowie men. The moonlight glinting off the blood on Blaze's knife handle was proof of the brothers' deadly prowess. She shivered and gazed at the handsome, lethal man on the reddish-brown sorrel.

They rode most of the night and the next day. Felice remained quiet, but that night when they were settled around the campfire, Felice let Noelle examine her legs. The doctor who had protected Felice with his life had closed the wounds and stopped the festering infection from spreading. Her legs were healing.

Shade offered to sleep next to Felice, but she shook her head. Noelle then put Mistletoe in her arms and hugging the cat Felice shut her eyes. Noelle made a bed next to her and glanced at Blaze who winked his approval. She whispered goodnight to him and prayed that somehow everything would work out.

· · ·

"WE SHOULD BE at the far edge of Gonzales," Blaze said, as he sat on Blue squinting into the afternoon sun.

"Felice," Noelle began with a smile at the silent girl, "this is where Blaze bought my purple dress."

"Maybe I can get you a dress like Noelle's," Shade said, but received no response.

Riding closer to town, Blaze grew concerned. The terrain in the distance didn't look right. And there was a reason. As surely as Noelle's purple dress was lost to the Alamo, Felice would not be getting a dress in Gonzales.

"Burned almost to the ground," Blaze said as they stared in disbelief.

"Santa Anna?" Noelle asked.

"No. We've traveled faster than his army can. He's behind us. Must have been Houston."

"Now what?" Shade asked, glancing over at Blaze.

"We find out what happened and then look for a place to camp," Blaze replied.

In a few minutes they met up with Mrs. Dickinson, her baby, Angelina, and Ben. Ben had to swear he was prisoner of war who'd been forced to cook for the men at the Alamo before Santa Anna would release him. Travis' slave, Joe, was with them now as well. Although women, children, and slaves were not considered Alamo rebels by the Mexicans, Joe had been detained. He'd escaped and had joined the other three on the road to Gonzales.

"Deaf Smith met up with us, too. He was sent by General Houston to determine the fate of the Alamo and report back here in Gonzales," Mrs. Dickinson said. "On the orders of General Houston, a Captain Sharpe and his troops burned the town so it wouldn't fall into the hands of Santa Anna."

After confirming Blaze's guess, they were told that Houston had been officially named Commander-in-Chief of the Texas Army. He had left his camp on the Colorado River and come as far west as Gonzales. He'd added a hundred and seventy-five volunteers to his ranks, bringing his numbers to five hundred. His job was to train these frontiersmen and farmers to be soldiers. Finding out Santa Anna was on the march east, Houston had turned around and retreated east toward the colonies.

Blaze had missed Houston by a week, that precious week when Felice lay in the hospital. Houston was now headed back to the Colorado River with Santa Anna on his heels and that meant Santa Anna was on their heels, too. They wished Mrs. Dickinson, Joe, and Ben the best of luck and made camp on the eastern edge of Gonzales. Around a crackling fire they ate a wild turkey they had snared. Felice ate little, then curled up on her bedroll with Mistletoe.

"Dammit," Shade growled. "We're right where you said you didn't want to be, in the middle of Houston and Santa Anna."

"I meant I didn't want to be between them with the girls in tow during their confrontation," Blaze said.

"We're still headed to Galveston Island," Noelle said. "Correct?"

CHAPTER 37

"CORRECT," BLAZE ANSWERED. "WE ARE GOING TO Galveston Island."

"Good," Noelle replied and lay down next to Felice.

TWO DAYS LATER, they came upon a sign stating that a man named Vazquez kept people and horses.

"Might as well see if we can sleep inside tonight," Blaze said as he reined in Blue near a jacal and barn. "Wait here."

Blaze knocked on the door. Soon, arrangements were made and inside a small barn, Noelle slid into Blaze's muscular arms. How right it felt whenever he touched her. Shade dismounted and eased Felice off her horse. She immediately pushed his hands away and stared at the ground. Noelle plucked Mistletoe out of the pouch and placed her on the ground. Hurrying to Felice, Noelle hugged her. Blaze and Shade unsaddled the horses and led them to the hay Vazquez had provided.

"This is my fault, Felice," Noelle said softly. "If we hadn't gone to the hill country, you wouldn't have been clawed by the cougar. I'm so sorry. Please tell me what happened in Bexar."

Felice neither confirmed or denied, forgave or confided.

She just floated out of Noelle's arms, picked up the cat and sat down in a corner of the barn. Noelle took charge of arranging the bedrolls and a short time later Señor Vazquez appeared in the doorway with plates of tamales. Settling in for the night, they sat down starved but Felice only ate mechanically.

"That's the same girl who told me so many times she could hardly wait to see you again, Shade." Noelle smiled at Shade, but he just shrugged.

"Has Vasquez seen any sign of Houston?" Shade asked.

"Yes," Blaze replied between bites. "They came through here, too."

With darkness about to descend, Blaze took the first watch. Noelle talked Felice into lying down next to Shade by promising she'd sleep on the other side of her. Blaze leaned against a bale of hay on the other side of Noelle. During the night, Noelle was drawn to the security of warmth and muscles.

"NOELLE," Blaze whispered, holding the beautiful redhead who had snuggled her way into his arms. "Wake up."

"Is it dawn?" she asked, sliding her slender leg between his.

"Almost. I wanna get going."

What Blaze really wanted was to tug her pants off, open the front of his and roll on top of her. The air was chilly. He'd like to warm up by making love to his sexy spitfire.

"Five more minutes."

"If you don't crawl off this bedroll, darlin'," he whispered in her ear. "I'm gonna strip your pants off."

"Promise?"

Blaze groaned from aching for her all night and the lack of privacy to do anything about it. He got up to saddle Blue as Shade yawned and picked up Buckshot's saddle. Once all four horses were saddled and everyone outside, Blaze tipped his hat in farewell at Vazquez. On the trail, the sun dawned in a cloudless sky. It was a good day to travel.

"Even though we're ahead of Santa Anna, dragging these travois is slower than we thought it would be," Shade said come late afternoon.

"I know." Blaze nodded. He didn't like the slowness of their travel either as they journeyed east. "Think about it this way, Shade, if the mantels weren't so heavy they wouldn't be worth as much."

Noelle smiled at Blaze and his spirits lifted. Without this woman to share his life, saving his land would have no meaning.

That night when they made camp, Noelle slept between Blaze and Felice, while Shade took watch. In the deep of night, during Blaze's watch, Noelle kept him company. At dawn, they were back on the trail. And so the days passed in peace.

"BEASON'S FORD," Blaze read from a sign one evening as they paused near the Colorado River. He dismounted to read the smaller print. "The sign says a Benjamin Beason operates a ferry at the river crossing and his wife, Elizabeth, runs an inn."

"Let's get rooms," Shade said.

"There's nothing I'd like more," Blaze said with a wink at Noelle. His loins had been raging for days. "But that would mean leaving the mantels unattended."

Shade cursed and agreed. At the crossing of the Colorado River, they saw dragoons in the distance on their same side of the river. It was the first time they had seen Santa Anna's army since leaving Bexar.

"You think they're tracking us?" Shade asked.

"They're tracking Houston," Blaze replied.

Once they were safely on Benjamin Beason's ferry and leaving the dragoons in their wake, Blaze found Mr. Beason to be a good source of information.

"General Houston and his troops rested here from March nineteenth through March twenty-sixth," Ben Beason informed them.

Blaze had never guessed they would reach Gonzales and now Beason's Crossing just days behind Sam Houston and the Texas Army.

"Is Houston still heading east to Washington-on-the-Brazos?" Blaze asked.

"Yes, via San Felipe de Austin on the Brazos River."

"How many troops does Houston have now?"

"Maybe six, seven hundred," Beason replied. "For what it's worth, I won't be using this ferry for dragoons."

"Much obliged," Blaze said.

Beason wished them safe travels as they got off the ferry on the east bank of the river. They soon made camp for the night and were sitting around a crackling fire when Noelle spoke.

"Since Sam Houston knows about the Alamo, you don't have to tell him yourself."

"I want to be sure Houston plans to make Santa Anna answer for what he did to Jim and Crockett and the others," Blaze said.

"I'm sure the Commander-in-Chief of the Texas Army will make him answer," Noelle said with a choke in her voice. "Since when do you lust for revenge?"

"It's not revenge I'm after," Blaze said and took Noelle's cold hand in his. "It's a reckoning of Santa Anna's wrongs. He should have taken the men who were sick or wounded or wanted to surrender as prisoners. Instead he slaughtered them. Jim couldn't even get out of bed and Santa Anna tortured Crockett before executing him."

"What's done is done," Noelle said.

"It's far from done," Blaze said in a lowered voice. "I wasn't there when Santa Anna took almost two hundred lives, but I will be there when Houston confronts him."

"I knew it!" Noelle yanked her hand from him. "I

suspected you were planning to help Houston make sure Jim didn't die in vain."

"I've been having second thoughts about going after Santa Anna," Shade said.

"I want a say in all decisions from now on!" Noelle snapped.

"Our goal was to find the treasure to save our land." Shade looked at Blaze. "Let's sell it and go home."

"We have the gold because of Jim. We lost family and friends at the Alamo," Blaze told them both. "Some goals are more important than land."

"I'm sick and tired of sleeping in Texas dirt!" Shade said. "I want to see our Louisiana plantation again. I want our damn house back."

"Shade, you can have my half of the house." Blaze said. "We'll see the plantation *and* the timberland again."

"Not if we're dead."

"Tell me everything, Blaze," Noelle said.

"That day in Carlos' shop, we agreed we'd go to Galveston Island together before going home," he reminded them with a smile. Noelle's lips pursed and Shade frowned. Directing his attention to Noelle, Blaze said, "I omitted the fact I plan to leave you and Felice with Lafitte and go after Santa Anna with Houston *before* we head home."

"Omitting that fact is the same as lying!" The gold in Noelle's greenish eyes sparked dangerously and her cheeks flamed bright red.

"I never expected to be this close to Houston along the way to the island," Blaze said.

"And now that we are?" Noelle asked.

"We're closer to Houston than to Lafitte. We'll catch up with him and maybe he can spare a couple of soldiers to help Shade get you girls to the island."

Noelle got to her feet and stormed away from the campfire. Shade shrugged as if it served Blaze right. Blaze felt drawn and quartered by the people he loved, both dead and alive, and by his own code of honor. Leaving the campfire he caught Noelle a few yards away. Taking her arm he led her under a tall tree. He leaned against the trunk and pulled her into his embrace but she freed herself and backed up.

"Every time there's an opportunity to be killed you walk right into the thick of it."

"And every time I live to walk away," Blazed said, hands resting on the hilts of his knife and saber.

"You're a fool if you think your luck will hold out forever," she said ominously. Her voice shaking, she continued, "Colonel Bowie wanted you to take your gold and go home, not die on some other battlefield. Why are you so determined to lay down your life instead of living it with me?"

"Dammit to hell!" Blaze yelled in frustration.

Noelle trembled, but stood her ground. Blaze took a deep breath and slowly let it out.

"I plan to live a long life with you, Noelle. But in war or in love, I have to do what I think is right."

One of the very first notions Noelle ever had in regard to Blaze Bowie was that she probably couldn't handle him, much less control him. She turned and walked away from the man she loved.

THEY CONTINUED EAST, pushing hard toward the Brazos River. Though every mile took Noelle closer to her grandmother, it brought Blaze closer to Houston. It was Shade's day to scout and he had seen Santa Anna marching just south of them. Houston's retreat lay to the north. Dragging the travois, they'd yet to catch up with Houston.

So it was that they secretly pulled a fortune in gold between two mighty armies.

Noelle had once thought to distance herself if Blaze planned to fortune hunt. Now he seemed to be distancing himself, making her feel she had already lost him on an inevitable battlefield. He hadn't taken her hand, much less kissed her since she'd walked away from him. Felice wasn't speaking and Shade was generally in a bad mood. Envisioning her dreams dying on a bloody theater of war, Noelle's heart and soul sagged in defeat.

Traveling in near silence, it seemed to be taking forever to meet up with Houston and nearing the Brazos River they were told they had just missed him. Again

"That's all right," Blaze said. "Even pulling the gold, we've gained ground. We're only two days behind him now."

The one who had told them about Houston was a sick soldier who lived in the area and had stayed home when the Texas Army continued east. On the upside, he had reported that Houston's ranks had swelled to nine hundred. He'd confirmed Houston was headed to San Felipe de Austin on his route to Washington-on-the-Brazos, by way of Groce's Landing.

"Nine hundred men free and on the march is a lot better odds than a hundred and eighty-eight men trapped inside a landlocked battleship," Blaze told the group.

"Yes, better odds," Noelle said.

They gave the horses a rest and then moved ever east through thickening groves of live oak and across prairies of tall green grasses. Noelle rode close to Felice, feeling responsible for her withdrawal. When she put Mistletoe's pouch on Felice's saddle, Felice smiled. A good sign, Noelle thought.

BLAZE WAS SCOUTING the day they reached San Felipe de Austin on the Brazos River. On return, his words slapped Noelle in the face.

"We're gonna cross the river and part company. Santa Anna's on this side heading toward Thompson's Ferry. They won't spot you if you're on the other side of the Brazos. Shade, you take the girls south and I'll catch you before you get to Galveston Island. All I'm gonna do for now is ride north and talk to Houston. I won't go after Santa Anna until I've got you in a safe place," he said, looking directly into Noelle's eyes.

Fear twisted Noelle's heart like a dish rag. If they went south and Blaze went north, would she ever see this gorgeous man again? Had the impending war already won him away from her? Well, she loved him and she would fight for him!

"I'll make my own decision!" Noelle said, shoulders squaring. "I'm going north. I came face-to-face with Santa Anna and I would like to meet Sam Houston, as well."

"That's not your choice to make!" Blaze replied.

"It's her only choice if I don't head south with her," Shade said.

"I don't need you to go north with me, Shade."

"Even though they're women, there's safety in numbers."

"You couldn't teach a hen to cluck with logic that stupid, Shade," Blaze said.

Heart pounding, Noelle nudged Betsy's flanks, leaving a livid Blaze in their wake as she, Shade, and Felice headed north.

ON APRIL FIRST, they arrived at Groce's Landing on the Brazos River, many miles north of San Felipe de Austin. They had finally succeeded in catching up with Houston! Blaze scanned the vast camp for him.

Blaze had hardly spoken to Noelle since her outburst. Her obstinate nature had once again crossed his equally strong will and this time he was furious. Things were so wrong, she didn't see how they could possibly ever be right.

Blaze Bowie?" a man called, breaking away from a crowd of soldiers. "I hear you're looking for me. I'm Sam Houston."

"Yes, sir!"

Blaze quickly dismounted and shook hands. Shade followed Blaze's lead and greeted Sam Houston with great respect. Noelle and Felice stayed on their horses as Blaze brought Houston toward them. Felice whimpered.

"It's all right, Felice," Noelle said. "These men won't hurt you."

Noelle noticed that Sam Houston was shorter than Blaze and not nearly as muscular. Instead of thick, dark blond hair brushing past his collar like Blaze, Houston's hair was dark and short, his hairline receding. What they had in common was a fierce determination in their eyes and a stubborn set to their jaws.

"Noelle Charbonnez, you said you wanted to meet the Commander-in-Chief of the Texas Army," Blaze said somewhat formally. "It's my honor to introduce you to General Sam Houston. General Houston, I'd like you to meet Noelle Charbonnez."

CHAPTER 38

"HAVING TWO PRETTY LADIES IN OUR CAMP IS A RARE TREAT," Sam Houston said. "It's a pleasure to meet you, Miss Charbonnez."

"Thank you, General Houston," Noelle said. "It's an honor to meet you, sir."

"This is our friend, Felice Herrera," Blaze said, smiling at Felice who remained silent.

Houston invited them to make camp, bidding Noelle and Felice good day and asking Blaze to come with him to headquarters.

"Shade, take the girls and pick out a place for our camp," Blaze said. "I'll be back later."

Noelle was left with a feeling of abandonment but Shade took the reins to Felice's horse and Buckshot and led the way to a copse of trees which promised some privacy. Shade helped Felice off her mare as Noelle dismounted. While Shade and a couple of soldiers watered and fed the horses, Felice just stared at the ground. Noelle hugged her sister and wondered if Blaze would ever hug her again. Would they ever laugh again? Would Blaze ever make love to her again?

The afternoon sunlight sprinkled through the tree branches as they made camp. About an hour later, Blaze returned, taking Shade aside. At first Shade appeared angry but then he suddenly whooped for joy and smiled for the first time in ages.

"General Houston says we should rest a couple of days," Shade said, swinging his arm around Felice's shoulders. She shrank slightly but didn't shove him away. "And then head to Galveston Island."

"What does this mean?" Noelle asked.

"It means Santa Anna has stopped pursing Houston," Blaze replied. "Houston knows, as we do, that the Mexicans headed south to Thompson's Ferry. So Houston's going to train and rest his troops here. While he's doing that he'll decide whether to keep retreating toward the safety of the United States' border at Louisiana or pursue Santa Anna in Texas."

"He should retreat toward Louisiana," Noelle said.

"Well, Noelle, when you're a general and the Commander-in-Chief of the Texas Army—"

"Shade." Blaze's brows furrowed and he shook his head. "These troops are out for Santa Anna's blood. They caught two Mexican couriers who admitted Colonel Fannin and his troops were captured by a Mexican general named Urrea. Urrea asked Santa Anna to grant clemency to Fannin and his men, but Santa Anna refused to show them any mercy."

"On Palm Sunday, a Colonel Portilla had all three hundred and forty-two of Fannin's troops shot pointblank," Shade said, sharing what had made him angry. "Survivors were knifed or clubbed to death. Colonel Fannin was blindfolded and seated in a chair. Fannin's last request was for his belongings to be sent to his family, to be shot in the heart and not in the face and to receive a Christian burial. And—"

"Stop." Blaze frowned at Shade.

"And what, Shade?" Noelle asked.

"You don't need to know," Blaze said.

Shade finished anyway. "Santa Anna's troops stole

Fannin's belongings, shot him in the face and burned his body along with the troops they'd executed that day."

Felice fell to her knees and covered her head. Noelle stared hard at Blaze, thinking he could be next. She knelt on the ground beside Felice and placed her arms around her. Noelle remembered Colonel Fannin had warned James Bonham of Mexican butchery and had stayed rooted in Goliad, instead of riding to the aid of the Alamo. Though Fannin's troops had wanted to fight they'd been held back and now they were all dead. She'd kept Blaze from fighting at the Alamo. Was he doomed to die at Santa Anna's hands...no matter what?

"Come on, Felice," Shade said, helping her to her feet. But she shook off Shade's embrace, turned to a tree and wrapped her arms around it. "Hell's bells."

"So General Houston will confront Santa Anna here?" Noelle asked, getting up and standing near Felice.

"Houston would have a mutiny on his hands if he doesn't stop Santa Anna in Texas," Blaze replied.

"Houston told Blaze if we're on Galveston Island, we'll be close enough to—" Shade began.

"Die," Noelle said.

"Maybe my death would suit you, Noelle," Blaze said irritably, hands on his hips. "You didn't want me to find the fortune that Jim made sure is one third yours. And you don't want me to see justice done by those who took you and your family in at the Alamo. You'll never love the kind of man I am. So, why do you give a damn whether or not I die?"

"I'm giving you my gold in exchange for taking me home," Noelle said in a stern voice. "I went into the Alamo to make sure you didn't die there. I want you and the lifetime of happiness you promised me. Evidently, you'd rather die than live with a woman like me!"

Blaze frowned at her and then stalked toward the river. God, he wanted that lifetime of happiness with Noelle. Despite his promise to live, he couldn't deny the possibility of being killed during the new, looming battle. And that was taking a toll. Her arrows of radiant smiles... he had not returned. Arrows of her sensuous touches... he had avoided. Each time he pulled further away, he was already dying a little.

In one Noelle Charbonnez he had met his match.

Shade followed him and they sat on the bank of the Brazos.

"You're the man I want to be and never will be," Shade said.

Blaze turned to Shade and they talked as they never had before.

UNDER THE PROTECTION of Houston's army, they rested for the next two days. Blaze bedded down beside Noelle, but kept his back to her at night. He remembered having told Noelle in the low barracks that Santa Anna might torture an enemy by not letting him make love to her. And damn, if that wasn't happening.

"BLAZE, Shade, you know where the enemy is, so stay clear of them," Houston said on the morning they were to leave. "Jim might roll over in his grave, but I'll get word to you on Galveston Island as to stopping Santa Anna."

"Thank you, General Houston," Blaze said and shook his hand. "We'll see you again soon, sir."

Blaze led the way out of the camp and they traveled south. One afternoon, when it began to rain, they took shelter under a huge oak tree beside a well. They dismounted and took time to fill canteens and water their horses.

"The main branches of this tree look like they're pointing in two different directions," Noelle said.

"East toward the Trinity River," Blaze noted and looked at the branches. "South toward Harrisburg."

"Whichever way we go, I'm glad we're going in the same direction," Shade said.

"Me, too," Blaze said, smiling at his brother.

As the rain let up, Blaze nodded for Shade to take the lead. Shade grabbed the reins to Felice's horse and headed south. Blaze held back and looked at Noelle.

"Is something wrong?" Noelle asked.

"Yeah," Blaze said. "I'm tired of not knowing which way to deal with you. Shade's convinced me I'm not the man I thought I was if I act like I'm dead, when you want me alive."

Confusion flickered across Noelle's face as he slid his arm around her waist. He pulled her off her horse and settled her sidesaddle across his lap. She put her arms around his neck and buried her fingers in his hair. Every vein in Blaze's body pulsed with life as he tilted her chin and claimed her mouth in a hungry kiss.

"Noelle, I need you," Blaze breathed. "I've missed you."

"Every time I smiled or came near you, it seemed to make you avoid me more so I stopped."

"I can't let you melt my resolve to do what I have to do," he said. "But I told you I'd prove myself to you and I realize keeping my distance isn't the way to do it."

"I thought you were immune to me, Blaze."

"Immune? I'm sicker'n all get-out from not having enough of you. I need a whopping dose."

"It's been three weeks since we made love in this saddle," Noelle said.

"Seems like three years."

"Do you think a dragoon had Felice?" she asked.

"Shade thinks so and he's blaming himself for leaving her with them. I told him he's not to blame."

"I agree. Felice might have died without the doctor's help. Shade mustn't feel guilty."

"He's hurting and he's handling it well. Despite what I once said about men flocking to your grandmother's house to court you, I would go crazy if I found out you went to bed with another man, Noelle. But to think you had been raped... damn, I'd kill him."

"Shh. You said I was a custom fit." Noelle tightened her arms around him and pressed her head against his. "That means I will never be with any man but you for as long as I live."

ON APRIL TENTH, they ferried across Galveston Bay to the island. It was late afternoon when Blaze reined in Blue at the hitching post of a large compound. Years ago, Mama had described this two story red house right down to the black front door and black flower boxes. On the roof amidst twelve gables a black cannon pointed out to sea. Also giving the house the look and strength of a fortress were ten foot tall stone arches. And surrounding it all was... a moat.

"Maison Rouge," Noelle said in awe as they paused between two towering palm trees.

"It might not be Lafitte's home any longer." Blaze dismounted and said, "Jim couldn't say for sure if he still lived here. But the moat tells me it's still the property of a pirate."

"The bridge over the moat tells *me* somebody needs to go knock on that big door." Shade dismounted Buckshot and stood at the hitching post.

Leaving Mistletoe in her pouch with Felice, Noelle slipped from the saddle into Blaze's arms. Shade waited at the hitching post near Felice as Blaze took Noelle's hand. They walked over the bridge and down a stone path.

"Mama said Jean Lafitte gave fabulous parties here," Noelle said, tightening her hold on Blaze's hand as they neared the front door. "She said everybody who was anybody visited Lafitte. Besides, Jim and Rezin Bowie, President Andrew Jackson was among Lafitte's good friends, his bon amis."

"Jim and Rezin sold that mantel to Lafitte sometime around eighteen thirty-two, but no one else has heard from him since eighteen twenty-three," Blaze said. "Maybe we'll find out why."

Coming to the freshly painted door Noelle lifted a shiny brass knocker, dropping it with a clang. No one answered. They waited. Nothing.

Blaze rapped his knuckles on the wood. Footsteps sounded and the door opened to reveal a striking man about six foot one pointing a flintlock pistol at them! From the grooves in his handsome face, Noelle figured he was in his mid-fifties. Black brows slashed above penetrating, *hazel* eyes. Curly, black hair, with a sprinkle of gray, reached his shirt collar. A thick mustache hid his upper lip and his beard was black.

"What do you want?" the man demanded, his brow furrowing into a fierce scowl.

"We're looking for Jean Lafitte," Blaze replied.

When the stranger cocked his pistol, Blaze swept Noelle behind him and Shade hurried forward.

"Who are you?" the stranger asked.

"I'm Noelle Charbonnez," Noelle answered, stepping from behind Blaze.

"Charbonnez?" The man seemed surprised. "What was your mother's maiden name, mademoiselle?"

"Yoder."

"Yoder!" Blaze and Shade barked at the same time.

"Of the Yoder Whiskey Castle fame?" Shade asked.

Noelle nodded as the brothers stared at her in stunned disbelief.

"The Yoder Whiskey Castle is not just *any* house on *any* hill, Noelle," Blaze said in amazement. "It's the biggest house, if you can call a castle a *house*, on the highest hill in all of Natchez."

"Did I not mention," Noelle looked from Blaze to Shade and back to Blaze, "Grandmother Yoder owns the largest whiskey business in the south?"

CHAPTER 39

"Papa!" Felice cried, stumbling down the stone walk. "I killed a man. And I am with child," she said fainting into the stranger's arms.

"Who'd she kill?" Shade asked.

"Don't know." Blaze clapped Shade on the back. "But we know who the father is."

"Do we?" Shade frowned.

"I believe you are coming inside," the man said, cradling Felice. He turned in the doorway and called, "Catherine?"

"Catherine?" Noelle mouthed to Blaze as they stood just outside. Quietly she asked, "Wasn't that the name of Jim and Lafitte's mistress?"

"Yes, maybe this is she," Blaze said

"Kitty!" boomed a voice from behind them at the hitching post.

Noelle turned as a heavy-set, towering man took hold of the pouch with Mistletoe's head poking out of it.

"That is Petit," said the man carrying Felice. "He is my cook's son. Petit helps keep the boat, horses, stable, house, and yard in good repair. He will treat your cat with kindness."

Relieved, Noelle and the others followed the stranger into a large and elegantly decorated foyer. A view of a wide staircase lay straight ahead. A gold mirror hung on a far wall and under it a fancy settee bookended by gilt tables.

Trailing their host into a parlor, the word opulence sprang to Noelle's mind. Rosewood and wrought iron furniture sat on thick, oriental carpets. A stone fireplace ran from floor to ceiling. Sunlight reflected off a crystal chandelier and flickered across wallpaper depicting a panoramic view of ships on the ocean. Noelle recalled how Mama always said only the very rich could afford wallpaper.

Their host put Felice on a sofa as a lovely woman entered the parlor wearing a plum colored, slightly belled dress. Her black hair was swept up in a chignon with tendrils brushing her neck. Brown eyes were warm with concern and full lips parted in a soft smile of welcome. Her skin tone was the same as Felice's. Possibly quadroon, she was stunning.

"Catherine, mon amour, we have guests," their host said in introduction. "This young woman has fainted because she is with child. Let's make our visitors comfortable and bring the señorita around."

"Oui, Jean." Catherine nodded and left.

She had pronounced the name with a French accent as 'Zhon', a soft 'j' version of John without emphasis on the 'n'.

"Please sit," their host said with a sweep of his hand toward two rosewood sofas.

Upholstered in deep burgundy brocade, the sofas faced each other. Between them a large glass table top was mounted on a silver sculpture of a ship. At both ends of the table were burgundy and gold striped chairs. Noelle sat down on the sofa with Felice. Blaze and Shade stood near the hearth adorned with a familiar looking mantle of pure gold. Catherine soon returned with a glass of water and placed a compress on Felice's forehead. When Catherine patted Felice's hand, her eyes fluttered open.

"Where am I?" Felice asked, looking from Catherine to their host. "Who are you?"

Noelle tensed and held her breath.

"You're inside the Maison Rouge compound within a colony known as Campeche," he said and took a seat in the winged back chair facing the fireplace.

"Campeche?" Felice repeated. "Mexico?"

"No, not the Campeche founded by conquistadores in Mexico," their host clarified. "Campeche founded by a pirate here on Galveston Island."

Noelle glanced at Blaze, but his expression was unreadable.

"This is my friend, Catherine," he gestured to the lady, "and I am...John Galveston."

Noelle noticed the hesitation in his voice. Was that his real name, she wondered. Noelle helped Felice sit up and Catherine handed her the glass.

"And what's your name?" Galveston asked, looking directly at Felice.

"Felice Herrera. I'm sorry I have caused so much trouble." There was wonder in her eyes. "You look so much like my papa."

"Coming from such a lovely young woman, I take that as a compliment," John said. "Where is your papa?"

When Felice hung her head, Noelle replied softly, "Carlos didn't make it out of the Alamo."

"Only yesterday, did we hear the Alamo fell," Galveston said.

"Si." Felice nodded. "First Mama died, then my stepmother, Trilby, died and now my papa is gone."

"I see." Galveston had flinched at the mention of Trilby's death. "I am sorry to hear that."

"I was clawed by a cougar and my house was taken over by Santa Anna's dragoons." Felice's voice rose slightly. "A nice doctor sewed up my wounds and put poultices on my legs but a dragoon shot him." Her eyes watered and grew glassy. "Then the dragoon was mean to me. He...he..."

Felice collapsed in tears, crying into the compress as Shade stalked out of the room. John sunk back in his chair as Catherine sat down on the other side of Felice.

"We all know what some men are capable of," Catherine said gently to Felice.

"No… no you do not know."

"I know a man whose beloved wife was raped by Spanish officers," Catherine said. "To avenge her, this man used his ships to plunder Spanish ships, making them pay for what they had done to his young wife."

Noelle hardly breathed. This was the story of Jean Lafitte told by Blaze. Whether he was recognizing the story or agreeing with Lafitte's actions or both, when she looked at Blaze again, he nodded just slightly.

"After that awful man hurt me, he turned his back," Felice said between sobs to Catherine. "I grabbed his pistol and made him pay! I ran, but a bearded officer and some other dragoons caught me. The bearded man said *His Excellency* was coming for me and shoved powder up my nose. But Shade and Blaze got there first."

Noelle felt ill. Their worst fears had been confirmed.

"Good for you, Felice," John said with a smile and a nod. "Sometimes one must personally make certain those responsible for injustices answer for their wrongdoing."

That was Blaze's philosophy about what had happened at the Alamo, Noelle thought.

"Now, you must forget about it, Felice," John said.

"How?" she asked in a small voice.

"Make this pact with yourself," he began, "when the face of that terrible man comes into your mind, you will replace it with the face of someone you love."

"Oui, ma chère," Catherine agreed.

"Excuse me, I need to see about my brother," Blaze said quietly and started across the room.

"I hope you will call me John, as my friends in Campeche do," John Galveston said, standing up. "I don't believe I've asked your name."

"Blaze," he said, extending his hand. "My brother is Shade and our last name is Bowie."

"Bowie." With a glance at the mantle, John smiled at

Blaze as they shook hands. "You would be a relative of mes amis, Jim and Rezin Bowie?"

"Yes, sir, their cousin," Blaze replied. "Jim told me to bring Noelle here to meet you shortly before he died in battle at the Alamo."

"Jim is dead?"

"Yes, sir." Blaze nodded with sadness.

"And Rezin?"

"Rezin wasn't at the Alamo."

"Jim and Rezin were always welcome here," John said softly as if remembering a long ago past. "We have many empty bedrooms and I hope you will stay with us as they once did. For as long as you wish."

"Thank you, John." Blaze smiled. "All things considered we had some good weather, we're ahead of schedule, and could use a couple of days' rest."

That decided, Blaze headed to the foyer and Noelle followed. They found Shade sitting on a three foot high stone wall surrounding the manicured front yard. Palm trees dotted the corners of the yard and the grass was lush. Red and white phlox and bluebonnets filled the window boxes.

"Red, white and blue; the colors of the American flag. You were right about Lafitte's loyalty to the colonies," Noelle said to Blaze.

Shade was staring at the bay they had crossed coming to the island. The gently lapping water of the gulf was a beautiful backdrop for this unique compound. Noelle stood on the lawn as Blaze straddled the stone wall.

"Is Galveston really Lafitte?" Shade asked no one in particular.

"Mama's description of him fits John Galveston right down to his hazel eyes and gold tooth," Noelle said. "Did you two notice the mantel?"

Blaze nodded. "It's carved with the ships Jim wrote about in his letter. Did your mother ever mention that Carlos resembled Lafitte?"

"No, but I wonder now if his resemblance isn't part of the reason Mama married Carlos. How can I ask him if he's my father?"

"Since Blaze most likely knew your grandmother represents a whiskey fortune, I'm sure he knows if Galveston is Lafitte *and* if Lafitte's your father."

"I didn't know about the whiskey," Blaze replied to Shade. "As for Lafitte, all I know is Jim thought Noelle favored him rather than Charbonnez." He looked at Noelle. "I see the likeness, too. Speaking of fathers, what are you going to do about Felice, Shade?"

"Nothing." There was a tick at Shade's eye and vulnerability in his voice. "I can't help it if she turned into a strumpet."

"Felice is anything but a strumpet!" Noelle snapped and glared at him. "She is devoted to you."

"Really?" Shade had listened to Felice's story from the foyer. "Then why didn't she shoot that dragoon before instead of after he had her?"

"She probably couldn't get to his gun until he turned his back," Blaze said with a frown.

"You don't deserve her love, Shade," Noelle said, shaking her head.

"Felice never said she loved me," Shade replied and shrugged.

"Si, I did," Felice said, as she crossed the lawn to them.

"You lied about your age the night we met," Shade said. "But you can't lie about saying you loved me because I know better."

"That same night I said te amo... Spanish for I love you," Felice reminded him with a smile. "Because I had been to bed with you, Shade, I'd already missed my monthly before the dragoon forced himself on me. When our baby is born, you will be able to see yourself in him or her." She placed her hands over her heart. "Our child will love you as much as I do and we could be a happy family."

"Are you proposing to me?" Shade asked gruffly.

"Si." Felice reached for his hand, but he crossed his arms over his chest. "I tried not to let you take me for granted," she clasped her hands over her heart and continued, "but I could not resist you, Shade."

"I told you I'm not the marrying kind."

"Shame on you for hurting Felice worse than any other man ever could," Noelle said.

"Is this how you prove to Felice that she can count on you?" Blaze asked. When Shade scowled at him, Blaze said, "On the Brazos River you were worried about her. What changed, Shade?"

"Everything about her was speculation then," Shade said in a strangled voice, not looking at Felice. "How would you be taking this if we were talking about Noelle and some bastard who'd had her?"

"I'd want to kill him all over again. But I wouldn't blame Noelle and I sure as hell wouldn't turn my back on her."

"Well, that proves I'm not the man you are and never will be."

Noelle placed a protective arm around Felice just as John called out from the front door.

"Blaze, Shade, I want to talk to you." John waved at them to come on. "*Spanish* whiskey's waiting for us."

"I'll be right there," Blaze said, glancing over his shoulder at John.

Felice held her head high as Shade stalked away and followed John into the house.

"There has to be an acceptable solution to all of this," Blaze said.

"Si, I will return to Bexar," Felice replied with no trace of self-pity. "I will live in Papa's house and raise Shade's baby myself. We will be muy bien."

"No, you would not be *very good*," Noelle said, taking Felice's hand. "You'll come to Natchez where you and the baby can live with us, Felice."

"Never." Felice shook her head. "The baby and I would embarrass Shade."

CHAPTER 40

"MAYBE SHADE WILL CHANGE HIS MIND WHEN HE HAS A chance to think it over," Noelle said, her distress over Felice, rage at Shade and terror of losing Blaze swirling her into such an emotional tempest, she wanted to scream.

"I thought over what you said about stopping Santa Anna and luck running out." Blaze frowned and ran a hand across his forehead. "If Houston sends for us tomorrow my niece or nephew could be born a bastard."

"Not if you and Shade do not go after Santa Anna," Felice said.

Blaze's silence was his answer.

"Then you give Felice and the baby the Bowie name, Blaze!" Noelle said, in sheer frustration.

"No!" Blaze and Felice replied at the same time.

"Felice, when Carlos put you on Shade's horse he expected us to take you home with us, not send you back to Bexar alone and pregnant. I cannot do that to you," Noelle said. "Can you, Blaze?"

"No, but when I once said that she'd have the Bowie name I meant Shade would marry her."

"I am sure he will not," Felice whispered.

Noelle was sure, too. Sure that if Blaze married Felice, he would eventually assume his husbandly rights with her.

Noelle couldn't live in the same town with Blaze and Felice, much less the same house knowing they were making love every night. But where would she go? And then she remembered. The Bowie brothers weren't the only ones with cousins. Grandfather Yoder had told her they had numerous relatives in Geneva.

"We'll make Shade marry you, Felice," Blaze said.

"I'd rather die," Felice replied and lifted her chin.

Noelle already saw herself sailing across the Atlantic Ocean to Switzerland.

And what if she, too, were pregnant, Noelle wondered. *I'm strong. I can raise a baby on my own.* If she had it all to do again, she would do nothing differently. Any scorn she might bear at having a baby out of wedlock would be worth it. She would proudly love Blaze's baby with all her heart.

"If I do this, the marriage would be in name only and end when the baby is born," Blaze grumbled.

Felice would take good care of Blaze and he would be a protective, loving father. Felice's baby would be Blaze's blood and they could have children of their own as well.

"Felice, you know how stubborn Blaze is. Once he makes up his mind, no one can change it."

"Te amo, Noelle," Felice said. "We will all live together and then I will seek a divorce as soon as my baby is born a Bowie and not a bastard. If I burn in hell for being divorced, so be it."

Felice was making sacrifices also.

"I'll ask John to arrange a wedding," Blaze said, unable to keep the anger out of his voice.

"Muchas gracias, Blaze," Felice said quietly.

Back in the house, Catherine escorted them through the foyer, down a hall and into a masculine study where John sat on a large black leather sofa, his feet propped on top of a seaman's trunk or... pirate's chest. And there in a big wing backed chair, was Shade downing the amber contents of a crystal goblet.

"Felice and I are getting married," Blaze said dryly.

Shade choked as John's brows shot up.

"I would have ventured that you and Noelle were the betrothed couple," John said to Blaze.

"Red hair... raven hair... Blaze takes what he wants, when he wants." Shade didn't look at them as his hands gripped the crystal goblet and arm of the chair.

"I can arrange for a priest or a minister to come to Campeche," John said, frowning at Shade.

Noelle's face was so deathly pale that Blaze's gut tightened but the moment she caught him staring at her, she smiled. He turned to John and muttered his thanks.

"We have not entertained for too long a time. Viviane, our cook, will love preparing for a wedding," Catherine said. "In the meantime her sister, Suzanne, our housekeeper, will see to your comforts."

"Catherine," John said, nodding. "I will have Petit bring down some of the trunks from the attic. Ask Suzanne to make up separate bedrooms for the gentleman. Perhaps the ladies wish to share a room."

John Galveston doesn't want a blood bath on his hands, Blaze thought, which might happen if he put him up with Shade.

Catherine excused herself and left with the girls. Blaze wanted Noelle back the moment she was gone. He needed to talk to her in private and promise her everything would be all right. Just when he could have made love to her in a real bed he was betrothed to another woman. Dammit to hell, he hoped this mess would work out.

"Blaze, my boy, sit down and have a glass of Spanish whiskey," John said, handing him a goblet. "You look as if you need it."

"Thanks," Blaze said and took a seat at the other end of the sofa.

"Some people call this Bad Luck Island," John said.

"Got that right," Shade said in a growl.

"But Jim and Rezin didn't think so." John chuckled.

"They made sixty-five thousand dollars in one year by smuggling slaves from this island into Texas."

"They've been condemned for that," Blaze said and took a drink of whiskey.

"So I have heard. But please remember, the Bowie brothers lived on the raw frontier where there was little to no law and order," John said with a wave of his goblet. "A man's fortune had to be wrung from the earth or the sea. And it is, after all, a legal practice in the colonies to own a slave."

"They wrung a fortune from the earth," Blaze said.

"Yes, I know," John replied. "Shade told me about your gold mantels. If we agree on a price, you will reap rewards on this island just as Jim and Rezin did."

"I'd like to keep the top half of my mantel," Blaze replied.

John suggested they have a look at them. He led them out to a red stable where Petit had unsaddled the horses and fed them. He had dragged the mantels into an empty stall. Petit sat on a bale of hay grinning and clapping as he watched Mistletoe play with a mouse.

"Magnifique," John said, examining the mantels. "Mine is carved in honor of a ship named The Pride."

"Since you gave me your half of the house, Blaze," Shade began with a cocky grin, "I'll mount my mantel over the brick fireplace in my front room where the Bowie coat of arms used to hang. And seeing as how you're betrothed to Felice, I'll let Noelle mount her mantel over the hearth in the master bedroom."

"Over my dead body, Shade."

"Happy to oblige," Shade said, squaring off with him.

"Enough." John held up his hands. "What is going on here?"

"It's none of your business," Shade sneered.

In a flash, John whisked a Bowie knife out of nowhere and put it to Shade's throat.

"You've made it my business by coming here," John said as Petit lumbered toward them. "You will use your tongue to speak in a civil manner or I'll cut it out of your hotblood head."

"No one has ever managed to put a knife to our throats," Blaze said, impressed by John's skill. "From what Jim told me, Lafitte could do it."

"Lafitte led a dangerous life. Conveniently, it is rumored he was killed and buried at sea in the Gulf of Honduras, on February fifth in eighteen twenty-three. Since his disappearance, I have led a quiet life."

"And you want to keep it quiet," Shade said.

John slowly sheathed his knife before instructing Petit as to trunks in the attic and placing them in the bedrooms. Smiling again, Petit nodded and picked up Mistletoe.

As if nothing had happened, John led them out of the stable and followed Petit back to the house. On a wide veranda overlooking the blue bay, he offered Blaze and Shade seats on wickerwork chairs. Through open French doors, hung with sheer lace curtains, John called to his cook. In minutes, Viviane delivered refreshments.

The sun was setting as Blaze gave John an overview of all that had happened from the time the bank manager had tried to foreclose on them in Vidalia, to the fall of the Alamo, to the Comanches, to meeting both Santa Anna and Sam Houston.

"I guarantee no bullets were found in Jim Bowie's back," John said, looking the brothers in the eyes.

"Jim sent a pile of dragoons straight to hell before they killed him," Shade said and ran his hands through his hair. "I hope the dragoon who had Felice is burning in hell."

"Oui, he is, Shade," John said.

Blaze wondered how they'd fallen into such familiar companionship with John. If anyone else had put a knife to his brother's throat, they'd have killed the man. Blaze guessed it was because Jim and Rezin were Jean Lafitte's longtime friends.

"Marcel and Trilby Charbonnez lived on this island for a

while," Noelle said, from behind them. "Do you remember them, John?"

As Noelle paused in the French doors, Blaze slowly came to his feet. He held his breath and stared.

A siren calling his ship to crash upon her shore.

More magnificent than the fiery sun slipping into the bay, her crimson curls cascaded around her shoulders and down her back. Shimmering emerald on her eyelids and a glittering gold gown magnified the green and gold in her eyes. The gown's neckline was daringly low, teasing Blaze with ivory cleavage. The sleeves were mere caps, the waist of the dress narrowed to nothing. The skirt draped her hips and satin slippers encased her feet.

"You're beautiful, darlin'," Blaze said, without thinking.

"Thank you," Noelle replied stiffly.

Shade remained seated, but John got up and held out his hand. Blaze smelled sweet lavender as Noelle walked across the veranda without giving him a second glance and took John's hand. With a rustle of petticoats and satin Noelle sat on the green-striped cushions of the sofa.

God, how Blaze loved and needed this siren's song.

"I can't thank you and Catherine enough for the loan of this gown," Noelle said as John sat down next to her. "It's beautiful, just like the dresses Mama said ladies wear in Mississippi."

"All that is within the trunks in your rooms is my gift," John said. "Catherine's wardrobes are so full I thought never to see these other Spanish gowns again." He added, "It is good to unlock and reveal the past."

"Felice is resting until supper," Catherine said, coming to the door. "Blaze, Shade, if you'll come with me, I believe Suzanne has baths and clothing waiting for you in your rooms."

Blaze smiled and Noelle turned her head. The heat of one of his grins could dissolve her resolve to let Felice marry him. Noelle's heart ached as Blaze left the veranda.

When it was just the two of them, John said quietly, "I knew Trilby and Marcel."

"Tell me about the man who knew my mother."

"He was a buccaneer who once gathered a thousand men, founded Campeche, and reined as governor on Galveston Island." He paused and gazed out over the bay. "He fought in defense of New Orleans in the War of Eighteen Twelve, but the colonies eventually pressured him to halt his privateer operations here on the island."

"What happened to him?"

CHAPTER 41

"In eighteen twenty-one, rather than turn on the colonies, some folks say he burned Campeche to the ground, boarded his favorite vessel, The Pride, and sailed away," John replied. "Within a couple of years, rumors widely circulated that he was killed in the Caribbean Sea."

Simply, but elegantly clothed in a white shirt and dark breeches, Noelle could easily imagine John as a knife-between-the-teeth swashbuckler.

"Mama often sat and stared out an upper window of my grandparents' house as if watching for someone to sail up the Mississippi," Noelle said softly. "One day in eighteen twenty-three, she stopped looking. Mama never seemed truly happy again. Perhaps she missed someone she had heard was killed."

"Perhaps. Trilby was, after all, married to another and her sterling reputation remained untarnished."

Noelle and John smiled at each other, their unspoken words saying they understood so much more after having shared their parts of the same story.

"Do you have children, John?"

"My son died of yellow fever in eighteen thirty-two."

"I'm so sorry," Noelle said and touched his arm.

"Merci." John nodded. "I told Trilby before you were born a child of mine might have red hair like my mother."

"Marcel had black hair and brown eyes." Noelle looked into John's eyes and realized that she had never seen anyone else with eyes the identical color of hers. "But he claimed his father's hair was red."

"Oui." John chuckled. "Marcel told that tale to Trilby and me *after* you were born." He tilted his head and said, "Timing is everything. N'est-ce pas?"

"Oui."

"Your mother was a woman to be loved and protected, not abandoned for the sea."

Noelle smiled at hearing he loved her mother as she'd hoped. "Marcel said I was not his child and Mama did not deny it."

"I never knew Trilby to lie," John said softly. "As you surely know, Marcel talked your mother into returning to Natchez when you were two. How I loathed seeing you and Trilby depart my island like beautiful birds leaving their nest." He sighed and then smiled. "In the parrot family, scarlet macaws are known for forming strong family bonds. I sent one to your grandparents' castle to remind Trilby that I would always be here."

"Supper is served, sir," an aproned woman said at the French doors.

"Merci, Viviane," John said. "Allow me to escort you to the dining room, ma chère."

Noelle's host rose and offered his arm.

"Mr. Galveston?"

"Please call me John."

"John?" she began, took his arm and paused. When he smiled she asked, "Do you have a daughter with red hair and hazel eyes?"

"What does your heart tell you?"

This enigma of a man seemed more fantasy than reality. Yet, here in Campeche, his colony where many loyal men still worked for him, she had found the buried treasure of her identity.

"My heart says yes." Noelle placed a hand over her heart. "I thought never to know for certain, much less meet him. But as far as the rest of the world is concerned, Jean Lafitte died in eighteen twenty-three."

"C'est bon, chérie," he replied and embraced her. "I will always be grateful to Jim for sending such a beautiful child to me and to Blaze for getting you here safely."

He kissed her forehead, stood her back and smiled. Noelle swiped a tear off her cheek and walked with him into a dining room where chandeliers glittered above a long, mahogany table set with crystal, china and silver. Coming in through another door was Felice on Blaze's arm. Noelle's calm shattered.

Blaze's tawny gold hair, still damp from his bath, shone in the warm glow from the chandeliers. His deep gray eyes glinted with silver intensity. His sun-bronzed face was clean shaven and would feel smooth against her lips. He wore a silvery gray shirt open at the throat with full sleeves flowing to wide cuffs buttoned at his thick wrists. Black breeches clung to his trim hips and muscular thighs. Polished black boots stretched over his well-developed calves to just below his knees.

A blaze of glory and she'd given him up.

John took Noelle to a chair as Felice stood on Blaze's right. Noelle gripped the back of the chair to steady herself. Shade sauntered in with Catherine on his arm, laughing at something they'd shared. Then Catherine glided to John as if he were the only man in the world and lightly kissed him on the lips. John seated her at one end of the table and then walked to the opposite end. Shade seated Noelle on John's right and sat between her and Catherine. Blaze seated Felice on John's left and sat across from Shade. Gazing at the betrothed couple, Noelle felt awkward.

"You look lovely, Felice," Noelle said and smiled.

Felice wore an olive dress that accented her skin and set off her shining black hair.

"So do you, Noelle," Felice said.

Though Felice's expression was pained with fear and regret, love for Noelle glowed in her dark brown eyes. Noelle did not know how she was going to make it through this dinner. John poured wine and suddenly Noelle knew exactly how she would endure it.

For every good mescal, for every ill as well.

She sipped wine before and after her soup and began a second glass during the entree of succulent roast pig and honey glazed yams. Finishing the second glass as the Crepe Suzette arrived, Blaze frowned at her. He shook his head when Shade poured her a third glass. She sipped it as a muscle worked in Blaze's jaw.

By the time their dessert of caramelized sugar, butter and *liquor* served flambé had been eaten, Noelle knew she was in trouble. She was glad she'd not finished that third glass of wine.

"Gentleman, whenever you're ready, let's have brandy on the veranda," John said.

"I'm sure Blaze wants to escort his fiancée upstairs," Shade grumbled, the effects of the wine slowing his speech. "I'll escort Noelle."

Shade got to his feet and pulled out Noelle's chair. She stood and suddenly knew only with help would she make it up the staircase to her room.

"Thank you for a lovely supper and your gracious hospitality," Noelle said to John and Catherine. Shade offered his arm and she smiled at the host and hostess. "I look forward to seeing you in the morning."

Catching a glimpse of Blaze, gray fire burned her as Shade gave her a tug. She wobbled on unsteady legs as Blaze crossed his arms over his chest. Turning away from his anger as Shade wrapped his arm around her waist, she left the elegant dining room with him. Reaching the staircase she placed her hand on the banister.

"You know what, Blaze? I remember straddling this banister and sliding all the way down it when I was a little girl...no, I think that was at my grandparents' house in Natchez."

"Shade," he corrected her. "Why don't we go to my room?" Shade scooped her up and was halfway to the second floor when he said, "You can straddle me and slide."

"Put me down!" she said in a firm voice. He did, but it happened so quickly she tripped down a couple of stairs. Shade bolted toward the second floor as a solid wall of muscle came up behind her.

"What do you think you're doing?" Blaze said as his strong hands gripped her waist. "Dammit, Noelle, you're full as a little tick!"

"Oui," she said as Shade disappeared. "Where's Felice?"

"Sober and downstairs with Catherine." Blaze took her arm as they climbed the stairs. "Where's your room?"

Noelle pulled away from him as they reached the second floor and weaved to the door to her room.

"Maybe Felice doesn't have a reason to drink too much," Noelle said.

"Really?" Blaze growled and opened the door.

"She's the one who's going to marry you," Noelle said, the wine and liquor loosening her tongue as Blaze led the way into the bedroom decorated with a brass bed, dressing table and upholstered chairs. Following him, she touched his arm and he turned to face her. "How long will it be before you make love to her?"

"I will make love only to you for as long as I live."

Noelle stared up at the gorgeous man who looked as much a swashbuckler as any pirate in the gulf ever could. She was so in love with Blaze she could hardly breathe.

"I would have made love to you every night in front of a romantic fireplace," Noelle said as she unfastened the buttons under the left arm of her dress. "I'd dreamed of," she tugged her arms out of her sleeves, "sleeping with my handsome husband in the castle's master bedroom suite." The gown gently puddled around her feet.

"Did you now?"

"Yes. Because after Grandfather died, Grandmother moved into a smaller bedroom leaving the master suite empty," she continued, sliding a petticoat strap off her right shoulder and then her left. "The master suite has French doors which open to a panoramic view of the Mississippi River." The petticoats slipped to her breasts, barely hiding the nipples. "My mantel, carved with its scene of a family, would have been perfect in the bedroom where I'd planned to make babies with you."

"We will have our own bedroom even better than that," he said with a sexy grin.

"Oh... but you would have liked the castle bedroom."

"Why?"

"Because I would have been waiting for you in our bed."

"Stop staying would have, Noelle. It will be."

"That highest hill, topped by the Whiskey Castle, is covered by thousands of acres of beautiful, dense forest."

"Yeah, timberland owned by me."

"What?" Noelle gasped, shaken from her alcohol induced reverie. "That can't be true, Blaze."

"Oh, it's very true. Apparently, your grandmother may not be in the best of health and maybe she's given up on you coming home because she sold all of her property to my family except for the castle."

"Is that why you said you were considering moving across the river to Mississippi?"

"Yes." Blaze eased her arms out of the petticoat and pushed it to her waist. "Let's get back to you waiting for me in bed."

"Not while you are married to someone else."

"It will be for a short time and in name only." His warm mouth met hers in a melting kiss. Noelle slid her arms around his neck and clung to him. "When I marry you it will be forever, darlin'."

Noelle's petticoats shimmied down her body, leaving her clad only in her silk camisole and underwear. Blaze groaned and lifted her out of the dress and petticoats as she twined her arms around his neck and wrapped her legs around his waist. Her lips on Blaze's, Noelle heard a small cough.

"I need to talk to you, Noelle," Felice said.

Noelle broke off the kiss and put her feet on the floor.

"I'll come back later, Noelle," Blaze said, turned and left the room.

Felice quietly closed the door and took Noelle's hand. Felice did most of the talking and Noelle did most of the listening. Silently, Noelle vowed to search for ways to make things right up until the last possible moment.

"Please go with Blaze when he comes for you, Noelle."

NOELLE SPENT the next two nights in bittersweet bliss and the days in anxious awareness. On this third night, a breeze from the open window had blown out the candle leaving the bedroom pitch black. Dreaming of Blaze, she was whisked from her bed and carried down the hall. Before she was fully awake she was in another bed being kissed.

By the wrong man!

"Hell's bells!" Shade almost shouted, jumping up and yanking her out of the bed. She tried to pull her arm from him as he rushed her down the hall and straight into Blaze's room, dimly lit by candlelight. "Stay outa my bed, Noelle. I love Blaze, even if you don't."

"I love Felice, even if you don't!" she said, yanking free.

"I thought I'd picked up Happy!"

"I know you love Felice! Why don't you show Blaze and Felice how much you love both of them by marrying her? Make Felice *happy*, Shade."

"Blaze and I should have never left home. Hell, the 'gators in the bayou were safer than you and Felice."

"I would think someone Colonel Crockett said was meaner than a 'gator and as noble as a horse would be man enough to handle a beautiful raven-haired señorita who loves him more than life itself."

"To hell with noble. I'm just mean." Shade frowned at the floor.

"Do you love Felice or not?"

"She's Blaze's fiancée now."

"You've blamed Blaze for being in his shadow. But you can't blame him for doing the honorable thing by Felice since you're *afraid* to do so!" Noelle gripped his arms and gave him a shake. "The woman you love, who is carrying your baby, is going to marry your brother unless you stop it!"

"I can't stop it." Shade slumped forward into her arms. There were tears in his voice as he said, "I can't."

"You're the only one who can, Shade." Noelle patted his back. "The only one."

CHAPTER 42

"I THOUGHT I WAS THE ONLY ONE, NOELLE," BLAZE SAID, standing in the doorway.

A black shirt was unbuttoned halfway down his chest, as if he'd been unfastening it on the way upstairs. He wore snug black pants and his black boots.

"How long have you been there?" Noelle asked, her voice trembling.

"Long enough," Blaze muttered, his expression as dark as a thundercloud. "I'd have come for you sooner, but John and I just finished dealing with the goldsmith. Where were you, Shade? Drinking and sulking?"

"This isn't what you think, Blaze," Shade said and quickly rubbed his watery, red eyes. "If it were, we sure as hell wouldn't be in your room."

Blaze raised his hand in a signal to stop and said, "Time is ticking against us. We only have a month to get back to Louisiana. Felice is pregnant, Sam Houston could send someone to get us tonight and Noelle wants to go home to see about her grandmother. Let's not fall out among ourselves."

"We've already fallen," Noelle said to the two men who had changed her and Felice's lives so drastically.

"What does that mean?" Blaze asked. "You and Felice and I are all going to live together."

"No, I told Felice she could live with *you and me*." Noelle shook her head. "I never agreed to live with *you and Felice*, Blaze."

"Felice agreed to it," Blaze said.

"She also agreed to burn in hell for divorcing you."

"She will not burn in hell," Blaze replied quietly.

"It's a moot point because the Catholic Church will never grant you a divorce," Noelle realized for the first time as she said the words. "*Never.*"

"The wedding's tomorrow." Blaze plowed both hands through his hair and in his gray eyes was the look of a trapped animal. "Why didn't you tell me you weren't going to live with me?"

"You told me the evening we crossed the Colorado River that in war or in love you had to do what was right. I know living with you and your wife wouldn't be right. We've made our beds and you'd better pray that Felice lets you into hers because you'll be there for life."

"Dammit!" Blaze roared. He paced over to a silent Shade and grabbed his shirt front. "When we heard about Lucy Ray and you thought I'd fathered her baby, you told me I should have married her. You are the father of Felice's baby and *you* should marry her!"

"Well, I'm not the man you are, now am I?" Shade barked and shoved Blaze back.

These were critical days and in the past, Noelle had not only inaccurately blamed the Bowies for her lot in life, but naively agreed to travel to Natchez with Buzzard. The most recent time Noelle had spoken too fast, she'd suggested Blaze marry Felice. Needing time to calm down and think, Noelle darted out of the room. She hurried along the hallway and down the stairs as fast as she could, picking her way through the now familiar house. She opened the French doors and a gentle wind billowed her long daffodil yellow gown as she padded over the smooth stones of the veranda and through the lush green grass of the yard. Crossing the arched bridge over the moat, she passed between the towering palm trees at the entrance to the compound. Rushing toward the bay, the sand felt good on her bare feet. She veered to her right and ran along the edge of the gently lapping water. Finally, she dropped to her knees on the beach knowing she could run no farther from her problems.

"Mistletoe," Noelle said in surprise as the cat scampered to her. "When I saw you last, you were prancing after Petit to the stable." Picking her up, Noelle sniffled and cuddled her pet. "The next time I see Blaze he will have asked Felice if she will honor his husbandly rights." Picturing Blaze making love to another woman was Noelle's undoing. Shoulder heaving sobs racked her. Even when Mama died, she'd not wept from a place of such soul crushing emptiness. Hollow. That's how she felt. It was several minutes before she managed to lift her head. In the distance, the moon shone down on the serene compound where utter chaos reigned. "I can't wait to leave."

"I can't wait to take you," came a startling voice from behind.

"Buzzard!" Noelle gulped and quickly stood. "What are you doing here?"

"I've been waiting on you. What took the Bowies so long to get here?"

"Our business in not your business," she replied coolly.

The moonlight revealed Buzzard's square head, ruddy features and blackened teeth with frightening clarity. Even six feet away his smell backed Noelle up a few steps.

"How come Blaze Bowie let you outa his bed tonight?" Buzzard asked with a sneer.

"If you came after the gold, you're out of luck," she replied, ignoring his question. She glanced back at Maison Rouge, furious with herself for running so far. "Some of the gold is promised to a buyer and the rest is going home."

"I don't want that heavy gold. That's why I let the Bowies

drag it here." His eyes glinted with malice. A sword hung from a ragged sash around his potbelly. "But I'll relieve them of the money they're collecting for it."

"They're not going to hand over their money to you."

"They will to get you back!" Buzzard walked toward her and bared his rotten teeth. "Yer papa can afford any amount I demand!"

"You're crazy if you think you can take on the Bowie brothers and John and come out alive."

"While we're waiting for 'em to pay, I'll be ruttin' between yer legs."

Noelle tried to scream but was cut off by his hand over her mouth. He grabbed a fistful of her hair and expelling a rush of hideous breath in her face, jammed the tip of a dagger to her throat. Swallowing meant being cut, a scream would surely bring death. Suddenly, Mistletoe squirmed out of Noelle's arms and dug her claws into the bandana around Buzzard's head. He used his knife-hand to catch the scruff of her neck and hurled both cat and bandana into the bay.

Suddenly free of the knife to her throat, Noelle cried out at seeing Mistletoe vanish into the sea. If only she had the knife Blaze had given her. What was it he had told her to do when Buzzard had her cornered in the Alamo?

Ram your knee between his legs, dammit.

Buzzard yelped and dropped to one knee, but still clutching her hair he dragged Noelle down with him.

"Try that again or scream and I'll kill you. Then I'll kill that arrogant Bowie you spread yer legs for when he brings the ransom for yer raped body," he snarled and backhanded her across her face.

Her right cheek stinging, Noelle fell onto her side in the sand and instantly Buzzard dug his fingers into her arm. Grimacing, he struggled to his feet, yanked her up and rubbed his crotch.

"We're goin' to my hideout down the beach."

For nearly a mile, he dragged her down the beach until they reached a burrow made of palm tree fronds lashed together with dried seaweed. Buzzard forced Noelle to her knees and shoved her inside. Salty stems scratched her skin as she quickly turned to face him. He hunched down just outside, blocking her escape.

"Shade won't pay to get me back if I'm soiled."

"Shade?" Buzzard snorted. "Blaze'll pay."

"Blaze is betrothed to Felice now."

"That's a pitiful lie." Buzzard sheathed his dagger and snorted. "Shade said Blaze has been hoisting his sail to plug only yer portal, so if Blaze marries anybody it'll be you."

"Felice is pregnant," Noelle managed to say, stunned by Buzzard's crudeness. "Blaze is going to do right by her because Shade won't."

Instinctively, Noelle put her hands to her stomach and the gesture was not lost on Buzzard.

"Blaze ain't marryin' her with his bread bakin' in yer oven." An evil grin split Buzzard's hideous face. "I'm gonna double the ransom."

"Forget about Blaze." Nose to nose with the stinking man, Noelle felt sick. "You take me to Natchez and my grandmother will pay whatever you ask for bringing me home. You won't have to kill anybody or be on the run from the law."

"Yeah, Maria claimed yer grandmother was rich," Buzzard said. "I'm still havin' you in the bargain."

"Like hell you will," came Blaze's ominous growl as Buzzard was grabbed from behind.

Noelle scooted to the opening of the burrow as Blaze sent Buzzard rolling across the sand.

"Noelle." John held out his hand and helped her to her feet.

Over the awful pirate towered latent fury.

Blaze's dark blond hair shimmered like gold in the moonlight, his deep gray eyes promising death. Armed with a knife and saber, the sea breeze fluttered his open, black shirt letting Noelle glimpse his broad chest. The black pants hugged his muscular legs and his booted feet were slightly spread. To Blaze's left stood Shade also armed. John moved to Blaze's right, flintlock pistol in hand, looking ready to kill. Petit joined them, cuddling Mistletoe.

Sprawled on his back, Buzzard scowled up at Blaze, then at Shade and sat up.

Looking for an ally, Buzzard said to John, "Ahoy, cap'n."

"I do *not* know you," John said. "And you have made an enemy of me with your actions. Many men have lived to regret that."

"One-on-one I can best any of you," Buzzard said and got to his feet. "I won't mind killin' a Bowie or the Pirate of the Gulf."

Shade snarled, "Nobody's ever bested Blaze or me."

"Yer first to die, Shade, you *turncoat*," Buzzard said, his hand near the handle of his sword.

"Bowie blood always runs thicker'n water," Shade replied coldly.

"I want to hear why you've dogged us since the day we met," Blaze said. "Speak and I'll let you try to fight your way out of this."

This was the mean-cussed-as-an-aroused 'gator side of Blaze that Davy Crockett had seen in the cantina knife fight. Be it Santa Anna or not, Noelle knew very well Blaze could carve up a man and leave him for dead.

"The day them cantina whores said the Charbonnez girl was rumored to be Lafitte's daughter, I knew there was a ransom waitin' for me on Galveston Island," Buzzard replied. "I was plannin' to take her the night of the first fandango, but you and Shade stopped by her shack."

"Hell, I wondered why you were wandering around in those cottonwood trees," Shade said.

"I knew if I snatched her after that you'd find me and take her back," Buzzard said to Blaze and glared at Shade. "So I pushed to come with you to the island. I figured to collect from you *and* Lafitte."

So there it was; the whole ugly truth revealed by an ugly man.

"Blaze said you were as savage as a meat ax," Shade said. "I should have listened."

"You whine worse than them cantina whores did over you Bowies," Buzzard hissed. "I hadta slit their sniveling throats to shut 'em up. Maybe you'd better keep yer other Mexican puta after all."

"You sonofabitch! Felice is not a whore!" Shade roared, lunging forward only to be stopped by John. "Let me at him, John."

"No, mon ami," John said calmly as if he'd been here a thousand times before.

"He's mine." Blaze stood back and drew his saber.

CHAPTER 43

"THE WINNER GETS THE MONEY FROM YER GOLD," BUZZARD bargained as he yanked his sword from his sash.

"Agreed," Blaze growled.

"When I win, I get the girl, too," Buzzard said, also pulling his knife from its sheath. "Lafitte must pay to get her back again."

"Jean Lafitte died in eighteen twenty-three, in the Caribbean!" Noelle said.

"To hell with Lafitte, then," Buzzard said, revealing his lie about knowing him. "Bowie, yer never gonna live to see the bread—"

"Noelle!" Felice wailed, running toward them with Catherine at her side. "Shade!"

Noelle had swayed forward when Buzzard almost blurted out her suspicion of being pregnant.

"Petit, keep the women back!" John ordered.

"Let's see you best me, Buzzard," Blaze said.

Weapons in both hands, Buzzard charged Blaze who nimbly sidestepped him. A wide circle formed around the two fighters as a chilling death match proceeded. Buzzard flung the knife at Blaze but he tilted his head and the blade dove harmlessly into the sand.

"Noelle can throw better than that. Hell, she knifed a cougar," Blaze said, taunting his opponent.

With a foul curse, Buzzard drew a second knife from inside his shirt and threw it. Blaze jumped out of the way and laughed.

"Yer gonna die now, Bowie," Buzzard said, waving his sword.

Blaze raised his saber and both men lunged, steel clashing against steel.

It was kill or be killed, Noelle.

If only Blaze's shirt weren't open, being dressed all in black would make him a harder target. But as it was, his naked heart was a bull's-eye for Buzzard's blade.

"Shade, do something!" Noelle said.

"Blaze is in his element," Shade said. "Just watch."

Blaze suddenly slashed Buzzard's wrist to the bone and as Buzzard hollered, Blaze deftly slit his other wrist. Blaze then dealt Buzzard's sword a mighty blow, knocking the man sideways. Buzzard shook his square head to clear it. But a second blow to the sword took Buzzard's feet out from under him and he fell on his back, heels in the air. Blaze kicked Buzzard's sword out of his hand before tossing his own saber to Shade. Blaze pulled the knife from Jim out its scabbard. Buzzard struggled to his feet and staggered sideways, blood draining down both hands.

"Blood loss makes an opponent an even easier prey," Blaze said.

"Pirate swore you Bowies had a secret you wouldn't tell nobody," Buzzard sneered, bleeding out.

"A secret well-kept is one kept close to hearth and home," Blaze replied, quoting Noelle.

As Shade flung Buzzard's sword into the bay, Buzzard yanked a small dagger from his pocket.

"Blaze, be careful!" Noelle cried.

Blaze tossed his knife from one hand to the other and raised his chin in challenge. Buzzard stumbled and Blaze lunged. In a blindingly fast move, Blaze buried his knife in

Buzzard's neck. Buzzard's eyes bulged and his dagger dropped to the sand. When Blaze pulled his knife out, Buzzard slumped to his knees.

"Show me mercy, Bowie," Buzzard said, blood coating his grimy teeth.

Blaze nodded to Noelle. "Like you showed Noelle?"

"Or like you showed Maria and Rosa?" Noelle spat. "Or Mistletoe when you threw her into the bay?"

"Kitty?" Petit frowned at Buzzard.

Cradling Mistletoe in his left arm, the giant walked up behind the all-but-dead Buzzard. He curled his mammoth hand around the back of the pirate's bloody neck and snapped it with a loud pop.

John shrugged and said, "Petit, please deliver Monsieur Buzzard to the Carancahua Indians."

Blaze swished his knife in the ocean, washing off the blood as Petit grabbed one of Buzzard's slashed wrists. Murmuring to Mistletoe, Petit easily began dragging Buzzard's body back down the beach.

"Blaze, are you hurt?" Noelle asked.

"Come here and find out, darlin'," Blaze replied, sheathing his knife.

"And do *not* come to our room tonight," Felice whispered and nudged Noelle toward Blaze.

Noelle drifted into Blaze's muscular embrace. Hugging him was sweet heaven after sheer hell. He let her go, picked up Buzzard's daggers and hurled them into the bay.

"They weren't *Bowie* knives," Blaze said.

"Then they weren't worth keeping," John said. "I remember how Jim and Rezin Bowie were always high entertainment." He chuckled. "I can see this next generation of Bowies is just as wild, with beautiful women who are not only courageous but unforgettable." He winked with a nod at Noelle and Felice while swinging an arm around Catherine. Hugging her, John said, "Did Jim impart the vein-slashing secret to you?"

"Actually, it was our mother who was half Natchez Indian and a midwife," Blaze replied.

"She said if we were gonna fight with knives, she wanted us to win," Shade said.

John hadn't expected that answer and his hearty laugh broke the tension of the night. Catherine wrapped her arm around John's waist and they led the way down the beach as Shade and Felice followed with Blaze and Noelle bringing up the rear. Far in the lead a whistling Petit cradled Mistletoe as they passed the compound with Buzzard's body leaving a sand path in their wake.

"John, I've never heard of the Carancahua Indians," Blaze said, taking Noelle's hand as they walked along. "Why would they want a dead pirate?"

"The Carancahua are cannibals," John explained. "They could be the reason this place is called Bad Luck Island."

"Once when Jean Lafitte hosted a party for Jim and Rezin, Sam, Jim's slave, was left in charge of thirty other slaves," Catherine said in a matter-of-fact voice. "But Sam fell asleep and in the morning all thirty slaves were gone."

"The Carancahua had 'em for breakfast?" Shade asked.

"Evidently," John said. "But I have made friends with them and they no longer take meals uninvited."

"There's damn good justice in Buzzard being eaten like carrion," Shade said.

"Absolument." John turned to them and his smile was all knowing.

"Oui," Catherine agreed. "Absolutely."

Everyone watched as Petit vanished into the night. Arriving at the white-sand beach that lay beyond the stone wall of John's home and grounds, Blaze stopped and pulled Noelle to his side.

"If you all will excuse us I'd like to talk to Noelle," he said.

"Bonne nuit," John said.

Shade nodded and wrapped his arm around Felice who

…heart thumped as she and Blaze stood in the
…t the edge of the water. Blaze placed both hands
…e and lightly kissed her right cheek, taking the sting
…. Then his lips covered hers and twining her arms around
…is neck, Noelle kissed him back, never wanting to let him go.

"Thank you for saving me from Buzzard," she whispered near his ear.

Blaze tightened his arms around her. "When Buzzard accused Felice of being a whore, he made Shade admit that she isn't one."

"Yes." Noelle leaned back and smiled up at him. "John said it's good that things are being revealed." She craved another wild kiss, but said instead, "Blaze, this is the eve of your wedding. We shouldn't be together." She was shocked when he laughed and sat down on the sand, pulling her with him.

"Noelle, Noelle," Blaze said with a sigh. "Don't you know Felice and Shade have been together in Shade's bed every night?"

"How did you find out?" she asked, wide eyed.

"Shade told me," Blaze said. "He was surprised as hell it was you and not Felice he plucked out of bed."

"That's progress."

"Maybe. He says Felice sleeps beside him, but that's all she'll do with him."

"Yes, she told me."

"Anyway, your cat streaked into the house sopping wet and all hell broke loose when we found only Felice in your bed."

"When you consummate your marriage, be gentle with Felice. She's afraid and nervous now."

"I'm not consummating any marriage except yours and mine."

"Goodnight, Blaze." Noelle kissed her fingertips and lightly touched them to his lips.

"I fought for you and I won," Blaze said, catching her wrist before she could stand. "Stay with me."

"I'd feel the guilt in the morning."

"But you'll feel the passion tonight."

Blaze's grin was hot and lusty and, God help her, Noelle knew he spoke the truth. She let him ease her to lie back on the sand. He stretched out beside her and she tingled with anticipation as he leaned over her, pulling the lacy décolletage of her gown aside to bare her right breast. His smile made her crave the feel of his lips on her skin.

Moonbeams at his back, Blaze kissed a fiery path down her throat. With the bay lapping near her toes, Blaze's mouth closed over her nipple. He groaned and Noelle arched her back. He suckled the other nipple through the gown and the sensation of the lace barrier caused a wanton yearning of having him deep inside her.

As if the heavenly bodies above desired the ones on the beach to become one, heavy clouds hid the moon covering Noelle and Blaze with nature's midnight blanket. She slowly spread her legs and his gentle fingers dipped inside her. She was more than ready for him. Blaze unfastened his pants and rolled on top of her. The tip of his manhood touched her where his fingers had just been.

"Blaze, we can't join our bodies mere hours before you join Felice in marriage."

"Yes, we can. Maybe Shade will come through."

"And maybe he won't."

Blaze grasped the hem of her gown and pulled it to her waist, lowered his head and circled her belly button with his warm tongue. She trembled as he nibbled a path downward. Noelle gasped as his lips and tongue played where only his fingers and manhood had created fevered friction. Such sizzling pleasure whirled between her thighs that her legs spread wider as she lost herself in his bold new kiss.

"Yes, Blaze." She buried her hands in hair holding him to her.

Wondering if the sand could catch fire, red hot passion swept over her in wave after wave of tingling sweet ecstasy. Blaze raised her hips off the sand as she writhed from the

max. She tossed her head back and forth
...is name as he kissed the vibrating folds of her
...od.

...mon, darlin'." Blaze smiled. "Let's go crawl in my bed
...d you can do to me what I just did to you."

"I'll race you there!"

In the cozy softness of his bed, she began by bashfully trifling with the hard length of his manhood. Quickly, she progressed to boldly kissing him and with pleasure he disappeared between her full, pink lips into her warm, wet mouth. Up and down she spiraled him into the clouds that had covered the moon.

"Up and at 'em," John called outside the bedroom door way too soon.

CHAPTER 44

"Blaze!" John said. "Are you awake?"

"Yes sir," Blaze replied and pulled a sleepy Noelle into his arms.

"A priest and a minister will be joining us for breakfast." As John's footsteps receded he said, "See you in the dining room."

"Let's get the ceremony over with, darlin'."

Blaze wondered when they would wake up like this again. Sheer white curtains fluttered on a warm spring breeze. Sunshine and sea air filled the room. What a perfect day for a wedding... if only he were marrying the naked beauty whose head lay on his shoulder. Hazel eyes misted but pink lips smiled at him. Her Cupid's arrows hit their target as always and Blaze's heart bled. He channeled his thoughts to her sweet mouth which had satisfied him so completely during the night that his flesh still felt fevered.

"Have you considered that General Houston might not send for you?" Noelle sat up and brushed her dark copper curls away from her eyes. Blaze was relieved to see only a tiny bruise on her right cheek. "In that case, you could wait until we got back to Natchez to marry Felice."

"Houston gave me his word he'd send for us." Blaze sat up, swung his legs out of bed and clenched his fists on his

have to make use of the priest's services
_?_."

_?_ John would invite the priest to stay on for a
until we see if General Houston sends for you."

"We can't stay on much longer because of our pending
foreclosure." Blaze stared at the floor between his bare feet.
"If Houston doesn't send for me by tomorrow, I'll have to go
find him," he said and felt Noelle tense at his side. "But
you'll be safe here no matter what. When I come back, we'll
travel fast since the gold we don't sell to John is being
shipped home." He leaned forward and rested his head in
his hands.

Noelle ran her fingers under his hair and gently
massaged his neck. It felt too good. He stood and stalked to
the walnut wardrobe in the far corner. She slid off the bed
and as pure feminine perfection neared, he turned away.
Stopping behind him, she molded her naked body to his and
flattened her hands to his chest. He wanted to take her back
to bed and forget the world.

"Why not confirm Houston's exact intentions toward
Santa Anna before you make good on yours to Felice?"

"Noelle." Blaze sighed, nudged her back and opened the
doors of the wardrobe. "Houston's intention is to stop Santa
Anna and soon."

"And soon I'll know if—"

"Know what?" he barked with a glare over his shoulder.
Loving her so much, he didn't want to hear she needed
more time to know if she loved him. "Nothing's going to
change." He nodded toward his bed. "Go put on your gown."

"I still have faith Shade will propose," she replied,
walking to the bed.

"I had faith you'd come to love me and we see how that
turned out."

Blaze tugged on a pair of pants. Bending over the washbowl on a marble top dresser, he splashed water on his face
and dried off with a small towel. Sitting down in a tapestry
chair he pulled on his socks and picked up a boot.

"One way or the other, we have to get back on the trail soon," he said.

"Don't count me in on the *we*."

"What?" Blaze looked up from tugging on his second boot. She was a vision of nakedness to drive a man insane; all auburn locks and ivory skin in a rumpled, four poster bed. "When we leave this island it will be together. You can count on that, Noelle."

"You'd better count on Shade sleeping with your wife. He'll blame you for stealing Felice from him. He will see himself as second best all anew and feel justified in bedding her. We know that you meant for Shade to give Felice the Bowie name. I want *you* to know that I truly never meant for you to do so in his place." Her throat ached, but she continued, "Independence and the freedoms you've fought for will become as lost and empty as the Alamo."

Blaze visibly flinched at that. "It's temporary," he said as if trying to convince himself. He stood, walked to her and grabbing the daffodil gown slid it over her head. He took her hand and led her to the door. He opened it and peered into the hall. "The coast is clear. Go," he said, but she shut the door. "What?"

"I understand your honorable intensions in standing by Felice," Noelle said. "But I am releasing you from your promise to take me to Grandmother. I will not travel with you and Felice once you're married. So, please don't make it difficult for me to leave after the ceremony."

"I'll admit it would be impossible for me to live in the same house with you and your *husband*." He squared his shoulders and said, "If you want to make a break until I'm free to marry you, I'll build you a house and—"

"You... will... never... be... free, Blaze! Have you forgotten the Catholic Church?"

He was sure trying to forget it. "John and Catherine aren't married and they're happy. If I can't get a divorce you could be my—"

"Mistress?" She cringed. "No. John's wife is dead. Your wife will be alive."

Nothing he'd ever suffered had prepared Blaze for the bleak despair he felt at this moment.

"It will be dangerous for you on your own." Blaze reached for her but she backed away and placed her hand on the doorknob. "Will you live with your Grandmother?"

"On the same side of the Mississippi River where you're planning to move?" In her laugh was a tinge of hysteria, which she cut off, shook her head and said softly, "No. I have relatives in Geneva, Switzerland."

"Good God Almighty," Blaze said, waves of shock washing over him. "I guess that's about as far away from me as you can get." He placed his hand over his heart as if that could keep her arrows from killing him. "Will you at least write and let me know you arrived safely? Let me know if... when you fall in love and get married?"

Silence.

"Noelle, I refuse to believe after all we've survived together, it's come to this end."

"We locked ourselves into this *inevitable end.*"

Blaze stood paralyzed with disbelief and defeat as this unforgettable woman walked out of his room and quietly closed the door behind her.

"WHERE'S YOUR *BETROTHED*, BLAZE?" Shade asked with a sarcastic smirk as he sat across from Blaze at the dining room table.

Shade had glared at the priest from the moment Blaze had said they'd need his services, rather than the minister's, since Felice was Catholic. Though he and Blaze were Methodist, Shade would have gladly married outside of his faith... *if* he were the marrying kind.

"Viviane took breakfast upstairs to the ladies," John replied when Blaze did not respond.

The priest wiped his pursed lips with a linen napkin and asked Blaze to tell him about Felice.

"Shade and I met Felice a couple of months ago in San Antonio de Bexar," Blaze said, without making eye contact with anyone. "The name Felice means happy in Spanish."

"And she makes you happy?" the priest asked.

"She will," Shade growled. "Hell, she'll make him happy every damn night, all night if he wants her to."

"Simmer down, Shade," Blaze said.

"Shut the hell up, Blaze!" Shade shot to his feet. "The smell of food is making me sick. No offense, John."

"None taken," John replied, but with a disapproving frown at Shade.

Shade stalked out of the dining room to the foyer and met Noelle coming down the wide staircase.

"Noelle, are you going to let Blaze go through with this farce?" Seeing she was deathly pale, he softened his tone. "Well, are you?"

"Blaze doesn't see it as a farce."

Noelle glanced toward the dining room then motioned to Shade and they walked outside. Coming to the stone wall, she sat and clasped her hands in her lap.

"He knows it's a farce," Shade insisted.

"He's accepted the fact this marriage is forever." Noelle gazed up at Shade. "He asked me to be his mistress."

"So be his mistress. You can get him to throw Felice out of his house and I'll take her in."

"We cannot let a child suffer any ridicule."

"Dammit! Nobody asked Blaze to be a hero."

"Nobody had to. He just is."

"Noelle, you need to do something."

"I will do something by moving to Switzerland and making my new home there."

So jolted he felt physically struck, Shade sat down and stared at Noelle. Not having this woman in their lives was unthinkable. Losing Noelle would devastate Felice and destroy Blaze. Shade would miss Noelle and realized he loved her like he would a little sister.

"The other side of the ocean would *never* feel like home," Shade said firmly and put his arm around her shoulders. "Blaze told me on the way to San Antonio that a *real* home is the freedom to live your life the way you want it to be, with people you would die for. You have the independence to leave, but you would never want to. After Blaze said that, I decided to turn over a new leaf." How vividly he remembered telling Blaze he wanted a raven-haired beauty, an exotic señorita. An innocent. He had found Felice and taught her everything. In turn, Felice had taught him that he didn't live in anyone's shadow. She'd told him more than once he was both the shade *and* the tree. He would die for Felice. "You can't leave us and move to Switzerland, Noelle."

"Remember to always love and laugh."

"We won't without you."

The front door to Maison Rouge opened and there stood the bridegroom.

"Staking your claim on Noelle, Shade?"

CHAPTER 45

"MI DIOS," FELICE SAID TO HERSELF.

Standing in the middle of the parlor, she was strangling the stems of her bouquet. Catherine had arranged Felice's hair in a chignon woven with turquoise ribbons. Turquoise lace trimmed the waist of the cocoa colored gown Felice had chosen to match the brown of Shade's hair. The gown's neckline hinted of her pregnancy-blossoming bosom and leg of mutton sleeves puffed at her shoulders. Felice's mounting anxiety had blunted her expression and despair had curled her toes inside the slippers topped with turquoise bows.

As the priest and a minister spoke with John and Catherine, Suzanne placed a crystal vase of fresh flowers on an ornate table and Viviane entered with silver platters of sweet breads and fruit, cheese and meats. Petit stood near a window petting Mistletoe.

Shade entered the parlor with Noelle on his arm. Felice wished for the thousandth time he had fallen in love with her as she had with him. Dressed in a white shirt, dark brown breeches and knee-length, brown boots Shade was so hermoso. She would have been the best wife ever to him if only he had given her the chance.

But no, he was going home and wanted his Natchez-

Under-the-Hill whores back. She swallowed her heartache by telling herself Shade would see himself in their baby. But even if he refused to see, she would free Blaze through whatever means necessary. Willing to burn in hell for divorce, she might as well burn for suicide, she decided. Noelle and Blaze would make wonderful, loving parents for her baby.

Blaze entered the parlor, his gaze fixed on Noelle, breathtaking in flowing gossamer. Noelle had chosen a deep gray gown because of Blaze's eyes. The tiny green and gold dots on the dress matched Noelle's hazel eyes to perfection and a scooped décolletage set off an ivory cleavage which would make any man's mouth water. Auburn curls simply swept to the nape of her neck and tied there with a single gray ribbon, rained down Noelle's back taking one's eye to her small waist.

"We are all here," John said from where he stood at one end of the gold mantel. "Shall we begin the ceremony, Father?"

The priest nodded and centered himself in front of the fireplace. Felice slowly made her way forward stopping before the priest. Blaze walked to Felice's side as Noelle moved behind them with John and Catherine. Petit, Viviane and Suzanne stood at the back of the room. Shade had stalked to the open French doors and crossed his arms over his chest. Felice figured he'd be gone before they said 'I do'.

"Noelle," Felice began, "will you stand beside me?"

"Yes, of course." Smiling, Noelle moved to her side.

Noelle glanced at Blaze. He was magnificent among all men. Stacked against the Napoleon of the West, the Commander-in-Chief of the Texas Army or the Pirate of the Gulf, Blaze knew no equal. His silky, dark blond hair was a dramatic contrast to the forest green, flowing shirt. It was open at his bronzed throat, cuffed at his thick wrists and tucked into his black breeches. Around his waist was a black sash and his knee-high, polished black boots were snug against his muscular legs.

Never giving Noelle a second look, Blaze stared straight ahead at the priest, duty bound. Catherine came up beside Noelle and John moved to Blaze's right. Gazing at the mantel, Noelle knew Jim Bowie would not be pleased with this situation.

The priest spoke and to Noelle it was the beginning of the end.

How had Blaze kissed her so intimately the night before and be marrying another woman a few hours later? How could she have so passionately returned Blaze's lovemaking in his bed only to give him up without saying she loved him?

Dear Lord! She hadn't told Blaze she loved him! He deserved to know... before, not after he was married!

"What part are we on?" Noelle asked urgently.

"Pardon me, young lady?" the priest said, frowning at her.

Noelle's skin suddenly felt two sizes too small. Felice's eyes glistened with tears. Blaze's brows were drawn in a menacing scowl.

"Have they said 'I do'?" Noelle asked in a small voice.

"No, they are not man and wife yet, but they shall be in a moment." The priest pursed his lips. "May we proceed?"

It's now or never.

"Well..." Noelle hesitated. Felice's soft smile encouraged her.

"Well what, Noelle?" Blaze asked.

"Blaze, do you remember Sick-Nick?"

Besides Blaze, only Shade would know who Nicky was. Felice had been in the Herrera's jacal the night they had run into Santa Anna outside the cantina.

"I remember," Blaze replied. "What about Nicky?"

Noelle's nerve faltered. She opened her mouth but no words came out.

"We will proceed now," the priest said.

"Au contraire mon ami, we will wait for her to speak," John said. "Noelle?"

Noelle nodded gratefully at John, squared her shoulders and looked into Blaze's eyes.

"Nicky will never send you a letter saying there's someone else. A lifetime of loving and laughing had to be with you. And only with you. Nicky loves you, Blaze Bowie."

"Better late than never." Blaze winked at her. "I needed to hear it in English to believe it."

So, he had known she'd said she loved him in Spanish with *te quiero mucho* and in French with *Je t'aime*. Good. She had finally told Blaze she loved him in every language she knew.

"Proceed now, Father," Noelle said.

"No!" Felice replied sharply.

"Petit!" Shade's roar filled the room. "Get Blaze outa my way!"

"Jean?" Petit looked at John who nodded. Petit lumbered to Blaze and took his arm. "Where do you want me to put him, Shade?"

Shade motioned for Petit to move Blaze to the right. The determination on Shade's face and the surprise on Felice's confirmed to Noelle that her step-sister had innocently succeeded in their long ago plan to break Shade of thinking he lived in Blaze's shadow. Felice held her head high as Shade stalked across the parlor.

For the second time in his life, Shade stepped in front of Blaze.

"Like you once told me, Blaze, you can't have them both!" Shade slid his hands under Felice's arms and lifted her off the floor. "Dammit, Felice!" He frowned, giving her a gentle shake. "Will you marry me?"

"Do you believe the baby is yours?" Felice asked.

"Hell, yes!" He put her feet back on the floor and said, "I know that baby is mine."

"About damn time," Blaze said.

"Such profanity at a wedding!" the priest said, crossing himself.

"Yeah well, you're not the first man of the cloth to think we're heathens," Shade replied as he grinned at Felice. "But we've found the ladies who could handle us."

"Will you give up all other women for me?" Felice asked. "You said once; that would be the day."

"This is that day, Happy."

"I love you, Shade, with all my heart." Felice looked up at him. "Do you love me, too?"

"Yes, I love you and I want only my raven-haired beauty to squeeze—" he whispered something in Felice's ear and then said louder, "and my heart. You make me *happy.*"

Felice flung her arms around Shade's neck and he pulled her against him, kissing her full on the lips. Blaze grinned and John chuckled as the priest crossed himself while the minister clutched his Bible and shrugged.

Smiling, Noelle pictured telling Blaze she might be pregnant and took an impulsive step toward him. Instantly, she feared he would be furious to find out she suspected she was carrying his child while planning to let him give the Bowie name to a niece or nephew. Not only that, her possible pregnancy would keep Blaze from going after Santa Anna and he would surely come to resent her for it.

She needed to escape this unexpected turn of events and consider her words. Carefully she backed out of the room and hurried across the foyer. As she put her hand on the knob of the front door, John's voice stopped her.

"Noelle, wait, s'il vous plaît."

Noelle paused and looked around.

"Do you not think Blaze deserves for you as well as Shade to do right by him?"

"I've done Blaze so wrong I don't see a way to make it right." Noelle's eyes watered.

"You found a way out of the Alamo. Can you not find a way out of this together?"

"I had Jim Bowie's help at the Alamo."

"You have had my help on Galveston Island, by giving the four of you time to work things out. I could have had a priest brought to the island the same day Blaze announced he was going to marry Felice," John replied. "I sent for the minister knowing the Bowies are Methodist."

Noelle wasn't surprised that John knew Blaze was Methodist. What stunned her was that John had deliberately delayed the wedding for days.

"Shade is about to do his part." John placed his hand over hers on the doorknob. She released her grip and he looped her hand through his arm. "Do yours, Noelle."

Blaze sauntered around the corner. "Is everything all right?"

"Oui." John lifted Noelle's hand to his lips, kissed it and left.

"I'm free, darlin'," Blaze whispered with a smile.

"Hey!" Shade called from the parlor. "Felice and I wanna get married before the baby is born. Get in here!"

"Come on." Blaze snared Noelle's hand. "They aren't good at waiting."

"Noelle?" came Felice's voice. "Tell Blaze that Noelle, not Nicky, loves him and hurry back here."

"Blaze," Noelle placed her hand over her heart and the words she'd yearned to say for so long tumbled out, "I love you so very much. Cupid's arrow hit me, too. I fell in love with you in Main Plaza. When I told you I might come to love you with time it was a carrot I tried to dangle to coax you out of the Alamo. Later on I hoped a baby would tie you to me and keep you from going after Santa Anna with Sam Houston. But—"

"Don't think I haven't done my best to tie you to me, too." Blaze's grin was lusty.

"But I've made some mistakes along the way."

"Because you're as noble as you complain I am," Blaze said, exonerating her so easily. "I told you the day you said you loved me there would be no turning back, we would get married within the hour. Remember?"

"Yes, and I said you couldn't be serious."

"And I told you I was." Taking her hands, Blaze said,

"With John's blessing, I'm asking you to marry me, Noelle. Will you?"

"Yes, Blaze." She smiled and squeezed his hands. "I will marry you."

"Do you want the priest or minister to marry us?"

"I was baptized Methodist."

Blaze placed a hand over his heart and with a lopsided grin said, "Me, too."

Noelle gently put her hands to his face, as he so often did to her. She gazed into his steely gray eyes and mouthed *I love you* then twined her arms around his neck. He planted his lips on hers in a wild kiss just as Shade and Felice called for them. They broke apart, laughed and hurried into the parlor. The ceremony began afresh and this time everyone was all smiles.

At the perfect time, John surprised everyone by handing a gold wedding band to Shade.

"Made from my part of the Bowie gold I bought from your mantel, Shade."

Obviously moved, Shade thanked him and slipped the shiny band on Felice's finger. The priest concluded the ceremony by blessing the bride and groom. Shade kissed his wife and then caught his brother up in a hug.

"Thank you for everything, big bad Blaze," Shade said. "I love you, brother."

"Same here, brother. Congratulations!"

"You were willing to sacrifice your happiness for me," Felice said, taking Noelle in her arms. "Te quiero muy mucho."

Hugs, kisses and claps on the back were exchanged as family and friends laughed, sniffled and thoroughly enjoyed the magical moment.

"Let us have the next wedding," John said with a smile.

Blaze strode back to the hearth. Catherine quickly whisked the conveniently placed fresh flowers out of the crystal vase and handed them to Noelle as the minister replaced the priest. Shade stood at his brother's side with his arm around his happy bride. Suzanne and Viviane dabbed their eyes. Mistletoe watched from her pampered perch in the crook of Petit's arm.

"Glide toward the preacher and me, beautiful lady," Blaze said with a smile.

John offered his arm to Noelle and they walked to her groom who never took his eyes off her. Blaze nodded respectfully at John and took Noelle's hand. Catherine looped her arm through John's and the wedding proceeded.

The minister was addressing Blaze and Noelle's intentions to cherish and honor, when galloping hooves were heard outside. The phrase *until death do you part* was on the minister's lips when the clanging of the brass door knocker interrupted. John excused himself and swiftly returned.

"Blaze, Shade, Sam Houston sent a scouting party to tell you it is time to stop Santa Anna."

CHAPTER 46

"We've got the Twin Sisters with us now!" a soldier shouted to them in San Jacinto.

"He better not be calling us girls," Shade said.

Blaze and Shade were bringing up the rear of the scouting party that had joined up with Deaf Smith. Smith was a man the brothers were glad to finally meet and whose scouts had been sent to Galveston Island. Only partially deaf, Erastus or Deaf, generally pronounced 'Deef' Smith was a revered spy. It was said Smith could read footprints like handwriting and smell a dragoon a mile away. A man of few words, Smith had once intervened on Jim Bowie's behalf when Jim had been attacked by bandits, had couried a letter out of the Alamo for Colonel Travis, had been trusted by Sam Houston to confirm the fall of the Alamo, and was determined to win Texas' independence.

"For those of you who don't know, the Twin Sisters are two six-pounder cannons," Deaf Smith said to Blaze, Shade and the others riding into Houston's camp.

"Yeah," said the soldier who had ridden out from camp to greet them. "The cannons are a gift to our army from the folks of Cincinnati, Ohio."

The tears in Noelle's eyes, when Blaze had kissed her goodbye, had hit him as hard as a cannon ball. Riding away from Maison Rouge, the bravest woman he knew had waved a courageous farewell to him as she stood at the hitching post. Damn he wanted her back in his arms.

The scouting party he and Shade were with had ridden hard, covering many miles while tracking the enemy. During the moonlit nights, they had pushed through live oaks dripping Spanish moss. When dawn broke this morning, Blaze had been amazed to find they were in the midst of a swampy forest of giant magnolias, rhododendrons and hyacinths. At ten that morning they'd swooped down on Lynch's Ferry, dumbfounding enemy guards and acquiring a Mexican flatboat loaded with flour. By noon they were in Houston's camp.

Blaze studied General Houston's choice for a camp. Opposite of a landlocked battleship in the middle of the mesquite prairie, they were surrounded by water now. Deaf Smith pointed. To their right was Buffalo Bayou some three hundred feet wide and fifteen to thirty feet deep. To their left was a marsh called Peggy Lake and behind them was the San Jacinto River. Some five hundred yards dead ahead was Santa Anna's camp.

"Let's find Houston," Blaze said to Shade.

It didn't take them long to locate Houston and thank him for sending word. He was glad to have them and saw to it that they were issued ammunition for the rifles they'd been given at the Alamo.

"How did you decide to come south to find Santa Anna instead of going east?" Blaze asked the general.

"Near New Kentucky there was a huge oak tree with limbs pointing east toward the Trinity River and south toward Harrisburg," Houston said." My men and I took shelter under the tree. I named it the Which Way Tree because that's where I decided to go south and stop Santa Anna rather than continuing east to seek help from the colonies."

"Was there a well beside it?" Shade asked.

"Yes, why?"

"We stopped at that big oak to take shelter from the rain and draw water from the well," Blaze replied. He vividly remembered telling Noelle he didn't know *which way* to deal with her under that same tree.

"I want you two alive to see the Which Way Tree on your way back to Galveston Island. So, be careful while you're here with us." Houston shook their hands and said, "Food's cooking boys, go eat."

As he ate, Blaze watched the flames in the campfire dance. In them he saw Noelle dancing with him at the fandango. From that night on he had known he didn't want to live without her. When he got back to the island he'd sweep her into his arms and take her to bed. Looking to the day he'd lay his hand to Noelle's pregnant belly and kiss her sweet lips, Blaze sighed. That was a picture of the luckiest man on earth.

It was only two hours later when dragoons were spotted wading toward them through the prairie grass. Their armor glistened and their bugles blared. With their own six-pounder, the Mexicans fired on Houston's camp. Houston traded shots and then as quickly as it had begun the enemy fire inexplicably died. A few feet away Shade was talking to a couple of the scouts who'd been with them at Lynch's Ferry. The scouts were anxious to fight and wished they knew why Santa Anna had pulled back.

Since arriving in this bayou a few hours earlier, Blaze smiled for the first time. Leaning against a large oak tree he recalled leaning Noelle against the cypress tree in the hill country and asking if she wanted to make love bayou-style. They would do that again when they got back home.

Suddenly Blaze knew what had ceased the enemy fire. He walked away from the tree and called to Shade who came over to him.

"Wanna go see who Santa Anna's taking his siesta with?"

"That's *exactly* why he called the fight off this afternoon." Shade's eyes narrowed with realization. "He came across a better offer."

"Let's go on a run to the enemy camp."

"Should we tell Houston we're goin' spying?"

"Nah, he might not let us."

"He'll think we deserted if we don't make it back."

"When have we not made it out of a bayou, Shade?"

"THERE'S ALWAYS A FIRST TIME," Noelle said worriedly to Catherine.

"They will not be shot," Catherine replied, seated on the wickerwork sofa. "Blaze has your gray ribbon and Shade has Felice's turquoise one. Shade said the ribbons would keep them safe."

"Yes." Noelle sat in one of the two white rockers on the veranda. "Before Blaze left he reminded me that Mistletoe's leather ribbon kept her safe at the Alamo and from Buzzard. Maybe Shade is right about ribbons being lucky in battle. But I would feel better if they had armor like the dragoons."

"Blaze did not have your ribbon when he bested Buzzard," Catherine said and smiled. "So now your ribbon will be his armor."

"Having seen Blaze win that fight makes me less afraid now than I would have otherwise been," Noelle said and nodded. "I hope Shade is as good."

"He is," Felice said, standing at the open French doors. She crossed the veranda and sat in the other white rocker. "Shade was as wild and furious when he bested the bearded officer as Blaze was when he bested Buzzard. The Comanches would call both Shade and Blaze; *el endiablado.*"

"Yes," Noelle replied, wondering how many more enemies the brothers would have to fight here in Texas.

John rounded the corner of the house and smiled broadly.

"What a lovely picture to see three beautiful ladies sitting on my veranda," John said, taking a seat beside Catherine on the wickerwork sofa. "The goldsmith just finished packing the gold mantels to ensure they will have a safe trip home with six of my best men."

"Thank you so much, John," Noelle said. She knew John had bought their gold not because he needed it to sell and make a profit, but because of his love of Jim, Rezin and Trilby. "What will you do with the gold?"

"Oh, I have plans for it," John replied with a nonchalant shrug. It was impossible to say what Jean Lafitte would do with such treasure. Whatever it was, this man lived like a king. "Already, I have had two beautiful wedding rings custom made. Did Catherine tell you how she measured your fingers?"

"Please tell us, Catherine," Noelle said, glancing at the shiny gold wedding band that fit her finger perfectly.

"Remember when I placed the ribbons around your fingers and asked you to hold them next to the dresses you intended to wear to the wedding?" Catherine asked. Noelle and Felice nodded. "When I took the ribbons from you, I creased them to indicate your finger sizes."

"You both have been unbelievably generous, kind and patient with all of us," Noelle said, smiling.

"It is our pleasure n'est pas, Catherine?" John asked the gracious and compassionate lady who shared his life.

"Oui." Love glowed in Catherine's dark eyes as she gazed at him. "We have not been so honored since a certain buccaneer joined Andrew Jackson at the Battle of New Orleans. New Orleans embraced the Pirate of the Gulf and the president gave him a full pardon."

"And then what happened?" Felice asked.

"The buccaneer founded Campeche," John replied.

"I'm so glad you have each other and this beautiful home by the sea," Noelle said. "I love you both and will always remember the two of you being so happy here together."

"Si." Felice smiled and nodded. "Me, too."

Felice then excused herself and went upstairs to rest. When she was gone, Catherine held out her hand to Noelle.

"I read palms. Shall I read yours?"

Noelle was afraid of what she might see but nodded and moved her rocker closer to the wickerwork sofa. Viviane brought refreshments and John looked on as Catherine took Noelle's left hand.

"What's in her future, Catherine?" John asked.

"Twins," Catherine replied, peering at Noelle's hand.

"Twins?" Noelle wanted desperately to ask if she was expecting twins at this moment, but was too shy to do so directly. "Really?"

"Catherine is never wrong," John said.

"Will our twins be boys or girls?"

"For that answer you must wait." Catherine studied her hand and traced a line with her fingertip. "I can see you will have a lifelong marriage where a river of happiness and fortune never runs dry." She paused and said, "And I see you are carrying Blaze's children even as we speak."

"I thought I might be expecting," Noelle admitted as tears gathered in her eyes. "I'm so happy."

"You will be blessed by a third baby."

Noelle thought of the three children depicted on her prophetic gold mantel.

"I can't wait to tell, Blaze."

"I CAN'T WAIT to get back to camp and tell Houston that Santa Anna's in his silk covered tent," Shade sneered, detesting the dictator, "pokin' and drinkin' champagne."

"In between pinches of opium," Blaze said around three-thirty as they rode back through Buffalo Bayou.

Just before four o'clock they met up with Deaf Smith and his scouts. The bridge at Vince's Bayou had been destroyed while Santa Anna dallied. Smith said there would be no more Mexican reinforcements and Santa Anna's army could not retreat. Taking out the bridge was a coup.

"Almost didn't recognize you boys with your necker-chiefs hiding that hair under your hats." Smith scratched his head and asked, "How'd you get those blue Mexican fatigues?"

"We stripped a couple of dead dragoons in a makeshift hospital in Bexar," Blaze replied. After they'd rescued Felice, they'd shoved the clothes into their saddlebags. He'd suspected the uniforms might come in handy and they had. "We look a little different because we went spying."

Deaf Smith was all ears.

"Santa Anna is under the misconception Houston is retreating," Blaze said.

Shade frowned. "So he's in his tent with a yellow rose named Emily Morgan."

Deaf Smith was impressed and that was a coup in itself. The scouting party was in absolute awe. After news of the Bowie brothers' spying spread through the ranks, a good portion of the Texas Army broke out in a raucous chorus of 'Come to the Bower' to describe Santa Anna's dalliance.

> *Will you come to the bow'r I have shaded for you?*
> *Our bed shall be roses all spangled with dew.*
> *There under the bow'r on roses you'll lie,*
> *With a blush on your cheek but a smile in your eye.*

TWENTY-FOUR HOURS LATER, on April twenty-first, the Commander-in-Chief of the Texas Army rode his dapple gray stallion, Saracen, to the front line. It was siesta time again at the Mexican camp and there appeared to be no lookouts. Blaze knew the dragoons were about to be rudely awakened.

"Get ready, Shade," Blaze said, atop Blue. He took off his neckerchief and pulled Noelle's ribbon out of his pocket. He didn't want hair, dirt or sweat blurring his vision. Foremost in his mind was going back to Noelle. He twined the ribbon around the neckerchief, tied the band around his forehead and set his hat atop it. "There's a battle royal on the horizon."

"I feel it, too." Shade did the same with his neckerchief and Felice's ribbon.

"You're right about Bowie blood running thick, Shade. You're the best brother a man could have. Thank you for making everything right with the girls."

"Thanks for making me the man I always wanted to be, Blaze."

"Let's stick close together and not let them spill much, if any Bowie blood."

"Agreed," Shade said. "I heard Houston spotted a raven flying from the direction of the Mexican camp and said it's a good omen."

Blaze hoped so. The Twin Sisters were loaded with chopped horseshoes. When those cannons were fired sleeping Mexicans would be sliced to pieces by razor sharp scrap-iron. Houston looked ready. Blaze braced himself.

"Forward my brave men!" General Houston shouted. "Charge the enemy and give them hell!"

Both cannons blew! Flames flew from rifles fired! Behind those weapons, troops raced forward on foot and on horseback. With a fife and drum urging them on men bellowed the song; 'Come to the Bower'. As quickly as napping Mexicans struggled to their feet, Houston's Texas Army of nine hundred and ten men cut them down.

"My God, it's gonna be an all-out slaughter!" Blaze yelled to Shade as they rode closer to Houston.

CHAPTER 47

"Hell yeah!" Shade shouted back to Blaze.

However, the Mexicans outnumbered them by almost five hundred and they kept coming. Blaze and Shade fired their rifles as rapidly as they could reload. The only orders to follow were those of survival; do not get hit with cannon grapeshot or musket minie balls.

One of the Twin Sisters gouged a hole through the breastwork of the Mexican camp and the swarming dragoons fell inside their own lines. Sam Houston galloped alongside Blaze and Shade.

Blaze called to the general over the roar of the battle, "Santa Anna's finding out what it was like for our side at the Alamo!"

With a nod at Blaze, the Commander-in-Chief raged, "Remember the Alamo!"

Everywhere the Texas Army began echoing battle cries of, "Remember the Alamo! Remember Goliad! Remember the Alamo!"

Houston and Saracen were the main target on the battlefield. Saracen was soon hit in the side and fell dead beneath Houston's rein. Blaze jumped off Blue and helped Houston to his feet. Houston quickly mounted Blue, the horse that had taken Blaze halfway across Texas and halfway home again. Drawing Mexican fire to himself and away from the Texas infantry, Houston charged toward the center of the Mexican camp.

"Come on, Blaze!" Shade shouted amidst the melee of killing, screaming, cannon blasts, and gunfire. "Jump up behind me!"

"No!" Blaze yelled and trading his rifle for his blades, motioned to Shade. "We'll have a better chance against these dragoons on foot."

Shade bailed off Buckshot and slapped the horse's rump, sending him galloping toward camp. The brothers then fought side-by-side expertly dropping the enemy with their knives and sabers as they moved ever forward. Making smaller targets on foot than on horseback, they didn't draw musket or cannon fire. But they were far from unscathed. Hand-to-hand war was a brutal fight for life.

Victory or death.

In the midst of the smoke-filled battlefield, Blaze saw a Texas victory in sight.

"Let's find out if Santa Anna's dead or captured, Shade!"

They headed into a new surge of enemy fire. They found Houston had been hit by a minie ball, his wounded leg draped over the pommel of a different horse.

"Damn," Blaze said to Shade. "Blue must have been hit, too."

"Parade, men, parade!" Houston yelled, trying to bring order among his troops. But the soldiers continued to fight with passion for the revenge they'd sought since the Alamo and Goliad fell. "Gentlemen! Gentlemen! I applaud your bravery, but damn your manners!"

"Where's Santa Anna?" Blaze shouted to Houston.

"Try Peggy Lake."

At Peggy Lake, Blaze and Shade found an organic bridge of horses and dragoons. It was there that the brothers witnessed the killing frenzy come to an end.

The entire battle had lasted only eighteen minutes.

. . .

"VICTORY TASTES SO SWEET," Shade said early the next morning, polishing off a biscuit.

On the Texas side ten men were dead and thirty wounded. The Mexicans' casualties totaled six hundred and forty dead, seven hundred and twenty prisoners, two hundred and eight of whom were wounded.

Santa Anna was not among them.

"I'm ready to leave for Campeche," Shade said as they stood beside their campfire. "I've got a wedding night coming to me."

"So do I." Blaze tossed out the last of the coffee in his tin mug. "But I'm going to find Santa Anna first."

Blaze had asked Houston about Blue and the general said the horse had thrown him. With hundreds of horses, dead and alive in the immediate area, Blaze had not seen Blue.

"How're we gonna find Santa Anna?" Shade asked.

"Santa Anna's too concerned with pleasure to suffer any pain. I figure he ran when he smelled defeat. If we look under enough rocks we'll find him hiding like the coward he is."

Blaze was given a horse and all day he and Shade helped the Texas Army scour the area for Santa Anna and round up prisoners. Evening found Blaze and Shade at Vince's Bayou. Under the remains of the destroyed bridge, Blaze spied a cowering Mexican. He and Shade dismounted and routed the man out of his rat hole. Hauling him up on solid land, Blaze's skin crawled. Disheveled, the man wore a blue jacket, a white silk shirt buttoned with diamond studs, white linen breeches, and red worsted slippers.

"Santa Anna," Blaze said calmly. "We meet again."

Recognition narrowed the prisoner's eyes just before he shook his head. Shade lunged and tackled him to the ground. Blaze quickly hauled Shade off the prisoner.

"We know you! We spied on you!" Shade roared as the coward cringed. "You're gonna pay for what you've done."

Santa Anna shook his head again and Shade said sarcastically, "Napoleon can't speak English."

"He'll understand this," Blaze said, grabbing Santa Anna's jacket and jerking him face to face. "Our name is Bowie. As in Jim Bowie!"

When Blaze released him, the prisoner stumbled backward with sheer terror widening his eyes.

"Because of you an innocent, pregnant woman was imprisoned in a hut and raped by one of your dragoons," Shade said as he yanked the man's jacket off his shoulder and put the tip of his Bowie knife to his heart. "Adios."

"No." Blaze raised his hand, palm out. "Santa Anna let his men kill Jim on his sick bed, but Jim had those five muskets. Santa Anna isn't armed. Let's not sink to his level."

Shade's voice shook with fury. "Santa Anna bragged about not giving or asking for quarter or mercy. He killed every last man at the Alamo and in Goliad. Why give him what he wouldn't give us?"

"Because taking those who surrender as prisoners is the honorable thing to do."

"He doesn't deserve it." Shade pushed the blade of his knife through the white silk shirt. "Let's kill him and be done with it."

"Sam Houston can't make deals with a dead man," Blaze replied with a cool head and an eye on the future. "Let's get this bastard back to camp."

Shade lowered his knife and spit on the prisoner's red worsted slippers as several Texas scouts hurried toward them, shouting they'd heard Santa Anna had escaped to Thompson's Pass.

"Santa Anna's right here," Blaze said.

Upon questioning by one of the Houston's Spanish-speaking scouts the prisoner swore he was not General Santa Anna, but a simple private. Several of the Texians hotly disputed Santa Anna's identity. Finding no one else under the bridge Blaze led the way out of the bayou, the prisoner following at the point of a saber. After a couple of miles the man said he could go no further. Shade was for putting a Bowie knife in his gut. Most of the other scouts agreed but Blaze said no and a man named Joel Robison yanked the prisoner onto the rump of his horse.

Returning to the battlefield, Mexican corpses covered the ground. This was exactly how Mayor Ruiz said it had looked at the Alamo when he had identified Jim Bowie's body for Santa Anna. Capturing Jim's enemy was the least they could do to honor his memory. Now, Blaze wanted Santa Anna's identity confirmed for Sam Houston.

They headed for the prisoners' pen. Nearing it, the captured Mexican officers slowly rose to their feet. In unison they shouted in regard to the prisoner, "El Presidente! El Presidente!"

"Victory for the deaths of Jim and Crockett and the others," Blaze said to Shade. "Let's find Houston."

A COUPLE of hours before daylight, Noelle awoke in Blaze's four poster bed. In darkness realization dawned. The ultimate test of her love had been in letting Blaze go with Houston's scouts. Would her hard won strength backfire on them now?

She regretted having once accused Blaze of wanting her for Grandmother's money. He had proved himself to her so many times; risking his life at the Alamo, saving her life from the cougar, rescuing her from Buzzard, looking out for Felice, and in marrying Noelle knowing well her inheritance could be forfeited.

"You are a blaze of glory... in and out of bed," she said softly to herself.

"Then sleep with me, darlin'. I'm tired."

Noelle couldn't believe her eyes as she turned her head toward the moonlit doorway filled with muscles. His neckerchief and her ribbon were twined around his neck, his handsome face smudged with dirt. His shirt was torn, his pants bloodstained and his boots dusty.

"Blaze!" she cried stumbling out of bed and wrapping her arms around him. "I love you so much. I will never ever, as long as I live let you go again." She stood on tiptoes and took his beard-stubbled face in her hands. "I feared you weren't coming back to me this time."

"Not come back to my wife?"

"I'm so glad we married before you left."

"Anticipating our wedding night made me fight all the harder on that battlefield."

"It looks like you almost didn't make it. Is Shade with you?"

An excited voice down the hall answered her question.

"Te amo muy mucho, Shade!" Felice said.

Hearing voices, John and Catherine came and welcomed the returning warriors. After a few minutes everyone returned to their rooms.

"Blaze, did you stop Santa Anna?" Noelle asked as she closed their door behind them.

"Oh hell, yes. We saw him turned over to Houston. He sniveled like the coward he is, begging Houston for mercy. Shade and I helped hold our soldiers back from any more violence so Houston could negotiate." Blaze's eyes narrowed as if seeing it all again. "Houston's reception of that dictator was so cold it didn't take long for Santa Anna to knuckle under to Houston's demands. Deaf Smith rode off with orders for a General Filisola to withdraw all Mexican troops from Texas. I wanted to hear that deal made to be sure the battle for Texas independence and land had been won."

"I am truly in awe of all you've accomplished."

Blaze shrugged, walked to the sofa and sat down. When he tried to pull off a boot, he winced. Noelle helped him pull off both boots and then began unbuttoning his shirt.

"You aren't going to like what you see."

"I love what I see when you're naked."

As she gently removed his shirt, he never uttered a

sound but pain flashed in his gray eyes. Blaze's upper torso was a mass of cuts and bruises.

"Oh, dear Lord, Blaze," Noelle said softly. "These are the wounds of riding into hell and living to ride out."

"We fought on foot because Houston borrowed Blue. True Blue threw him, but he found me right before we left camp. Petit's seeing to him and Buckshot now."

Noelle took his scraped hands in hers. "I'll kiss each hurt and make you well."

Eyelids drooping, Blaze said, "I'll hold you to that, darlin'."

She kissed his hands and tenderly placed her cheek to his raw knuckles. She then brought the washbowl, stood between his legs and gently washed his face, arms, chest, and back. He stood so she could strip off his pants, leaving him naked. His lower body wasn't as badly bruised as his torso. The blood on his pants didn't belong to him.

"I didn't lose any valuables in battle," Blaze said and yawned. "I'll be assuming my husbandly rights the minute we're in bed."

"I'll hold you to that," Noelle said, wrapped an arm around his waist and walked him to the bed.

Blaze sat down and swung his legs into bed. Resting his head on a feather pillow, he pulled Noelle in beside him and closed his eyes.

"Remember the night we made love in your saddle?"

"Of course," he replied.

"Well, I have some news." She hesitated for a moment. "We made a baby that night."

"What?" he asked, opening his eyes.

"In fact, Catherine read my palm and says I'm carrying twins. She even told me that we'll have a third baby by the time our twins turn four."

Gray eyes misting, Blaze leaned over her and flattening his hand to her pregnant belly, he kissed her lips.

"I'm the luckiest man alive. I love you, Noelle Bowie."

. . .

A FEW DAYS LATER, Blaze thanked John, Catherine, Petit, Viviane, and Suzanne for all they had done for them. He and Shade had graciously refused John's gifts of two small gold cases. John, however, would not accept no for an answer and placed a case in Blaze's hand. On top was a carving of a ship titled, *The Pride*. Inside was a nautical compass. On the top of the case John presented to Shade was a different carving of the same ship and inside was a second compass. John explained he had owned the two unique compasses for many years but commissioned their cases to be made by the goldsmith along with the wedding bands.

"On land or at sea, you will never lose your way home," John said to the brothers.

Catherine then asked Noelle and Felice to choose a gift to wear with their wedding bands from a chest full of bejeweled rings. Noelle chose a small ring embedded with a tiny dark stone. Shaking his head, John chuckled and Catherine nudged Blaze to choose. The ring he picked was a pear shaped ruby surrounded by canary diamonds.

"Red for your hair," Blaze said with a smile.

"Yellow for yours." Noelle smiled.

With Catherine's help, the ring Felice and Shade picked out was an aquamarine stone with diamond baguettes on either side. Felice said it would always remind her of the sea and surf where Shade told her he loved her.

"Magnifique," John said.

"Oui," Catherine agreed, hugging John.

It was an emotional bon voyage on Galveston Island.

CHAPTER 48

"My grandparents, Jason and Dorothea Yoder's, house." After whispering those words Noelle looped her arm through Blaze's and edged closer to him in the buggy. They'd been stopped by an imposing iron gate supported on either side by an eight foot tall stone wall. "My grandfather designed this place to resemble the Swiss castles he always admired in Geneva. Mama said he was a visionary."

"It's one helluva castle," Blaze said, staring it through the decorative gate bars. "Jason Yoder was a master builder. I'd like to have done business with him."

Sometime between February tenth, at the fandango where Blaze had said he intended to marry her and May tenth which was the current date, Noelle had decided Grandmother would welcome her with open arms. Now that she was here, she wasn't so sure.

They'd reached Vidalia, Louisiana the previous afternoon. The bank was Blaze's first stop, but it had closed for the day. Along with Shade and Felice the Bowies' plantation was their second visit. Approaching the outskirts of the estate, charred land and scorched trees surrounded the remains of the burned sawmill and farm buildings confirming the fire that had forced the brothers to the brink of bankruptcy and killed their parents.

In the distance, a majestic white Greek Revival plantation house with forest green shutters stood sun dappled by maple and magnolia trees. Six fluted marble columns, twenty-five feet high and twelve feet apart supported the cedar shingled roof over the wide porch of the spectacular mansion. Drawing closer, bullet holes in the oversized forest green front door were proof of misdirected violence.

Inside the palatial house, the Bowie home was none the worse for wear. Later, the four of them had celebrated their many victories with supper at the best hotel in town and then spent the night there.

On this morning, Blaze and Shade had found the bank still closed. Noelle and Blaze had dropped Shade and Felice back at the Bowie plantation. Now, they were on the highest hill in Natchez, Mississippi.

"I've never been this close to your grandparents' house. I didn't realize this property had a wall and a gatehouse," Blaze said. "Did anyone ever man this entrance?"

Noelle thought a moment. "Yes. But when I lived here there was just a fence instead of the stone wall. A man and his wife lived in this gatehouse. He was a lively fellow who played a fiddle and was quite a yarn spinner."

"Davy Crockett worked here?"

"No." Noelle laughed. "His name was... umm... Adam Williams!"

Behind them flowed the Mississippi River. They had traveled a carriage path through a forest, Blaze's forest, to this grassy rise which had just rolled into view. In back of the castle, Blaze's timberland spread as far as the eye could see.

"May I help you?" a man suddenly asked, stepping out of the gatehouse and squinting through the iron bars.

"Yes, sir, we're here to see Mrs. Yoder," Noelle replied.

"Mizz Yoder doesn't allow visitors in to see Yoder Castle," the man replied.

"We're here to see Mrs. Yoder herself," Noelle said.

"Well... she doesn't see people."

"And why not?" Blaze asked.

"Because," the slender man, maybe fifty years old said, scratching his head. "She's ancient!"

"I'm her granddaughter," Noelle said.

"Little Noelle." The man's jaw dropped. "I should have known you by your red hair. Don't you remember me?" He tapped his chest. "It's Adam. My wife, Dannette, is still the cook up at the big house. We haven't seen you since your Mama took you away when you were seven." He unlocked the heavy gate and pushed it open.

"I do remember you, Adam. I guess I've changed a bit," Noelle said with a smile. "I'm Mrs. Bowie now."

"Tarnation!" Adam's brown eyes danced. "I sure 'nough wanna be there when you tell Mizz Yoder that you're back and married."

The horse's hooves and buggy wheels clicked over a cobblestone drive as they entered. The sides of the road, which curved in a wide half-circle, were dotted with moss covered trees. The grounds were not as immaculately manicured as Noelle remembered. Centered in the front yard was an ornate fountain adorned with a winged Cupid and his arrow, but no longer ringed by dark copper irises.

"So that's where you got the arrow you shot me with," Blaze said.

"That same arrow hit me, too," Noelle reminded him softly. "I loved to run through the grass, hop through the irises and dance in Cupid's fountain. It gave the gardener fits."

"Gardener's gone and the fountain is broken now," Adam spouted, catching up alongside them.

"Adam, we'd have given you a ride," Blaze said and slowed down.

"I'm spry," Adam replied, waving a fiddle in the air. "But the gardener's stiff as a board on accounta he's dead. Mizz Yoder's too tired to hire a new one."

Adam then sprinted past them. There was bare dirt where buttercups, foxglove, scarlet catchflies, day lilies, and trumpet flowers once flourished. One of Grandmother's favorite windows in the house looked out on a side yard where Noelle would swing in a tree swing and play in her little house on a low tree limb. Reminiscing those good childhood times of the past was over for the moment as the Yoder Castle loomed ahead.

A dark red roof dwarfed tall trees to touch the blue sky. The enormous three story light gray castle was rectangular with a splash of southern architecture mixed into the design. Six chimneys rose from the roof and a second floor balcony swept across the front of the mansion. On both the first and second stories, sets of French doors separated huge windows. Supporting the balcony, stone pillars stood like sentries on the stone porch. Between two of the pillars, was a rounded tower with a dark red roof all its own. Atop the tower, an American flag fluttered in the breeze. In the center of the tower, the main entrance to the castle, was a large dark red door bearing a polished brass knocker and door handle.

"What do you think?" Noelle asked.

"I think I should have stopped by when I was seventeen and met the little seven year old who lived here." Blaze chuckled. "It would have saved me the trouble of hauling her back from Texas."

"The seven year old would have fainted at the sight of you!"

"What happened to Adam?" Blaze asked as he reined in the horse and buggy to a stop.

"He always enters the house through the back door where Dannette has her kitchen," Noelle recalled.

Blaze got out of the buggy to help Noelle. "You look beautiful in your new purple dress. I want to show you off to your grandmother."

"I want to show you off, too," Noelle said, smiling at him. Clean shaven, dark blond hair shining he wore a black suit, white shirt, black boots and a charming smile. She grabbed his hand and said, "I'm nervous."

"It was your mother's last wish for you to make amends with your grandmother. You'll be fine."

After Blaze knocked, a dapper middle-aged man in a dark suit opened the door and Adam came around from in back of him.

"There she is, just like I told you, Walter! Little Noelle who is Mizz Bowie now! Let 'em in!"

The butler stood back as Blaze escorted Noelle into the elegantly wallpapered, marble-tiled foyer. A maid rushed down the left side of wide staircases that resembled a horse-shoe. From a twenty foot high ceiling, and centered between the dual staircases, hung an enormous chandelier. Under it was a cherrywood table upon which a Waterford crystal vase held red calla lilies and white cherry blossoms.

Closer now, Noelle recognized the maid as Zelm, Walter's wife.

A flustered Walter hurried down the hall and ducked into a room on the left. A woman, wearing a white apron, appeared around a corner at the back from the kitchen.

"Hello Dannette." Noelle smiled at the woman coming toward them.

"I thought Adam was yarn spinnin', but it's true." Dannette's brown eyes were wide and filled with tears. "Our precious girl has come home."

"Mrs. Yoder will see you now," Walter said.

"Do you want to see your grandmother alone?" Blaze asked.

"No, I want you with me," Noelle said, holding onto his hand.

"Hard to believe little Noelle has a husband." Dannette sighed and shook her head.

Noelle and Blaze followed Walter with Zelm, Adam, and Dannette on their heels. They paused at the double doors of a two story library decorated in creams, greens and gold. Floor-to-ceiling bookshelves took up a good portion of the wood paneled walls. A spiral staircase provided access to books on the second story.

Walter announced them and moved aside. Blaze allowed Noelle to enter first and then Walter quietly pulled double pocket doors together behind them. Noelle took Blaze's hand again.

On their far right French doors opened to a large side yard. Two sets of burgundy leather, wing backed chairs stood on both sides of the French doors.

Straight ahead, two Victorian sofas faced each other in front of a massive stone fireplace. The sofas rested on a thick green, cream and gold carpet which covered most of the polished, hardwood floor in the middle of the library. Above the fireplace was an oil painting of a beautiful brunette and a little girl with long copper curls.

Everywhere Ming vases, porcelain statues and priceless antiques adorned shelves and tables. Crystal candle sconces were mounted on walls and hanging from the ceiling high above were crystal chandeliers.

To the left of the hearth and bookcases was a large window draped in green. Gold tassels held the curtains back revealing a view of the Mississippi River.

Sunlight spilled through this window to fall across a tiny woman dressed in somber brown. Sitting in Grandfather Yoder's favorite throne-like cushioned chair, feet resting on the matching footstool, she petted a big orange cat with one hand and held a cane in her other one.

"Hello, Grandmother," Noelle said softly.

"Where have you been for thirteen years?" Grandmother asked abruptly as they approached.

"San Antonio," Noelle said. "Didn't you know?"

"No, I did not." Her hair was snow white and her body wizened, but her eyes were vivid blue. "How'd you get here?"

"He brought me." Noelle smiled up at her husband and then back to the elderly woman. "Dorothea Yoder, I'd like you to meet Blaze Bowie, my husband as of last month."

"Mrs. Yoder," Blaze began, "it's a pleasure to meet you, ma'am."

Grandmother squinted up at Blaze. "Are you the same Bowie who owns half the territory on both sides of the Mississippi River? The same Bowie, whose timberland borders my property right up to the iron gate and stone wall? The same Bowie whose sawmill burned down?"

"Yes, ma'am. I plan to build a new sawmill."

"You lost your barn, silo and farm equipment in a fire." Grandmother frowned. You're the Bowie who planned to grow crops for mash and give me competition in my whiskey business?"

"That would be my brother, Shade Bowie."

"Did you leave Vidalia because of the death of a swamp girl named Lucy Ray?" Grandmother asked and pointed the gold handle of her cane at him.

"No, ma'am," Blaze replied. "Shade and I left Louisiana for another reason."

"Good, because Lucy Ray's mother admitted she knew the father of Lucy's baby was one of her nine brothers. Shame drove Lucy to suicide. Rufus Ray shot and killed a couple of the sons before turning the gun on himself. Mrs. Ray died of a heart attack and the rest of their swamp scum scattered."

Surprise crossed Blaze's face. "How do you know all of that?"

"I own the newspaper, young man!" Grandmother rapped her cane. "It's my business to know things."

"Such as Noelle's whereabouts for the last thirteen years?"

Noelle's eyes widened and she smothered a grin as Grandmother's wrinkled face grew pinched. A vaguely familiar cackle intensified the glare Grandmother gave Blaze before looking back at Noelle.

"Are your mother and Marcel with you, Noelle?"

"Noelle! Noelle!"

The sudden screeching of her name, like the cackle, came from the second floor of the library. Noelle smiled.

Alighting on the banister at the top of the spiral staircase was a large red, blue and yellow bird.

"Where'd that parrot come from?" Blaze asked.

"He's a scarlet macaw from Galveston Island," Noelle said. "Hello, Jackson."

"Hello! Hello!" Jackson parroted, walking back and forth along the banister.

"Noelle!" Grandmother interrupted. "Please answer my question."

"Marcel was killed by Comanche Indians and Mama died of cholera," Noelle replied, returning her attention to the tiny, but formidable woman. "It was her last wish for me to come here."

"I hope your mother died happy." Grandmother bowed her head and petted her cat.

"Happy?" Noelle asked. When Blaze squeezed her hand, she took a calming breath. "Mama was destitute. We lived in a hut a quarter of the size of the gatehouse. It had a thatched roof and dirt floor."

"Trilby could have come home at any time." Grandmother's head snapped up.

"She didn't know that." Noelle shook her head. "She thought you wouldn't forgive her for choosing Marcel over you."

"Trilby was a daydreamer and headstrong." Grandmother shrugged. "She loved adventure and despised me."

"She didn't despise you," Noelle said. "She wanted you to know she loved you until the end."

"Do you despise me, Noelle?"

"I don't really know you, Grandmother."

"It's high time you get to know me!" The elderly lady rapped her cane again and the cat bailed off her lap. "Your grandfather, Jason, is gone, your mother is gone and you're the only family I have left. I've waited a long time for you to swing in your tree swing again."

"It's a little late for that, now," Noelle said gently.

"You and our children can swing in it, Noelle, when you

come to visit," Blaze said as he wrapped an arm around her shoulders and gave her a squeeze.

Grandmother's sharp eyes riveted to Noelle's flat stomach. "Did Mr. Bowie sow his seed in your fertile ground, young lady?"

"Yes, I'm due around Christmas."

"So you put the cart before the horse by marrying without my approval." Grandmother frowned and Noelle could almost see the wheels turning in her head. "And you conceived before taking vows." She turned to Blaze. "Got any money for rebuilding that sawmill, Mr. Bowie?"

"Yes, ma'am. I do." He crossed his arms over his chest.

CHAPTER 49

"I will match every penny you put into rebuilding your sawmill Mr. Bowie, so you make it twice as big," Grandmother said.

"Just because I'm married to Noelle, doesn't obligate you to make an investment," Blaze said.

"I would have given you the money even if you weren't married to Noelle." Grandmother paused. "I'll take care of your brother as well."

"I don't understand, but no thank you," Blaze replied.

"Just hear me ou—out, Mr. Bowie. Walter! I know you're on the other side of the doors!"

"Yes, ma'am?" Walter said, slowly opening a door.

"Fetch those chairs over there." Grandmother waved a wrinkled hand toward a black walnut secretary flanked by two black walnut chairs. "Put them here for my guests and ask Dannette to prepare tea."

When they were seated and the door closed again, Dorothea Yoder began where she left off.

"My former bank manager is the one who tried to foreclose on you and your brother."

"*Your* former bank manager?" Blaze asked, his hands clenching into fists. "What do you mean?"

"I mean my late husband, Jason, started the bank and I

still own it, young man. Spencer, our former bank manager—"

"Yes." Blaze held up his hand. "Shade and I know Spencer." He turned to Noelle. "Why didn't you tell me your grandmother was the one trying to foreclose on my house and land?"

"I didn't even know she owned the newspaper," Noelle replied. "Much less the bank."

"Hush!" Grandmother gave two hard raps of her cane on the floor. "Trilby wouldn't have mentioned it because they were sore subjects with Marcel, the mudsill, who was always scheming to find quick money. Marcel, that worthless, no account miscreant—"

"Please don't, Grandmother."

"Marcel Charbonnez was not your father, Noelle and I'm a blunt, old woman. So don't take offense when you finally hear the whole truth."

"Let's get it over with," Blaze said.

"I intend to!" Grandmother nodded sharply at Blaze and turned to Noelle. "Marcel wanted your grandfather to allow him to run the bank. Jason told that crooked as a dog's hind legs swindler absolutely not!" The feisty lady rapped her cane twice on the floor for emphasis. "When Charbonnez tried to worm his way into managing the newspaper, I told him he couldn't track an elephant in snow, much less track down news. So that popular as a muddy dog at one of our Saturday night soirees in the ballroom took to living at the distillery trying to personally guzzle up all the Yoder profits!"

After that tirade, Noelle realized Marcel's treasure seeking was the tip of the iceberg of traits her grandparents had not appreciated about her mother's first husband. They hadn't liked, respected or trusted him.

"Marcel would have run your businesses into the ground," Noelle agreed softly.

"Yes, he would have!" Grandmother gave another sharp nod of her head and two raps of her cane. "I rejoice that your surname is no longer Charbonnez!" With that stated, she gazed over at Blaze. "Spencer's wife wanted that new plantation showplace of yours, Mr. Bowie, so Spencer tried to ruin you to get it."

Blaze's jaw clenched as he got up and paced away to the fireplace. There, he turned with a menacing glare and asked, "Are you saying Spencer burned my sawmill, the barn, Shade's silos, and farm equipment? All of it?"

"I'm afraid so." Grandmother winced as Blaze's eyes narrowed dangerously. "I'm truly sorry."

"Dammit!" Blaze's oath shook the window panes. He swept back his suit jacket and placed his hands on his hips. "Your banker murdered my mother and father in cold blood!"

"Yes, he did," Grandmother said. "I'll make things up to you and your brother."

"You can't make up for two lives lost," Blaze replied as he stormed toward the library doors.

Noelle turned to her grandmother." Do you know what your bank put Blaze and Shade through?" she asked with a tone of anger she'd never heard in her own voice. "They went to Texas because Jim Bowie was their last hope of finding the money to save their land."

"Noelle, stop." Blaze shook his head. "Let's go."

Noelle frowned at her grandmother. "Blaze and Shade could have been killed in the Alamo along with their cousin, Jim Bowie, and their friend, Davy Crockett. Blaze and Shade helped Sam Houston stop the ruthless Mexican dictator, Santa Anna. When Blaze and his brother returned from the battle at San Jacinto, they were covered in blood and bruises. That's not to mention facing down Comanche Indians in the Texas Hill Country, killing a cougar to save three lives and rescuing me from a kidnapper."

"Was Spencer caught?" Blaze asked, standing in front of the pocket doors.

"Yes," Grandmother replied quietly. "I became suspicious and at my prodding the sheriff investigated. He found out

Spencer had boasted in Natchez-Under-the-Hill of setting the fires. Spencer's chirping put a noose around his scrawny chicken neck. After he was hanged, his money grubbing widow ran up the gallows to fish through his pockets. She tripped and fell to her death. In the meantime, your loan was wiped off the books."

"The lives of Tyler and Dawn Bowie were worth one hell of a lot more than anything we owed your bank, lady!" Blaze said, seething with anger.

"Of course, they were. But I want to repay my debt."

"Blaze doesn't like debt either." Noelle stood up and turned to him. "Yes, let's go."

"No! Please!" Grandmother said. "Adam!" she snapped. "I know you're out there, too. Fetch a couple of glasses and pour Mr. Bowie and me double shots of whiskey. Noelle, Mr. Bowie, let's sit by the fireplace. Please."

Blaze didn't move a muscle, but when Grandmother struggled with the footstool and tried to stand, Blaze helped her to a sofa in front of the hearth. Noelle took a seat on the other one and Blaze stood. Walter returned with a teapot and teacup just as Adam entered the library with glasses of Yoder Whiskey. He handed one to Grandmother, but Blaze refused. Walter poured Noelle's tea.

"Will there be anything else?" the butler asked.

"Yes." It was Blaze who answered, taking command. "Please see that we have privacy, Walter." When Walter and Adam were out of the room, Blaze turned to Grandmother. "By God, you're lucky I'm not out for revenge. If I were, I'd *burn* your bank, your newspaper and your distillery to the ground."

"You sound just like my husband, Jason, and I don't blame you," she said. "But you'd be burning your wife's, property. Everything goes to Noelle and her husband, if he's a man I approve of."

"I don't give a damn what you think of me."

"Blaze, I didn't come here to start a feud between you and Grandmother," Noelle said. "I came to end the one between my mother and grandmother. I'm tired of all the fighting, aren't you?"

Blaze scowled. Jackson flew down from his perch to the top of his fancy birdcage in a far corner of the cavernous room. Apparently at peace with each other, the cat ignored the macaw and moseyed across the room where it sat on the thick carpet near Grandmother's feet.

"If there is to be war then in war as in love, I must do what I think is right, Grandmother." Noelle smiled at her husband. "I love Blaze and I'm going to spend the rest of my life with him."

"Obviously! Or you wouldn't have married him before obtaining my approval."

"I'd begun to hope I'd live in the castle again but—" Noelle's voice broke.

"But what?" Grandmother rapped her cane.

"But never without Blaze."

"I want you and Mr. Bowie to live here and raise a family." She lifted her whiskey glass in a toast to Blaze. "Yoder's Whiskey built this castle, the bank and the newspaper. You and Mr. Bowie can have it all."

"I plan to build my own house," Blaze replied sternly.

"I know you could build a house that would put this one to shame." Her blue eyes were sharp and focused on Blaze. "The one you and your father built is magnificent. Your father was a savvy businessman and from the profits I hear your sawmill made, you are too, Mr. Bowie. For that alone I approve of you, not to mention that you don't want my money or that you're descended from royalty."

"Royalty?" Noelle asked, looking up at Blaze.

"I hid the Bowie family coat of arms in the attic before we left for Texas," Blaze said. "How do you know of the Bowie ancestry?"

"Everybody around here knows it," Grandmother replied. "Jim and Rezin and Tyler Bowie were men after Jason's heart." Grandmother sighed. "I only wish one of them had captured Trilby's heart. But no, she eloped with Marcel the mudsill, we disowned them and they fled. On Galveston Island she met Jean Lafitte and fell in love with him. You were conceived aboard The Pride, Noelle. Did you know that?"

"No."

"Well, now you do. Jean was Trilby's one true love. You don't resemble your mother much, so you must favor Lafitte," Grandmother said, smiling at Noelle and sipping her whiskey. "After she and Marcel returned when you were two, she had Jason put the dark red roof on this house and fly the American flag. For the next five years, Trilby hoped it would bring a patriotic Lafitte sailing The Pride up the Mississippi River to claim her. We heard Jean had died shortly after your grandfather passed. I didn't want to deal with the mudsill by myself so I paid Marcel off to get rid of him. Never did I dream he'd convince my daughter to take my little granddaughter and sneak out in the middle of the night."

"Noelle, are you all right?" Blaze asked, placing a hand on her shoulder.

"Yes," Noelle said, looking over at her grandmother. "It almost sounds as if you and Grandfather approved."

"Approved of Jean Lafitte?" She tilted her head and laughed. "Yes, of course we did! Where do you think your grandfather got all of his money, Noelle? In the late seventeen hundreds, Jason Yoder was the famed Swiss pirate chief, feared by rivals and emulated by cohorts. Jason named the macaw Jackson because of President Andrew Jackson's pardoning of Lafitte, a fellow pirate. After the turn of the century, when Jason mysteriously vanished from the sea, he put his bounty into an American whiskey business. Our empire grew from there!"

"This is a lot to hear all at once," Noelle said softly.

"Fair enough." Grandmother raised a wrinkled hand in surrender.

Needing a moment, Noelle lowered her gaze to the cat

and it came toward her. Rubbing against Blaze's leg on its way, the cat then stopped at Noelle's feet.

"His name is Nick o' Time," Grandmother said. "A couple of years back I was taking a walk around the grounds and came upon a kitten and a fox. With my cane, I scared away the fox in the nick of time. I had the fence removed and the stone wall built to protect Nicky."

"Nicky." The name put a lump in Noelle's throat. As she petted Nick of Time Nicky, she glanced at Blaze who smiled just a little. "I had a cat named Mistletoe, but I left her in Campeche."

"Ahh... yes... Lafitte's colony. Is Jean really dead?"

"Depends on who you talk to," Blaze said.

"Pirates are known to have aliases," Grandmother replied. "Jason Yoder wasn't my husband's name at sea. Only visionary pirates disappear and retire at the height of their career to live in peace and prosperity."

Blaze nodded and said, "Jim asked me to take Noelle to Campeche."

"Good for Jim. He and Jean were thick as thieves." Grandmother smiled at Blaze. "No offense."

"We were treated like family on Galveston Island and made lifelong friends," Blaze said.

"Our friend, Petit, loved Mistletoe and that's why I left her with him," Noelle said.

"I love you, Noelle Katrina. In case you forgot, you and I share the same middle name." She held out a blue-veined hand to Noelle. "Please move in and share your life with me."

Noelle got up, walked around the table and sat down beside her grandmother.

"I would never keep Noelle from visiting you, Mrs. Yoder," Blaze said. "But we aren't living here."

"Hell's bells, boy!" Grandmother said and rapped her cane. "I'm eighty-three years old. Moving in now will keep you from having to build a house somewhere only to move in here after I die, which might be any damnable minute!"

"Hell's bells! Hell's bells!" Jackson echoed pacing back and forth atop his birdcage.

Blaze flung his arms wide. "You've never laid eyes on me before today. What makes you think I can run a distillery, a newspaper, a bank and a sawmill?"

"You're a Bowie!" Conviction rang in her voice as she stared up at him, "You can do it with one hand tied behind your back."

"Why didn't you just sell the businesses when you sold the timberland?"

"You didn't sell out when times were hard."

"With all due respect, Mrs. Yoder, I'm thirty, not eighty-three."

"Selling the castle and businesses would have meant giving up hope that my granddaughter would come home to inherit." Grandmother smiled at Noelle.

Blaze conceded that with a nod as Noelle rose and moved to his side.

"Blaze, think of the good you could do on both sides of the Mississippi River with your know-how," Grandmother said. "Envision all the jobs you could create with all these businesses."

"I would start by changing things at the bank."

"Then it's settled?" Grandmother asked.

A breeze blew in through a large window which framed a massive oak. An uneven swing was tied to a left branch and a little weathered house looked ready to fall off a right one.

A Which Way Tree.

"Why not let Noelle and your children inherit their Yoder birthright?" Mrs. Yoder urged.

Birthright hit home with Blaze. He'd fought hard to save his home, his land, Texas land, and now Noelle's home was at stake.

"Is living here something you truly want?" Blaze asked Noelle.

"Far second to you," she said and took his hand.

"Please say yes, Mr. Bowie," Zelm said, pushing open a pocket door. "Mizz Yoder won't live much longer if she keeps fretting about the businesses."

Walter joined his wife and added, "All of us who work here would treat you properly and with the utmost respect if you were to move in, Mr. Bowie."

"Apparently, privacy wouldn't be part of the deal," Blaze replied dryly.

Adam opened the other door and Dannette said, "We'd pamper your wife, help with the baby, take care of the house and grounds, and I'd cook and bake anything and everything you wanted every day."

The four members of the staff then backed out of the library and Walter pulled the pocket doors closed.

For so long, Noelle's home was a rancid shack. She had lost Trilby and Carlos forever and bid farewell to John and Mistletoe. Blaze knew she would give up her grandmother and this house. She had sacrificed enough.

Noelle squeezed his hand. The hope on her face and Mrs. Yoder's twisted Blaze's heart. He sighed.

"I guess my gold mantle will fit over this hearth as well as it would fit over the hearth I planned to build."

"Thank you, Blaze." Noelle's hazel eyes misted with happiness. She kissed him and then whispered, "I'm the luckiest woman alive."

"I'll bet Blaze Bowie is a wild stallion in the bedroom, isn't he, Mrs. Bowie?" her grandmother asked.

"Grandmother!" Noelle gasped and then smiled up at Blaze. "He's a blaze of glory."

EPILOGUE

NATCHEZ, MISSISSIPPI 1841

BLAZE LOOKED UP AT THE PIRATE SHIP, A REPLICA OF THE Pride he had built from his sawmill's lumber, in the oak tree. Noelle's weathered playhouse had been moved to the ground and refurbished. Fondly called Maison Rouge, it was red with a black door and black window boxes over-flowing with red and white phlox and bluebonnets. Above it, sailing across enormous branches, The Pride's bow pointed toward the Mississippi River. Two years prior, when John and Catherine had visited, The Pride and Maison Rouge received high praise from a man uniquely qualified to bestow it. Seemingly afloat in an ocean of green leaves the Bowie twins co-captained the ship. Christmas gifts in December 1836, they had just passed their four and a half year mile marker on this Fourth of July late afternoon.

"James Tyler Bowie! Jean Rezin Bowie!" Blaze called to his sons. "Don't lean so far over the starboard and stern or I'll make you walk the plank!"

"Yes sir!" they replied in unison.

Two blond boys, smaller versions of their father right down to their gray eyes, nodded and instantly obeyed. Blaze heard giggling and turned to Noelle sitting in a new swing hanging from the sturdiest of enormous limbs.

"Isn't your papa fierce?" Noelle asked the baby in her lap.

"I can be," Blaze said, putting his hands to his hips.

"Yes. You certainly can be." Noelle's sultry smile took his breath away.

In the landscaped backyard, protected by an eight foot stone wall, Noelle held a miniature of herself named Olivia Katrina. The little girl, born on Thanksgiving Day, a month before the twins turned four, was seven months old now. Wearing a navy blue dress with white dots, Noelle was a vision of red, white and blue, femininity, sensuality and love. Copper waves cascaded down her back. Olivia was dressed the same, her blue eyes sparkling and strawberry blond curls framing pink cherub cheeks. Blaze was drawn to his girls in a heartbeat.

"Swing us, Blaze," Noelle said.

Blaze leaned down and kissed her. She tenderly touched his face as he kissed the top of Olivia's head. Moving behind them, Blaze pulled the ropes to the swing.

Amongst blossoming magnolia trees, fuchsia crape myrtles, lemon lime hydrangeas, milky white gardenias, sweet honeysuckle, and red roses, a flower-scented breeze fluttered long red waves and baby fine curls.

On the other side of the wall, maidenhair ferns blended in with the thick forest of a frontiersman. So often in the dark days at the Alamo, Blaze had dreamed of having Noelle at his side as he looked over his land. Since moving into the castle in 1836, he had built a barn for buggies and tools, a large stable and had fenced in a pasture for Blue, Betsy, a couple of ponies, and several winning race horses.

Behind the house, he had attached a wide veranda, similar to the one on Galveston Island. Noelle had decorated it with thick red and blue cushions on white wicker-wood. In the front of the castle, the grounds were once again as well manicured as Noelle had kept them in her memory. Red and white phlox and bluebonnets grew in dark red window boxes and copper irises circled Cupid's fountain which once again flowed from an underground stream.

Proof that he had made the right decision by moving into the castle and taking over the businesses was Noelle's happiness. She had achieved her stable life with peace and security. Her kisses were no longer salty with tears but sweet with laughter. She was a loving mother to their children, gracious hostess to family and friends, and passionate lover to him.

God, he was a happy man.

Dorothea Yoder reveled in watching the twins sail The Pride and encouraged them while they learned to ride their ponies. She was elated as the newspaper's circulation shot up, as the bank earned the finest reputation in Mississippi and as the twice-as-big sawmill provided more jobs than any other mill in Mississippi and Louisiana. She adored Shade and his plantation supplied the brothers' now co-owned distillery with all the mash needed for Yoder's Finest Bourbon Whiskey and for Bowie's Secret Recipe Scotch. Shade was a wealthy man in every way.

Thanksgiving Day, when Olivia was born, Dorothea had tearfully thanked Blaze for bringing Noelle home and sharing his family with her. She loved Blaze, would rap her cane and tell anyone and everyone that she and Blaze were thick as thieves. Blaze was saddened when a week after Olivia's birth, Dorothea died in her sleep.

"Good thing Papa sent Adam to open the gate. I think I hear a horse and buggy, Olivia," Noelle said to the baby. "Your Uncle Shade and Aunt Felice are coming to celebrate Independence Day and Papa's birthday with us."

"Muchas felicidades, big bad Blaze!" Shade shouted a moment later.

Strolling down the walk of the side yard with Shade and Felice was a child wearing a coonskin cap. The boy, whom Shade had once claimed to doubt was his, beelined for The Pride.

"Hello, Uncle Blaze, Aunt Noelle, Olivia!"

"Hello, Davy!" Blaze said as Noelle waved Olivia's tiny hand.

Named David Carlos, the little boy, a month older than the twins, had Shade's brown hair and the Bowie gray eyes. The twins shouted with delight as Blaze gave Davy a boost into the tree ship.

"Come to Papa, Olivia," Blaze said to his daughter.

Blaze took his baby girl and she wound her arms around his neck as Noelle stood and looped her arm through his. They then joined Shade and Felice on the veranda to visit and watch the children play. The women took seats and Noelle opened a chest of toys brought by John and Catherine to celebrate the birth of the twins. The men stood, each holding a baby girl.

"Alicia Dawn, say hello to Olivia Katrina," Shade said, holding his little year and a half old daughter. Pretty and sweet like her mother, Alicia had brown eyes and raven hair.

Walter served liquid refreshments and, taking seats on the veranda, the brothers and sisters relaxed on this pleasant summer evening. While the boys sailed The Pride, Nicky padded onto the veranda, stretched out and watched the little girls play. After they had finished their drinks, Adam opened French doors and called to them.

" Dannette says your supper celebration is ready!"

Squeals erupted from three little boys as Blaze and Shade got them down from the tree. Blaze picked up the twins and ran with a laughing boy under each arm. Placing Davy on his shoulders, Shade sprinted after Blaze.

"Come on, girls!" Blaze shouted with a laugh.

Noelle and Felice gathered up the girls as Blaze and Shade put the boys down on the veranda. Zelm washed little hands and faces before leading the boys into the dining room which easily seated twenty.

"Do you ever think we're dreaming, Noelle?" Felice

asked with a choke in her voice. "Who would have thought we would ever be so happy?"

"I knew we would be this happy the day we married Blaze and Shade," Noelle said. "We have all that Mama, Carlos and John wanted for us."

"You are the finest sister anyone could have," Felice said.

"As are you."

Noelle's eyes lingered on the finest husband anyone could have. Blaze's dark blond hair touched the collar of a white shirt reminiscent of those he'd worn on Galveston Island. Fawn colored britches hugged his thighs.

Blaze's steely gray eyes met Noelle's. As they did now, his eyes glinted with love whenever he looked at her. The tender touch of his strong hand or a whisper from his deep voice always stirred butterflies in her stomach and never failed to pull her to him.

"This reality is far better than any dream I ever had," Noelle said as she walked to Blaze.

Blaze wrapped her and Olivia in his sinewy grip of iron and they let Shade, Felice and Alicia enter the house ahead of them.

In the parlor, Noelle had added new carpets and draperies to compliment the antique furniture. In the library where Blaze met with businessmen and politicians, he'd mounted the Bowie coat of arms over his gold mantel. On the mantel, Blaze had placed the case of gold holding the pirate ship compass. In the glittering ballroom where quartets played and people waltzed, it was well known that Blaze and Noelle danced only with each other.

As Noelle once envisioned, Blaze mounted her gold mantel over the fireplace in their bedroom. She had chosen a large four poster bed, much like the one in which they'd consummated their marriage on Galveston Island, for their private suite of rooms. Down the hall, the twins shared a big, sunny room filled with two beds, two rocking horses, cowboy hats, storybooks, building blocks, army men, whirligigs, tops, and other toys. In the nursery, between Noelle's infant cradle and childhood canopy bed was the same rocking chair Grandmother had used to rock Noelle as a baby. The portrait of Noelle and her mother now hung on a wall near the rocker.

Perched on the hill, inside and out, the Bowie castle was unforgettable. But what mattered to Noelle was that it housed her pride and joy; Blaze and their children.

Now, on his thirty-sixth birthday, looking as commanding and comfortable as she always knew he would, Blaze sat at the head of the long, dining room table. When supper was over they enjoyed a red, white and blue birthday cake. The party then moved to the library where gifts were opened, cousins played and Jackson watched from his second story perch. On a Victorian sofa, Noelle relaxed in the crook of Blaze's arm. Shade had brought Blaze a case of scotch. Walter soon arrived with a silver tea service and poured tea for the ladies.

As they reminisced of other celebrations, the talk turned to May of 1840, when Blaze, Noelle, Shade, and Felice had attended Sam Houston's marriage to Margaret Lea in Alabama. Though a memorable time, for Noelle the best weddings would always be the two marriages in the middle of a pirate colony.

"You were right about leaving Santa Anna alive that day at San Jacinto, Blaze," Shade said. "El Presidente was only too happy to order his troops out of Texas in exchange for Houston sparing his life."

"The battle at San Jacinto is being called one of the most decisive battles in history," Blaze said. "Travis was vindicated by Houston making sure Santa Anna's victory at the Alamo cost him more than it was worth."

"And Houston did it under the headquarters' oak tree with a wounded leg," Shade said and chuckled appreciatively. "I still can't get over the story in your newspaper about Santa Anna getting into a fight with the French and losing his lower left leg to a blast of grapeshot," Shade said.

"It's certainly ironic since Santa Anna proclaimed himself the Napoleon of the West," Blaze replied.

Noelle hugged Blaze and smiled at Felice, knowing how dangerously close they had all come to losing each other during those perilous days and nights.

An explosion sounded just before Walter and Adam suddenly appeared at the open pocket doors.

"Fireworks!" Walter announced.

"Fireworks! Fireworks!" Jackson flew from the top of the spiral staircase to the back of Grandfather's throne-like chair as if to watch through the window.

Adam played the Star Spangled Banner on his fiddle causing Jim, Jean and Davy to follow him like he was the Pied Piper of Natchez. Holding Olivia with one arm, Blaze swung his other arm around Noelle as Alicia toddled between Shade and Felice holding their fingers. On the front lawn, everyone in the household gathered as fireworks, shot off from the levee along the Mississippi River, burst with brilliance across a cloudless, evening sky.

As the fading colors drifted away on a breeze, goodnights were said. Shade hoisted a drowsy Davy into the buggy where Alicia already snoozed in Felice's lap. Shade slapped the reins to a big bay as Adam waited at the gatehouse. Walter came for the twins and Zelm took a yawning Olivia. Tonight they, instead of Blaze and Noelle, would tuck the children into bed.

"The new desk I bought for your office at the sawmill is not your only birthday present, Blaze," Noelle said as they lingered alone under the evening stars.

His lusty grin seared her heart and soul. "Give it to me, darlin'."

"Bayou-style or saddle-style?"

"I'll race you to the backyard."

Minutes later, facing her husband and saddled across his lap in the tree swing, a soft sigh escaped Noelle as Blaze groaned her name. Heartbeats slowly returned to normal.

Their bodies still one, a balmy breeze fluttered their hair and helped cool their fevered flesh.

"How right it is the Fourth of July is your birthday," Noelle whispered, smiling at him. "You are the essence of righteous independence."

"To my redheaded fireworks, the rockets' red glare can't compare."

"I love you so very much, Blaze Bowie."

"My eyes pulled me to you that day in Main Plaza and my heart was lost the moment you spoke, Noelle Bowie."

"Someday we'll tell the children how we found each other at the Alamo."

"Making love to you beside the eighteen-pounder is my only good memory of the Alamo."

"We will always love and laugh." Noelle kissed the man who had fought so nobly for her, for his land and for Texas. "So whenever we think of the Alamo, we'll only remember the passion."

A LOOK AT: TAME THE WILD

BY LYNN ELDRIDGE

On New Year's Eve 1905, Genevieve Morgan attends a ball at the
elaborate Palace Hotel in San Francisco hosted by Seth Comstock,
the newest, most eligible bachelor in town. Desperate to escape the
infamous bordello she inherited, Genevieve hopes to charm and
marry Comstock. Easier said than done for a nobody fish in a little
pond who cannot waltz. As Seth catches her eye, Genevieve prays
he has a warm personality to take the chill off his cold smile. If only
there was someone to give her a few lessons not only in dancing
but in the art of seduction.

Seth warns his twin sister, Selma, to distract Harriett Peak, a local
journalist who wrote about the Nob Hill house he claims he's
building, so that he can make Genevieve his teammate for a
midnight scavenger hunt. Genevieve is not to suspect this ball is for
her benefit. Enter Luke Harper, a riverboat gambler who is staying
at the hotel while he unloads a horse ranch he won in a high stakes
poker game. One glance at the beautiful siren with lilac cat eyes and
Luke goes on his own kind of hunt.

As the music stops and dancers switch partners, Genevieve finds
herself in the arms of this man, so gorgeous he rivals Adonis. The
thought crosses Luke's mind to never let her go as she stomps his
feet. No, he's leaving soon. But finding out she wants to marry the
host, Luke's gut warns him that Genevieve is headed for serious
trouble. Will Luke vanish into the wild or strike a deal with
Genevieve, who is anything but tame?

AVAILABLE NOW!

ABOUT THE AUTHOR

Lynn Eldridge is a former president of the West Virginia Chapter of Romance Writers of America and earned an honorable mention in their Golden Heart Contest. Lynn is the author of several historical and contemporary romance novels including, Desire in Deadwood, Remember the Passion, and Tame the Wild. Her next book, soon to be released, is Skyrocket to Surrender, and she is currently working on another historical romance titled Hearts and Mountains. In addition to her writing career, Lynn is a licensed clinical therapist and dedicates one day a week in an outpatient behavioral health facility in Charleston, West Virginia.